When the Clocks Stopped

Separated by two centuries, two young women confront evil and intrigue.

M. L. EATON

 May all who read this book be richly blessed.

Published by Touchworks Ltd. A company registered in England, no. 03668464.
Registered Office: 67 London Road, St. Leonards-on-Sea, East Sussex TN37 6AR.

A catalogue record for this title is available from The British Library.

ISBN 978-1-4716-2189-5

This is the first book in the Mysterious Marsh Series.
The second book, *When the Tide Turned,* will be available in early 2014.

For my daughters

Sophie Jessica and Laura Davina

With love and pride

'Time is dead as long as it is being clicked off by little wheels; only when the clock stops does it come to life.'

William Faulkner
American Novelist 1897 – 1962
Nobel Prize for Literature 1949

Prologue

The silver light of a gibbous moon shimmers on the new green leaves of the ash tree. The horse stamps and jerks his head, jangling the bridle. I sway with the movement, soothing him instinctively. The sweetish smell of horse is thick about me as I wait at the crossroads. Stiff as I am in every joint and sinew, my body screams for me to dismount and stretch my legs, but I cannot. Some intuition, some sense of impending destiny, holds me motionless. I am aware it will not be long.

I flinch as the expectant hush is broken by the screech of an owl, eerie in the stillness that binds me to the saddle. She circles silently above me, seeking her prey. I watch until she glides away into the blackest shadows, where the sacred ash grove huddles beneath the escarpment.

My eyes seek the hallowed place where the Earth Mother is still honoured by man and maid on the sacred feast of Beltane; the ash grove to which they come at dawn, clad in white, and garlanded in green. May blossoms wreathe their brows as they stand side by side under a living canopy for their hand-clasping, their ceremony of rejoicing in union, the celebration of life itself in dance and song. This is the seven-treed sacred grove to which my beloved and I came not long ago; there we swore an oath to honour our love and there later, alone beneath the moon-silvered leaves we became one in the flesh.

It grows cold now, and I shiver. The horse pricks up his ears, listening intently. A small sound trembles towards me; perhaps no more than a fluctuation in the air current. Then the nightingale's exquisite song fills the air with beauty. It is the signal. Jack's signal.

I fire my weapon into the sky and wheel about, pulling sharply on the reins. We race off into the night. Lying close to the horse's back, my head beside his ear, I ride hard. For a moment or two, as we gather speed, I choose those places where the low light gleams through the covering of cloud. I catch the sound of hooves in swift pursuit and know I have been seen. Now I guide my good companion into the gloom of the darkest shadows, allowing him to choose his own footing on the causeway. He gallops on.

I risk a backward glimpse. Shapes pursue us; legless in the mist rising from the Marsh, centaurs ride hard in a bow-shaped line. The triumph and excitement of the men who chase me is almost palpable. How long were they lingering near the crossroads where I myself had waited?

I let the gelding have his head because he knows these levels well. His hooves drum into the earth and I crouch low in the saddle, horse sweat hot-smelling in my nostrils. As I cling to his mane, I chance another glance but see nothing. I am sure we are gaining on our pursuers, but have they ridden yet into the trap where the Marsh is quicksand and will swallow horse and rider whole?

The moon is hidden now and I have no bearings. All I hear is a thrumming, thrumming, thrumming — and I know not whether it is my heart beating in my ears or the sound of pursuit. All I can do is ride.

- 1 -

Of Dreams and Aspirations

I woke with a start, heart pounding and stomach churning. As I reached for the memory of the dream it sank away into the mists of the past. I knew this one of old. It had been part of my childhood, visited me more seldom in my teens and in my twenties it had returned to the realm of shadows. Suddenly and vehemently it had come back. I had woken up in this fashion for the past three nights when, as now, the luminous dial of my alarm clock showed twenty minutes past midnight. I sighed. Why had the nightmare returned? Was there a message or a reason?

An internal fluttering brought me back into the present. I would worry about the meaning of the dream in the morning, if I remembered. I went back to sleep.

Much to my surprise, I was early for my appointment. I had raced across the Marsh from Rye in my old black Ford Anglia, double-de-clutching from third gear into second on the most treacherous corners, and had made the journey in record time.

I was glad of the coolness as I entered the bank. It was late April — the month of sunshine and showers — but this was 1976, the year that was to be the hottest on record in this corner of south-east England. There had been few showers but plenty of sunshine. Although it was not yet eleven o'clock in the morning and I had driven with wide open windows, the air inside my car shimmered with heat. I checked my appearance in the rear view mirror and wished I hadn't. My hair was a mess and a sheen of dust clung to my sticky face.

As if by reflex, the bank manager emerged from his office just as I walked in the door, my fingers busily trying to rake my mane into some semblance of tidiness. He greeted me with a kind smile and a firm, short handshake.

Mr. Stone was a short, tubby, balding, middle-aged man with a round head and rounder glasses, thick bottle-bottom lenses masking his pale blue eyes. His eyes twinkled — or was it the light catching his lenses?

"Come in, come in, Mrs Dawkins."

He ushered me into the room from which he had appeared and drew back an armchair from his leather-topped desk.

"Do sit down, my dear."

As I literally dropped into the chair I was aware that my pregnancy was obvious. The conservative part of me had hoped that it was hidden under my tartan smock.

I discovered I was nervous.

"Er ... Mr Stone, thank you for seeing me."

How silly you sound! my internal critic sneered. *As if he wouldn't see you when you'd made an appointment.*

"I'm delighted to see you, of course," Mr Stone responded gallantly, his smile deepening as he seated himself on the other side of his desk. "Tell me, what can I do for you, young lady?"

"We've banked here since we came to Rype," I began.

"Yes, I know."

"And before that, at the Ashford Branch."

"Yes, I know that, too."

Mr Stone raised his eyebrows encouragingly, his head to one side, reminding me of an inquisitive sparrow.

"Well, as you can see, I'm going to have a baby," I said haltingly.

"Yes, I can see that. Congratulations." His smile widened and I actually blushed.

My internal critic mocked: *Blushing. How ridiculous, Hazel! You're twenty-eight years old and you've been married for three of them.*

I made a braver effort: "So I'll be giving up work soon, and it might be a little difficult financially."

"I have a note here that your husband works for Fathom & Deep in Ashford — a good firm that — and that you work in Rye at Farthing & Change. I presume you're a legal secretary?" Mr Stone sounded genuinely interested.

"Actually, I'm a solicitor." My mouth was never happy with that word, my tongue always slurring it into something resembling 'sister'. "I mean I'm an assistant lawyer," I corrected.

"A solicitor? Really? How interesting!" he exclaimed, rubbing his hands. The smile was replaced by surprise.

"Oh! I'm glad you think so, Mr Stone. As I said, I'll be giving up work to have the baby and we — my husband and I — might need a little latitude. Do you think we could have an overdraft?" The last few words came in a rush.

"I'm sure we can agree something. We need a solicitor in Rype. A solicitor. Well I never. A solicitor, indeed! Who'd have thought it?"

He seemed for a moment to slip into a little reverie of his own. I was used to this reaction because in 1976 few women were in the professions and in the legal profession fewer still. On meeting me, most of the clients of the old-fashioned firm where I worked believed I was one of the secretaries. When they discovered I was a Solicitor of the Supreme Court — my full professional title — reactions varied, the usual ones being surprise, bafflement or resignation.

Mr Stone recollected himself. Leaning forward over his desk, he remarked in a confidential tone:

"We need a solicitor in Rype, Mrs Dawkins. The bank encourages its customers to make Wills. And personally, I believe they're *most* important documents. My customers certainly need legal advice about them. Why, only this morning I was advising a farmer on the topic. Would you be interested?"

"But, Mr Stone, I'm having a baby. I'm going to give up..." This conversation was not going in the right direction.

"Don't worry about that. You'll soon be bored at home, an intelligent young woman like you."

"Perhaps," I allowed. "But I think I'll have my hands full for a while."

Those hands found themselves comforting 'the Bump'. My unborn child was my reason for becoming a stay at home wife and mother — my dream for as long as I could remember.

Mr Stone interrupted my abstraction, dragging me back to the present: "When, exactly, is the baby due, my dear?"

"In the middle of June. I'm hoping to give up work in a month's time."

"Good, good," he nodded. "So you'll be working with Farthing & Change until late May, I take it?"

"Yes," I agreed.

Mr Stone made a note.

"Good, good," he approved, and I relaxed a little. "Leave it with me, my dear Mrs Dawkins," he went on, his voice soothing but his eyes gleaming wickedly — and it was definitely his eyes and not his spectacles. "Don't worry a jot. I'll find someone to look after the baby for you. In fact, I know just the person. She's been looking after other people's children for years. What do you say?"

No! I screamed inwardly, but I found myself saying: "I can't — I'd need all sorts of things! A filing cabinet, and a typewriter to begin with and..." I floundered.

"You can have your overdraft, Mrs Dawkins," he interrupted. "How much do you want? A thousand pounds?"

I gasped and tried to mask it with a cough. Bruce and I had discussed our financial situation at length. We had decided a facility of five hundred pounds would be plenty. Bruce, who had qualified as an accountant in Australia, was head of the accounts department in a local factory. A thousand pounds was a third of my annual salary, a quarter of his.

"Thank you, Mr Stone, that would be most helpful."

"No need to thank me, my dear." The bank manager smiled. "I'm pleased the Bank can be of service and *delighted* that Rype has a solicitor."

Oh dear. How had this happened? Did he really expect me to start giving legal advice? Or to make Wills?

"But I *am* giving up work to have the baby," I reminded him.

"Think it over, my dear. Or may I call you Hazel? Have a word with your husband — think it over together. Two heads are better than one, you know. I'm sure that together you'll make the right decision."

He stood and held out his hand. As I gave him mine, relief that I had achieved my objective flooded through me followed by a flash of annoyance at his assumption that I needed my husband's permission to start my own legal practice. I concealed my irritation, pushed my chair back and rose to my feet.

"Very well," I smiled with feminine guile. "I'll speak to Bruce about it. Thank you again."

In the twinkling of one of Mr Stone's eyes, the door was opened and I was ushered out, my head a whirl of possibilities.

Outside, despite the cool breeze, the car door-handle was hot to the touch. I caught my tights as I slipped behind the wheel. Slipped — but only just. My girth was increasing daily.

I drove back to Rye exultant. Although I hoped that we would not need it, the overdraft facility would cover any shortfall in our income when I left work. That was one worry less. Mr Stone's indication that he would like me to set up a legal practice was of more concern. I was giving up work to start a family and that would take all my time.

I had only six more weeks in the office. After that, I was looking forward to several small luxuries: resting in the afternoon; having supper ready when Bruce came home; an immaculate house, a tidy garden. I would have time to think of names for the baby, to read all the baby books piled beside my bed, to talk of babies to my mother while we knitted tiny clothes: and when the Bump was no longer a bump but a baby, I would do anything, everything, always be there, smiling, for my child. Motherhood was all I had ever wanted apart from the love of the great chunk of red Australian sandstone who was my husband. I vowed to myself that I would be the perfect wife and mother.

Don't be so silly! You can't be perfect. You're in love with the whole idea of motherhood. The reality will be very different. My common sense tried to reassert itself, but I seemed to have no space in my mind for anything other than children.

Resolutely changing my thoughts, I felt my heart beat faster as the dream from the night before returned vividly to memory. I recalled the urgency of my nightmare mission. I remembered it reflected in the palpitations of my heart as I woke with a churning stomach, but I knew that there was something more — some recollection that slipped away before my mind could grasp it. I ransacked my memory.

A crossroads with an ash grove nearby. Surely I knew the place, had seen it recently? Ah, I had it now — a place where three roads met behind the coastal village of Lightchapel and close by, under the old cliff that marked the shore line from long ago, a stand of tall trees. I remembered driving past one windy day on my way to Hythe and wondering at the threadbare rags and ribbons fluttering from the ash trees' lower branches.

"You have a lot to learn about the customs of these parts, my duck!" Our next door neighbour Horace had chortled when I mentioned it to him. "Marsh women still seek the blessing of the tree spirits of the Ash Grove."

"But why tie rags to the branches?"

"Each rag represents a wish, or a vow, or a thank-offering for a wish come true. When Christianity was imposed on the Marsh folk they paid lip service to it, but the old ways have always been honoured in secret and now some of the old festivals are being revived."

I was intrigued. "What festivals?"

"The Celtic Festivals of the old religion. They're celebrated on the cross-quarter days and begin at night at the full of the moon."

He ticked the names of the festivals off on his fingers: Lammas, Samhain, Imbolc, Beltane. *Beltane* — that had been the word in my dream.

I had noticed years ago that the dream only came during the moon's second quarter, ceasing to trouble me when the moon's face was full. Last night, a gibbous moon had hung low in the sky, its silver fingers caressing my face as I leaned on the window sill. Reluctantly drawing the curtains to block its light, I had calculated that the moon was still waxing but that within three nights it would begin to wane.

Too soon, I drove into the outskirts of Rye. Returning to

concerns about my work and the many matters that needed my attention, I banished all other thoughts and dismissed any idea of starting a legal practice. That was the last thing I wanted.

- 2 -

Of Memories in Sunshine

Summer threw its languorous spell over me as I stepped out into the freshness of an early morning in late May. Bruce had left for work in his usual whirl of half-asleep-ness.

"Bye, darling," he mumbled as his lips aimed for mine but connected with my left ear. "Enjoy your first day off."

He had remembered that much in his semi-comatose state but I still had to chase after him with his briefcase. My first day off. The pure luxury of it! I was still in my nightgown as I wandered round the garden. During the time that we had lived here, Bruce and I had worked hard in the garden and it now looked much as I had envisioned on the day we first discovered Rose Cottage. I made my leisurely way to the vegetable plot, pausing to touch the rosy beginnings of the fruit on the apple trees and to admire the rear of the house, its newly white painted walls set off by the yellow and purple pansies overflowing the window boxes. Their fragrance wafted to me on the morning breeze.

"You're doing very well," I encouraged the broad beans. Neat rows of green shoots were appearing almost as I looked at them.

The telephone was ringing.

"Let it ring," I told the blackbird who was eyeing me hopefully. He bowed and flew off.

Silence reigned in the garden; there was no traffic noise, no phones ringing or typewriters clacking, and after their divine singing in the dawn chorus, even the birds had quietened. All I could hear was the blackbird's melodious song and the hum of bees amongst the yellow-faced pansies and sweet-smelling wallflowers. My thoughts wandered back to the day when Bruce had come into my life — or rather, when I had fallen into his....

Tripping over the step into the snug bar of The Royal Oak in my home village of Waterham, I'd cannoned into his arms. I had come home to spend the weekend with my parents and my father had seized the opportunity for a celebratory pint at the local pub while my mother cooked the usual gargantuan Saturday lunch.

While I had blushed and stammered with embarrassment, my father had congratulated the tall, tawny haired, blue-eyed stranger on catching me with such alacrity. Soon they were deep in conversation, my father applauding Bruce's sporting skills while I tried to make myself invisible. Bruce had smiled at me over my father's shoulder: the smile was followed by the flutter of an eyelid. My composure had returned and my heart had flipped — a flipping from which it had never recovered. After years of trying to find someone with whom I wanted to spend the rest of my life, I'd fallen in love, headlong and completely, in the winking of an eye. Literally.

It turned out that Bruce was staying with my parents' next door neighbours whose son he had met in Australia. All I remember of that week-end is a blur, but by the Monday I was as sure as eggs is eggs that I'd met the man I would marry.

He was broad shouldered and good looking, true; but he was also an enigma. There was an attractive air of mystery about him which I'd put down to his foreignness. Not that he was really foreign. His upbringing on the East coast of Australia had been similar to mine, but nonetheless there was a frontier quality to him — a quiet grace, slow speech and the fact that I was never sure exactly what he was thinking. It had found these qualities, attached to his strong physical presence, very attractive. I had been drawn under his spell and soon found that I was thinking of him every moment that I was out of his company. He was like a drug, one that I couldn't do without. But, as it turned out, he was equally taken with me.

The only fly in the ointment had been his flat-mate, Joanna.

During the year of our courtship, while I had been completing my Articles of Clerkship in a solicitor's office in Sussex, I had spent most of the limited time I had available with Bruce. As a constant visitor at the flat he and Joanna shared, I'd observed how easy they were together — teasing each other unmercifully, sharing Australian slang and joking in what seemed a foreign language. I'd found myself wondering why Bruce wanted me around when he had had this blonde, blue-eyed nurse as a friend and flatmate. Not just blonde either: she was slender and tanned, too. I knew I was shapely, in a buxom English sort of way, but next to her I felt very plain with my green-pond-water coloured eyes and turned-up nose, not to mention the curly dark hair that would never hang straight and shiny like hers.

Joanna had always been very hospitable towards me, but I'd felt like the proverbial cuckoo, uneasy about intruding into their relationship — until the day Joanna and I quarrelled. Although the original subject of our dispute was something quite minor, my simmering jealousy made me yell words I would never have otherwise said. Joanna had laughed when she'd realised that I was so insecure about my relationship with Bruce, thinking she wanted him all to herself.

"I don't believe it. What would I want with that great, goofy thing? You can have him. With my blessing. He's not bad as a substitute brother but I prefer an English gentleman, thank you very much."

"Are you *sure* I'm not getting in the way?" I'd asked.

"Honestly, I wouldn't have him if he was the last man on earth," she had replied, sobering. "Besides, I wouldn't get a look in anyway. He's head over heels in love with *you*. Surely you can see that?"

I shook my head in disbelief, and she came and put her arms around me.

"Watch how his eyes soften when he looks at you. And how his voice changes. Believe me, he's in love with you. But don't you dare hurt him or you'll have me to deal with. He's like a brother to me ..." and her eyes had filled with tears as she told me of the brother she'd lost to a motorcycle accident when she was fifteen.

From then on, Joanna and I had been the best of friends. In fact, it was thanks to Joanna that we now owned our collie-cross dog, sometimes called a mutt or a mongrel but, in my opinion, far too aristocratic to be either. Bruce had been away on business and I had been spending the night on the sofa in Joanna's Hampstead flat when a little bundle of black and tan fluff with sandy eyebrows had sneaked in through the French window and crept into my arms. And that had been that: the puppy had stolen into my heart as well as into my bed.

Finding us together the following morning, a surprised Joanna had informed me that the puppy belonged to her next door neighbours who were anxious to find her a home. To my glee and their mingled sadness and pleasure, within a couple of hours the little scrap was named 'Poppadum', nestled into the neck of my coat and taken by bus, rail and road to a new life in Kent. She had since grown into an intuitive and generally well-behaved pet of medium size and intelligent mien. Her true breeding was unknown but to me she was all that I'd ever wanted in a dog.

Thinking of Joanna made me smile. I turned towards the house and remembered the time we had found it. Joanna had been visiting us for Christmas ....

At the time, having returned from a prolonged working honeymoon in my husband's native Australia with sufficient deposit for a small house, Bruce and I were staying with my parents while we sought for jobs and somewhere to live.

Joanna had arrived from London; the final leg of her journey courtesy of my father who had collected her by car from the station at Ashford.

Poppadum was stretched before the fire in my parents' sitting room when she heard the car door slam and Joanna's voice. She leapt up instantly, barking with excitement, her wagging tail leading us to the hall. She launched herself at the newcomer as soon as the door opened and Joanna, heavily laden with a large box and a bag from which Christmas paper peeped, staggered under the onslaught. Quickly recovering her balance she put the box down behind the door with obvious relief.

"Aw! But it's great to see you, you great galah!" she remarked, fondling Poppadum's ears. "And great to see you, too." She beamed at my mother, scattering flat Australian vowels amid us all. "Christmas in the English countryside. What a treat! Thank you so much for inviting me, yet again. You know I love London, but it's bonzer to get out of the place for a while. Especially when the rain is falling vertically and the tube isn't running."

My mother was all concern: "I'm sorry you've had such a horrid journey. There's a fire in the drawing room. Do come and warm yourself."

"Thank you, Betty. I'll be right there. Soon as I've got these Chrissie prezzies organised."

Joanna was already piling presents around the Christmas tree, which took up much of the space in the octagonal hall, when my father came in with Joanna's overnight bag, jingling his car keys in his pocket.

"That bloody tree takes up too much room," he complained, taking off his streaming macintosh and allowing it to drip onto the chequerboard tiled floor.

After patting her companionably on the shoulder in greeting, Bruce picked up Joanna's suitcase and shouldered it as if it were light — which, knowing Joanna, was most unlikely.

"I bet you're really missing that hot South Australian sunshine? And talking of wonderful Australian things, I hope you've brought some of that wonderful South Australian wine with you." He eyed the carton she had shoved behind the door.

"Of course! And Victor ..." smiling broadly at my father, she dipped a hand into the box and brought out a small, square, purple packet covered in gold writing and maroon seals. "Look at *these*. Port-dipped cigars! Specially from my father to thank you for putting up with me."

Dad looked slightly bewildered.

"Port-*dipped* cigars," he repeated. "*Port*-dipped! What *will* they think of next? I need a cigarette to recover."

He pulled a packet of twenty Guards from his pocket and offered one to Joanna who hesitated but declined with a shake of the head. She knew I didn't smoke. I hated the smell of cigarettes with a passion, despite the fact, or possibly because of it, that both my parents smoked. With a sixty-a-day habit, my father was seldom without a cigarette between his fingers; my mother smoked less and with a certain elegance; unusually, neither Bruce nor I smoked at all.

"Come on, Joanna, this calls for a drink," Dad commanded, chuckling effulgently as he led the way into the room my mother always referred to as 'the drawing room' and which the rest of us called the sitting room. He was always glad of an excuse to down a whisky and having an attractive girl in the house was not merely an excuse, it was a very good reason.

Joanna followed my father while I waited for Bruce to return from depositing our friend's suitcase in the spare bedroom. Noticing that the large mirror that hung opposite the front door was again hanging askew, I adjusted it.

'My hair is like that mirror,' I thought. No matter how often I straightened it, my unruly mop constantly curled. The comparison made me grin. The grin improved me, even if it was a bit too wide and there was a lump in the middle of my lower lip.

'Actually,' I thought, as I inspected the lump more closely, pouting for the purpose, 'it *has* flattened quite a bit.'

"There you are, Honey." Bruce threw his arms round me. "Why are you practising pouting in the mirror? Are you planning to seduce me?"

He kissed me, pulling my offending lower lip with his teeth.

"Irresistibly sexy," he whispered huskily.

"We'd better rescue Joanna from Dad," I said after a while. Bruce sighed.

"Okay, if you say so. But stop looking at me with those bedroom eyes of yours or I won't be able to concentrate on the conversation."

- 3 -

Of Future in the Fire

Tonight the child glimpses the future in the fire. She is nine years old and her mother has set her to stir the thick soup in the cauldron, to make sure that it neither sticks nor burns.

Embers glow red beneath the cooking pot as she sits beside the inglenook, ladle in hand, watching the steam rise from the stew. Her eyes are wide, seeing without seeing. The vapour dances, conjuring figures from the nothingness. Figures which leap from the dark-shadowed roadside as horse-drawn vehicles materialise from the mist. Quickly they move the contraband from the waggons, rolling barrels towards the cut, the hidden track beside the road. If she strains, the child hears their thunderous rumbling.

She is aware that it is night — a night when the moon's face is turned from the earth and the owl's eerie hoot echoes around the Marsh. The waggons trundle on ... but now there is a flare of scarlet, a man falls from a footboard and masked horsemen canter in, rein in sharply as incoherent flashes of white and red light up the darkness, reminding her of stars shooting across a black night sky. The firearms' sharp reports are slower to reach the child's ears across the void of time. She drops the ladle and covers her ears but her eyes grow ever wider.

The waggons are surrounded. Men continue to fall or spring or vault upon their foes. Now there is a commotion and confusion such as she has never seen or heard. A horse rears, neighing, striking out with its forelegs. Red blood blossoms on a greenish face slowly turning as knees buckle and the body drops, falls to the ground, is trampled under hooves of iron.

Someone has cut the pack horses free and they gallop away; silk and tea flowing and falling about them like hay pitchforked from the hayloft.

Now hands grab at carthorse reins, frightened horses fidget unbalancing the silhouetted figures wrestling above them. A punch. A whack with a stave. A man falls, screams as his leg is broken by the rear wheel — and the waggons are captured. In a crescendo of sound and action she sees the long whips crack above the frightened carthorses, sees the rolling whites of their eyes as they lumber away on shaggy-skirted feet, tall figures rising above them, laughing with scorn. The last rider wheels his steed one-handed, flames shoot from his musket and a dark-shirted man claps hand to shoulder. The horseman gallops off, his hoots of derision mocking the groans of the wounded. The stillness of the night drops down once more ... and the child cries out for her mother.

"What ails thee, child?" Her mother runs in from the garden, root-vegetables bundled in her apron. Onions and carrots skitter across the floor as she pulls her sobbing daughter away from the fire-basket, grabs the ladle and stirs the pot vigorously.

Only then does she cradle the child close.

"Shhh, my treasure, shhh. What is it ails thee?"

The little girl draws breath and tries to tell.

"The fire ... I saw ... I saw ... in the fire...." The sobs break out again. Her mother shakes her firmly but her voice soothes:

"Hush, hush my child!"

The sobs subside a little as the child whimpers.

"'Tis Pa! Pa is mighty hurt ...."

- 4 -

Of the Marsh in Winter

Bruce and I had determined to visit Rype-in-the-Marsh on the following day, although it was Christmas Eve. A friend of my parents had recommended it as 'a charming little town with a very friendly community.' After consulting the local newspaper, I'd soon realised that, although the ancient town had been of great importance in medieval times, it was now isolated in Romney Marsh, away from main roads and some miles from the nearest large town of Ashford. Property prices were comparatively low. It seemed a good place for house-hunting.

My mother had fortified us for our journey with a breakfast of boiled eggs, soldiers of home-made toasted bread soaked in butter and many mugs of coffee made with milk. Poppadum was keen to come with us. When I told her to stay with my parents she resorted to looking pathetic, head down and her tail between her legs. Amused though I was, I ignored this flagrant attempt at blackmail, knowing that my mother would comfort her with a biscuit as soon as we had left.

With some trepidation, I pulled the starter on my old Ford Anglia. Fortunately the night had been frost-free and the engine caught almost immediately needing only a little encouragement with the choke. Bruce scrunched up his long legs and pen-knifed into the back seat. Joanna sat beside me so that she could enjoy the scenery. Both passengers snuggled into the rugs that my mother had warmed for them on the Aga.

It was a chilly, damp morning and the sun was struggling to throw off its night-time eiderdown of cloud as we drove through narrow lanes winding between high, bare hedgerows. Here and there clumps of trees stretched their branches towards the sky, the rooks' nests in them making a pattern like inkblots on blotting paper. At the top of the cliff that looms over the Marsh and marks the old shore line of Saxon days, we seemed, for a moment, to be suspended in space. A broad expanse of flat land stretched before us as far as the eye could see, patch-worked with shimmering, sparkling hedges awash in soft pink mist which merged into a sky of pale, pale blue. I drove carefully along the narrow road which looped down the steep hillside, braking hard on the corners to slow our descent.

A blush of mist rose to greet us. Shimmering droplets clung to the boughs of the willow trees which leaned over the dykes, droplets which caught the light from the low sun and sparkled rosily in the gentle light. The dykes twisted with every turn of the narrow road, thin rivers of mercury lined with silver spikes of reeds and rushes.

I pulled up and turned off the engine. Bruce and Joanna, who had been sparring like the quasi-siblings they were, fell into a startled silence when the car stopped. The magic of the English countryside in winter flung its spell over us. All was quiet; for once, there was no traffic. A watery sun fingered the occasional tall, bare tree and a naked church spire rising ghostlike from the haze. We drank in the transient beauty of the Marsh in hushed appreciation. For me, the moment stretched into infinity.

None of us spoke as I re-started the car and drove slowly on, the road uncoiling before us through acres of flat marshland, the reed tangled dykes our constant companions. Much later, quaffing our pints of bitter before a roaring fire in 'The Three Chimneys', we agreed that we had all succumbed in a trice to the allure of the Marsh.

We drove into Rype along a narrow lane which meandered amongst trees that seemed to rise taller and taller as we approached. We came upon a house half-hidden by an evergreen hedge on a sharp bend, then a straggle of other houses before we reached a T-junction. On the other side of the junction stood the church of All Saints known as the Cathedral of the Marsh, its warm, grey stone glistening with the same brilliance as the sparkling hedges which had escorted us into the town.

"Which way?" I queried, hauling the car to a stop at the T-junction. The road curved round the churchyard to left and right but there was no signpost.

"Left," said Bruce.

"Right," said Joanna.

"Left it is!" I said, and turned right.

By the time Bruce had reminded me that I did not know my left from my right (a fact of which I was well aware but always denied) we were crawling down Rype's High Street. The medieval buildings crowded together as though for warmth. Small shop windows beckoned from their black-and-white timbered façades, punctuated here and there with a thatched cottage or brick-fronted public house, together providing the picture postcard look of a typical English market town. Further along, the street widened, cottages giving way to larger, detached, more modern buildings, Georgian, Victorian, nineteen-thirties, post-war. Unexpectedly, huddled opposite a patch of vacant land, an ancient house appeared, its roof set at differing heights and angles. White weather boarded and red-tiled, it stood close to the road looking empty and forlorn, even at a distance. A 'For Sale' sign hung askew from a gatepost.

I stamped on the brakes, swung the car sideways off the road and leapt out of the car before either of my stupefied companions could utter a word.

There was no doubt about it. It was *my* house. It crouched along the pavement, long and narrow, with small windows almost at ground level and bigger dormer windows above. In the middle of the roof a huge chimney climbed skywards: a smaller one rising on the building's far left. The house was supported by brick buttresses, around and over which old roses scrambled, naked now of all but their thorns. A low brick wall, painted white, ran along the pavement in front of it, curving round at either end to touch the house itself. A little wicket gate spanned the opening onto a short brick path leading to a black front door. A small painted sign nailed to the door read 'Rose Cottage'.

"What made you jump out of the car like that? Not that house, surely?" asked Joanna as she came to stand beside me. She looked at Rose Cottage as if it would bite. "God, I thought it was cold in the car but it's bloody freezing out here."

Bruce had managed to untangle his legs and struggle out over the front seat.

"I hate two-doored cars," he declared, limping towards us. He exaggerated the limp as he caught my smile. "I'm probably crippled for life after being bottled up like a pound of pears in a preserving jar and all you can do is grin!"

Placing a heavy hand on my shoulder, he ratcheted himself up to his full height. I regarded his antics with amusement but the house held my attention. As I turned back towards it, Bruce peered round me to get a better look at my face. He groaned.

"Don't tell me. You like the look of this house. You must be mad." I hoped he was still teasing.

"It seems empty," I said hopefully."Let's knock and see if we can view."

"Surely you can't expect people to show you round on Christmas Eve?" Bruce was aghast.

"I'm sure it's empty," I countered as I craned my neck to look around. "There are no lights on. The curtains are open downstairs. And they're open upstairs too."

"There's no smoke from the chimney," Joanna chimed in. "And they'd certainly need a fire today."

I stepped up to the front door and banged the knocker. The flat sound came back to me with that slight echo of reverberation which indicates a room devoid of furniture.

"There's no furniture in here." Joanna confirmed my intuition. She had climbed over the wall to peer into the window, her nose pressed close to the pane and her hands tunnelled like binoculars. "There *is* an inglenook with a copper hood and a disgusting coloured carpet and...yes, stairs."

I knocked again, even harder, and rang the doorbell insistently. Nothing. No creak or shout or sound of footsteps. Only that flat echo. The place was deserted.

"Okay. We can't view it today. Let's go and find a pub."

Ignoring Bruce's proposal, I whisked along the pavement and through the side gate, a big black-boarded affair. The others followed, Joanna eagerly, Bruce rather reluctantly. A big, overgrown garden stretched before us. Bruce was mumbling something under his breath. I thought I caught the words 'woman' and perhaps 'pig-headed' but I was far too excited to listen or make my usual retort.

"Isn't it beautiful?" I breathed. "I know it's uncared for — but just look at those old brick walls and the orchard of fruit trees. Apples, mostly, I think. And there are damson trees over there."

I pushed through a gate well-armed with old brambles.

"A secret garden. The perfect place for a vegetable plot. Imagine. Humped rows of potatoes here."

I ran to the right of the orchard, spreading my arms wide, already seeing the crossed bean poles, twiggy rows of pea sticks, rows of broad beans, lettuces, the lacy greens of carrots.

"I think there's a stream at the bottom by those willow trees. And we could build a barbecue right here." I stamped on the overgrown patio near the apple trees as I spoke. Bruce stopped the stream of enthusiasm issuing from my lips by the simple expedient of kissing me.

Joanna had tactfully wandered away towards the house. As far as I could tell from this distance, she was surveying it with curiosity. I caught Bruce's hand and gave it a squeeze before tugging him back towards the building.

"It's not straight at all, is it?" Joanna remarked. "It's all higgledy-piggledy. Look, it's got a small window there, a large window here, a medium sized one by this great stable door and that ... that seems to be a hole."

I peered into the hole, an asymmetrical room which followed the line of the boundary wall. Widening towards the back, it boasted blank walls on three sides, no windows and no door, only a gap where the fourth wall should have stood. An oil tank took up most of the space.

"Hooray!" I whooped with joy. "It must have central heating."

Bam. Bam. Bam. Bruce was crashing on the back door with his fist. It sounded as though he was trying to knock the place down.

"They *must* have heard that," I exclaimed, slightly embarrassed. We waited. Nothing.

A deep voice said: "It's empty. They've moved to Sandwich."

We all jumped guiltily. The voice belonged to a chap in a red woollen hat who was peering over the fence to the right.

"Th ... thank you," I replied. "Do you know where we can get the key?"

"Sorry, duck. Agent's closed for the holiday. But you might find a window ..."

He tapped the side of his nose knowingly, tipped his head in the direction of the house and disappeared from view. We all waited, rather chastened, in case he should re-appear but he didn't. Joanna shivered, something she did very well and convincingly.

"Are we going to find a way in or are we going to the pub?" she asked.

I had been surreptitiously checking windows for their security.

"Look this window is loose," I blurted, as Bruce said "Pub!"

"I mean the *catch* is loose," I corrected, demonstrating by pushing the window a little. "With luck, if I pull it this way, I can squeeze my finger in and lift the latch ... there! All it needed was a little encouragement."

The window swung open; the aperture measured about eighteen inches square. Closer inspection revealed a tiny washbasin inside, beneath the window.

"No wonder the glass is obscure. It's the lavatory." I observed, heaving one leg over the windowsill before either Bruce or Joanna found the breath to remonstrate.

A very short time later I was reflecting that this had not been one of my cleverest ideas. Not only had the point of the latch caught me in a tender place but I still had the wash basin and taps to negotiate. And somehow I had to get my body, head and my second leg to follow the first. Ouch! However, I was committed beyond return. So, biting my lip to keep myself from saying some very rude words, with a little wriggling in places that often wriggled and a lot of bending in places that didn't often bend, I found myself inside with my second leg stuck over the basin. A backward hop and I reached the wall; now I had just enough room to bring in my other leg and set my second foot to the floor.

- 5 -

Of Things Seen and Unseen

My back against the wall, I surveyed the compact room. It possessed a modern white toilet as well as the minuscule basin I had first encountered. The walls were wallpapered in a tiny mauve flower pattern printed on a white background. Although I might not have chosen that particular paper, I could live with it. I shook with that sense of exhilaration experienced by generally law-abiding people when they do something illicit.

I opened the door and found myself in a small lobby. The bathroom was to the left, similarly papered; the bath and basin new and white. The shaggy, beige carpet covered the side of the bath as well as the floor. Novel, I thought.

The door out of the lobby led into the white-walled living room which took up the whole of the width of the house, from front to back. It was empty, except for brown velvet curtains and Joanna's 'disgusting' carpet, a vivid print in yellow and brown — to me it was contemporary and exuberant. Black beams criss-crossed the low ceiling but I hardly noticed them because there, in all its glory, was a huge inglenook fireplace with a beaten copper canopy. I could hardly breathe for delight.

"For God's sake, let us in, Haze. We're freezing to the bloody bone out here," Bruce shouted, thumping away on the back door.

I started, the spell broken. Straight ahead of me was a wide doorway, through which I discovered the kitchen, narrow like a galley. I recognised the big stable door on the right.

"I've found the back door," I called. "But it's bolted top and bottom and the lower one's stuck. Wait a moment."

I yanked hard on the jammed bolt. It shot upwards and the door flew back towards me. Two pale faces, pinched with cold, stared at me for a moment before their owners jostled each other in the doorway as they rushed in.

"It's not much warmer in here, but at least it's out of the wind," Joanna noted, pushing past Bruce. Turning right, she found a door, opened it and stopped short.

"Look at this, will you?" she exclaimed. "It's a real old-fashioned larder with a meat safe and shelves."

I peered in behind her and for a moment, despite the shelves and wire netting at the unglazed window, it seemed more like a porch than a larder. I received the impression of oilskins and sou'westers against the wall and and sea-boots flung into a corner. Odd, I thought, frowning. I closed my eyes for a second and when I opened them it was a bare, old-fashioned larder.

"It's Old Mother Hubbard's cupboard," I joked.

"Sure is — not a bone to be seen! But I *can* see you making jam and chutney and mincemeat and lemon curd," Joanna predicted. "And storing it all in here for your twelve children. Speaking of children, where's Bruce?"

Bruce had turned the other way and I found him surveying the inglenook, rubbing his hands together to warm them. As I watched, he lifted his right hand to pull at his lower lip, a habit to which he resorted when he was considering something. I crept up and hugged him from behind, making him jump.

"This would take a huge fire," I said, swiftly checking the gap between the low-beams of the ceiling and his head, relieved and glad to note that there was an inch or two between them.

I turned my attention back to the room itself. On the wall beside the inglenook, stairs rose towards the upper storey. At the foot of the staircase the door to the kitchen stood open. The door opposite opened into the lobby that led to the bathroom and cloakroom. Revolving slowly, I counted two other doors. This room was clearly the hub of the whole house.

Joanna had followed me and now her eyes gleamed mischievously as she raced me to the first door. She turned the handle. The door swung inwards.

I gasped. For there at the window, sitting in a rocking chair with her mouth a little open and her chin resting on her chest, sat a very old woman. The low sun made a thistledown halo of the white hair that had escaped her bun and glanced off the gnarled hands resting on the crocheted rug which covered her knees, emphasising their frailness. Her eyes were closed; but opened – wide, opaque and blind – as I entered. A smile lit up her face, deepening the lines around her mouth and eyes.

Joanna completely ignored the room's occupant. She was twirling, oblivious, in the centre of the room.

"Say, Hazel, this would make a fabulous study."

I took a step towards her.

"Joanna!" I hissed, jerking my head towards the rocking chair.

"What?"

I repeated the movement, widening my eyes at her.

"What?" she said again.

Exasperated, I signalled urgently with my eyes, swivelling them back and forth in the direction of the window.

"What *is it*?" Joanna sounded puzzled. I gave up.

"I'm so ..." I began apologetically as I turned towards the old lady.

I never finished the sentence. The room was empty. The sun was still shining through the window, accentuating the dust that had gathered on the panes and highlighting the nails in the floor boards. White walls and bare boards, a large window and a porcelain sink in the far corner. That was all.

"What is it? Are you all right?" Joanna asked, frowning.

"It's ... nothing." I shrugged uncomfortably. "This is not very interesting. It's just an empty room. Let's see what else we can find."

We left the room together – but I could not resist a backward glance. Dust danced in the sunbeams: the room was bare. Only a hint of lavender scent, swiftly fading, and the memory of thistledown hair and a sightless smile. I smiled myself, feeling a vague sense of benediction. I followed Joanna to the other door realising that it must lead to the lobby-cum-porch into which the front door opened and from there a door into ....

"Dining room," I cried, "With a hatch through to the kitchen. I've always wanted a dining room with a hatch."

I looked around. On the plus side: it had a hatch, the far wall was panelled in wood; two alcoves bore massive bookcases; one window overlooked the street, the other the garden; the carpet was passable. On the minus side: the plaster of the ceiling was coming down. There was a sizeable downward curve in it by the garden window.

"Only kept up by the paper," said Bruce, who had followed us and was about to poke it with an exploratory finger.

"Don't!" I remonstrated, with visions of dust enveloping us.

A scraping at the window made me jump guiltily but it was only a bare rose branch, tapping the window as the wind increased. The tap, tap, tap discomforted me a little, reminding me that we were trespassing. I suggested we explore upstairs, out of sight.

The stairs, steep and dangerous, led up from the inglenook room to a small landing. I opened the first door and found myself in a room which reached up into the rafters and took up the whole of the eastern end of the house. A casement window graced each of the three outside walls. I skipped to the farthest, most eastern one.

"Look! There's the church nestling in the trees at the end of the High Street," I exclaimed.

"You can see the *whole* back yard from here," announced Bruce from the southern window. "And ... yes, you're right. There *is* a stream at the bottom of the garden."

"Can you see fairies, too?" I teased.

Bruce threw me a look which combined scorn and amusement.

"I like the high beams in this room," I said.

"Rafters," corrected Bruce, pulling himself up to his full six feet two. "I'm glad I can stand tall in here. Downstairs is a much closer fit."

Joanna followed us as we explored the rest of the first floor. There were two more bedrooms. The first one led off the landing. Boasting a dormer window, it was the same shape as the dining room beneath it; the other, which led out of it, was smaller with a large sash window. It was situated over the black hole, echoing its trapezium shape.

I suppose, looking back, they were only rooms, but my

imagination had already filled them with babies and toys. Bruce and I returned to the big room where I envisaged a huge double bed in pride of place.

"I think this house likes us," said Bruce, reaching for my hand. "Do you really want it, darling?"

"Oh, yes," I breathed, quite overcome.

"There's a coal bin here ... and an old mangle." Joanna's muffled exclamation reverberated from below: she must have been investigating the back garden.

Bruce and I shared a hug.

"So do I," he said. "Let's have a proper look round while we're here."

I was a little apprehensive when we approached the old lady's room but she did not reveal herself a second time. Bruce seemed very interested in the corner by the sink.

"See those marks on the wall? I think there used to be a fireplace here, or perhaps a copper. The flooring's comparatively new."

"Oh yes, of course." Now he had pointed it out, I could see exactly where the fireplace had once been. Another thought struck me, one that might explain why the old lady was here, looking out into the street, rather than by the inglenook.

"I suppose this may have been a separate cottage. They used to be one room up and one down," I said, deciding against mentioning the old lady.

Apart from that one room, the rest of the downstairs was carpeted. Not to our taste, perhaps, but the carpets were good quality and fairly new. It seemed the beaten copper hood above the fire had been added recently. I stooped beneath it and stood up inside, gazing up the chimney to the sky. The wind came down to meet me.

"Plenty of ventilation," I joked. "The chimney needs a cowl, that's all."

The wind gusted and, for an instant only, my ears caught a few plaintive notes of unfamiliar birdsong. I gave myself a mental shake, remembering that songbirds seldom sing in winter. I ducked out from under the hood. Bruce had gone into the kitchen; I could hear him teasing Joanna who had apparently been testing the plumbing.

"There's no hot water," she was saying.

"The central heating boiler's been turned off," he told her. "I expect the water has, too, in case it freezes. It *does* freeze in this country, you know. You're not in Oz *now*. You're in the land of the Pommies, the country of warm beer. Talking of which ...."

I knew he was itching to get to the pub but my feet remained stubbornly where they were. I needed a moment or two on my own. The whole house felt warm and welcoming despite the lack of heating and the cold draught that blew down the chimney. The old lady's smile still lit the deeper recesses of my mind as I imagined children and adults huddling round the huge fire when the winter winds blew from the East, a great black cauldron of stew bubbling over a huge driftwood fire. I could imagine wet clothes set before it to dry — in fact the smell of wet wool permeated the room, endorsed with the warm fragrance of lamb stew and salted wood. I felt slightly dizzy.

"Are you there, Hazel?" Bruce asked as he poked his head round the kitchen door. "Have you seen enough for now? The pub is definitely calling. We can discuss everything more sensibly over a pint."

Pulling myself together, I agreed it was time to go. I shooed Bruce and Joanna back into the garden and re-bolted the stable door. After checking to make sure that we had left no trace of our visit, I eased myself gingerly over the basin and out of the tiny window. I closed it as securely as I could.

The neighbour with the red woollen hat was waiting for us as we came out of the side gate.

"They've only been gone about a week," he said, nodding his head in the direction of the house. "It's been on the market a while. They're asking too much, I expect. Nice people, done a lot of work."

With a quick "Happy Christmas!" he was gone, head down to the wind and his hands buried in his pockets.

"Happy Christmas!" we called back, almost in unison, as we made a bee-line for the car.

"I'm far too excited to drive," I declared. "I'll go in the back."

"Great," laughed Bruce. "Now, *at last*, I get to go to the pub. There's one back in the High Street that I happened to notice on the way through. Not that you were listening."

"Do something with your daughter!" was Bruce's greeting to my parents as we all tumbled, laughing, into the kitchen. "She's been driving us mad all the way home. She's seen a house she likes and she's determined to have it, come hell or high water. I've never known her like this. My ears can't take the strain."

I was kneeling on the floor pursuing my usual ritual of greeting Poppadum, her head down in my lap. Usually I flipped her over but not this time. Instead, I leapt up and pretended to box Bruce's ears.

"I'll give you sore ears!"

Poppadum nudged my bottom with her nose. I jumped. Bruce grinned.

"No, *naughty* girl," I admonished her, patting her head absently as I turned to my mother. "It's called 'Rose Cottage'. It's a long sort of building. Black and white. And beams. I'm not sure how old it is but probably a couple of hundred years. I think it was two or three cottages originally ..."

Bruce laughed. "See what I mean? *Do* something, *please*."

My father winked at him knowingly.

"... Three bedrooms, an inglenook *and* a larder." I continued, ignoring him. "It's wonderful, Mum, you should see it."

"If I'd known you were going house hunting I wouldn't have been able to resist coming with you," she responded smiling. "I can see you've found something special. Tell us more."

I think she may have regretted that invitation because Joanna and I started talking over each other, the volume increasing exponentially. My father clapped his hands over his ears and remarked to Bruce that he knew a good place to lie low until it had all blown over. My mother held up her hands.

"I think you'd better go and see the Estate Agents when they open after Christmas. Rose Cottage sounds perfect. But now ... *food*." She dived into lower oven of the Aga and brought out a wonderfully fragrant casserole. "Into the dining room with you."

After dinner, when my father had retired to the sitting room to watch the news on television, Bruce and Joanna tackled the washing up, Bruce almost up to his armpits in soapy water and Joanna wielding the drying up cloth. I took my mother back to the dining room for a private chat.

"Something strange happened at Rose Cottage," I told her. "I know the house was empty, but I saw an old woman sitting in a rocking chair by a downstairs window. I could see her so clearly. Her white hair done up in a bun, her veined hands, the rug on her knee, her eyes ... I'm sure she was blind. But she smiled at me in *such* a way. It was as if she knew me."

"How intriguing! Did it worry you?"

"It was strange," I said slowly. "Somehow it felt comfortable ... almost familiar. As if she were welcoming me home."

"You obviously liked the house itself?"

"Yes! I love it. I'd love to ..."

"And you'd be happy to live there even if you had to share it with that old lady?"

"Yes, and I'm sure she'd like it too."

"In that case, I can see no problem," said my mother.

"Do you think the old lady was a ghost?" I'd asked, intrigued.

"I think it's almost certain." Mother's smile had a knowing quality.

"There's something else," I went on. "I told Bruce that I'd travel in the back of the car because I was too excited to drive. He got into the driving seat but of course the seat was too far forward for him. He went to move it back *after* he'd started the engine, pressed the accelerator by mistake and we started to go backwards *fast*. Bruce was leaning forward and didn't notice. I heard a short, hard, rapping sound and a shout of "HALT!" I'm *sure* I didn't shout and I *know* Joanna didn't, but Bruce heard it and told me to keep my hair on." I swallowed.

"Go on, darling."

"Bruce braked hard and the car stopped. But if it had been a moment later ... a lorry was going past at full speed and we would have reversed right into it ..." I hesitated.

"Yes?" she prompted.

"I ... I twisted round in the back seat and ... *You* might believe this, but thousands wouldn't! I'm *sure* I saw a face in the window – and a hand waved at me."

"And you think it was the old lady?"

"Yes. I'm *absolutely* sure it was. The face was in that very window where she was sitting. But the thing is ... I *know* that house was empty. There can't have been anyone there. And whoever heard of a ghost knocking on a window?"

"*I* have, now," said my confidante, that smile playing around her lips again. "How intriguing! We shall have to see what the future holds. *If* you buy the house."

Of course, Bruce and I did buy the house, old lady and all. We moved in three months afterwards. We were very happy amidst the dust and disorganisation of essential repairs although we were seldom home, each of us working long hours to pay for the building work.

I sometimes felt a beneficent presence around me but nothing more.

- 6 -

Of a Long Ago Dream

Rosy is shaking me awake.

"What, what?" I cry, the dream fast receding. I grip it in my memory, loath to let it go, its strangeness exaggerated in my waking.

"Thou wast striking me! And yelling. See — Mary is crying. And thou hast even woken little Jane."

From the end of the bed which I share with my sisters, two woeful little faces stare at me. Jane regards me solemnly, her eyes huge. Tears are dribbling down Mary's cheeks. She creeps close to me, her chubby little arms twining round my neck as she sobs. She snuggles close: my neck is wet with her tears.

"A ... Ann ... Annie." Her chest heaves but her weeping is lessening as I pat her back. "W ... what madest thee cry out like that? It affrighted me."

"It affrighted me more," Jane declares, still solemn.

"I was struck!" Rosy is indignant, her red hair flaming in the moonlight.

"But it affrighted me most," Jane repeats stolidly.

"Wast thou affrighted, Annie?" Mary whispers in my ear.

"'Twas but a dream," I soothe.

"But thou wast affrighted, Annie?" Mary pursues.

"Not as affrighted as me," Jane insists. "I was very, very, very affrighted."

"But I was struck and affrighted!" Rosy is still indignant.

"Shhh. You'll wake Ma and Pa."

I know there is only one way to quieten them, so I whisper to them all to draw close and I tell them of my dream.

'I found myself floating down the stair and transported to the parlour. It was cold for there was no fire in the grate, indeed there

was no grate. Our parlour it appeared, yet bare of all trappings other than the rocking chair in which I was sitting by the window that gives onto the High Street. I blinked — for it seemed that sunlight had slanted into twilight. I saw only shapes moving through a December fog. I blinked again. It made no difference, my eyesight so feeble I could barely make out the familiar street. Yet 'twas not familiar quite, for there were odd, tall, square houses where the common fields should be and the road ran hard and black. Noisy carriages passed by that shook the very walls. For an instant, I discerned people who walked close by, only to dissolve once more to shadows.

Strange it was, to feel so decrepit and so very ancient, my bones stiff in my body and my eyes dim.

The door opened and a young woman flung in — but a woman dressed as I have never before seen. She was bundled in a strange coat of a vivid hue, her long fair hair a-hanging uncurled or dressed though she was clearly a maid no more. She did not greet me — indeed it seemed she was unaware of my presence.

She was followed shortly by another young woman whose clothes sang with colour through the murk. I saw not clearly yet I was aware of her curious apparel. Her legs were cased in wide breeches of bright pink and her jacket — for she was dressed like a man — was patterned in green and vermillion. In that same peculiar fashion I was aware that her hair was cropped short and curled, dark and close as the fleece of a new-born lamb. She saw me and smiled — then turned away, speaking strange words, familiar in meaning yet unlike these I utter now. A strange scent came from her, such as I have never smelled. It was not of Nature, yet not unpleasant. And as her fragrance surrounded me, I found myself fading, fading, fading into the very air. I was adrift in grey mist when, abruptly, I was lifted up as if moving through a tempest, so strong was the force.

Of a sudden, the squall — for such it must have been — flung me back in the rocking chair, facing the glass — and my eyes were keen once more. The woman and some others were mounting into something like a carriage, for I saw the door open and the woman climb inside. But there were no horses. A rumble, louder by far than the turning of a cartwheel on a gravel road, and the machine shot backwards towards me. I started — for I feared the impact on the very window by which I sat. And in that moment a huge monstrous snorting thing roared down the track, faster than a runaway horse. Yet the moment was strangely slow as if Time stood still. As if in a dream within the dream, I felt the force of a disaster about to happen, I saw the danger clear — then Time gathered speed once more and before I knew I was a-shouting and a-banging on the glass ...'

And Rosy is shaking me awake.

- 7 -

Of Possibilities and Probabilities

The recurrent dream from my childhood had started again a few days before my meeting with Mr. Stone. It had followed the pattern that I'd recalled, coming nightly for about three days over the dark of the moon. But at full moon a couple of weeks later I'd had another dream and then they'd come thick and fast. From some I woke with my heart beating fast only to find that the dream had dissipated into thin air leaving me with the impression of danger, but no more. Others were more distinct and I would remember a few details. Many of them my memory refused to record. Violence and fear were the overriding themes. But through them all was threaded a bird's song — the beautiful nighttime anthem of the nightingale. And a love story.

Why had I been thinking of that bird's melody this morning? I had barely framed the question when I remembered the few notes of song I had heard when I first stood in the inglenook and looked up the chimney into the ice blue sky of winter. Was it because I'd been recalling the day we discovered our home? Were the nightingale's song and the cottage linked somehow to my dream? Surely not. That would be surreal. But then, the whole experience of being at home on this, my first day off work, was peculiar.

A comment from someone close by brought me firmly back into the present, reminding me not only that I was standing in a sun-drenched garden in May, daydreaming, but also also that our boundary was shared with the Fire Station. I overheard the voice of one of the firemen.

"Did you hear all that noise last night?"

"What noise?" a second, older voice queried. "I don't remember hearing anything."

"Impossible not to, I'd have thought," the fireman replied. I remembered his name was David.

"Well I didn't hear anything."

"It was close to midnight so I expect you were snoring. I definitely heard a loud noise — like thunder that seemed to come from everywhere at once. Funnily enough, it sounded like horses stampeding."

"Oh yeah?" Heavy cynicism from the other.

"Yeah."

"You must have drunk too much last night, I reckon."

"Okay. Let's say I dreamed it." David. Resigned.

They moved away, still chatting. I stood still, recalling a strange sound in the night. I'd thought it was thunder, although I recollected neither the flash of lightning nor the sound of rain falling. The grass was dry, too. But now I vaguely remembered the sound of horses galloping through the night.

The telephone started ringing again. I ignored it for a while but the caller did not ring off this time. I supposed I would have to answer it. I went indoors with a sigh but put on my brightest voice when I picked up the receiver.

"Hello, Mrs Dawkins speaking."

"Hello Mrs Dawkins. Good morning to you! It's Paul Stone from the bank, here. May I call you Hazel?" He didn't wait for an answer. "I've found that baby-minder I promised you." What baby-minder? My silence must have indicated my puzzlement. "You remember I mentioned her when we last met?"

"Er ... yes," I said doubtfully. Surely it had been a suggestion in passing, intended only if I should want to start practising law again after the baby was born?

"She came into the bank yesterday so, of course, I mentioned you to her. Her name is Mrs Green and she's very experienced. Knows a lot about children because she has five herself. I said you would phone her today and she told me she can see you tomorrow. She lives close to you."

He rattled off her telephone number and address, said goodbye and disconnected instantly. Nonplussed, I put my hands protectively to my protruding belly.

"If he thinks I'm going to let you go to just anyone *he* thinks is okay, he's got another think coming," I reassured the Bump. The comment was acknowledged by what felt like a shrug of the baby's shoulders. I closed my eyes and sighed another long sigh. My mind went back to that evening in April, after my appointment with the bank manager....

Over a supper of omelettes, new potatoes and the very first salad leaves from the garden, I had regaled Bruce with a full account of my visit. He had listened to me in silence apart from a munching sound as the lettuce disappeared.

He fixed me with his 'I am considering' look, the sun catching his red-gold hair and making it into a shining halo. I was reminded of my mother's description of him: 'that golden man you married' she'd said.

'How I love you!' I'd thought, 'I hope the baby is exactly like you. Except that if it's a girl it would be better with my nose. Yours is much too big.' All thoughts led back to the baby.

"Did we get the overdraft?" Bruce asked.

"Oh yes," I'd answered. "Even more than I asked for. A thousand pounds!"

"You could give it a whirl then," he'd suggested with a lop-sided grin. "If it doesn't work out we won't have lost much."

My mouth had fallen open. I'd been convinced that he loved the idea of me being at home, as his mother had been. It made him the sole wage-earner and head of the family. Surely that was how he wanted it to be? Or so I had thought.

"But the baby?" I'd gasped. "It will take all my time and I want to put my feet up and talk baby talk ..."

"You can do all that, Hazel. But we both know you'll be bored within six months."

"I suppose it would be good to know a baby-minder," I'd admitted. "Just in case."

"Don't do it if you don't want to," Bruce had responded, smiling a very knowing smile. "I very much doubt Mr Stone will send you any work anyway — but we'll manage, come what may."

When the Clocks Stopped

I came back to the song of the blackbird and opened my eyes. Mrs Green's telephone number was still written on the notepad in my hand. It seemed that circumstances were against me being a stay-at-home mother.

Mrs Green answered the telephone almost immediately.

'Wow! She's efficient,' and 'Oh dear, now I can't get out of this.' The two thoughts were simultaneous.

"Marigold Green," a brisk voice answered.

'Oh dear,' I thought, wondering whether to pretend I'd dialled a wrong number.

"Hello?"

"Er ... hello, Mrs Green. I'm Hazel Dawkins. Mr Stone gave me your number and asked me to phone you ...." My voice trailed away.

"Oh yes. Of course. *Dear* Mr Stone." The voice seemed to relax into a smile — a smile with a soft Cornish burr.

"You see," I began. "He seems to think I need someone to look after my baby ..."

"That's what I do, duck," she interrupted. "Done it for years. I love babies and children. I'd have to meet you both first, though."

"Of course," I found myself agreeing. Oh dear, oh dear and triple oh dear. I did *not* want a baby minder. I wanted to look after my own child, all by myself ... but I found myself agreeing to call round at eleven o'clock the very next day.

I didn't mention it to Bruce when he arrived home, hot and tired. If I didn't mention it to him, it might never happen.

The following morning was as beautiful a summer morning as its predecessor. Very hot and sweaty in my best smock and maternity trousers, I waddled along the High Street towards Mrs Green's house. I found myself continuously rehearsing my speech. I knew exactly what I was going to say:

"I'm sorry to have put you to this trouble. I really don't want anyone else to care for my baby; but when Mr Stone rang me I thought it would be very rude to say no."

So far, so good.

I came to a neat white gate set in a white picket fence. The garden was trim. Maybe a little too trim, I thought — but, as I walked up the path to the front door, I caught a glimpse of the back garden which contained a swing and a see-saw and seemed well-scuffed by children's feet.

I was about to put my finger to the bell when, all of a sudden, the door was thrown open and a sleek, black cat was forcibly ejected into my path.

"Out with you, you ... oh!" A round, cuddlesome woman had materialised on the doorstep, the sun glinting in her lustrous dark hair. The cat landed on all four feet and disappeared round the corner. Mrs Green viewed me with consternation.

"Yes?" she said defensively, "Hello ... er ... you can't be ...?"

"Mrs Dawkins," I hurriedly introduced myself.

"Goodness me!" responded Mrs Green, eyeing my resplendent belly. "You haven't even had the baby yet."

"No, but Mr Stone ..." My voice, and all my good intentions, trailed away.

"I see. Cart before the horse again. Typical man," she scoffed. "Well, come in."

She backed away from the door to let me pass into a narrow hall. Feeling apprehensive, I followed her into a large sitting room that was full of sunshine.

"Do sit," she said, motioning to a huge brown sofa as she sank into an arm chair of similar proportions. She looked me up and down with a pair of knowledgeable but kindly blue eyes. "Would you like a cuppa?"

"No thanks." Tea made me ill, but I wasn't going to admit that. "I only came ...."

"Because Mr Stone told you to," she finished for me, with a touch of empathy.

"Yes," I nodded. "He said that a solicitor was needed here in Rype. He also said he'd organise everything for me. But I wasn't expecting it to be so soon."

"I realise that," she smiled. "Mr Stone likes to get things done quickly, but babies take their time, don't they? Anyway, since you're here now, let's get to know one another a little. When's the baby due?"

"June. Only three weeks to go now."

"It's your first isn't it?"

"Yes. Mr Stone said you have five of your own."

"They're mostly grown up, now. My eldest is in the Army and my youngest is nine. I'd have liked more but the doctors said any more would kill me. Now I look after other people's children before they're old enough for school."

"How many little ones do you look after?" I enquired.

"At the moment I look after only one little girl. She's two years old and comes to me three times a week while her mother works in a shop." She hesitated for a moment. "From the way Mr Stone was talking, I thought you needed me urgently. *Now*, in fact."

"I'm sorry," I apologised. "But yesterday was my first non-working day. At the moment I want to look after my baby myself."

"Good. I'm pleased you feel that way. When Mr Stone told me about you I got the impression that you weren't happy in your pregnancy, that you didn't want to give up work. I see that I was wrong." Her wonderful warm smile lit up her face. "I'm glad I was wrong."

She cocked her head a little to one side.

"Maybe you should come back after you've had the baby. If you change your mind, that is. Anyway, now you're here you might as well have a look round and I'll explain how I work, just so that you know."

That evening, I waited until Bruce had finished his supper and was nursing a cup of tea between his hands.

"I found a baby-minder for the Bump, today," I said casually.

"*What?*" He slurped his tea and choked in astonishment.

"I know, I know," I agreed, when his coughing fit had subsided. "I said I was going to be an at-home mother. I still want to be ... and you agreed we could manage financially ... but Mr Stone organised it. So I had to go and meet her."

"Who is she? What's she like?"

"She's about ten years older than me." I answered the second part of the question first. "She has five children of her own. She's plump and pretty with dark brown hair and very blue, smiley eyes. I liked her. Her name is Marigold Green and her husband is Martin. I haven't met him yet."

"Why this sudden change of plan?" Bruce still looked puzzled.

"No change. I'm still planning to take this time off to be a proper mother. I think she was rather surprised to see I was still pregnant. She suggested I go back after the baby's born, *if* I still want someone to help."

"Okay. Maybe that's a good idea. What's the house like?" He was more interested than I'd anticipated.

"Very clean and comfortable, apart from a disobedient cat. A garden that children can really play in. Lots of knickknacks and ornaments in the sitting room but she says that children soon learn not to touch them. I liked that."

"So you think it's a possibility?"

"Yes," I agreed, easing my way round the table to kiss his cheek. "Just a *possibility*, though."

Bruce grabbed my hair in mock exasperation and kissed me very thoroughly and satisfyingly.

The following morning I was in the garden, enjoying the sun's caress of my hair, when the phone rang. It rang for a long time before I answered it.

"Hello, Mrs Dawkins. Good morning to you, Hazel," came Mr Stone's cheerful voice. "Did you go and see Mrs Green?"

"Yes, I did."

"Good, good!" He sounded pleased. "And did you ...?"

"I'm going to see after the baby's born," I said firmly.

"Quite right," he commented, a knowing chuckle in his voice. "Quite right."

- 8 -

Of Sounds in the Night

A pale finger of moonlight strayed across my eyelashes, teasing my eyes open, as a plaintive melody poured over me. I moved my head so that my ears were clear of the muffling pillow and lay in the near-dark, awash with liquid sound.

I slept fitfully these days, turning from side to side in an effort to get the Bump comfortably balanced. Damn! I needed the toilet. I would have to get up. Bruce's legs lay over mine, pinning me to the bed. Accustomed as he was to my erratic sleep pattern, I knew I had only to push him gently and he would change position without waking. I nudged and he re-arranged his limbs, releasing me with a grunt. A glance at the bedside clock revealed it was five minutes to midnight.

Wondering if I would ever be able to slip easily out of bed again, I cautiously heaved myself up on one elbow, swung my legs round and eased myself out from under the sheet. It was unseasonably hot and now I was awake I needed a glass of water as well; but first, I tiptoed to the window and looked out onto a garden swathed in moonlight. Nothing stirred; even the white cherry blossom below mesmerised by the music pouring from the heavens.

Enchanted myself, I leaned on the sill until the nightingale's song drew to a close and the hushed night seemed to sigh. I sighed too; I could put off the call of Nature no longer.

Feeling my way along the wall, I descended the flight of stairs, catching my breath as a shadowy pattern of moonlight danced on the far wall of the sitting room. There was no breeze, nothing to make the plants outside sway so wildly. Then came a sudden laugh, instantly hushed in a very inebriated fashion, and a soldier fell off the low front wall with a thump, a wail and:

"Shit!"

"Sod it! You bloody …."

"Shhhh."

I'd reached my destination and the sheer bliss of relieving myself was overtaken by a desire to laugh. Soldiers on their way back to camp after a night at the pub — the Red Lion was their favourite watering hole — could not resist trying to walk along the low wall in front of the cottage.

Now I was thirsty. I repaired to the kitchen and was drinking a glass of water when a very different sound made me jerk and the baby kick. A single shot — so loud it reverberated round the kitchen. The noise of a galloping horse filled the room, quickly receding along the High Street towards the open Marsh. I rushed from the kitchen to the sitting room and peered out of the window. The buttresses spoiled my view, so I opened the front door and ventured out into the moonlight.

To the left, the High Street ran straight for the quarter of a mile to the church. It was deserted, bathed in the light of the full moon. To the right, the street curved as it hooked into the road to Rye. The army camp was a little way to the left of the junction, its entrance hidden by the buildings opposite. Again, there was no movement, no sign of life at all. The soldiers who had tried to balance on our wall must have been the last ones back to barracks that night.

The scent of pansies and heartsease pervaded the still air, their perfume mounting in intensity. A presentiment of impending doom filled me with misgiving. Deafened by the pumping of my heart, I fled back inside — but now the house itself was stifling with foreboding. I struggled to breathe through a blanket of moisture as trails of luminescence materialised within the darkness wherever I turned my eyes. Blinking rapidly, I fled into the sweetness of the moonlit garden, where peace and tranquillity reigned again, and my pulse steadied.

As I took a lungful of the night's fragrance, the nightingale resumed her hymn to the beauty of the moon and Time stood still, holding me within its spell. I was dimly aware that the nightingale had stopped singing and the night had grown silent again but I stood there, lost, until the weight of the church clock's bell ringing out the hour stole into my consciousness. Surely it couldn't be a whole hour since I woke? Standing there I counted the chimes. Twelve. Midnight. How could that be? It had been almost midnight when I awakened, and I was sure I had been downstairs for longer than a few minutes.

A whispering tremor winged its way through the moonlight, and Time ran again, confirmed by a swift succession of kicks in what my father termed 'the breadbasket'. I shivered, drawing my voluminous nightgown closer around my body as I retreated into the kitchen, hoping that the strange atmosphere had dissipated. Sure enough, the house wrapped its usual comforting presence round me.

Poppadum appeared from her bed, asking to go out. I was faintly surprised that she had not responded to the sounds of the shot and the horses. Usually, when the moon turned its full face towards the earth, Poppadum would hurtle outside at the first opportunity; indeed, at any time the opening of the back door was a signal for her to dash into the garden in search of squirrels, cats, foxes or anything that moved. Poppadum hadn't appeared when I'd first come downstairs, nor when I'd stepped out of doors. In fact, until the church clock had struck the midnight hour she might not have existed.

I decided that heavy pregnancy must have made me fanciful.

Suddenly the solid security of my husband's warm body felt irresistible. I called the dog back into the house and tiptoed up the stairs and into the bedroom. A moonbeam stroked his burnished curls as I snuggled into Bruce's reassuring ordinariness.

The clock ticked on. It showed ten minutes past midnight.

The sun's rays woke me; light and the dawn chorus together were better than any alarm clock. I checked the clock: a minute or two past six o'clock. I had managed to get through the whole of the last six hours without having to get up again. The thought had hardly reached my consciousness when the Bump kicked me hard in the bladder as if to tell me that I had no chance of drowsing now I was awake.

Bruce's face was hidden below the sheet in an attempt to hide from the light. I was tempted to ruffle his hair but stopped my hand halfway to its destination. Let him sleep for another half-hour.

"Wasn't it a beautiful night?" I whispered to the Bump as I descended the stairs again. "Did you feel the strangeness too? It wasn't only me, was it?"

The Bump lay quiescent, enjoying the ride downstairs. As I reached the foot of the stairs Poppadum came to greet us in her usual gentle fashion, pushing her nose gently into my left palm.

"Where were you last night?" I asked, remembering. Poppadum pricked her ears at the sound of my voice but made no answer.

"Never mind," I said. "I'll let you out again now."

I opened the back door and Poppadum flew out with a series of little barks, chasing sparrows from the lawn.

"That's more like you," I said to her wake as I headed to the bathroom.

I was making breakfast — egg, bacon, mushrooms and fried bread — when Bruce put his still ruffled head round the kitchen door half an hour later.

"*Stone the crows* but that smells good," he enthused, emphasising the Aussie expletive. "I love a woman who smells of breakfast. And talking of breakfast, do we have time for a quick snack of another kind?" He caught me to him and nuzzled my neck.

"Not now, you fool," I chided him, with a sharp backwards movement of my buttocks into something quite hard. "Maybe later when you're dressed. I never could resist a man in a collar and tie ... and no trousers ...."

The fat sputtered in the pan. Too late, I averted my head with a twist to the right and managed to connect hard with his chin. Bruce released me instantly. By reflex action, I turned off the gas.

"Ow!" I spat out. The fat had caught my arm and Bruce's jaw was as hard as rock.

"Ow!" Bruce's exclamation was followed by an unrepeatable expletive as he rubbed his reddish stubble and somewhere lower at the same time. He caught my eye and grinned.

"Come here, woman," he demanded. "Put that down." He took

the slice from my hand, put it on the draining board and kissed me very hard. "I'd better get washed and dressed before you can do any more damage," he said, slapping me playfully on the bottom as he disappeared into the bathroom.

It was only after he had left for work, washed, shaved, suited and tied and well filled with breakfast, that I realised I had not mentioned my odd experience during the night. I shrugged to myself.

'It was just a dream. Forget it,' I told myself.

I turned my mind to my meeting with Marigold. It had made me think again; she was the kind of loving, natural mother I wanted to be myself and I'd felt instantly that if I were going to leave the Bump with anyone she would fit the bill perfectly. And then Bruce had reminded me of how much time and effort I had put into qualifying as a solicitor.

I had been the first girl from the Grammar School to apply to read law at university. My headmistress had been scathing in her dismissal of the idea.

"Teaching or nursing," she'd declared. "Those are the careers for you. You must face it, Hazel. Mark my words, you will *never* achieve a university place, let alone in law, and *certainly* not at such a prestigious university as Bristol. I suggest you change your options. Set your sights lower, my girl."

"Yes, Miss Jones," I'd said, demurely acquiescent while seething inside. But she hadn't finished with me.

"This school," she'd haughtily insisted, "Has been extant for the cream of intelligent girls since 1909. Many have gone on to Oxford and Cambridge. Many more have done well at other universities and teachers' training colleges. They have read subjects in both the arts and the sciences but not *one* — I repeat, *not one* — has attempted the impossible task of applying to read law. What makes you so arrogant as to think you can do this?"

I had listened in silence, my feelings very mixed — I was cross, uncomfortable, nervous and anxious — but this question brought my anger to the surface.

"My father, Miss Jones," I'd replied stonily. "My *father* believes girls should have a profession. He went to Bristol and he wants me to go there too."

"It's my belief that your father views your academic achievements through rose-coloured spectacles," my headmistress observed caustically. "It is, of course, your decision. But I fear you will be drastically disappointed. You may go."

Her opposition — for such I had perceived it — had worked as reverse psychology: I believed myself honour-bound to prove her wrong. And I did. I was accepted as an undergraduate to read law at Bristol University. As one of nine women students among a hundred men, I really enjoyed my time at Bristol. After three years of interesting study, I'd received an Honours degree sufficient to exempt me from the first part of the Law Society's Solicitor's Qualifying examinations.

Next, I needed to find Articles of Clerkship — the contract between a solicitor and his apprentice. I was fortunate that it was no longer the norm for the clerk to pay for his Articles, as had been the case until only a few years previously. Nowadays an articled clerk usually received a small wage as well as training and was not generally required to pay. However, finding Articles proved a difficult task; no firm wanted to risk the cost and time involved in training a woman only for her to later marry and leave work to bring up a family. Even when I finally achieved an interview with a local firm I was informed that I would not be considered for the position unless I signed an undertaking that I would not marry for three years from the date of my engagement by the firm. Incensed, I refused. I found out later that the position had been filled by a young man I knew, who had no formal qualifications and who was not required to sign an undertaking.

As I was beginning to lose hope, my aunt suggested that her solicitor husband might be prepared to employ me. I spent a month on trial in my uncle's office at the end of which I was still in the dark as to whether he was prepared to retain me. I went home for the weekend feeling dejected.

My father met me at the door.

"Well done, Old Girl!" was his greeting as I kissed his stubbly cheek. He was grinning from ear to ear. "I've had James on the phone. He tells me that my daughter is actually quite intelligent and much more practical than he expected! He asked my permission to offer you 'Indentures'."

I was overjoyed and I had accepted the terms he offered me — a small salary of nine pounds a week and one week's holiday a year — with alacrity and gratitude.

The word 'Indentures' that he had used was unfamiliar to me.

"An Indenture," Uncle James explained, "Is a legal contract document made between two individuals. It's usually a contract of employment or apprenticeship. Here, in our case, it's the old-fashioned way of describing 'Articles of Clerkship' or 'Articles' for short."

"I'd rather gathered that. But where did the term come from?"

"Ah! Now should I tell you or make you look it up?"

The solicitor pursed his lips as he considered, looking at me over his spectacles with mischief in his eyes. Then he continued:

"The term comes from medieval times when a contract was written out twice on the same sheet of vellum. The vellum was then divided into parts by cutting it in a zigzag line. Each individual, or party, retained a part."

"Why do that?"

"Because, in law, the two parts had to fit together perfectly in order to constitute a valid contract and to settle any dispute as to the its terms."

I had signed my Articles of Clerkship and committed myself to two years of hard work and intense learning, of late nights and early mornings and, most of all, of excitement and fascination with the law and how it affected everything and everybody in some way, almost daily.

Afterwards, when the two years were up and my articles completed, I had spent an unpaid year at the College of Law in London. Rising early and going to bed late, all the hours in between were spent in lectures or cramming into my brain the eight subjects, including Accounts, for the Law Society's finals. During that time, I had only weekends in which to see Bruce and even the thought of marriage was dismissed until I had passed the exams. As we celebrated my freedom from all the years of study and the fact that I was qualified at last, Bruce proposed. I accepted and we arranged our wedding. Two days after our nuptials, I was formally admitted as a Solicitor of the Supreme Court.

It was a professional requirement that I had to have worked as a solicitor for three years after qualification before I was able to 'set up my plate' and practise on my own account without supervision. It had taken me almost ten years but I had done it.

'And now,' I thought, 'do I really want to give up the law and all its fascination? Especially when I have the opportunity to start my own practice?'

When Bruce came home that evening he found me wedged between the door and the bookcase. Opening the door without looking, he trapped me behind it.

"What are you doing there?" he asked, baffled.

I managed to get myself back to my usual size by taking a deep breath. It helped me to shout, too.

"What do you think I'm doing?" I exploded. "I'm looking for a book, of course."

"What book?"

"This one!"

I held up a book on birds. I had located it as he put his key in the lock, which was the reason I had been crouching behind the door, trying to reach the book from the bottom shelf of the bookcase.

"That's a book about birds," Bruce stated, still sounding puzzled.

"Yes," I agreed, launching into explanation. "You see, I had a chat with Horace next door. He tells me that this house used to be called 'Nightingale Cottages' back before the First World War. Apparently, before all the other houses round here were built, this house was ... er ... were? ... Anyway, two or three cottages were knocked together to make this house. The part on the side where the little bedroom is above the Hole was a net hut."

"Net hut? What on earth is that?" puzzled Bruce.

"It's a place where fishermen can dry their nets and mend them. It used to be a sort of tunnel, open at both sides with a roof over the top so that the draught dried the nets. The odd thing is that we're quite a way from the sea here — at least a couple of miles — and net huts are usually close to the fishing boats that use them."

"Interesting," remarked my husband. "Now may I come in?"

"Okay."

I moved away from the door. Bruce automatically ducked his head in order to miss the low beam as he came down the two steps from the tiny lobby into the sitting room. He dropped his briefcase onto the nearest armchair and came towards me, his lips puckered in a kiss. I offered my cheek; my mind was elsewhere. I was looking at those two steps.

"I see," I exclaimed. "That would have been the front door into this cottage and the dining room door would have been the entrance to the other cottage. I wondered why there was only one inglenook and that it was in this room. I'd have expected another fireplace back to back with it but there's only one place where a fireplace could have been in the dining room, isn't there?"

Bruce surveyed me with the annoying, quizzical air he adopted when he had not the slightest idea what I was talking about.

"It must have been on that flat piece of wall between the alcoves where we have the books. You know? Where the wood-panelling seems a little loose. Let's open it up and see if there's a fireplace there. It would have been in the perfect place, backing onto the net hut to help to dry the nets."

"Darling," said my dearest drily. "This is all very interesting, I know, but, if you're looking for fireplaces, why did you want a book on birds?"

"Well, obviously, I wanted to find out something about nightingales."

"Er ... any particular reason?"

"This house was called Nightingale Cottages. There was nothing else here except the fields and that track outside until the town spread this way — and that wasn't until about thirty years ago."

"So?" Bruce was still wearing a baffled frown.

"Why was it called 'Nightingale Cottages' do you think?"

"They liked the name? The chap who built them was called Nightingale?" He was guessing just to tease me.

"It's the name of a bird, idiot!"

He looked at me, a little hurt, and I remembered that he was Australian. I didn't know what a Galah was until he told me; naturally he didn't know the names of the less common birds.

"Horace said they used to be heard a lot around here, but he hasn't heard one for years and years. Almost as long as he can remember."

"Well, he's probably deaf. How old is he?" I knew Bruce was trying to steer me away from this peculiar conversation about birds.

"I don't know, but that's beside the point. The thing is, I think I heard one last night, at around midnight. It was a hauntingly beautiful sound, but I've never heard a nightingale sing myself, so I wasn't sure." I held up the book. "I was hoping to find something about the nightingale's song in here. I'll look later."

"Is there another name for a nightingale? One I might know?"

"Shakespeare called it Philomel — there's that sonnet of his I used to quote to you when we were dating. You remember? 'As Philomel in summer's front doth sing, but stops her pipe in growth of later days ...'"

"'Not that the summer is less pleasant now than when her mournful hymns did hush the night ...'' he continued.

"'But wild music burdens every bough and sweets grown common lose their dear delight.' Exactly!"

"Well, now we've sorted that out and finished quoting poetry at each other, do tell me..." he pleaded, holding up his hands in prayer. "Pleeease tell me! What's for dinner, Haze? I'm famished. And don't tell me it's nightingale stew because I won't believe you!"

Much later, Bruce had gone to bed. Having promised to follow as soon as I had finished laying the table for breakfast, I was about to turn off the lights when I spotted the bird book lying on top of the bookcase. The volume was quite old and tattered, well-thumbed and with a page or two turned down. As I smoothed those pages I found that one bent corner marked a page headed 'Nightingales'.

'Generations of poets have been inspired by the song of the nightingale, remarkable for its tonal richness, variety and volume. Sometimes, but not always, delivered at dead of night, the song consists of short phrases and single notes, usually repeated, often with increasing volume. Some notes are piping while others have a flute-like quality. The short song period lasts only from mid to late April until June.'

It seemed I was right. I was thrilled to think I had heard a nightingale at last. It was the right time, dead of night, the right time of year and the song I had heard was very similar to that described.

'A shy bird, the nightingale is generally found in open deciduous woodland where plenty of cover is provided by dense undergrowth of bramble, or by thickets of thorn bushes.'

Interesting. The Marsh was an open territory of fields defined by dykes and ditches. Brambles and nettles grew in profusion but in patches, not in a large wild area; woodland was sparse apart from the ubiquitous, water-loving willows which overhung the ditches and the hawthorn trees planted along the dykes to prevent erosion. Thorn trees were vital to the Marsh: not only did they stabilise the dykes that had been thrown up, centuries since, to defend the Marsh from the sea, they were literally woven into them when the dykes were holed by the tides. Indeed, it had once been a capital offence to cut hawthorn down for any other purpose.

'Made of dead leaves, lined with grass and hair, the nest is constructed on or close to the ground. It is usually hidden in brambles or nettles.....'

I found myself thinking sadly of the nightingale's nest near or on the ground, its protection being only the brambles or nettles surrounding it, and of the plethora of cats in the neighbourhood, thugs out to kill after dark. Nettles and brambles would prove but little protection. Poor nightingales. No wonder their songs were heard so seldom.

I closed the book and put it back on the shelf. Wondering whether I would ever again hear a nightingale sing, I took my weary limbs upstairs to bed. I was woken not by the moonlight nor by a bird's mournful hymn. This time I woke abruptly from a dream.

- 9 -

Of Death and a Vow of Vengeance

'Twas not my Pa's wounding that I had seen in the steam. He comes home weary and worn that night, with burnt black patches on his shirt and wild, wild eyes. Nay, 'twas not my Pa.

But grief weighs heavy in his shoulders and his arms. For there is held the bloody form of my brother Harry. A form that stirs not, lies still and broken where my father lays him tenderly upon the settle. His breast is blackened from the powder, black-red blood sticks to his fair hair where his lolling head is caved in from the stone on which he fell. A bare bone sticks out, wildly angled from his shin; his breeches hang in crusted rags.

I run to him, my hands reach out to tend him. His blood, still warm, sticks dark and red to my fingers. In horror, I turn away, run to put my back to the wall, can only stare unbelieving at my gory hands.

A moan, such as a beast would make when separated from her calf, and my Ma falls to her knees beside the corpse. For such it is. And though we are well aware of the risk that our Owlers run to keep us fed and warm when the wild Marsh winds blow icy in the winter's chill, still we are unprepared for tragedy to strike so close. So very close. At the beating heart of our family. For Harry is the son who bears his parents' hope, the brother whom all his sisters cherish. He of the flopping hair and grin as mischievous and cunning as the fox which takes our fowl. Harry of the tender heart who stoops to comfort little Mary; in whose tender hands unmothered fledglings tremble trustingly. He who can steal a single egg from a moorhen's nest, the bird quite unaware. Harry who over-looks the sheep at pasture and drives the foxes from the flock. Harry who assists at lambing; who pulls the living young from dying ewes and raises lambs who, motherless, would perish. Now it is he who lies here, lifeless in the parlour.

My sisters weep. Ma's grief, unshackled, shakes her uncontrollably. Pa's shoulders droop and his reddened eyes water, dark specks littering my mother's pinafore. Before me they group in sorrow, lending support to each other, loud in their lament.

But I turn away. I weep not. My eyes are dry. Yet the grief that burns in my breast is no less for my lack of tears. I am vastly angered and my grief is more than I can tell. For my brother who is closest to me, who is my helpmeet and my goad, is dead. No more will he push me in the ditch or tie my apron strings to the chair. No more will he laugh me out of anger or tease me from my tears. Or stoop to play with the little girl to whom he is a hero.

This night, in my tenth year, I take a mighty vow to join the Owlers and avenge my brother. The brother who is but two years my senior, whose warrior heart is great in his thin breast and whose ambition is to be the greatest Owler the Marsh has ever known.

I know who killed him. His murderer's face shone clear amongst the flames and 'tis imprinted in every detail on mine eyes. I know what I must do.

But tonight I creep to the net hut and there, alone, I admit my pain. I howl into the night, my bloodied fingers twisting in my hair.

I woke with the warm, metal smell of blood in my nostrils, my hands still feeling the stickiness, feeling blood all over me, as if I were lying in it, too. I turned to Bruce, half expecting him to be dead and his eyes glassily turned to the ceiling, but he was lying on his back, breathing loudly. Dead to the world, true, but not to the living.

The dream's tentacles were around me still. My heart leaping in my chest, I felt the sweat bead on my brow and realised that the stickiness I felt was merely sweat. Merely sweat! How horrible.

I made my way to the bathroom and washed my face and hands under the cold tap. Stripping naked and taking a flannel, I soaked it in cold water in the basin and scrubbed the perspiration from my body. Afterwards, I splashed myself with rose water, its fresh perfume lifting my spirits, banishing the gloom and horror.

Feeling better, I took myself and an idle Bump into the sitting room. I had seen it so clearly in my dream. The floorboards had been bare and the settle made of wood: shutters had covered the windows and the stairs had been enclosed by a wooden partition, not open to the room as they were now. But it had definitely been here, here, by the fire, that Pa had laid the body of my brother, Harry.

My brother?

I looked around and made comparisons. It had been modernised of course. Clean brick walls and the newly-shining copper hood took the place of the old black spit, the sooty stewpot and the metal griddle. I sniffed. I caught the faint smell of the beeswax polish I had tried yesterday. There was no whiff now of onions cooking, nor the warm close smell of sweating bodies. But my nostrils still remembered the metal odour of drying blood to which I had awoken, the redolence and atmosphere of the dream. The odours did not dissipate, rather they grew in intensity.

I had been half-dreading the feeling that had pervaded this room the night before, sure it would be there again, but there was no trace of that still strangeness. Tonight it felt loved, safe and cosy, as indeed it was. The memory of the dream, so sharp a moment before, began to fade. I turned over and drifted back to sleep.

- 10 -

Of Clients and Secrets

The telephone shrilled. Head buried like an ostrich in the darkness of my pillow, I was so comfortable that I couldn't move. I waited for Bruce to rise up and answer it but there was no movement beside me.

The phone rang and rang. Surely he was going to answer it? I poked him simultaneously with my foot and elbow but connected with empty space. I lifted my head and opened one eye. The sun was hot on the dented pillow beside me, illuminating a small hand-written note.

The phone continued to ring. Bother! I had finally found a comfortable way of lying – on my stomach with my arms crossed under my breasts – to keep the weight from both tender parts of my body. I attempted to lift myself to a crawling position but I could not feel my arms or hands. Collapsing back into the mattress, I managed to turn over in a whale-like manner, taking the sheet with me. The phone stopped ringing as feeling began to return; pins and needles ran up and down my arms as I picked up the note.

Dearest,

You were sleeping so well that I didn't have the heart to wake you. I'll be home at the usual time. Take care of the Bump.

SWALK X

Gosh! What *was* the time? I glanced at the clock. The hands showed five and twenty to ten. Shaking the alarm clock made no difference; its hands trembled a little but stayed stubbornly in the same position. I stretched luxuriously, blessing Bruce for letting me sleep in.

It was definitely time I got up. I yawned, screwing up my eyes, as I stretched again. When I opened them, my eyes fell on the note that Bruce had written; grabbing it, I kissed the X where I knew his lips had touched. SWALK was a word we used as a code, probably in common with hordes of other people. The letters stood for 'Sealed With A Loving Kiss'.

The phone shrilled again. Propelling myself across the room I managed to catch it on the fourth ring.

"Hello Mrs Dawkins – Hazel. Good morning to you. It's Paul Stone, from the bank. I'm sorry to call you so early but I have Mr and Mrs White here and they need to make Wills urgently. Would you be able to see them this morning?"

My head was in a whirl so I only managed an "Er ...?"

It didn't matter because he rushed on. "They could walk along to you, now, if that's convenient?"

Convenient? I thought of my unwashed body and wild hair. 'Definitely not' my mind screamed, but once again my lips had other ideas.

"Good Morning, Mr Stone." I was amazed at how cool I sounded "I'm afraid I'm engaged at the moment but I could see them at half past ten, if that would suit?"

Half past ten? I must be mad. I detected a short but muffled conversation. Then Mr Stone's voice again:

"Thank you, Mrs Dawkins. They'll be with you at half past ten. It's Rose Cottage, isn't it?"

"Yes."

"I know where it is. I'll give them directions. I'm obliged to you for fitting them in at such short notice. Goodbye for the present."

He put the handset down. I looked in disbelief at the black receiver I was holding and then slammed it home and jolted downstairs fast.

By half past ten, amazed by my own celerity, I was washed, dressed, brushed, and made up with eye pencil, mascara and lipstick – all I had time for – into some semblance of normality. I had pushed a reluctant Poppadum, who had been expecting a proper walk, into the garden and had run the carpet sweeper and a duster over the hall and dining room. I'd even found an official looking pad of paper and a fountain pen.

I stilled my racing heart and sank into the rocking chair. Phew!

I was ready.

There came a timid tap at the door. Poppadum merely raised a fawn eyebrow. I peeped out of the window. The view was obscured by the rampant yellow rose but I could see a man's hat and a pair of very sensible ladies' shoes.

Rat-a-tat-tat. Someone else must have grabbed the knocker. Poppadum's ears perked up the instant before she threw herself at the sitting room door, barking wildly. I grabbed her collar and dragged her away.

"Quiet!" I boomed. She obeyed reluctantly, grumbling. "Sit! Stay there."

She slid to the floor, keeping her eyes on me as I raced to the front door and threw it wide. An elderly couple stood there hand-in-hand, looking slightly nervous.

"You must be Mr and Mrs White," I said, with my best welcoming smile. "Do come in."

"Good morning," the gentleman greeted me. "Mrs Dawkins?"

Poppadum and I replied together — she with a conversational growl from behind the door and me with a "Yes." I ignored the growl and continued: "Mr Stone said you'd be here at ten thirty. And here you are. Please ...."

I backed into the dining room feeling Poppadum fuming behind the other door. I mentally warned her, on pain of certain death, not to make another peep. The thought must have reached her; I heard a long sigh and a thump as she lay down.

Mr White glanced at his diminutive wife:

"Yer seem to 'ave a very big dog, Mrs Dawkins. My wife is ... not fond of dogs. 'E won't come near, will 'e?"

I realised that they were so nervous that they would run back up the High Street at the slightest provocation. I suspected that they were as scared of me — or at least of what I represented — as they were of the dog.

"No, no. I promise. I've shut her in the other room. Do come this way."

My smile returned, having slipped earlier without my permission. There was no answering smile from either of them. If anything, they looked even more nervous as they followed me into the dining room.

'How do I put them at their ease?' I wondered.

I needn't have been concerned for my feet did it for me. As I turned to indicate a chair, I tripped over something invisible and started tottering backwards. Mr White grabbed me instinctively and, to my horror, I found my bulk, off balance, pulling him towards me.

Luckily the table stopped our backward progression – but I was halted before Mr White could stop himself and he cannoned into the hardness of the Bump and ricocheted backwards towards his wife. She held up her hands to ward him off. Fearing he might fall, I caught his arm. We stared at each other for a moment – and then he chuckled and I collapsed in helpless giggles. Mrs White was quivering; for one brief moment I wondered if she were about to collapse – until I registered that she was laughing silently. None of us appeared any the worse for our encounter.

Gasping for air, I could only speak in short bursts:

"What ... a way ... for a ... solicitor ... to greet ... her first clients!" I stuttered, "Please forgive me."

"Mr Stone did say as yer was a most unusual solicitor," chuckled Mr White.

"Yes, and 'e sed we'd find yer very friendly," added his wife, still breathless with silent laughter.

In the sitting room Poppadum snorted.

"Maybe we should all sit down now?" I suggested when I had regained my breath. Laughter threatened to break out again at any moment. I picked up the pad of paper and poised my pen above it, struggling all the while to compose myself.

I chose the carver at the end of the table. Now smiling broadly, Mr and Mrs White sat side by side on my left. I noticed that they were holding hands again.

"Thank yer for seein' us so quickly, dear," said Mrs White.

"My pleasure, Mrs White," I replied. "As you can see, I'm having a baby next month and I'd planned to give up work for a while, but Mr Stone is very persuasive. I gather that neither of you has an existing Will?"

"Nope," responded Mr White. "I'm still not keen. Seems ter me that as soon as yer makes a Will, yer dies."

I stopped myself from sighing. That old chestnut. It was always the same; no-one realised the importance of making a Will while of sound mind and healthy. Many people seemed to believe that to make a Will was to sign one's death warrant or perhaps they were so afraid of death that they simply ignored its inevitability.

Mrs White appeared to be less vexed than her spouse.

"Now, now, dear. Yer knows we 'ave ter realise we'll die some time," she admonished. "Not terday, not termorrer, nor even next year, p'rhaps — but I'm sure Mr Stone's right ter send us ter Mrs Dawkins. If we does it now, it'll be one less thing ter worry about."

She looked at me unswervingly as she continued:

"Mr Stone speaks 'ighly of yer, me duck. 'E said yer'd 'elp us organise this very quick. It's urgent, see, 'cos my 'usband 'as ter go into 'ospital the day after termorrer. It's 'is prostrate, yer see."

"I see." I bit my lip to stop it curling in amusement at her mispronunciation. "In that case it would be best to get the Will made quickly, I think. Then there will be one less thing for you to have on your mind."

I turned my attention to Mr White, noticing his sallow complexion and obvious anxiety. His hand trembled a little and I became aware that he was in severe discomfort; Mrs White had recovered quickly from her apprehension about Poppadum and now demonstrated an indefinable air of being able to cope with anything life threw her. My heart went out to them both.

"First, I need to check one thing. Are you *sure* that *neither* of you have *ever* made a Will before?" I asked.

"No," was Mrs White's swift response.

"Long ago, in the Army," said Mr White, with an air of embarrassment. "Before I'd even met Phyllis."

"Did yer?" Phyllis White was amazed. "Yer never told *me* that. Well, I never!"

"I imagine it wouldn't be valid now," I interjected. "Marriage annuls a Will, so it would be void anyway."

Then I noticed Mrs White's cheeks reddening and a saucy smile curving Mr White's lips. Looking from one to the other, I perceived that I had made a faux pas.

"Oh, I see ... I've made a mistake. I'm so sorry."

They weren't married. How could I have been so indelicate? How could I rescue the situation? I rushed on:

"In that case, it may be even more important to make a Will now. Have you been together long?"

"Forty two and a bit years!" exclaimed Mrs White. "Long enough. Eh, Archie?"

"Indeed! Congratulations," I responded, thinking fast but silently: 'Mrs White will have no automatic entitlement to any part of Mr White's estate since she is not his wife: she will, at best, only have a claim. I suppose there's a distinct possibility that the Will Mr White made in the Army is still valid? At least it will be if he made it when he was on active duty, even if it wasn't correctly witnessed.'

I came to the swift conclusion that the sooner they made their Wills the better; I could make sure the Wills reflected their wishes and that they were executed properly. And then any previous Will would be revoked.

"Tell me what you would like in your Wills," I pressed.

"Well, we ain't got much," said Phyllis. "I've made a list ov things. 'Ere."

She drew a slightly grubby piece of paper from her handbag and handed it to me. Mr White raised an eyebrow at Phyllis and put his hand in his pocket. He drew out a recent bank statement.

"That's what I've got," he said. "And I've marked what I want ter go ter 'oo."

I looked at the two pieces of paper. They represented two very different things. Phyllis' showed the contents of their house and two small savings accounts, one with the Post Office and the other with the Hastings and Thanet Building Society. On the other hand, Archie's statement showed a large five-figure sum invested through the bank.

I did a swift mental calculation and realised that there would be very considerable assets in Mr White's estate. It seemed very likely that Estate Duty would be payable and, since she wasn't married to Mr White, Phyllis had very little protection under the law unless ....

"It seems that all these savings and investments are in your sole name, Mr White. Are any of them held in joint names?"

He shook his head. "Phyllis never wanted ter know 'bout that sort ov thing. Wonderful manager, she is. I give 'er me pay-packet and she gives me back enough for a flutter on the 'orses. That's where that's all come from. Couldn't tell 'er I won, could I? She wouldn't 'ave let me 'ave me pocket money."

"So all this is ... your winnings?" I was astonished.

"Yes. Thought I 'ad all the luck. Steady job, winnin' on the 'orses, nice 'ome, Phyllis, children and then this flippin' — begging yer pardon! — cancer come from nowhere." Mr White lapsed further into Kentish. "A little discomfort goin' — if yer knows what I mean — then it stops completely and they puts in a flippin' — begging yer pardon! — caffitter. Ooh what a relief that was — and two flippin' days later I'm flippin' 'avin' a flippin' operation. It's a bloody flippin' nuisance, when all's said and done!" His sallow cheeks had reddened considerably in the course of this speech.

"I'm very sorry ..." I began.

"I've written down there all that I 'ave and 'oo I want ter 'ave it." He cast a wary look a Phyllis, who, apparently shocked into silence, had been peering at the statement on the desk in front of me.

"Give it ter me!" She shouted as she grabbed the much-folded, whiter piece of paper from the table. "Yer never, ever told me 'bout this, neither! Look, *thirty thousand* pounds! We could 'ave bought our own 'ouse, we could 'ave ..." And, much to my concern, she burst into raucous sobs. "Oh, 'ow could yer, 'ow *could* yer ... yer knows 'ow much ... An' after all I've done fer yer ..."

I handed her the box of tissues I kept on the bookshelf. She pulled out a handful and blew her nose, noisily and very definitely.

Archie sighed, but his voice grew stronger. "I knew it — now yer'll go on and on 'bout 'ow much yer've done fer me."

This was too much for Phyllis:

"So I 'ave, yer ungrateful bastard! *And* 'ad 8 children of yours — not to mention that skinny lad you got on Dierdre what she don't look after properly and as stays with us — *and* brought up em up on next to nothin', *and* made all their clothes, *and* done cleaning for Mrs Jupp *and* gone fruit pickin', potato pickin' and every other sorta pickin'! Worked my fingers ter the bone, I 'ave and *never* asked fer *nothin*! And all the while yer've bin saltin' away this and puttin' away that and, I expect *havin*' it away with ... OW!" she ended sharply. "What'd yer do that for?"

Her husband must have kicked her under the table, for she bent down to rub her leg. Okay, I thought, we've loosened the emotions, now it's back to me.

"You've obviously had quite a shock, Mrs White," I soothed. "I think a cup of tea would be a good idea. Do you take milk and sugar?"

"Milk with two sugars, please — an' the same fer 'im." She jerked her thumb at Archie.

I retreated to the kitchen, leaving them to sort things out between themselves. Fortunately, I had anticipated that a cup of tea would be required during the course of the morning and had filled and boiled the kettle in readiness. It was still quite warm so I set it on the hotplate and replaced the whistle, hoping that its screech would give my clients time to compose themselves before I sailed in with the tea.

The phone rang. I caught it to my ear immediately.

"Hello Mrs Dawkins. Good morning, Hazel!" Unmistakably Paul Stone. "I need to have a word about Mr and Mrs White."

"Too late, Mr Stone! They're with me now."

"I thought you should know that they're not actually married." He hesitated.

"I've discovered that, Mr Stone," I said drily.

"Has Mr White given you details of his investments with the bank?"

"Indeed he has."

"Oh, so you know ...?"

"Yes, I think I have all the information I need for the moment, thank you." The kettle emitted a shrill whistle. "I'm about to make them a cup of tea. I must go. So sorry. Goodbye."

I flung the receiver down, rushed to lift the kettle from the heat but took my time making the tea. I rattled the cups as I left them by the hatch and when I re-entered the room my clients were quiet again; Archie had his arm round Phyllis and she was looking at him lovingly, her eyes still wet. It was a poignant scene. I cleared my throat.

'It's all right, dear," Phyllis said, smiling at me, seemingly back to her previous self. "Archie and me've decided we've bin together too long now to argue over things like 'oo 'as the money. At least 'e saved it. Anyone else would 'ave put it back on the 'orses and blown it all!" She smiled at Archie, an affectionate, slightly sad smile. "We've just got ter get on with gettin' 'im better so we can enjoy it. 'E ain't goin' ter get away from me now."

Archie squeezed her shoulder and took his arm away. He looked distinctly drained and more than a little grey, but he grinned roguishly at me as I handed him his tea.

"Life in the old dog, yet!" he crowed. "Let's get on wiv it, so's I can go 'ome and get ter bed."

"I do advise you to make a more complicated, more tax-efficient Will when you're feeling better," I said, trying to be tactful. "I suggest you make a very simple Will for the moment. So I only need to know what ..."

"Well, I wants Phyllis ter 'ave it all, a course." Archie interrupted. "*No-one* could've looked after me better — even if she do 'ave a naggin' tongue in 'er head and a vicious swipe wiv a tea towel!"

"Only when I 'ave ter, my man!"

"And Mrs White? Do you want to do the same, to leave it all to Mr White?"

"But *I* ain't got no money, 'ave I?" She was smiling at me in a rather tolerant fashion as if I were simple. Oh dear.

"Not much at the moment, certainly; but — if Archie dies first — who would you want to have the money then?"

"Well, first, he ain't goin' ter die. And next, I wouldn't flippin' care would I? Not if Archie was dead."

I discarded the idea of trying to explain anything about the more complicated part of making a Will. A simple Will would suffice. Any outstanding matters could be dealt with after Archie's operation. I had to be pragmatic. If he died soon it would be necessary to make another Will for Phyllis anyway, since she would have inherited a great deal of money. There might be some Estate Duty payable on his death but that was a comparatively small consideration since Phyllis would inherit much more than she had expected earlier in the morning.

"I want ter make sure Phyllis and the children are orl right if I ... don't make it." Mr White said, making it easy for me.

I had seated myself back at the table. Of themselves my hands naturally formed a steeple on which I rested my chin. It might be a hackneyed lawyer's attitude but it always assisted my thinking process.

"Very well, this is what I advise," I said, with as much authority as I could muster. "I will make a simple Will for each of you in which you leave everything to the other and then, when the second one of you passes away, to your children — including Dierdre's son, I presume? Is that all right with you so far?"

They glanced at each other and then chirruped "yes" in unison.

"You will need an executor. I expect you know that an executor is someone who carries out the legal side of dealing with the estate?" They both looked at me blankly. "That's all the money and property you leave." I explained, hoping I was not lapsing into too much legal jargon. "It can be the same person who benefits under the Will, or someone else whom you trust. In fact, since you already have an account there, you might like to consider the bank as an executor. "

"Oh yes. Der yer think Mr Stone would?" Mr White seized on this suggestion. Phyllis nodded.

"I'm afraid it wouldn't be Mr Stone," I interjected. "The bank has a whole department to deal with such things. They are very efficient but sometimes rather impersonal — and can be quite expensive."

"Would *yer*?"

I was in a fix here. I knew Mr Stone was required to achieve a quota of Wills in which the bank was appointed Executor, part of a recent marketing strategy. He had recommended me to the Whites on the unspoken, but quietly understood, basis that I would help him reach his quota. Most solicitors saw Wills as a future source of earnings and always recommended their own services. At least I did not have that consideration; I was merely drawing up some Wills to make a little money before the baby came. I had no intention of building a firm that would last for generations but, on a personal level, I wanted to help this engaging couple.

"I could, but I suggest that it would be simplest to appoint the other of you as executor. Then, when the time comes, you can take the Will to Mr Stone, or *any* solicitor you like, to help you with the probate ... the administration ... the winding up of the estate ..." I floundered. Four eyes surveyed me blankly.

"When someone dies," I tried to elucidate. "There is a lot to do. Most people worry about the funeral and believe the rest takes care of itself. But there is a great deal to do, unfortunately. The executor has to give a sworn account to the Inland Revenue, called an Inland Revenue Affidavit. It lists the value of all the assets ... things they owned ... that were in the name of the deceased ... I mean the person who has died. The Affidavit is sent to the Court of Probate, with another document that the executor has to swear, before what is called a Grant of Probate is given to ..."

"I'd no idea it were so complicated, duck," interjected Mrs White, looking quite flummoxed.

"Mr Stone'll do it all," said Mr White. "Put *'im* down, Mrs Dawkins, or the bank, fer the ex ... ex ... ex ..."

"Very well," I said, saving him. I made a note to talk about executors again at another time. "I'll draw up a very simple Will for each of you in which you leave everything you have to each other and appoint the bank as executor. Are you happy with that?"

"Yes, thank yer, Mrs Dawkins. And can yer make it so we can understand it, please? None ov that lawyer-speak?"

Once again I bit my tongue. Contrary to common belief, solicitors did not choose to write in riddles and were not paid by the word. As a result of legal cases too numerous to mention, the Court itself had decided what terminology and wording had proved most efficacious for conveying the right meaning.

"I'll do my best, Mr White. However, when you appoint the bank as executor there is a set clause that I have to use. Now, it's most important that your Wills are signed before you go into hospital. Would you like me to bring them to you tomorrow?"

"Er ... yes." Mrs White nodded.

"You will need two witnesses to be present," I continued. "I can be one but perhaps you would ask a neighbour to be the second witness?"

Mrs White thought for a moment, frowning, and then her face cleared:

"I'll do it fer Archie an' 'e'll do it fer me," she declared.

"No, I'm afraid you can't," I said, shaking my head. "You see, if you witness a Will you can't take any of the money left to you by it."

They looked at each other, and then back at me, apparently mystified. I hurried to explain:

"It's a safeguard to make sure that no one forces someone else to make a Will, or forges their signature," I explained. "The two witnesses have to be independent, adult and preferably not relatives of the person making the Will."

"Orl right," said Phyllis, still looking a little perplexed.

After a good deal of hand shaking and many thank-yers, they left, having agreed that I would call at their house at eleven o'clock the next morning. I breathed a sigh of relief, released Poppadum from her incarceration in the sitting room, and took my cup of cold tea into the summer-scented garden. I needed a breath of air before I sat down to type up their Wills.

- 11 -

Of an Encounter in Songster's Wood

Harry is gone and Annie is bereft. Listlessly she goes about her chores and schools her sisters in their tasks. She watches as her mother's grief bows her shoulders and ages her face until it is as expressionless as the stone within her heart.

Annie takes no comfort from her sisters, though she is warm in her caring for them. She speaks to them of Harry singing loud in heaven, more tunefully than ever he did in the choir in church. She describes the angels who surround him and the brightness of his golden hair, the happiness of cherubs who play hide and seek with him and the chair upon which he sits and waits for them to join him in the game. But her heart, too, is a stone and her grief lasts longer than a year and a day.

It is a warm and sunny morning in May when Annie gathers the wild garlic in Songster's Wood. Her skirt is tucked up and her feet are bare, her toes curling in the damp earth. She places the garlic carefully in the basket on her arm, their bulbs shielded within it. A sudden sting on her bare arm. Annie goes to brush away the bee but none is there. She rubs the arm and bends again to her task. A small pebble glances off her skirt. She turns in the blink of an eye and there, sitting upon a low branch in the sycamore nearby, is a boy whose eyes glitter with mirth. In his hand is a sling. Annie is not mirthful. She is still grieving, content in her bereavement and the purpose it has given her. Her eyes narrow.

The boy chuckles.

"Thy visage is as sour as milk on a thundrous day," he declares. "Why for?"

"My brother wast murdered." Annie's eyes darken. Her sisters would be wary, but not Jack.

"'Tis well known," he said. "And 'tis last year's news. The days have lengthened twice since he fell and he is now become perfect to all who speak of him. But 'twas not truly so."

"How can'st thou say it? Harry was a perfect brother!"

"Not true! He was but a boy like me, like any other. And he ..."

Annie is not prepared to argue. She falls upon him in a temper although the only part she can reach is his bare foot. She pulls him by the ankle with both her hands and her scrawny weight is just enough to unbalance him. He falls upon her, bearing her to the ground beneath him. The garlic scatters but much is squashed beneath them. Its distinct aroma, surprising in its strength, surrounds them.

Jack is the first to move. He leaps up lightly and offers Annie his hand. Scornfully, she ignores it and pushes herself to her feet. Her dress is stained, reeking of garlic and she has lost the only hair ribbon in her possession. Her chestnut locks cascade over her shoulders. Jack's eyes widen for she is the fairest maid he has ever seen. He endeavours to make amends.

"Beg pard..." he begins, bowing in the courtly manner in which he has been schooled..

But Annie's rage has not been dampened, rather it has been fuelled. She is incandescent, her cheeks flaming and her hazel eyes alight.

She sets upon him with her fists, boxing his ears, hitting his chest, his face, his arms, any part of him within range of her flailing arms. Jack leaps backward but she follows, sobbing with rage and beating, beating, beating as if he is a carpet set upon the washing line. He is sore tempted to put up his fists but is aware that it was he who taunted her to such viciousness — much as he is coming to regret his words. Eventually a tree root trips his backward progress and he topples so sudden that she is taken off-balance and tumbles upon him. The shock silences her and for a moment they gaze eye to eye. He feels her soft budding breasts hard-pressed to his chest and senses the stirring response in his breeches. Then her breast heaves and she springs to her feet, picks up the squashed basket and is gone on winged feet.

Or so it seems to Jack who, winded, punched and unable to move, can only watch her swift departure. He glances ruefully at his attire, knowing he will be sore berated by his mother for the ruination of his school clothes. But that is as nothing to the strange feeling that fills his young heart and the ardour that engorges his loins. There is a red mist before his eyes through which he can see only Annie, beautiful and passionate in her fury.

Jack! Jack! Jack!

My head is full of Jack. My temper and my anger too. All revolve round him. How dare he say what he has said. How can I cease to grieve for my dead brother? How can I cease to live for vengeance? Yet am I not a stupid girl who has no means to fight? To kill? I stamp the life from the garlic in my path.

I see Jack's teasing stance and his face as I pummel him and something in me responds ....

He is the Squire's son. This I know. I know because my mother is his mother's friend and confidante. We girls are banished upstairs when Mary comes to speak to Ma but we creep down and, sitting on the bottom stair, press our ears against the staircase door.

Jack is Squire's son but he is not acknowledged as such, save that the Squire pays for him to go to school. His mother worked at the big house as a chamber maid and his sickly wife knew nothing of the passion that Mary and the Squire shared in his poster-bed, its thick drapes tight drawn.

I learn how Jack was conceived and born and how, at first, the Squire swore never to see Mary again and to keep him only to his spouse — save that they remained childless and rumour told of the boy-child born to Mary. He could not keep himself from demanding the boy brought to him while declaring that on no account should the child's mother accompany the babe. Yet Mary loved the Squire full well and he reciprocated her ardour, though he would deny it even to himself. Thus, when Mary's mother brought the infant to him, Squire could do naught but weep with joy upon his son and Mary could not but drop her shawl, reveal her presence and declare her love. And Squire pressed her to his heart and swore that he would keep faith with her so far as he may in decency so do. Yet he stopped short of acknowledging his son for the sake of his wife, an invalid for whom Squire cared deeply.

Thus Squire found Mary a husband — a footman from amongst the staff at the big house, a Londoner, no less — who was paid handsomely to give the Squire's whore a decent name. Yet he was a drunkard who could not forget her dalliance with the Squire and took great pleasure in taunting her with harsh words and his fists upon her tender parts. Often it was that she was seen with a black eye or a livid bruise upon her cheek. She bore a child each year to this man of violence but none of the children she bore him held so much of her heart as Jack.

Poor Jack, known as a bastard yet unacknowledged by the Squire, disciplined by his mother's raging husband should he seek to protect her, sent to school far away; the while all his brothers and his peers ran barefoot through the fields and on the shore and learned to fish or overlook the sheep or yet some other means of keeping hand to mouth. And when Jack returned to Rype they jeered at him and teased him sore for his book-learning and his fancy words and thoughts.

Indeed, my heart softens for I see that Jack is but as I, myself. For he has no father as I have no brother and needs must he watch his mother's sorrow and forbearance as I must watch the grief my parents bear and yet deny.

And so I flounce back to where he sits upon the bruised garlic, its odour overpowering his eyes so that they are red and running from the fumes. He comes lightly to his feet and sketches a mocking courtly bow in my direction. And my anger springs again — for how dare he taunt me so? Me of the bare feet and the torn and dirty apron. So I set upon him with my fists and rain more blows upon him till he catches my wrists and holds me well away from him. I try to kick his shins but he leaps out of range, yet holding me fast. A fighting light gleams in his blue eyes but he forebears to strike me. He merely holds me thus and waits till my anger turns to frustration and thence to sobs. He sets me free but keeps a distance between us.

"Shalt thou and I be friends?" he questions.

"Wherefore?" I demand, rubbing my wrists which still burn.

"For thou hast courage and a mighty temper! And I wouldst sooner have thee as friend than foe."

"If thou shalt swear to treat me as an equal and ne'er again mock me?"

"I shall so swear if thou shalt swear ne'er again to take your fists to me — for I am sadly bruised."

For answer I spit upon my hand and hold it out to him. He spits on his and we shake hands for all the world as if we were about to engage in fisticuffs.

Then I am off running across the field with a basketful of bruised and stinking garlic. And he is shrugging and making his way home.

- 12 -

Of Wills and Words

Perhaps I dream .... I find myself in a place that appears to be the chamber where I sleep with my sisters yet it is bigger, different, as if the room that Ma and Pa share has been added to it. The sun is shining through the casement onto a table at which a young woman sits with her back to me. Her hands are moving and a strange tap-tapping noise fills the room. At her feet lies a black-and tan bitch of medium size. The dog seems to sense my presence, for she raises her head, her ears pricked. Her eyes look straight at me, through me: she sniffs the air in a puzzled manner.

The tap-tapping stops suddenly. A noise like the fast rolling of a barrel, and a crumpled ball of paper is tossed angrily over her shoulder, in my direction. The woman holds her head in her hands and blasphemes. But I see her shoulders heave. I move to comfort her, as if she were one of my sisters, when a door bangs and I am gone....

Some hours later, I ripped a sheet of paper from the typewriter, screwed it up and threw it on the floor in a fit of pique. Poppadum jumped and let out a surprised 'woof'.

"You may well woof," I told her, my hands still shaking. "I wish I could bark, too. That's the fourth piece of paper wasted. I wasn't made to be a typist. Damn!" I buried my head in my hands, feeling tears of frustration trickle through my fingers.

"Damn and damn again!"

The muffled expletive was more of a sob than an exclamation. Who was this silly over-emotional woman? Well, obviously, it was me. Poppadum nudged me with her nose and then put her head in my lap. I peeked between my fingers and saw her looking up at me. It made me laugh. I caressed her soft fur with my fingertips.

"Thank you, sweetie-pie," I said out loud. "What would I do without you?"

It was not at all what I had been feeling about my canine companion a few hours earlier when she'd barked at the postman and attacked each letter as it was pushed through the letterbox. My mail was not fit to be filed — her teeth had penetrated every sheet. Nor had she been popular when I'd had to shut her in the sitting room because she had frightened Mr and Mrs White.

I was sitting at the table that I'd positioned so that I could look through the bedroom window eastwards towards the church. On it I'd placed a filing tray and the small portable manual typewriter my brother had bequeathed to me when he had emigrated to Australia a couple of years previously. The typewriter had been second-hand when he acquired it, on the basis that it would be used only for typing the odd invoice or letter. The "s" key stuck very easily and the ribbon was hard to acquire and even more difficult to fit. I'd struggled to put in a new ribbon that afternoon before endeavouring to type the Wills for Mr and Mrs White.

It had not gone well.

The front door slammed and Bruce yelled: "Hello? Hazel? Where are you?"

"Darling, I'm up here — very hot and bothered."

I heard a thud as Bruce dropped his briefcase and came leaping up the stairs two at a time. He swept me into his arms and held me as close as he could, baby permitting. I felt better instantly.

"I love you being here when I come home," he said into my hair. He took a deep breath. "Your hair smells lovely even if you *are* hot and bothered. I know why you're hot but why are you bothered?"

The baby kicked him and he moved away with a rueful smile.

"These stupid Wills. See — I've drafted them here in biro." I showed him the lined pad with my close-packed writing on it. Several crossings out and amendments showed where I'd wrestled with the wording. "I took most of the morning doing that and I've been trying to engross them all afternoon."

"Engross?" he queried, frowning in puzzlement.

"You know. Legalese for 'fair copy ready for signature'."

"Trying to? What's difficult? Has the typewriter been playing up?" He loosened his already loose tie and, after pulling it off over his head, he started undoing his shirt.

"No ... not really ... apart from that stupid sticky 's'... No, it's me! I know I *started* to learn to type but I've never had to do it properly because I've always had a secretary. Now I have to engross Wills on this special paper. Look."

I held out a piece of the heavy, blue-grey paper. He threw his shirt on the bed and took the Will engrossment paper from me.

"I can see it's thick. Why is it doubled over?"

"It's special *Will* paper. See — the front has 'This is the Last Will and Testament' printed on it." I pointed to the words printed in large mock-copperplate writing. "It's a huge sheet, folded into two, because you can't attach anything to a Will, even another page."

"Why not?"

"Because it would give rise to the legal presumption that the Testator intended to change the contents of his Will — so it would be invalidated to prevent any misrepresentation of the Testator's wishes."

Bruce was looking at me as though I were talking complete gobbledegook.

"Anyway," I pressed on. "I have to use this paper and I have to type down this page." I pointed to the front with the heading. "Then this one," I turned the page and indicated the page on the left of the crease. "Then this one." I ran my finger down the opposite page and turned it over. "And here on the back I have to put the name of the Testator and a space for the date when the Will is signed and witnessed."

"Ah," nodded Bruce. "Complicated then."

"*No* ... it should be simple! But if I make a mistake in the typing, the whole engrossment is ruined because a mistake may invalidate the Will."

"So what exactly is your problem?"

"*After* I've typed the whole first page *perfectly*, I keep messing up the second one. And the page creases when I turn it through that *horrid* machine. I don't think the typewriter likes the double thickness. And — worst of all! — I *have* to have *two* of them ready by tomorrow." I finished, my voice rising in a wail.

Bruce had stripped to his underpants.

"*Poor* Hazel," he cooed as he made for the door. "I need a cool bath now. I'll mull it over in there and see if I can find a solution. But I warn you — I don't mull well when I'm hungry!"

"Mull? Hungry? I'll ... I'll ..." I gave up trying to think of a threat and threw his clothes at him, laughing, but he jerked the door shut and escaped.

True to his word, Bruce did mull it over in the bath.

"You've already drafted the Wills. Suppose I read them to you? That would save you having to look up and down all the time. I expect you would even type more quickly."

I kissed his head as I handed him his plate of cold ham and salad. I was so glad the weather was hot. We could exist on salad. No cooking required. But I'd baked some potatoes in their skins, thickly encrusted with salt, because Bruce didn't think a meal was a meal unless it included potatoes. I sat down and passed him the butter.

"That's a good idea. Maybe we could do it in the cool of the evening?"

I was watching him lavishly plonking butter on his potatoes as I wished I felt like eating; there was simply not enough room. I picked at a piece of ham. What I really wanted was a very large Mars bar.

"In the bedroom, eh? Great idea." He leered at me. I must have looked horrified because he grinned. "Don't worry, I know you won't be feeling like making love — but you have been warned. I shall be keeping a tally for afterwards."

"Being pregnant is not very sexy." I patted my belly. Much as I had loved being pregnant up to now, I was really feeling the heat and the lack of mobility. My ankles felt as if they were tree trunks. I looked down at them ruefully, sure they were swollen.

"You look wonderful to me, darlin'!" The response was a little slow in coming because he was ruminating on a large mouthful of buttery potato. The salad was looking a little forlorn; most of it was sitting on the side of his plate, uneaten. He gestured at my middle with his fork. "And if you're able to make a Will as well as a baby, you must *be* wonderful, too."

When the sun began its descent behind the willow tree, we made our way upstairs and settled down to work. Shadows crept along the wall and a cool breeze from the open windows fanned our cheeks. Unfortunately it had also ruffled my papers, most of which were strewn across the floor. Bruce picked them up and I shuffled them into order.

"I'll have to order some proper files," I remarked. "It's lucky I brought the Will paper home from the office. I did it only because I thought *we* needed new Wills now that we're going to be parents. The trouble is," I continued, "I've only got these four sheets left, so I daren't make any more mistakes."

"You won't," Bruce replied. "I'm here to help."

He settled me into a chair that was now a little too small for me. Gingerly, I inserted a doubled sheet of Will paper into the machine, turning the cylinder slowly. For once it came through perfectly, without a single crease down the fold.

My helpmeet picked up my draft and began to dictate: "'This is the last Will and Testament'... you don't have to type that it's already printed ... 'of me Archibald Shakespeare Galsworthy Marlowe White' ..." He grinned. "What a name! 'of 5 Coronation Gardens, Rype, Romney Marsh in the county of' .... Shouldn't there be a comma after 'me'?" he queried, looking over my shoulder.

"Nope." The denial issued instantly from my lips as I continued to bash away at the typewriter. "There's no punctuation in Wills."

"Really?" He was most surprised, "Why ever not? How do you know how to read them?"

"Exactly. You can change the whole meaning of a passage with punctuation. There's a whole tranche of case law about the meaning of a comma in a certain place, so the convention is to use no punctuation at all."

"I can understand that bit I just read out," he commented, his eyes skipping down the page. "But what about this? '*I give, devise and bequeath*' ... do you *need* three words? ... 'my blah, blah, blah ... *unto and equally between* ... isn't that obvious? ... *my children* ...

blah blah ... *provided they attain the age of twenty one years provided always that if any of them shall predecease me or not be proved to have so survived me leaving a child or children him or her surviving who shall attain the age of twenty one years such child or children shall take and if more than one equally between them the share or shares in my estate to which his her or their parent would have been entitled had he or she not so died as aforesaid.'"*

He had run out of breath.

"Can you read a little more slowly?" I teased. "I can't type that fast!"

He smiled but not very deeply. "Honestly, Haze, I don't understand it. If I can't — and I'm *quite* clever — then how can anyone else?"

I sighed. I seemed to be sighing a lot recently.

"That's why it's best to go to a solicitor to make a Will," I explained patiently. "*We* understand it, you see! If I had the time I'd explain it but, for now, please pretend you're a tape recorder."

"Okay Here goes. '*Whereby I revoke all former Wills*' .... What is it, Hazel?"

I'd stopped typing and closed my eyes. Somewhat belatedly a thought had worked its way into my mind.

"I've just remembered that this is confidential and I haven't given you the confidentiality lecture or sworn you to silence."

Bruce looked amazed.

"*What*? You *are* joking? I'm your husband."

"No. No, really I'm *not* joking. Everything between a solicitor and her client is confidential. We have to make this very clear to everyone in the office, from the cleaner to the cashier and *especially* to the secretaries. Now, unfortunately, you're not a tape recording machine so I will have to make you swear to keep this completely confidential. You are not to tell *anyone* anything about this, even in fun."

"Sure," he said. "I understand that, but you must admit that Archibald Shakespeare Galsworthy Marlowe White is a *most* amusing name."

"Please don't joke about it," I begged. "I'm deadly serious. I could be struck off the Roll of Solicitors if I divulged anything. I was taught not to recognise a client even if I passed them in the street — because they might not want anyone to know they've been to see you. *Honestly*." I stressed the last word as I saw his face light up incredulously. "I can't even tell Mr Stone anything and he knows everything about Mr and Mrs White and even sent them to me."

"Okay, Haze, relax. I can see how important this is to you."

"Not to *me*," I interrupted. "To *my clients*. But of course it's important to me, too. I'm a member of a respected profession and I have to make sure that I keep that respect. *And* I have to keep the professional standards I swore to uphold when I was admitted. You remember, surely?"

He had been there when I was admitted as a Solicitor of The Supreme Court. We had been married only two days before the formal ceremony of Admittance. Kneeling with my hands clasped between those of the judge who administered it, I had sworn an oath that was as clear to me and as binding as my marriage vows. The formality and beauty of the ceremony had impressed Bruce who had added that he was very proud of my achievement.

"*Of course* I remember and *of course* I won't divulge anything." He took my hands and replaced them on the typewriter keys. "Now, where were we? Oh yes, '*I give, devise and bequeath* ..."

It took over two hours but I eventually held two perfect Wills in my hands, one for Phyllis and one for Archie. I also had a somewhat bemused husband.

"If you're going to do more of this, I think you need some proper equipment," he said, hoarse from dictation. "Not only files, but a proper tape recorder with earphones and a foot peddle, and, I suppose, paper and typewriter ribbons."

"Next week," I agreed. "Or next month. But right now I need to stretch my legs."

So we set out, hand-in-hand, with Poppadum ahead of us on the lead. It was almost dark, that soundless time when the veil between the worlds is thin and easily perforated and strange things can happen, especially on the Marsh.

- 13 -

Of a Mighty Smiting and a Shot in the Dark.

There is a sliver of new moon this night, a silver crescent laced with indigo clouds that race across a winter's sky; clouds that threaten ever more ominously towards the West. The fishermen amongst us are mumbling of storms and ill luck when we are brought to a sudden halt by well-armed, mounted men obstructing our path, the ancient smuggling road well hidden by the dyke. We recognise the notorious and much-feared Eaglewood Gang whose members are as vicious as they are ruthless. Of that we are sure, for no other smuggling band in all of Kent and Sussex could raise so large a force. And force it surely is — for they block the lane ahead four horsemen abreast and many score behind them. Scarce have we reined in our mounts, the waggons still rolling forward, than as many men again fall upon our rear. They are a disparate company, not least in size and weapons: many, indeed, are drunken men roiling to do violence a-plenty.

One man draws to the front of this army. A strange man this, seemingly as wide as he is tall. His mount's back is swayed beneath his giant weight and his feet dangle, stirrup-less, barely a foot from the ground. Big John is he, the Eaglewood blacksmith. His shoulders are sore misshapen from the hammering of his trade; and his heart is as black as the soot in the chimney of his furnace. Some whisper that he is the Devil incarnate. For 'tis said he cavorts before his forge at the full of the moon, naked but for his Blacksmith's apron, brandishing a pitchfork in his hand and flaunting a tail that bears an arrow at its end. Some joke that his male parts are so large that it takes his two hands to raise his member to relieve himself and, when erect, no woman can accommodate him.

High and threatening, Big John raises the blacksmith's tongs he bears in his left hand — and laughs his devil's laugh.

"What have we here?" he asks, — sardonically, to be sure — for have we not already paid for safe passage for our tea through their country?

"Why, 'tis tea and silk, as we agreed," replies our leader, Will the saddler, kicking his horse forward close enough to see the hairs upon Big John's nose.

"Agreement is it? What agreement might that be?" and Big John, feigning surprise for all to see, turns to his drunken troop who raise their armed fists aloft and cry:

"None. None. Save blood alone!" or words to that effect.

Will allows his gaze to rest upon the place where Big John's beetle brows meet.

"On Michaelmas' Eve we paid our dues to run our goods through thy country. I have witnesses." His voice is even but I see the tick in his cheek and know him to be afeared.

"Nay, we do not make agreements," quoth Big John, shaking his head as if in disbelief.

"We take what we want!" a reedy voice declares from behind the giant. A hand rises, armed with a musket.

"Thou know'st ..." Will continues, apparently unbowed.

"Nay, we have no agreement with the likes of thee. But we will relieve thee of the trouble of carting our goods yet further," quoth Big John.

"We have paid our dues, as did our fathers and their fathers before them."

"Nay, we like not that custom. It stands no longer."

"I say it stands yet!" cries Will, rising up in his stirrups and turning back towards his band of Owlers. "What say you, Owlers of Rype?" But there have been murmurings and back-slidings and many of the Owlers have slipped away into the darkness of the moonless Marsh, so he is met with a rustle of discontent, no more.

"Thy fine fellows have slipped the leash!" guffaws Big John.

"Not so!" Will declares stoutly.

"Move aside. The goods are ours for the taking."

"Not while I stand!" Will rejoins, ready to fight or fly — but

alas not ready enough.

"So be it then."

And with that utterance Big John brings down the devil's tongs upon poor Will's head and smites him to the ground, bleeding copiously, his near foot still hooked into the stirrup. Will's bay horse snorts, rears and kicks out with his hooves at Big John. The giant smites him too — sharp upon the nose with the tongs and brings his sword, battered and old as it is, hard down upon the horse's flank. 'Tis over in an instant. The horse screams and takes off at a gallop into the night, bleeding hard. He drags the saddler by the foot, his yells and shrieks bloodcurdling in the darkness.

In the distraction provided by the fleeing horse, I spur my mount. Black Bess flies after Will's bay stallion, hoofbeat for hoofbeat. The stallion's head is down and he is set upon a course, blinded by the savagery inflicted on him, seeing not the ground he covers. Will's screams grow longer, louder, hoarser — then cease abruptly. Black Bess swerves. The saddler's horse is halted, screaming in agony, his foreleg hanging shattered. I catch his bridle, the poor beast quivering in every sinew, eyes rolling in his head. But I am come too late — for Will is dead, his head mangled black and scarlet in the flickering light of the moon between the clouds. I disentangle his foot and lay him down upon the turf.

Meanwhile, our Owlers are vanished into the dark, leaving their covered waggons for the taking. The Eaglewood Gang exults. Keen to intimidate all within the town, they whip the carthorses to a canter through the very streets of Rype. Townsmen and women shudder at the noise, concealing themselves behind closed doors and curtained windows. They see not the cumulus clouds scudding dark and ghostly across the sickle moon.

Beneath their tarpaulins, the waggons hold but a tenth of our goods, bulked up with straw. For Will's plan is to deceive those who would trick and rob us — we who run the gauntlet of the moon, the sea, time and tide, pirates, swindlers and the full force of English law. We who run the risk of press gang, prison, injury, and death. And all for to keep our families fed and sheltered through the seasons of rough weather and foul tide — when the fish swim not, crops fail, the Marsh ague takes young and old and a murrain falls upon the sheep.

No fewer than one hundred tubs of brandy were earlier thrown into the sea beside the lobster pots. Casks which Owlers' tub-men are e'en now recovering; loading them fast upon the string of pack ponies hidden amongst the fishing boats that are drawn high up upon the beach. Thirty five ponies will trot inland along the path to Lightchapel, there to be swiftly unladen in the ash grove. Soon the tubs are hidden, rolled deep into the caves mined by Roman soldiers, ages since.

Meanwhile, many hands lug oilskin bags of tea and silk from hiding places close to the shore, bags soon stowed within the narrow barges which lie upon the dark and greasy water of the King's ditch. Within the hour the merchandise reaches the edge of Rype. Willing volunteers convey those goods from barge to bank and thence to a cellar cache; a place from which men, sworn to secrecy, bear them beneath the sleeping town towards the church. For generations, goods have passed this way through passages and tunnels and into the crypt beside the crypt — the whereabouts of the entrances and exits kept secret since time immemorial.

'Twas a dangerous plan, as likely to inflame as to befuddle, and I, Jack, had had reason to fear that all may not go as we hoped. I had spoken of my misgivings to Will. But he had laughed at my timorousness, slapped me upon the back and bid me be of good cheer for I should be entrusted as his lieutenant. An honour I had deemed it. For only recently had I returned from France whence my father, the Squire, had sent me, requiring that I learn the language and the customs of the country, the better to oversee the French side of the Owlers' trade.

Yet I had not foreseen so great a calamity as good Will's death. Now, too late, I understand the weight of the responsibility Will bore upon his shoulders and know that it behoves me to act fast and purposefully.

For there is another pressing task I must perforce perform this night — and one which makes my heart weep, for Will's stallion stands dejected and in pain, white bone sticking through the bay hair of his forelimb. I hug his neck one-armed and whisper in his ear. I press my musket to his temple. A single shot and he lies dead upon the earth beside his master.

So have I put Will's stallion out of his misery, but the agony of Will's widow and children has not yet begun. Soon I will send word to her, and choose waggoners to bring the corpses home to Rype. Yet first I must enact another duty.

I reassure Black Bess, who quivers by my side, and breathe into her nostrils. I remount and ride for Squire's stables where she shall receive a feed of good, warm mash, ere I change for dinner. Tonight, the Squire has bidden the Captain of Dragoons and the Revenue Officers to his board and hearth. My presence is required.

- 14 -

Of Moonlight and Shadows

Dusk had deepened into night. Poppadum was in the lead as we strolled up the High Street in companionable silence, each wrapped in our own thoughts.

The just-over-full moon rode high and clear, charging the shadows with mystery and shedding its brightness along the road.

"You're very quiet, Haze. Penny for them?"

"I was thinking of all I had to do at Farthing & Change," I whispered back. "And that was when I had a secretary and the support of the firm."

"Different now, then," he teased, tapping his chest with his free hand. "Now you have *me*."

He turned to face me and the moon shone over his shoulder directly into my face. He must have seen something there for he backed me into the doorway between the greengrocer's shop windows and put a finger under my chin, raising it so that he could look into my eyes. His head blotted out the moon. In the darkness I felt the roughness of his fingertip on my cheek as he gently removed a tear from under my left eye. He bent his head to kiss me tenderly on the lips. Poppadum chose that moment to pull on the lead, whining softly.

"Never doubt yourself, Hazel," Bruce said huskily. "You're good at *everything* you do. I'm proud to have a solicitor as my wife ..."

He broke off, for a strange sound echoed through the night. Horses were galloping down the road towards us, their hoofbeats growing louder and louder as they came towards us, fast. Very fast. So fast that Bruce instinctively spread his arms, protectively crowding me back into the shop doorway. Poppadum was already crouched beside me, panting, hackles raised and ears flattened.

Galloping hooves grew closer. Louder ... louder ... and louder still. A crescendo, the noise deafening, sweating horse smell overpowering.

I pulled myself up on tip-toe to look over Bruce's shoulder, fully expecting to see horses streaming past, and saw ... the gleaming face of the moon. Nothing else. As the sound faded, the smell of horses lingered. Bruce stepped out into the road followed by a sheepish but inquisitive Poppadum. Moonbeams illuminated the bewildered look on his face as he rubbed his eyes.

"Wha ... what was that?" His hand moved from his eyes as he ran his fingers through his hair. "Did *you* hear it?"

"Hear it? How could I not?"

Poppadum whined softly.

"Shhh!" I held my finger to my lips. A faint jingling, like a horse's harness.

"There." It came again. "Did *you* hear *that*?" I whispered.

Bruce turned to stare up the road towards the church. I peered round him, my eyes following the direction of his gaze. The roundness of the cobbles in the road reflected the moonlight which threw a gleaming pathway to the church door.

I found myself holding my breath. Poppadum pushed her cold nose into my hand. Resonating softly through the night, came the sound of a single lame horse, walking away from us towards the church gate.

"That?" Bruce mouthed.

The shadow was dense on the other side of the road and I knew that the rider was keeping carefully to the margin of darkness, out of the moon's revealing light. We stared at the crossing of Cannon Street and the High Street, the length of the ancient book shop from the church gate and the only place where the bar of blackness was broken. I stared so hard that I was forced to blink, and in that fleeting moment I thought I saw a shadow edge round the building. Darkness fell suddenly, as if someone had switched off the electricity, but it was only a cloud obscuring the face of the moon.

Bruce and I risked a glance at each other — and a sliver of light flashed between us and was gone. Our eyes flew back up the road to the church. No sound. Then the mere suggestion of a creak such as a church door might make.

Quietness settled around us. The church clock began to strike, melodiously. We were held in a spell, counting the strokes. Twelve. As the last toll faded away into silence, the shadows shivered while the night seemed to shimmer and then sigh. Its quality changed.

Poppadum shook herself from nose to tail. The moon showed its face again, revealing the same road, the same buildings and Bruce, bewitched, as if turned to stone on the pavement. I shivered violently and threw myself against him. He came out of his reverie just in time to catch me.

"God! What was that?" I asked.

"What do *you* think that was?" He spoke at the same time.

"You must have heard horses, surely?" I was coming back to earth now, reassured by the normality of Bruce's arms encircling me.

"I really thought we were going to be mown down. But it must have been a trick of the wind or a motor bike ..." Bruce said, shrugging.

"Wind? Motor bike? Don't be silly! There wasn't any wind and certainly no motorbike," I said scornfully, certain I had heard the drumming of hooves. Many, many, many of them. "It sounded like a horse race to me. Explain that."

"Okay, it sounded like that to me, too. And I can't explain it." Bruce sounded as puzzled as I felt.

"Did you *see* anything?"

"No ... no, not really. I don't think so. The flash of a torch, maybe."

"I thought I saw a shadow slip towards the church door and then a sliver of light as if the door had opened a crack," I admitted. "Did you?"

He grinned at me. "So you did see something! Why ask me then? All right, I agree, I saw the same thing. Something strange must be going on."

I shivered again, less violently, and felt an answering tremor from within. Suddenly I just wanted to go home.

"I'm tired out. Let's go back home."

"Good idea, Haze. What fantasies you spin! Goodness knows *what* you'll imagine next."

We headed home with Poppadum pulling anxiously on the lead. Bruce put his arm round me and our steps fell into rhythm. I allowed my head to rest against his shoulder.

- 15 -

Of Birdsong and Kisses

My head is pillowed in Jack's lap. He teases my eyes awake, tickling them open with a bluebell culled from the carpet of wild hyacinths that surround us, filling the air with perfume as dusk falls. Jack leans back against the old oak that blows with ribbons, some newly bright, some faded; ribbons are tied upon every bough close enough to be reached on tiptoe from the bank in which the ancient tree was planted centuries since; the bank which marks the boundary of Songster's wood. The sentinel's bark, gnarled with age, appears woven grey and rippling in the twilight. Its roots cling to the earth like witch's fingers, swollen and twisted, but its leaves are soft and newly yellow-green, fresh with the moisture of Spring. Tomorrow we will stand together in the ancient grove for it will be the feast of Beltane. There we will be hand-clasped, promised to each other. Tomorrow we will consummate our love: but this eve is for weaving spells and reminiscing.

Jack bends his head, his lips touch mine — and in that moment a full-throated, liquid song bursts forth from the bough above.

"A nightingale!" my darling says. "A nightingale for thee, my Annie."

"Ssshhh." I press my fingers to his lips.

The nightingale's song is interwoven joy and sadness, entwining our hearts, plaiting together the themes running through our lives: the torment of grief, the thrill of discovery, the glee in shared pleasures, the sadness of parting, the joy of first love, the fear of disaster, the thrill of adventure, the simplicity of content. The nightingale sings and my love kisses me ... kisses me until the songster's pipe is ended and I am breathless.

Then Jack raises his head and from his lips spill trills and thrills and stops and runs and pipes and notes that delight my heart. The song ceases for a second time as he draws my hand to his lips, kissing each finger and my open palm.

"For thee, my dearest Annie. The nightingale's song shalt ever be our signal. Thou shalt know when I am close even if thou sees me not."

- 16 -

Of Testators and Nonchalance

I was up early next morning after a disturbed night. The sound of hoofbeats and the nightingale's pure song intertwined into a semi-dreaming consciousness, that strange state that is neither waking nor sleeping. With that, and the general discomfort I experienced lately, I slept fitfully at best.

However, the dawn brought another of those shining late spring days when the early sun makes sparkling jewels of the dew and the birds compete with each other in the loudness and beauty of their songs. Revelling in the newness of everything, I stepped into the fragrance of the morning garden. My toes sank into the cool softness of the grass, still spangled with diamonds of dew. The sun, shining from a clear blue sky, was warm on my head.

The odd happenings of the past few days seemed nigh impossible in the sunlight. That Bruce had also experienced the sound of ghostly horses stampeding down the High Street had reassured me that I was not going completely mad. There must be some explanation, but where would I find it? Galloping horses and gunshots brought to mind the many tales I'd heard of the smuggling gangs who had infested the Marsh in the eighteenth and early nineteenth centuries, when the gangs warred between themselves. I knew that the Revenue Officers had experienced great difficulty in enforcing the law and that sometimes there had been pitched battles between them and the smugglers. Unfortunately I knew no detail. I made a mental note to do some research on Marsh history in the local library.

As I entered the kitchen, I knew Bruce had risen — the pipes from the hot water tank banged when the hot water was running. When I peeped into the bathroom he was standing at the basin, stooping a little to peer into the mirror as he shaved. He swivelled towards me, razor in hand, one cheek still covered in shaving foam. He smiled, the foam making his smile seem lop-sided. Morning was not his most communicative time. We usually conversed in monosyllables until after breakfast, but today he asked:

"Did you sleep okay, Haze? After all that excitement? You need to take care of yourself and the Bump, you know."

"I'm fine," I responded, kissing his shaved cheek, which just happened to be closer to me than the lathered one. "I'll put the eggs on to boil. They'll be ready in five minutes so *be there*."

I ducked away. A moment later a splat announced that a wet flannel had missed its aim at my disappearing grin.

Two hours later, dog walked, and myself washed, dressed, made up and in business mode, I took myself and the Bump for a slow walk along Park Street, a quiet road that ran parallel to the High Street, to call on Mr and Mrs White. In my briefcase were a pair of Wills for signature or, as we solicitors would say, 'execution'.

The term *execution* was inextricably linked in my mind with King Henry VIII's decapitation of his wives, servants and allies. However, lawyers used it as a simple way of describing a process: 'to make valid by signing in the way required by the law'. As with many other legal procedures, there was a certain ritual to execution, rules that had to be obeyed to ensure that the Will was legally binding.

According to the law of England and Wales, no Will was valid unless it had been dated and signed by the testator (a word meaning 'any person who makes a Will') in the presence of two witnesses who were both adult (over eighteen years of age) and independent of the testator. I recalled that the Latin word 'testare' meaning 'to testify' was the root of the word 'testator'; the word 'testare' reflected the fact that, under Roman Law, a man swore an oath on his honour as a man — on his manhood or, more precisely, on his testes. The thought made me grin.

My amusement grew as I reflected on the legal term 'he died intestate' which meant 'a man who died without having made a legally valid Will'. Such a man must be lacking in two very important respects, I thought crudely. I laughed to myself, taking a belated peek around to make sure no-one was in earshot. My thoughts continued along this track: a woman who died without having made a Will was called a testatrix and died intestate despite never having had testes on which to swear. But I sobered as I reflected on the reason for the term. When this part of the law developed it was legally impossible for a woman to own property, and thus only a man was able to dispose of his possessions by Will. In the case of married women, that had continued to be the case until the Married Women's Property Act was passed by Parliament in 1882.

My meditations on the singularity of English law came to an end as I approached the Whites' home in Park Row, off Park Street. It was in the centre of a row of terraced Victorian cottages built of red brick under black slate-tiled roofs.

Phyllis opened the door, looking a tad surprised to see me on the doorstep.

"Good morning, Mrs White," I greeted her. "I've brought your Wills for signature, as I promised."

"Oh! 'Mornin', Mrs Dawkins," she responded. "I was expectin' the doc, 'atcherly. Archie's not very well terday."

"I'm sorry to hear that. Is he well enough to see me, do you think? It's important that he signs his Will as soon as possible."

"Yes, I 'spect he'll be the better fer it. Yer go up them stairs. 'Is room's straight ahead."

She moved aside to allow me access and I had put a foot on the first step of the staircase before I realised I had forgotten to check something.

"I hope I won't take long, Mrs White, I just need to read Archie's Will to him to make sure he understands it. I'm afraid there's no escaping some legal language and I may need to explain some of it to him," I said, grimacing a little. "The only problem is that I need another witness. I can be one, but ..."

A loud knocking on the door made us both jump.

"... we need two," I ended limply as Phyllis opened the door.

Doctor David Hadley stood on the doorstep, a battered medical bag in his hand. An older man of sixty five plus, hefty of build and grey of hair, he had been a well known rugby player in his youth. He was the senior partner in the local medical practice and over-due for retirement; but his wealth of experience and matter-of-fact bedside manner — sometimes matter-of-fact to the point of rudeness — were reassuring to the older inhabitants of Rype-in-the-Marsh.

"Good mornin', Doctor," Phyllis greeted him, a little obsequiously, bobbing as if she were about to drop him a curtesy.

"Good morning, Doctor Hadley," I echoed. He inclined his head curtly in reply, apparently expecting me to be leaving since it was plain that the tiny entrance hall was scarcely big enough to accommodate us all; however, he must have caught my last words.

"Two what?" he asked in his trademark brisk manner.

"Witnesses for Mr White's Will," I explained, equally briefly. "I can be one, but we need another."

"I presume I can do that for you," he said, the brief flicker that passed for a smile crossing his features. "But I must see my patient first. Lead on, Mrs White."

They ascended the stairs, Phyllis speaking in hushed tones to the doctor. I was left in the hall. 'Hall' was a very grand word for the tiny space at the bottom of the stairs, I thought, as I looked around for somewhere to sit. There was no chair, so I lowered myself onto the second stair and waited, surveying the small area. On the wall, to the right of the front door, there were two rows of hooks smothered in coats and anoraks of all sizes, an untidy row of shoes beneath them and, to the left of the door, a number of books piled up roughly on their sides, the spines facing towards me.

"A Pageant of India," I read, turning my head sideways. I was sure my parents kept a copy of that book on their own bookshelves and that I'd dipped into it from time to time. Interested, I scanned the others:

'*Gardening in the Shade*', '*Good Housekeeping Cook Book*' — both useful but not very interesting — a collection of slim volumes with names like '*The Passionate Bee Keeper*', which I dismissed as lightweight romantic novels. Right at the bottom of the pile was a book that looked intriguing, the gold lettering on its faded red dust cover indistinct. I stood up and bent over, almost standing on my head in an effort to read the title, squinting a little. '*Haunted Towns and Villages of Kent*'.

"They're fer the jumble." Phyllis' voice came from the landing above. "Someone brought 'em fer Archie ter read but he ain't interested. If yer want 'em, just take 'em."

"Thank you," I said, slightly embarrassed at being caught in such an unprepossessing position, "I ..."

Dr. Hadley came out onto the landing beside Phyllis.

"You can come up now, Mrs Dawkins," he instructed peremptorily. "Mr White is ready to do the necessary."

I grabbed the Wills and took them upstairs, past the doctor and into the bedroom. Archie was sitting up in bed looking exhausted, but with a certain gleam in his eye which indicated to me the likelihood of a swift recovery from the operation scheduled for the morrow. I had a sneaking suspicion that it was pure funk which had sent him to his bed, partly from the fear of surgery but also from the superstition that making a Will was likely to kill him.

I showed him the Will, read it out to him and explained its terms in detail. I dwelt on the point that he would need to make a new Will if he married, even if he married Phyllis. I asked if he had any questions: he shut the eye nearest me in a wink.

"Not about the Will, duck. Leastwise, not now."

I handed Achie a clipboard and indicated where he should sign the Will. He did so laboriously, tongue poking out in concentration. I dated the document and proffered it to Dr. Hadley who witnessed it and passed it to me to do the same. Once executed, I folded the Will and put it carefully into the envelope I'd typed in readiness. I dated the envelope too.

"Glad that's done, duck," said Archie from the bed. "Thank yer fer arrangin' it so quick like."

"A pleasure," I responded, laughing inwardly as I remembered my fit of temper over the typing of it. "You make sure you hurry up and get well now ... so I can make a longer and better Will for you." I saw a sudden gleam in his eye and forestalled him. "Yes, and charge you the earth for it, too."

We bade each other farewell and the physician also took his leave. I shut the door firmly behind us feeling certain Archie was itching to get out of bed and into his clothes.

"Can you spare another minute or two to witness Phyllis' Will, please?" I said to the doctor.

He nodded terse agreement. Phyllis ushered us into the dining room, a poky space behind the small front room where I swiftly ran through the same formalities as I had with Archie, reminding her that the Will would be invalidated if she married. Three quick signatures and it was done.

Dr. Hadley bade us a brusque farewell and left. Before I departed, I reminded Phyllis that I would deposit the original Wills with the bank and send her copies of them. I would also keep a copy of each Will in case it were ever needed. Then, with suppressed excitement, I gave her an envelope containing the first bill I'd ever submitted in my own name.

As I was leaving, Phyllis plucked a book from the pile by the door and pressed it into my free hand.

"Do take it, duck. I seen yer lookin' at it." She smiled, but there was a sadness in it. "I want ter thank yer fer doin' this so quickly. 'E may joke, but I knows it's bin a-worryin' Archie, not 'avin' a proper Will."

"He'll be fine now," I assured her. "The funny thing about making a Will is that it concentrates the mind on living."

I stepped out into Park Row, documents and book safely stowed in my briefcase, wondering how best to obtain the copies I had promised Mr and Mrs White. I was so used to taking Wills back to the office and asking my secretary to photocopy them that I had forgotten that I no longer had access to a photocopier.

'Damn!' I thought, 'how stupid!' but the chastising thought had barely made its way through my synapses than I realised that the simplest method was to take the originals to the bank for photocopying. This sensible thought required sensible action; I would take them now. Even better, I would call into the library on my way. I relished the joy of the library's coolness; it was close to midday and the sun was beating down in a way which had now become customary.

A tall brick building with large arched windows and an arched door, painted blue to match the window sills, the library was a very impressive building for the size of the town. It overlooked the little park in the centre of the Rype which was always full of flowers and often crowded with youngsters.

Unfortunately, the library door was locked. I looked around for some indication of the its opening hours and discerned an almost illegible notice propped up in one of the windows. Peering over the iron railings which guarded the frontage, I managed to decipher the words 'Back in 10 minutes' scrawled on a piece of cardboard.

When would the writer return? I pondered. Ten minutes could easily stretch into an hour in this lazy little place. I turned the brass door handle to check, pushing hard. It didn't budge. Frustrated, I looked around. A man was sitting in a white saloon car parked on the other side of the road, beside the park.

He was smoking, his elbow resting on the window frame. Curls of blue smoke from the roll-up cigarette drifted from its tip. The man screwed up his eyes as he slowly inhaled. The sun danced off the heavy gold rings that adorned his fingers. He was clearly waiting for someone or something; perhaps for the library to re-open. I crossed the road towards him and smiled my most ingratiating smile.

"Good morning. I wonder if you can tell me when that notice was put in the library window?"

He had drawn his cigarette hand inside the car as if to spare me the smoke.

"Thank you," I said. "How considerate of you."

He stared at me for a moment or two. Something about his look was offensive, threatening almost, transfixing me like a mouse before a python. He narrowed his pale, pale eyes and I noticed that his pupils were dilated. Then he smiled. It should have been an attractive smile, for he had a well-formed mouth and white even teeth, but it held something that was singularly unpleasant.

"No," he sneered. "I don't know and I don't want to know."

Despite my discomfort, I asked, in what I hoped was a beguiling manner:

"Have you been parked here long?"

"Long enough. Why d'you want to know?"

"I thought you might have noticed if ..."

"I have absolutely no idea why you're speaking to me," he interrupted, taking another pull at his cigarette. He blew the smoke in my face. "Go away, there's a good girl. Run along."

I breathed in sharply, deeply incensed, patronised and insulted all at once. Not a good move. His smoke, sweet and fusty with a rotten edge to it, was pulled deeply into my lungs. I fell into a fit of coughing, so bad I feared I'd never breathe again. Through it I heard the car accelerate away.

I sat down hard on a nearby bench. Sensitive though I was to cigarette smoke, never before had I suffered such a paroxysm. Gradually, I regained my breath but the disgusting smell-taste remained. I fished in my pocket for a peppermint. My hand brought out a selection of bits of wrapping. Just my luck. I delved a little deeper and this time my hand discovered a fluffy, white sweet. I wiped the fluff off and sucked the mint hard. That was better.

- 17 -

Of Smugglers and Smiths

I was hot and short of breath when I reached the bank. Helen, the chief cashier, immediately invited me into the inner sanctum.

"You look done in, Mrs Dawkins. Do please take a seat and catch your breath. Mr. Stone's out visiting a customer so we can make ourselves comfortable in here until he gets back."

She sat down in her superior's chair and leaned back. I sank gratefully into a chair and drew the Wills out of my briefcase.

"These are the original Wills I've made for Mr and Mrs White," I explained proudly. "Mr Stone said it was urgent so I've just been round to their house to get them executed."

She took the Wills from me, turning the envelopes over and frowning slightly. I realised she was not sure what I expected of her.

"Mr and Mrs White have asked me to leave them with the bank for safekeeping," I told her. "Unfortunately, I don't have a photocopier and I've promised them copies. Would you be good enough to take two copies of each, and give me a receipt for the originals?"

"Of course." Helen gathered up the original Wills and headed for the door. "I'll be back in a jiffy."

Left to my own devices, I leaned back and studied Mr Stone's bookshelves. There was only one row of books, mostly to do with accountancy, economics and banking. They looked pristine, as if they had never been opened. The rest of the bookshelves were home to an array of periodicals about banking; my eyes slipped sideways in search of something more interesting and alighted upon a slim, well-thumbed volume half-hidden by his telephone. The title had once been written in ink on the brown-paper cover but some mishap had occurred and it was now a long smudged blot. Intrigued, I was unable to resist picking up the book. It fell open in my hand at Chapter 3, headed '*Smuggling*'. Serendipitous indeed. My eyes flew along the page.

'Romney Marsh was the birthplace of smuggling in southern England. Fine grazing for hundreds of thousands of sheep was supplied by the fertile land that had been reclaimed from the sea. For centuries, the export of the wool from their backs was both highly taxed and badly policed. In days when the common people suffered many privations the opportunity to avoid tax provided an open invitation to smuggle.

In 1275 the Crown imposed a tax, called the Great Custom, on wool leaving England. This proved to be such a significant source of income to the Crown that the tax was doubled in 1298, and successive administrations tinkered with the laws and duties according to their need for funds. Wool was a very valuable commodity and commanded a high price on the Continent and it is therefore believed that illegal wool exports from the Marsh commenced very soon after these restrictions were imposed.

Nonetheless, the amount of wool smuggling from Romney Marsh fluctuated in response to the laws and to market forces. Thus, when there was high demand in England there was less incentive to smuggle. In the 15th century, when wool prices fell as a result of diminished demand and producers found it difficult to make a living from the home market, it was inevitable that smuggling would increase.

In the 17th century the problem assumed epidemic proportions and attention focused on Romney Marsh as the centre of the trade. In 1660 wool exports were forbidden, and two years later the death penalty was introduced for smuggling wool. The legislators of the day probably saw this as a major deterrent, but it simply made the Marsh smugglers, known as Owlers because they carried out their nefarious pursuits in the dark, even more desperate....'

'Not very surprising,' I thought. 'If you're going to hang for smuggling wool, why hesitate to shoot your pursuer?'

I heard a sound from behind. I shut the book and pushed it back behind the telephone feeling as guilty as if I had stumbled upon someone's diary. I could feel my cheeks flaming as Helen came back with the receipt and the photocopied Wills but she didn't appear to notice.

As she handed the photocopies to me she said: "I'm sorry to trouble you, but I have two customers at the counter who are expecting to make their Wills today."

"Oh?" I enquired.

"Apparently it's a misunderstanding. Mr Stone said that he would make arrangements for them to consult you and suggested they call in to the bank this morning. I don't want to presume, but since you're here ...?" Helen left the last part of her sentence hanging.

"I'd be delighted to see them," I assented. "Shall I come and speak to them? I think I have some time tomorrow if that would ..."

"I was rather hoping you would be able to see them now. You see, Mr Smith seems to have thought that was what Mr Stone meant."

"Oh!" I tried to recollect whether I'd left the dining room tidy.

"I'm sure Mr Stone would be happy for you to use his office," Helen suggested. "But only if you have the time, of course."

Relief coursed through my veins. I checked my wristwatch but only for show; I knew I had nothing important on my agenda for the day.

"If you're really sure Mr Stone won't mind, that would be perfect."

Five minutes later I was sitting behind Mr Stone's desk with a pen and paper kindly supplied by Helen, and two new clients, Mr and Mrs Smith, settled across from me.

Taking their instructions took no more than half an hour, for the Smiths had come well prepared with all the information I needed readily available. They had clearly thought about their requirements and simple basic Wills were all they wanted. I was relieved that I would not have to spend the whole of the rest of the day typing complicated Wills.

I explained to Mr and Mrs Smith that they would need to come to my house to execute their Wills and we arranged a date and time. I bade them goodbye thinking that the only outstanding thing about the reserved but determined couple was that they were beige; their hair, skin, eyes and clothes were all the same colour, in different shades — beige. I took my leave of Helen and walked home, happily without incident.

Poppadum gave me her usual effusive greeting, rushed round the garden and finally came to rest close to me. I poured myself a large glass of cool water and downed it in one gulp. Collapsing onto the sofa, I wondered briefly if I had inadvertently drowned myself, since I seemed to have doubled in size. I put my feet up and reposed with a cushion supporting my back, glad of relief from the constant struggle between my breasts, my lungs and the Bump, which all vied for space like overstuffed furniture in a parlour.

I pulled out the book which Mrs White had pressed on me. The dust cover belonged to some other volume: this book proved to be about the history of violent crime, including a whole chapter on Romney Marsh. I had scarcely begun reading before I found I was nodding off, my chin dropped onto my chest and dribble edging out of my lips. The book closed itself and began a slow slide to the floor. Bump aimed a kick at my chin, missed and thumped my bosom before doing its slow turn. Opening a bleary eye, I watched as my belly bubbled up one side and then felt the peculiar sensation as the baby trembled and shook itself into a new position.

Poppadum had moved her head and was regarding me with a questioning look.

"You're right. Time for a rest."

I heaved myself to my feet again and tottered into the kitchen where I grabbed a hard-boiled egg from the fridge, chopped it with mayonnaise and chives, added some lettuce and slapped it between two slices of granary bread. It was delicious — so delicious that I propped myself against the draining board and devoured it there and then. Licking the last of the creamy dressing from my lips, I climbed the stairs longing for my afternoon snooze. Poppadum padded silently behind me.

I slipped into sleep like a lascivious girl welcoming her lover.

- 18 -

Of A Nightingale's Summons

I am sitting in a rocking chair by the inglenook, the baby nursing restlessly at my breast. I feel restless, too, but there is nothing I can do — nothing to alleviate the seething anxiety within my chest. The baby is fussing, spitting out my nipple, not nursing properly. I take a deep breath and find myself praying, praying that my Jack will be home soon. He had promised. Really promised me this time.

The weather is warm, so the fire has been damped down to a glimmer. I know it is late, too late. Jack should have been home by now. Strong, dark haired and handsome, there is no-one in the world like my Jack. Always full of laughter and bravado, so sure of himself.

I feel my love fly out to him, I feel myself fly to him as if I am a nightingale, small and brown. My mate is calling me, singing, singing, singing his beguiling spellbinding melody. Calling me to him as if I had no will of my own, my little wings carrying me onwards, onwards towards his tender attention. All is well, all must be well, for he is singing me to him.

And then I am in the tavern, and Jack is standing, tall and vital, at the bar, tankard of ale in hand, joking with his comrades. He spins towards me as my thoughts reach out to him and I am there, alone now, as all else vanishes, my arms outstretched towards him.

'Jack,' I cry his name, but no sound issues from my lips ....

'Annie, my Annie!' The words hush into my heart ....

His special crooked smile lights up his face as he strides one long step towards me, his own hands reaching out to me. A loud report, the smell of gunpowder overcoming the stench of stale beer, and my Jack crumples to the floor ... blood, blood, blood is everywhere.

I kneel beside my love. I hold him into my arms, cradling his dear head against my heart as he tries to speak but red, red blood bubbles up, choking him, smothering the life from him ....

Even my babe is forgot, abandoned to its crying on the sawdust ... all I can smell, can feel, can taste, can see ... is the blood ... so much blood ... the blood that pumps his life from him, from me, from our babe....

Once again I woke with the warm, metal smell of blood in my nostrils. Once again I felt the viscosity of drying blood all over me. My heart was breaking. I felt the blood pump out of it, gushing round me. I turned towards the place where Bruce should be and it was empty. Empty? Why could that be? My heart leapt in my chest, settled a second and missed a beat. I could feel the uneven palpitations bumping though my whole body ... and then I realised it was the baby within. It was only the baby kicking. Of course Bruce was not there. I had been having an afternoon's rest.

I shook my head, bringing myself firmly into the present. But still it took me a while to rise and even then the stickiness and the red iron smell of blood was still clinging to me.

I went slowly downstairs and took a long, cool bath before I began to prepare the evening meal.

- 19 -

Of The Smell of Death

"Good God! What's that?" The words fell out of my mouth as someone thumped thunderously on the front door.

It was the next morning and I had just come in from walking Poppadum. Her lead was still in my hand as I rushed to open the door before it was shattered, Poppadum growling behind me. A stout, grey-haired lady nearly fell into my arms. She was very flustered, almost shouting, talking fast and furiously. Poppadum started barking.

"I must see the solicitor. At once! It's *most* urgent! Very urgent! I must see him *now*! Tell him *at once*!"

She waved her hands and her voice crescendoed to a bellow as she endeavoured to make herself heard over Poppadum's fury.

"*At once*! *Mrs Pendant*. My name is *Mrs Pendant!*"

So far my efforts to quieten Poppadum had proved utterly ineffectual; Mrs Pendant's flapping arms serving only to inflame the dog's need to protect me. Catching a glimpse of teeth bared in a ferocious snarl, I grabbed Poppadum hard by the collar, stroked her gently and whispered to her.

"It's all right, Old Girl, quiet now."

Poppy grumbled, but quietened. I addressed Mrs Pendant:

"Do come in and have a seat ..." I began soothingly, still holding the dog's collar.

"*No! No*. I can't sit down. I told you. *It's urgent*!" she boomed, so close to my ear that I actually flinched. "I *must* see him at once!"

Poppadum made a distinctly threatening noise somewhere between a growl and a bark.

"Shush!" I admonished her, as she eyed Mrs Pendant

speculatively. The latter had followed me into the sitting room. Slightly deaf in my right ear, I motioned her to an armchair.

"Please tell me ..." I tried again.

"No, I can't tell *you*. I *have* to speak to the *so-li-ci-tor*," she said, spelling it out for me as if I were simple. "My business is *private* and *urgent*."

She was becoming so agitated that I had a real fear that she might have a stroke and drop dead on the spot. I raised my voice.

"I *am* the *so-li-ci-tor*! Now, Mrs Pendant, *please* take a seat and I'll be with you in a minute."

She looked at me curiously for a moment and then dropped into the armchair like a stone.

"Would you like a cup of coffee or a glass of water?" I asked, heading for the kitchen with Poppadum.

"No. No, thank you." Her voice had dropped a couple of octaves.

I hung up Poppadum's lead and settled her in her basket, warning her, on pain of instant decapitation, to stay there and to stay quiet. She showed her disapproval by turning round and round before she lay down with her back to me, but with a wary eye on Mrs Pendant. I filled two glasses with water, placing them through the hatch into the dining room. When I returned to the sitting room Mrs Pendant was sitting straight-backed in one of the armchairs, looking uncomfortable.

"Sorry about the noise, Mrs Pendant. Poppadum is very protective of me at the moment. Let's go through here into what serves as my office."

My new client heaved herself to her feet as I led the way into the dining room. I was grateful for my glass of water. I was parched; and sipping it gave me time to collect my thoughts. Mrs Pendant accepted her glass from me absent-mindedly, taking a quick sip as she moved to the window, her eyes raking the street outside as if she were looking for someone.

I allowed myself a moment to survey her. Some of her greying curly hair, escaping the neat French pleat, twisted around a beautiful complexion, though now rather hectic in colour. Very bright blue eyes were inspecting me.

She had been surprised that I was the solicitor. I presumed that she'd expected someone older, probably a man. I was as accustomed to this expectation as I was to the dismay and disappointment that often surfaced when I proved to be a young woman. I'd recently applied to join the Kent Law Society; my application apparently causing some consternation among my fellow solicitors because approval of my application was slow. It was made clear to me, in no uncertain fashion, that I was fortunate indeed that an older lady who practised near London had set a precedent — for it transpired that I was only the second lady solicitor to become a member of that esteemed Society. I was aware that there were not many local solicitors and certainly very few who were women as young as I, let alone pregnant and in a small town like Rype.

I held out my hand.

"Shall we start again? How do you do, Mrs Pendant?" I smiled what I hoped was a reassuring smile. "My name is Hazel Dawkins. I've been qualified as a solicitor for a little over three years."

"How do you do, Mrs Dawkins?" she replied, shaking my hand very firmly but briefly. "I am indeed sorry to have disturbed you, but something has occurred — it's most urgent."

She ensconced herself into a chair on the other side of the dining table while I wedged myself into the chair opposite her.

"Please tell me more," I requested.

She was so wound up that she could not sit still; she fidgeted with the pen I had placed in front of me, her eyes following the movement of her fingers. After a long moment of silence she offered me the pen. I took it. She leaned forward and spoke in lowered tones:

"I have a problem with my neighbours. I've known for a long time they've been trafficking Pakistanis into the country because I hear things at night. Footsteps, people shuffling around, whispers."

I must have looked askance because she looked at me sideways, her well-modulated, cultured voice strengthening, as she continued:

"Oh, they try to keep it quiet. But I've *heard* them. Often ... yes

... very often. And sometimes I have even seen them passing beneath my window. It's not easy to see them because they dress the poor creatures in black, and their skins are so dark. But I see the whites of their eyes ... they are *so* afraid. Oh yes! They try to keep them quiet. *But I know.*"

"Mrs Pendant, are you s ..." I was beginning to wonder whether she were a little deranged. She waved my interruption aside with an imperious hand and raised her voice.

"*Of course* I'm sure. That was what you were going to ask, were you not? They all ask the same thing ... everyone I dare to talk to. Even the police. Do you think I would come ...?" she broke off, taking a deep breath, and I seized my chance.

"You've been to the police?" I asked.

"Yes, yes! I told them all I'm telling you. I've told them of the lorries that come to take them away. I've told them that Pakistanis are smuggled into the loft. I've told them that I hear noises in the night — muffled footsteps and shuffles. And sometimes a muffled cough or a cry ..."

Her voice died away as she fixed my eyes with hers. Her eyes were wide and her pupils dilated, very bright. She shook slightly. With a shock, I recognised her heightened mental state. 'What does one do with a lunatic — perhaps a schizophrenic?' I thought in panic.

But she had not stopped speaking.

"... but no-one believes me. No-one will *do* anything. And I ... I have to admit ... I'm frightened. I don't like to admit that. I'm a proud woman, unlike some of these namby-pamby nitwits that live round here. But I *am* afraid. I'm sure I'm being followed," she divulged, her hands trembling.

"I'm sorry," I tried again, putting a hand over hers. She shook it off impatiently.

"I don't want sympathy!" she exclaimed angrily. "I'm trying to get you to *do* something. Let me spell this out to you as concisely as I am able. My next door neighbours bring in Pakistanis. How, or by what means I do *not* know. I only know they take them up into the attic ... into the loft which runs over my bedroom. I can't get up there — I have no access. How *they* get them up there I don't know either."

"But why do you think ...?" I started.

"Think? *Think*? I don't have to *think*! I *know*. I'm telling you! *Listen* to me. They keep them like *slaves* up there. Yes — just like the black slaves in the old sailing ship days. As a rule, they lie there, quiet. They are soon collected and taken away — to London, I expect," she swallowed, noisily. "But last week, someone *died* up there!"

This was too much for me. "But how do you know that?"

"There's a patch on my bedroom ceiling. I've watched it grow. It's the shape of a human form. And there's the smell. I know the smell of death when I smell it!"

"Er ... Mrs Pendant ..." I tried to forestall her, but she was in her stride now.

"I was a matron in a Singapore hospital in the war when the Japs overran it. Then I was a POW — a prisoner of war — for nearly four years. Oh, yes! I know the smell of death all right!"

"You were in Changi ...?" I was taken aback, thinking that what she must have suffered in a Japanese prisoner-of-war camp would be enough to unbalance anyone's mind.

"Indeed! But before that I ran the whole show at the Kerdang Kerbau hospital. That was in the days when nurses were proper nurses — not glorified air hostesses that just take temperatures and blood pressure. We used to deal with the birth and death every day. They were all brought to my hospital, until Singapore was taken and then .... But what are you going to do about the Pakistanis?"

I thought it best to counter with another question.

"You say you've told the police? This really is a criminal matter, not a civil one."

"Of course I've told the police. I've told you that already," she said heavily.

"What did they do?" I queried.

"Sent some young constable round to have a look. I told him all I knew — which is just what I'm telling you. All he did was to go and talk to the neighbours. I don't believe he went into the roof."

"Why not?"

"They must have spun him some tale. I expect the neighbours told him I was deranged and, no doubt, he believed them. I suppose I seem like a resentful old biddy." Her shoulders slumped, but her voice strengthened again. "But I know what I hear. *And* I know what I see. I hear the noises. I see the whites of their eyes. And I know what I smell, too — and it's the *smell of death*, I'm telling you."

She paused for a moment and then went on more quietly:

"I know you don't believe me. I know I sound deranged. But, believe me, I am *not* the fanciful sort, generally. This whole affair is very disconcerting and not a little frightening."

"Did the police report back to you?"

"Yes. They were not at all helpful. They said they'd investigated but had found no evidence of anything suspicious. But that was *before* the death. And the smell! I can't sleep in my own bedroom because the smell is so bad — with that big, dark shape on the ceiling made by all the body fluids."

"*If* there's been a murder, it's definitely a case for the police," I said firmly, in the hope of avoiding further comments about the smell of death. I was beginning to feel quite queasy.

"The police won't do anything. I told you, I tried. They think I'm a time-waster. I'm resigned to it. Young people nowadays have no respect for their elders. But I know the neighbours have no right to use my loft space. Now that *is* a civil matter."

"Perhaps ..." I began.

Snorting with annoyance, she jumped to her feet and cried distractedly, "*No* 'perhaps'. I *must* do something. *You* must do *something*."

She was walking up and down the room. My eyes followed her as I tried to think of something to say, let alone do.

"I don't quite see what ..."

"Just come round to my home. See the mark I'm talking about. *Smell* the *smell*! Talk to them. *Demand* to go up in the loft to inspect it. They must be made to stop this dreadful trade."

I was beginning to feel completely out of my depth. Never before had I been confronted by a mad woman in my office, let alone in my dining room, and I had certainly never heard anyone mention the smell of death before. This was a far cry from my usual round of wills and conveyancing which, although they could prove emotive on occasion, were matters that produced emotions with which I was used to dealing. Insanity was quite another thing.

"Please sit down, Mrs Pendant. I need to take a few details."

My firmness seemed to calm her and she reseated herself while I took down her name, address and telephone number and made a few notes of dates and times. The ordinariness of it calmed me as well.

"From what you've told me, Mrs Pendant, this is really a criminal matter and should be reported to the police. Now I'm going to ring the police and I would like you to tell the constable exactly what you've told me."

"He won't beli ..."

"He will have to take it seriously if he knows I do. I'll accompany him to make sure he inspects the loft, and then I can see if I believe you have any civil claim against your neighbour. Are you happy with that?"

I began to feel in control of the situation again. Mrs Pendant felt it, too:

"Yes. Very well, you may call the police. But I *will* require you to be present and to advise me. What will your fees be?"

"Shall we see if there's anything I can do, first? I'm not sure that I can help you. If I can't, I won't make a charge." It appeared generous, I hoped, but I didn't want to be retained by this strange woman unless there was something I could do – and there was some substance to her accusations.

"Thank you. How kind of you. Will you make that phone call now?"

"Yes, of course," I replied as I picked up the receiver and dialled the police house. Neil, the local constable, was not there but his wife said he would be back soon.

"I'd be very grateful if you would ask him to telephone me as soon as he returns. Thank you." I put the receiver back on its cradle with a click.

"He won't ring," Mrs Pendant prophesied. "They all think I'm out of my mind. But I really do know the smell ..."

"Yes, yes, Mrs Pendant," I interrupted hurriedly. "But I didn't mention you. And Neil always rings me back. There's not a lot I can do for you until I speak to him, so would you like to go home? I'll telephone as ..."

"No!" she cried, leaping to her feet again and amazing me with the ease with which she moved her bulk so swiftly when I had such difficulty with my swollen belly. "No, I'll wait here. They saw me come out. They may have followed me here. And they've got a lot to hide. I'll wait here."

Mutely, I passed her glass of water to her. She might have been followed – goodness me, she was making me nervous now. We were sitting there, silently sizing each other up as we waited for the telephone to ring. When it shrilled, only a couple of minutes later, we both jumped.

I answered it immediately.

"Hello Mrs Dawkins, I hear you need my help."

Neil was a young, fair-haired man who knew practically everyone in Rype. I had not consulted him professionally before but I knew him reasonably well because we both served on the committee of the local youth club.

"Yes, Constable," I said, thinking it best to speak formally. "I have Mrs Pendant here. She has a problem and would be grateful for your help. She believes a crime has been committed."

"Not the Pakistanis again?" I could feel the sigh in his voice as I hesitated. "Surely, it can't be?"

"Yes, you are quite right, Officer," I confessed. "I wasn't involved before, but this time I think it may be serious."

The long sigh he fetched was quite audible to me. I hoped Mrs Pendant had not heard it. I pushed the receiver still closer to my ear.

“She’s as nutty as a fruitcake,” Neil declared. “I’ll be with you as soon as I can.” My heart sank at the thought of spending more time waiting.

“Within five minutes, do you think, Officer? Mrs Pendant is most anxious.”

“I’ll be there,” he promised.

True to his word, Neil arrived five minutes and twenty-three seconds later. By that time I had managed to reassure Mrs Pendant that he would take her complaint seriously. I had also confirmed that I would personally inspect the roof space on her behalf. I sincerely hoped that the neighbours would be available; to arrange another time might prove difficult and, in view of what Mrs Pendant had said, I wanted to inspect the property adjoining hers when the occupiers were unprepared for the visit.

Neil took off his helmet to enable him to walk through my low front door. Looking both very handsome and very friendly, he shook Mrs Pendant’s hand.

“Mrs Pendant is concerned that her neighbours are using her roof space for illegal purposes,” I informed him, retaining my formal manner. “She tells me that there is no access to the roof space from her property, although of course, she owns it. She’s not sure what her neighbours are using it for but thinks it may be to cultivate drugs or to store stolen property. I suggested that she should contact you but she fears you may be of the opinion that she’s wasting your time. I assured her that you would take this matter most seriously.”

He nodded, giving me a speaking look. “Of course.”

“I have also advised her that I should inspect the property, and the deeds, so that I can make sure that one reflects the other. If she owns the roof space to which she has no access, she may wish to take remedial steps.” Gosh. I was sounding formal even to my own ears. I spoiled it by grinning. “So I thought we could assist each other by visiting it now."

"Right. Let's go." He headed out of the door, replacing his helmet once outside. He had come on his bicycle which lay against the low wall.

"You go on ahead," I suggested. "I'll accompany Mrs Pendant. It's not far."

We walked the short distance to the house known as 'Old Owlers' in fairly companionable silence.

Ten minutes later Mrs Pendant and I rounded the corner into Draper's Road. Neil was talking to a youngish, pleasant-looking blonde woman who was standing on the steps of a wide old building that stood back from the road, separated by some distance from its nearest neighbours. Surveying the property closely with my conveyancer's eye, I guessed that it was originally a hall house and at least four hundred years old. Clearly, it had originally been built as a single dwelling, then later extended and subsequently divided into two smaller residences.

The woman turned towards us as we approached. I noticed that she was wearing heavy make-up, her foundation a touch too dark for her skin, her eyelids and eyelashes darkened too. She wore bright red lipstick.

"Hello, Mrs Pendant," she said before turning her charming smile on me. "You must be Mrs Dawkins. I'm Petronilla De Cham. Call me Petronilla." She held out a red-nailed hand. "I'm sorry my husband isn't here. He's away on business. Neil tells me you would like to check the roof space for Mrs Pendant. That's fine. We've just cleared it out, so you timed it well."

She was still smiling; but there was something in that smile that was just a smidgeon too fulsome. For the first time, I wondered if there were any truth in Mrs Pendant's story. After brief greetings from my new client and myself, Petronilla led the way up to the loft.

"It's true, you can only access the loft from our side of the house. I suppose it's a legacy from when it was all one house, before it was divided into two. I'm not sure when that was. Do you know, Kate?"

I was amazed that she addressed my client so familiarly; I certainly wouldn't have been comfortable doing so. Mrs Pendant had stressed that her Christian name was Catherine. She did not have the air of a 'Kate' at all.

"Actually, my name is Catherine," she corrected, plainly annoyed by the familiarity, and I was pleased that my judgement in this small thing was correct. "No, I have no idea. The property had been divided before I came here. As you know, that was over twenty-five years ago, not long after the War."

We had been climbing the stairs during this conversation and had now come to a crooked door on the second floor which opened onto a narrow, winding staircase, boarded on both sides, that led to the loft. I noticed a cupboard let into the side of the staircase wall, the sort that used to hold candles and candlesticks for those venturing upstairs. The stairs to the attic were steep and uneven, dimly lit by a single lightbulb. I had expected the loft to be similarly lit but when Petronilla flipped the switch as we entered, artificial daylight flooded the place.

I noticed that it smelled stuffy and damp but that was all. No dead body nor any stain on the floor where it might have lain. Perhaps significantly, the whole area had been floored comparatively recently; it was also very clean. Petronilla had mentioned that they had just cleared it — still, there was something a little odd about the place. Was I imagining it? Or was there a feeling that the place had been vacated recently?

My eye caught a glint from the floor. I picked up the small piece of metal, shaped roughly like a doughnut, and handed it to Petronilla. Close to her, a livid bruise down her left cheek was just visible beneath her dark make-up. Her eyes narrowed as she took the object, her right one more than her left and I noticed a flicker of pain. I guessed her eye-shadow hid a black eye. She took the object and moved quickly away from my scrutiny.

"Thank you," she said. "I wondered where I'd lost that button. I must have caught it on something when we were cleaning up here."

I was about to comment that there was not much to catch it on, and that it looked more like a washer than a button to me, but thought better of it, and said instead:

"Thank you for showing us up here, Petronilla. Can you show me where the dividing line is between the two properties? Is it marked in any way? *Mrs Pendant,"* I stressed the surname, "Needs more storage and is thinking of dividing off her half and making a separate access to it from her side."

"It would make it a much smaller space," Petronilla observed. "I don't think it has ever been divided and I have no idea where the correct boundary would be. In fact I believe *we* own the flying freehold."

"That's interesting," I commented. "Mrs Pendant has instructed me to check her title deeds to her property, so I'll be able to ascertain the precise position. If she has legal title to half the loft and decides to go ahead with a division, I'm sure she'll instruct a surveyor to make sure there are no structural ramifications."

"At least she'll know there are no Pakistanis on *her* side then," she remarked.

Mrs Pendant bridled but said nothing. I watched Petronilla closely; her fixed smile stuck to her lips as if glued in place, but she paled a little and the bruise became more apparent, despite the concealing cosmetics. Neil was ready to go.

"I think we've seen all there is to see. Is there anything else you want to check?" he asked.

A thought struck me.

"Where do the pipes run, Petronilla? Maybe the water running is what disturbs Mrs Pendant."

Petronilla looked away but not before I'd noticed that her smile had disappeared.

"I really have no idea. There must be a tank somewhere, I suppose. I think it must be above our heads, up in the roof space. Where's your tank, Catherine?"

"It's in the roof above the back extension," she answered stiffly.

"Time to go," I said. The stuffiness, heat and damp came together in a noxious brew: my head whirled. I clutched the wooden bannister on the way down.

Reeling into the sunlight, I had no option but to sit down abruptly on the doorstep. The whole street was going round and round in a most peculiar way. Mrs Pendant took control.

"Hazel needs a chair. Quickly, Neil! And a glass of water, Petronilla." To me she commanded, "Open your knees, my girl! Here, put your head down as far as you can."

I felt a slight pressure on my neck as my head came into contact with my smock and the baby took the opportunity to kick me on the chin.

I wasn't sure if it were pure embarrassment, or the chair, or the water, but when I raised my head the street came slowly into focus again. I took a deep breath and considered standing — everything revolved fast around me and once again the world was blotted out by blackness.

When I came to, I found myself lying on a unfamiliar settee in a strange room furnished in the Chinese style. Neil was gazing down at me with a furrowed brow and Mrs Pendant was quietly taking my pulse.

"It's all right, Mrs Dawkins. You fainted, that's all. Caused by the heat in the attic, I expect. The constable kindly carried you in here. You were only out for a few minutes. Stay there quietly and rest for a little longer — the baby's fine."

I couldn't believe that Neil had actually carried me. I was such a lump. A fireman's lift would have been difficult, I thought, chuckling to myself. At that moment the baby decided to turn over. I felt and watched my tummy bulge up at one side and then slither over to the other. 'Are you a boy or a girl?' I thought fleetingly, but it didn't matter at all, as long as the baby kept moving.

After assuring himself that I was not likely to give birth there and then, Neil said his goodbyes and left.

"Since I'm here, Mrs Pendant, may I look at that stain on your bedroom ceiling?"

"I'm not sure you should take the stairs yet," she replied. "But I would be *most* appreciative if you would."

"I think I'll try," I said, pushing myself to my feet.

That was fine, the room stayed still. I took a tentative step. No problem; the floor remained at the correct angle. I took another step, and another.

"Yes, I'm all right," I acknowledged. "I'll take it slowly this time."

I was pleased I did because it gave me time to survey the staircase. Mrs Pendant's half of the house contained the upper part of the original staircase, an elegant curved affair with a carved bannister and wide stairs with low rises. Beautiful paintings hung on the walls and a red Chinese cabinet graced the half-landing.

Her bedroom occupied the whole of the front of the first floor: another elegant room furnished in the colonial manner. Although the carpet was slightly worn it was of thick Chinese silk and the colours were still fresh; it must have been stunning when it was new. The curtains, slightly faded where the sun had bleached them, were of leaf green Chinese silk and embroidered all over with flowers.

I noticed the strange smell at once. Nauseatingly sweet with a rotten quality. I risked a glance at the ceiling. Sure enough, a great dark stain covered half the ceiling. Amorphous and spreading, it might well have once represented the shape of a body — but then it could also have been Africa, clouds, or even, at a push, a sailing boat. I wondered whether to take a deeper breath but quickly reflected that it was probably better not to push my luck, so after that one, brief glance and quick sniff, I made my way carefully back down the stairs.

Mrs Pendant was watching me carefully as I descended.

"Did you see the stain?" she asked. "Did you smell that dreadful stink?"

"I *do* see what you were complaining about, Mrs Pendant," I said carefully. "It *does* appear that *something* has leaked through from the roof space we've just seen next door. Do you have your deeds here, by any chance? If so, perhaps I could take them with me? Then I could check the legal situation with regard to the roof space, if you'd like?"

"No, Mrs Dawkins," she replied. "I keep the deeds at the bank, but I'd certainly like you to check the legal situation for me. I'll collect them from Mr Stone tomorrow."

"Thank you," I said. "And thank you, too, for taking care of me. I think I'll go home, now. If you have any more problems, do call Neil. I'm sure he'll come to help you. In the meantime, I'll see if there's anything I can do that will help."

"Thank you for coming," she responded. "And for taking me seriously. Not many people do."

- 20 -

Of Sickness and Health

I thought about many things as I walked slowly home, most of them connected to Mrs Pendant. My one overriding feeling was that I was missing something. Not surprising, I thought. I was still feeling sick and woozy although the fresh air was gradually restoring my senses,

'What made me faint?' I asked myself as I reflected on the suddenness of my collapse. 'I've never done *that* before.'

'Well, you did,' said the other, more reasonable, part of myself. 'Probably because you're pregnant and the weather's very hot. That loft was airless, and it was a very steep climb up those stairs.'

'Don't be stupid! I've never passed out in my life – even when I've had one too many – and I don't intend to start now.' This part of me wasn't feeling very reasonable.

'There was a very peculiar smell up there, if you remember? Damp and fuggy. With something else behind it. Something I can't quite put my finger on ...'

The memory of a sweetish, brackish odour permeating the loft combined with the recollection of the rotten smell in Mrs Pendant's bedroom seeped back into my nose causing a renewed wave of nausea.

"Finger?" My other self snorted. "Nose, more like. Actually, there was an unusual smell. Something I haven't smelled for a long time."

The more I tried to capture what had disturbed my olfactory organ, the more nauseated I felt and the more the odour seemed to drift away from my memory. I turned into Park Street to take the slightly shorter way home.

"Good Morning, Mrs Dawkins – Hazel." The call came from

across the road. I could not mistake that greeting, nor the voice. I did my best to smile as Mr Stone, that kindest of bank managers, crossed over and shook my hand.

"I do hope you're well?" he enquired.

"Not very," I responded frankly, trying to breathe deeply as I fought the sudden heaving of my stomach. "I'm finding the heat a little difficult."

Mr Stone was all solicitude. "You've gone very white. Come over here, into the shade," he said, taking my arm and guiding me into the little public garden that edged this part of Park Street. "Sit down here for a while, take the weight off your legs."

I sat down. I was very aware of the line of perspiration along my upper lip and the wetness under my fringe. He seated himself beside me and looked into my face with concern.

"Never known it so hot at this time of year," he remarked. "It's only early June and the temperature's already up in the eighties."

"I'm not used to carrying so much weight or having so little room to breathe." I tried to laugh but it came out more like a sob.

"Oh, my dear," Mr Stone said, patting my hand. "Don't speak, just take a few deep breaths and you'll feel better in no time. If you don't mind an old man and four-times father giving you advice?"

I had my eyes closed while I concentrated on using my breath to settle my stomach, so I simply nodded to indicate that I had no objection at all.

"I'd suggest that you wear something cooler and preferably do not go out in the mid-day sun. You know: 'Mad Dogs and Englishmen ...' or, in your case, Englishwoman. *Not* a good idea."

"No, I know," I agreed, beginning to feel better. "I've been very silly. But I had to make an urgent site visit and it took longer than I expected."

I was not going to mention that I was blowed if I was going to buy any clothes that I would only wear for a month. I definitely had no intention of staying this size for long.

"I'm feeling much better, now," I smiled, and it was true. "It's not far home and I'm sure I'll make it."

"I'll escort you, just to make sure."

Mr Stone rose to his shinily-shod feet and offered me his arm. I heaved myself up and put my hand through it. We set off slowly.

"Actually, I'm glad I've had the chance to see you away from the bank, Hazel. I was wondering how you were getting on? I know I've sent a few people along to you. Are you managing all right on your own? Do you need anything? A secretary, perhaps?"

"I'm doing fine at the moment, thank you, Mr Stone. I still haven't finally decided whether to set up my professional plate."

I used the old-fashioned words for setting up a legal practice. Solicitors were forbidden by their professional rules from advertising for business. It was permissible only to put up a small plate, usually brass, giving one's name and profession; after that one simply waited for clients. Although, as a solicitor, I was permitted to put one advertisement in a local newspaper indicating that an office was opening, the rules forbade me from advertising legal services and from paying a commission in return for an introduction.

"I mention it because I saw a customer yesterday who has two small boys. She's a very experienced legal secretary but has been at home for the last six years." Mr Stone turned towards me. Magnified by his glasses, one eyelid fluttered. "She tells me she's looking for some part time work, now her youngest is starting school."

I laughed. "How kind of you to think of me, Mr Stone. I must admit I'm finding it a little difficult without a secretary. I'm not the world's fastest typist."

"Well then?"

"Not yet," I said hurriedly, "I haven't made a final decision. And I don't want to do more until I know how I'll cope with a baby."

"I think she'd be happy to do just a few hours if and when you need her."

"Thank you so much, Mr Stone. I really *do* appreciate the work that you've sent me but I don't want to make any commitments to anyone."

"I understand," he said. "But when you change your mind ..."

We'd reached Rose Cottage, so I took my hand from his supporting arm. Wondering if it were permissible to kiss his cheek, I came to the swift conclusion that decorum demanded that I merely shake his hand.

"Thank you for looking after me, Mr St ..."

"Oh, I think you know me well enough now to call me Paul," he suggested. "Are you sure you're all right now?"

"I'm absolutely fine! But I certainly won't be sorry to get back to my normal shape," I responded, thinking gleefully: 'Less than three weeks to go until the baby's due.'

Poppadum must have heard our voices because she started barking. Mr Stone watched me put my key in the lock and took his cue, raising his voice to make himself heard above the din:

"Good. I'll leave you then. But before I go, I must tell you that Mr and Mrs White were very pleased that you completed their Wills so quickly. They said that they even understood what you were saying! In fact, they said they'd never before understood *what* a solicitor was talking about."

I could feel my grin spreading across my face.

"Thank you so much for telling me." I *did* kiss him. On the cheek.

Poppadum stopped barking as soon I opened the door from the lobby. She seemed to know I had no intention of going down on my knees in our normal mode of greeting. She backed into the sitting room and waited until I had lowered myself into the nearest chair. Then, at my signal, she came and buried her head in what was left of my lap. I pulled her ears gently in greeting.

"You must want to go out," I told her.

I pulled myself to my feet. She followed close behind as I waddled into the kitchen and opened the back door for her. She rushed outside instantly. I balanced the Bump on the draining board and ran myself a glass of cold water from the tap. It tasted divine. As I watched Poppadum chase a butterfly I thought how lucky I was to have so much — everything I had ever wanted, including the chance to put my feet up in the afternoon.

Poppadum had soon had enough of the heat and came in before I whistled her. She escorted me up to the bedroom, where I opened the windows, drew the curtains, pulled back the summer covers and lay down for a moment. Utter luxury. I shut my eyes ....

"Hazel? Poppadum? Where are my favourite girls?" I woke up to hear Bruce's voice. I also heard the familiar thump as he threw his briefcase down.

"Up here," I yelled. Heavy footsteps on the stairs.

"Are you all right?" he asked concernedly as he came in. He took my hand in his, holding it as he studied me with a frown between his brows. "You look rather peaky."

"I'm just hot and tired," I explained. "What time is it?"

"Half-past four," he replied, looking at his watch. "It was so sweltering I decided to come home early and bring some work with me."

I made to get up.

"No, you stay here, Haze. For the first time you look really red and uncomfortable. What have you been doing?"

"I'll tell all later. Now I need to make our dinner."

I made as if to get up but not convincingly enough for Bruce. Shaking his head, he sat down on the bed beside me. Poppadum came and put her head on the bed too, looking at me with mournful eyes. He stroked her head.

"I *told* you. Stay there. I'll rustle up something for us to eat."

Poppadum turned hopeful eyes on him and bounded towards the door, wagging her tail. I laughed.

"That's better," my beloved approved. "I'll feed the dog, have a quick shower and work my wonders in the kitchen. You stay here. I'll be back."

"Thank you, darling," I said, meekly shutting my eyes again.

Bruce was a very good cook when he could be bothered. He ushered Poppadum out of the room and closed the door slowly and carefully. I closed my eyes and for the second time that afternoon I drifted into sleep.

Wonderful smells ascended the staircase, crept under the door, assailed my nostrils and brought me back to reality. I realised I was famished. A moment later the door was kicked open and in came my hot and sweaty husband bearing a tray laden with a luscious dish of ... something. It smelled deliciously of garlic and spices.

"Curry and rice," he declared. "Made with everything I could find. Looks a bit peculiar but tastes *good*! Here, eat this and then get up — but *slowly*."

He left the tray and went away. I heard him banging around in the kitchen to the sound of the news on the radio and I was glad he could enjoy it without my having to listen. The news was sad and depressing. The Cold War loomed large in our lives — I was bringing new life into a very uncertain world. I shivered with gloom but instantly chastised myself. There was no point in worrying about world affairs when there was nothing I could do to change them.

Instead I turned my attention to the curry. My hunger satisfied, I felt so much better that I hardly noticed I didn't have the heartburn I dreaded might be the result of such spicy food. A different nagging feeling intensified — the Bump hadn't tickled my ribs internally as it usually did after I'd eaten.

I'd become used to the constant awareness of the little being within me. It was a very symbiotic relationship, me and my child, part of one whole. That was the problem: the baby was so still, too still. It hadn't moved since — when? Anxiety filled me. I racked my brains in alarm.

'Do not panic ... breathe.' I admonished myself. 'and again ... deeply ... breathe.'

I tore into the dining room where Bruce was enjoying his curry, his nose deep in the newspaper and the radio blaring from the table. He half stood at my sudden entrance, his face the picture of concern.

"Darl! What is it?"

"The Bump ... the baby! It isn't moving." I was distraught.

"Come, sit here," he directed, drawing a chair well back from the table for me.

"I can't move!"

He came to me, took my hand and led me to the chair, pushing me gently down into it. Kneeling at my feet, he put his ear to my belly. He pressed it there for nearly a minute. I held my breath and closed my eyes. Suddenly, taking us both by surprise, our child acknowledged his presence with a little squirm, and I opened my eyes wide. Bruce smiled. I burst into tears. He took his head away and gazed up at me.

"It's all right, Haze. He was just having a nap." The almost-dad had a funny, lop-sided grin on his face. "But what d'you know? I heard my son's heart beat." There were tears in his eyes and his much-loved voice shook.

"Really? Could you really?" My voice was shaking, too, with relief. Bruce often put his hand on the Bump to feel those strange, mysterious movements within but he had never put his ear to my belly before.

"Of course I could." He was delighted. "But I don't think I'll put my face down there again right now. I don't want a black eye!"

The babe was well awake now and kicking so hard that my smock looked as though it was hiding a bagful of ferrets. I looked at it in astonishment. The Bump was turning and kicking and squirming and writhing ....

"Whoa," I gasped, as I doubled over from a jab in the stomach. "That felt like a knee *and* a fist. Must be a boy."

"*My* boy! *My* son!" Bruce grabbed me in delight, despite his reservations, and got kicked for his pains. "Wow! He sure packs a punch."

He pretended to be knocked back into his chair, picked up his fork and went back to his curry.

"Okay, woman of mine, that's sorted. Tell me," he beseeched, finishing one mouthful and shovelling in another, speaking round it so the words came out muffled. "What's all this about? What's been going on today?"

I leaned one elbow on the table, the other hand soothed the Bump. A wet nose pushed reassuringly under that hand. And I told him everything.

"Don't complain to me about an uneventful life, ever again," said Bruce mock-severely when he had heard me out. "I think you've probably had rather too much excitement today, what with the Smell of Death Woman, gallivanting about in lofts, fainting in the street and starting an affair with the bank manager. And all while you're in the last few weeks of breeding!"

"Seriously, though," he added. "I know it's been particularly hot today but you haven't fainted before. I suggest you see Mark tomorrow, just to check up."

Mark Wilkinson was our G P — the initials standing for General Practitioner of Medicine — and the youngest doctor in the Rype medical practice which he had joined not long before we bought Rose Cottage. A charming man in his mid-thirties, slim, neither tall nor short, with long-lashed dark eyes and black hair that flopped over one eye, he certainly had a 'way with the ladies', as my father put it. He and his wife, Sue, had become friends of ours almost as soon as we had been introduced by a mutual acquaintance. They were very sociable and gave the most interesting and boozy dinner parties in Rype. Luckily for me, Mark's speciality in the medical world was as an obstetrician, and he had kept a watchful eye on me throughout my pregnancy.

"Yes, I think that, for once, I'll take your advice," I conceded.

"Bravo! That's a first," Bruce crowed. I was very tempted to kick him but preferred to have the last word.

"Well, if I'm going to start an affair," I said. "Which, by the way, I consider a very inviting suggestion — I think Mark would be a much more enticing prospect than Paul Stone!"

- 21 -

Of Parting and Meeting

Jack and Annie are become near inseparable when he is returned from school each Summer. He teaches her to read and write a little and to figure out sums in neat fashion. She teaches him of the secret places in the Marsh where wild garlic blows in Spring, and the early greens of dandelion and burdock peep, of ground elder where it runs wild along the ground — the bitter herbs that bring health back in Spring after the meanness of Winter is past.

In Summer they gather the seaweed from the shore and go a-shrimping in the shallows. Jack teaches Annie to set a fishing line as he has been taught in school. The fisherfolk laugh to see them perched upon the sandbank with their lines out to sea, and taunt them for their meagre gains. When Annie's father is amongst the fishermen the pair are set to help haul in the fishing nets, fish a-leaping and a-jumping in their desperation to be free. Now and then they help wind the windlass that hauls the boats far up the shingle beach. Annie teaches Jack to gut fish and to suspend herring to smoke over the slow fire that preserves bloater and kipper.

In late summer they gather elderberries and haws from the hedgerows to make the possets against the winter cold and the sweet black berries of the brambles to mix with wind-fallen apples from the orchard. They harvest hazelnuts from the hedges and chestnuts from the floor of Songster Wood. They search out pinecones beneath the few stunted pines along the coast and drag driftwood from the sea and beach to build the inglenook fire high and salt-smelling in the winter cold. From the ditches they pull the reeds for thatching and collect the mud to mix with horsehair for caking upon the lathes as plaster. Many, many are the gifts of

Nature that they find. When Jack returns to school and writes of his ice-cold dormitory, Annie searches out the white blossom of wool upon the gorse spikes, wool which she cards and spins and knits into a scarf for Jack's Yuletide gift.

As like or not they bring their separate armies of siblings — his four younger brothers and her three little sisters — to assist, but always it is Jack and Annie who command their troops and, when their work is done, they play hide and seek, or tip and run, or hare and hounds. Jack and Annie ever out-hide and out-run the others so they may steal a moment together. A moment to play a trick, or tell a joke, or tease each other. A moment only — and it is over in the twinkling of an eye. Never do they dare to look straight into the other's eyes or touch a hand. Somewhere deep inside their hearts they sense that they belong together but they know it cannot be. For she has a vow to fulfil and the Squire has plans for Jack to become his steward.

And so they grow to the time when Jack leaves school. His mother's husband is knifed to death in a drunken brawl in the Three Chimneys. In the same month the Squire's ever-ailing wife ceases to breathe her delicate breath and both are buried in the churchyard of All Saints.

The Squire finds comfort in the tall black-haired, blue-eyed son he has sired and grants the boy's mother a place in his household. The young man is sent to France to learn to trade in goods both legitimate and contraband. Annie's mother loses her confidante and Annie is deprived of her companion and her friend.

- 22 -

Of Questions and Answers

I rang the surgery first thing in the morning.

"May I have an appointment to see Dr. Wilkinson, today, please?" I asked the dragon of a receptionist. "It's Mrs Dawkins."

"I'm sorry, Mrs Dawkins, Doctor is booked solid this morning. Is it urgent? You may be able to come and wait until the end of surgery."

I pulled a face but there was only Poppadum to see it. She looked away with a disdainful air as if to say I was no puppy of hers or I'd display better manners.

"It's not urgent. But yes, I think it *is* important. I fainted a couple of times yesterday." Nothing like piling it on as thickly as I dared. "It might be the heat but I *am* very near term."

"Very well, Mrs Dawkins. Surgery ends at half past eleven. I suggest you come at eleven fifteen. I'll tell Doctor."

I was feeling much better. I had woken early to tumultuous birdsong and yet another shining morning of blue sky for as far as the eye could see. Neither nightingale nor dream had disturbed me: I had slept the sleep of the dead that night. I shuddered at the thought. So did the Bump, who responded to my every thought this morning. Delighting in the familiar movements within me, my heart sang as I ambled along to the doctor's surgery.

When Rype had been self-governing, the old building that was now the surgery had been part of the Town Hall. I traversed a lengthy corridor to the waiting room, reporting to the tactless receptionist before I took a seat. She gave me a small square of wood, painted green, which bore the number eleven. I gathered Mark was using the green surgery today. A glance at the pegs on the wall showed me that the number eight was dangling from the green peg. I would have a while to wait.

The smallish waiting room was packed and I wished I'd come later, for, despite the benign weather, everyone seemed to be coughing and snuffling. The only seat left was next to a thin old man, weatherbeaten rather than tanned, who sat leaning forward with his elbows on his knees. He knuckled his brow in salutation. I smiled at his politeness as I crammed myself into the space between him and a large woman who was trying to deal with sniffling recalcitrant twins.

"Sorry," I apologised. "There's just too much of us at the moment. We can't fit into our usual space." I patted the Bump.

"Don't worry, duck," he replied, with the flicker of a smile. "I'm waitin' fer my wife an' she's a lot wider than yer. Not surprisin' after havin' seven children, I s'pose."

I recognised him then. He mowed the grass opposite Rose Cottage, often accompanied by hordes of children. I had heard that his family had lived in Rype for generations.

"I'm Hazel Dawkins," I introduced myself, awkwardly offering him my hand. "I live at Rose Cottage."

"I know," he said, looking me straight in the eye as we shook hands. "M' name's Bert Oddly. Not bin there long, 'ave you? At Rose Cottage?"

"A little over a year. We love the place. But, tell me, do you remember when Rose Cottage was called Nightingale Cottage?"

"Ah, that I do," he responded. "But it were called Nightingale Cottages," he stressed the plural, "on account o' there bein' three cottages there, see?"

"Three? Really? They must have been very small."

"I s'pose they were, but most people lived in one up and one down cottages then. I was born in number three, by the net hut. M' brothers and sisters, too. We was all born there."

"Why was it called Nightingale Cottages? It's such an evocative name compared to Rose Cottage."

"Well," he said, eyes gleaming. "It were on account of them nightingales, yer see."

And he lapsed into teasing silence.

"Yes? Ordinary nightingales?"

"Yep! Ordin'ry nightingales. Very ordin'ry they looks, too, just small and brown and hiding away most of the day. But at night, when they sing, it's a different matter. A *very* different matter."

He winked, the flutter of his eyelid so fast that I could have been mistaken, had he not also tapped the side of his nose with his index finger.

"Mr Oddly, you're teasing me. What *do* you mean?"

"Now let me see," he paused and I thought, uncharitably, that he was trying to work out which fable I was most likely to believe. "When I were a lad, Nightingale Cottages were all on their ownsome down there. The High Street stopped at the end of them Victorian terraced 'ouses. There were nowt but fields beyond and a copse of chestnut and hawthorn what'd been there time since. Nightingales lived in that copse — 'twas called 'Songster Wood' on account ov 'em — and 'twas said that a curse would fall on any who chopped down them trees. Save in time of emergency, o' course." He was warming to his theme. "Thorn trees was used to mend them dykes, see?"

"The dykes? Those wide ditches that are all over the Marsh?"

"No them ditches is just that — ditches. The dyke is the *bank* made to defend us from the sea. Good thing was that when they made them dykes, them made them ditches too, and them ditches grew into a good drainage system. You'll never see a flood on the Marsh, mark my words."

"Why thorn trees?" I had already shown my ignorance, so I might as well carry on questioning him. Besides, I was very interested.

"They grow on the Marsh when nowt else will. Salt 'ardens the wood."

I had wondered why there were few tall trees on the Marsh but I had come to realise that the strong, salt winds that blew in from the sea stunted everything in their path. Even the hardy hawthorns leaned away from the prevailing southwesters, their branches streaming northeast like windswept hair.

"I see, I didn't know that," I acknowledged. "How interesting. Did nightingales nest in the copse?"

"Ah," he agreed, in the Kentish affirmative. "'N' other things, too."

"What other things?"

"'Twas said that them trees 'id those who 'id from the long arm of the law. For generations — from highwayman to smuggler. Ah, and 'tis also said that the signal for the all clear was the song of the nightingale."

I shivered, half with unease, half with presentiment, as he continued:

"Not that I niver 'eard no nightingale, meself. Except once, at the full o' the moon, 'bout forty years a-gone. There's the missus. I'll be off. 'Bye."

He tapped his forehead in that odd gesture of respect and took his spare frame over to where a big, jolly-looking woman stood making arrangements with the receptionist. I found myself smiling for they looked for all the world like Jack Spratt and his wife.

The waiting room had gradually emptied during my conversation with Bert Oddly and now there were only two patients left, myself and an old lady with a bandaged foot and a crutch. She was reading a magazine intently, mouthing the words as she read, her hand grasping a green marker with the number ten showing. Checking that my own marker still bore the number eleven, I settled down to wait.

Dr Peter Hunsford — a charming man, grey of hair and eye, older than Mark, and slightly stooped — came out of the blue-doored surgery and approached the reading lady.

"Good afternoon, Mrs Clements. Would you mind seeing me instead of Dr. Wilkinson?" he asked, his smile for her also encompassing me. "I've seen my last patient this morning and Dr. Wilkinson is likely to be busy for some while."

"Oh, no, Doctor," she said, clasping her hands and looking adoringly at him, making it clear he was a favourite of hers. "It's just a check up for this silly ankle of mine."

"Let me help."

Doctor Hunsford offered Mrs Clements his arm in the old-fashioned courtly way that Mr Stone had proffered his to me. She purred as she took it but I noticed that she put most of her weight on the crutch. They had just made their slow exit from the waiting room when a rough-looking young man in a leather jacket that was studded, torn and dirty, flung himself out of Mark's surgery and thumped his fist on the reception desk. The receptionist jumped and glared at him.

"Another appointment. Soon as possible." His voice was rough but there was a tremor in it.

"Doctor has told me that you are to have only one appointment a week. Do you have your prescription?"

He signalled 'yes' with a nod.

"Then I suggest you take it straight to the pharmacy. They close in less than half an hour." She turned her back on him and he stormed out. She sighed and opened her eyes wide.

A buzzer sounded and a green light flashed on the wall above the green peg.

"You can go in now. That was Dr. Wilkinson's last patient."

I realised I had been staring.

"Thank you," I said, already walking away. I knocked on Mark's green surgery door.

"Come in," called Mark's warm voice with its lilting Welsh accent. I entered. He looked up from his desk and darted round to set a chair for me, steadying me as I sat down.

"Hello, Hazel. What brings you here?" His eyebrows drew together as he regarded me. "You look in the pink of health."

"Quite literally!" I grinned. I opened my arms to display my loose-ish, pinkly-floral, summer dress to full advantage. It was the only one that came near to fitting me.

He grinned in reply. "Seriously, Hazel, what is it?"

"Bruce suggested I come so that you could check everything is okay with me and the baby. You see, I fainted twice yesterday. *So* unlike me, though I know it was very hot and I'd been out in the sun..." The words tumbled out of my mouth. "Then I went to sleep *all* afternoon until I realised – quite suddenly – that the baby hadn't moved for ages. I was sooooo fright ... fright ... frighten ... ed."

Much to my horror, tears coursed down my cheeks and my last words became sobs. I hid my face in my hands and tears trickled through my fingers.

"All right, Hazel," said Mark, concerned but firm. "Remember how well you've been in this pregnancy. There's absolutely no reason you should have any problems now. Tell me, has the baby moved since yesterday?" He put a kindly hand on my heaving shoulder.

"Yes," I gasped from behind my hands.

It had never been my gift to weep beautifully. When I cried it was not only my eyes that grew red. The whole of my face was a sea of blotches, I just knew. I was sure my nose was running and I had no tissue. Mark pressed a perfectly ironed white handkerchief into my hand, almost causing me to relapse into more tears at his kindness. I restrained myself sufficiently to mutter thanks, dab at my eyes and blow my nose.

Mark walked over to a corner of his surgery, drawing a curtain aside to reveal a couch.

"It's all right, Hazel. If the baby's moving there's probably no cause for concern whatsoever," he said gently. "But I'll give you a once-over just to make sure. Come over here and make yourself comfortable. How long is it now to term?"

I realised he was asking questions to help me to compose myself; he knew when the baby was due because I had noticed him examining my medical record.

"Twenty second of June. Only two-and-a-bit weeks to go," I answered obediently, moving over to the couch.

I saw him inspect my ankles as I sat down. I looked at them too.

"Nice ankles," he commented, "No sign of swelling, but I'll still take your blood pressure."

A quarter of an hour later, I had been tested, prodded and examined very thoroughly.

"Very good," said Mark. "You seem to be in perfect health but you *are* a pregnant lady nearing term. That means that your organs are squashed up under your rib cage and I expect you find it hard to breathe fully. Apart from that, I can find no problem whatsoever."

"Thank you," I said, preparing to leave.

"However," he continued, surveying me with a quizzical air. "I know for a fact that you're not subject to fancies or fainting or false alarms, so why did you faint? What *were* you doing?"

"A client instructed me to inspect her property. There is some sort of neighbours' dispute and she was very upset so I thought it best to go along straightaway. It was very hot in the sun and I had to climb steep stairs when I got there. It was the roof-space that was the source of the problem, you see. The attic was particularly stuffy and there was a smell I can't quite describe — but I wasn't there long and it was absolutely empty."

"God! Who quibbles over roof-space?"

"It was very important to my client," I said defensively. "I'm not at liberty to tell you why without her consent, of course. Anyway, it was easy for me to measure, and now I can compare it with the deeds."

"You said a smell? What sort of smell?"

"Fuggy and damp — almost herby. It reminds me of something but I'm not sure what." I spoke slowly, endeavouring to remember. Funnily enough, just thinking of that smell made me queasy.

"Had they been doing any work up there? Maybe it was something chemical, like a woodworm treatment?"

"It was empty, true." I spoke slowly. "But I don't think it was a chemical smell."

"I only ask because I'm interested. I'm researching — informally, of course, and only for my own edification — the effect of exposure to common chemicals on individuals in different states of health and ... er ... condition." This last with a glance at my abdomen.

"Well, something affected me, I suppose," I replied. "Maybe it was only heat and stuffiness and being unable to get my breath after all those stairs. I feel like a complaining old lady. But I must admit that I'll be very glad when the next couple of weeks are over."

"Don't you find it exciting now you're close to term? You know, I've been delivering babies for years but I never get over the wonder of it. Make sure you have the baby on a Thursday — it's the day I'm on duty at the hospital."

"How kind of you. But I'm not sure I can manage a Thursday — I'd prefer a 'Sunday's Child', for 'the child who is born on the Sabbath day is bonny and blithe and good and gay'!" I quoted.

"Talking of bonny and blithe, are you feeling better?"

"Yes ... yes, thank you," I replied. "But I need a mirror after my histrionics."

Mark motioned me towards a looking glass hanging on the back of the door. My mascara had run dreadfully but otherwise my little makeup seemed intact. I did my best to get rid of the smudges on my cheeks; my fingers came away black but my eyes looked better. I turned back to my doctor with a smile.

"Do you have a moment? There's something else I'd like to ask you. It's got nothing to do with medicine."

"I always have a moment for you, Hazel," he joked. "Seriously though, it's the end of surgery so I do have some time."

"I had the chance to talk to Mr Oddly in the waiting room and he told me that he was born in our house. It was number three Nightingale Cottages then. That was interesting, of course. But then he said something even more interesting — that the nightingale's song was used as a signal by the smugglers. Have you heard anything about that?"

"No, I'm afraid I know nothing of nightingales," he replied. "But I do know a bit about smugglers. Of course, most of the tales concern the eighteenth century shenanigans between the smuggling gangs and the Customs Officers, or Preventatives as they were called. I expect you've read Russell Thorndike's Dr. Syn books?"

I nodded. "I've got most of them. I've only read the first one because I've been saving the rest to read while I'm a lady of leisure. I think Mr Stone has other ideas, though. He's certainly keeping me busy."

A shadow crossed Mark's face.

"Take care, Hazel," he advised. "Make sure you get your rest – you will be very busy when the baby arrives, you know. I don't think you should take on too much at the moment. Take an afternoon nap and read Dr. Syn."

"Okay, Doctor, I will. What were you saying about smugglers?"

"The old stories make one think that smuggling's a thing of the past, but actually it's always gone on. It still does today. And the smuggling gangs are still as violent and brutal as they were then, so don't get some romantic notion of it. It is vicious."

I found this very exciting. So did the Bump, for I received a series of little kicks that made me hiccough.

"What makes you think it's still going on?" I asked.

"Hazel, I *know*. There are some very nasty people indeed involved in a smuggling and people trafficking ring on the Marsh. I don't know who they are but I do know some of them operate from Rype."

He was deadly serious.

"Don't raise your eyebrow at me, Hazel," he cautioned. "It's all very well when someone brings in the odd bottle of wine or some cigarettes. That's harmless and may be a bit of fun. But these people mess with people's lives – they bring in drugs and get the youngsters hooked on them and that's *bad*." He paused long enough to make sure I was aware of his emphasis. "But the heinous crime is people trafficking."

"Yes, I know," I said, serious myself now. "But that doesn't go on around here does it?"

"Hazel!" he admonished. "How far are we from France? Where do you think they land these people?"

I had not given people trafficking a thought. I was one of those who believed that the Police and Customs and Excise would deal with that. Mark didn't wait for a reply. He ploughed on:

"There are a few individuals around here who are in the thick of it. They charge these poor people extortionate sums to bring them over from the continent in a small boat and land them at out-of-the-way places as they have always done with contraband. They are brought ashore after dark; hungry, wet and cold. They are stored, like the goods they are, somewhere no-one will notice before they are shipped off to a city like Manchester or London."

"You *do* know a lot about it. How come?"

"I'm called out often, usually at night, when Customs find people illegally entering the country. Sometimes they're found on the shore. At other times they're discovered stowed away under the floor of a lorry where they're packed like sardines. They may be abandoned by a lorry driver who takes off if there's a problem. The poor wretches are left to starve or suffocate. Yes," he gave a long sigh, "I've seen some ghastly things. I have absolutely no sympathy for those *criminals*."

"What happens when they get to London?" I asked.

"They're given a 'job'. Job? It's slave labour. They're forced to work for very low wages — at jobs no-one else would touch, mind you — to pay off the 'debt' they owe their 'rescuers'. If they're female and passably pretty, they're sold to a pimp and into prostitution. Some of the girls doing that are as young as nine. It's iniquitous!" He thumped the table with his hand.

"Oh! I didn't realise." I felt very naive.

"Don't get involved, Hazel," he warned.

"I was just interested in the old legends. I've never worked in criminal law and I don't intend to start now. Strictly civil and non-contentious, that's me!"

I was glad when he chuckled.

"Sorry, Hazel. I'm raising my own blood pressure and probably yours as well. Time for a break. How about a sandwich at the Three Chimneys?"

- 23 -

Of Wells and Clocks

The Three Chimneys had the advantage of being right next door to the surgery. It also boasted a walled garden and good beer. Mark escorted me to the former and went in search of the latter for himself. I settled for homemade ginger beer — a non-alcoholic alternative to my favourite half pint of bitter.

I made straight for my favourite corner of the garden where a table had been placed under the spreading branches of a copper beech tree. Obscured from the rest of the garden by a bend in the warm red brick wall of the boundary, one could observe without being noticed. However, I chose that particular place because it was the coolest; the day was as hot as its predecessor and I had no intention of fainting again. Sinking onto a cushioned wooden chair, I put my feet up on another, closing my eyes and letting the peace of the place wash over me.

Here in the centre of the little town of Rype all I could hear was the buzzing of the bees and the song of a blackbird in the tree above me. The scent of wallflowers floated on the breeze which rustled the dark red leaves of the tree above. I sighed with content, rejoicing in my luck to be here on a 'working' day and relieved of my cares about the baby.

The Three Chimneys was a medieval building whose front elevation to the High Street had hardly changed in four hundred years. Not so the rear which had been extended and extended again over the centuries, so that the roof was not one but many, of different sizes and at differing heights from the ground, their one common factor being red Kentish peg tiles spotted with moss. The walls were painted white and interlaced with such a webbing of black beams, drainpipes and gutters that the overall impression was of a cat's cradle.

Window boxes and a plethora of hanging baskets, suspended from every available surface by wrought iron brackets, were full to overflowing with sweetly scented pansies and heartsease, their brightly-painted yellow and violet faces set off by a backdrop of dark green variegated ivy. In a semi-circular flower bed beneath, the last of the season's tulips blazed in red and gold. I looked around this haven of fragrance for the wallflowers whose scent had first assailed my nostrils and found them growing along the top of the old wall. Other fugitives were furtively peeking out from nooks and crannies along the edge of the wall where the mower could not quite reach.

A door closed with a sharp click and Mark came out, bearing a frothing tankard in one hand, a glass of fizzing liquid in the other and a menu tucked under his arm. I hurriedly lowered my feet. Mark made his way along the uneven narrow brick path behind the tulips and across the sea of still-green, unevenly-mown grass. He placed the drinks on the table. I pulled the menu from under his arm.

"Thank you," I said, with feeling. "I'm parched — actually, I'm famished, too. Cheers!"

I raised my ginger beer in salute and gulped down a third of it. It was cool and delicious.

"Me, too. Cheers!" He grinned, raising his tankard. He downed half his pint in one and wiped the froth from his top lip with the back of his hand. "That was good. Now what will you have to eat?"

I had been studying the menu at top speed: my decision was instantaneous.

"Chilli-con-carne please."

"*Chilli-con-carne*? Are you sure?"

"Absolutely. I need something spicy."

"Spicy eh? You must be carrying a boy. Well, we have to humour you at the moment, I suppose. Though I think you might find it a bit indigestible?"

"No, it'll be fine. Honestly," I insisted.

"Right, I'll go and order. I'll be back in a jiffy."

I leaned back, closing my eyes again. I drifted into a daydream on the scent of wallflowers.

"A very odd thing happened to me yesterday."

The words were spoken close to me. A man's voice, light in timbre.

Startled, I jerked awake and looked around. A young couple had taken one of the tables near the tulips but they were leaning across their table, holding hands and speaking in tones inaudible to me. Otherwise the garden was empty. The voice must have come from behind the wall, no doubt its owner unaware that he could be overheard.

"Really? What was it?" Another man's voice, this one deep and melodious. It sounded familiar but I couldn't quite place it.

The first voice came again, hesitantly now. He sounded older than the other.

"I'm a little embarrassed to tell you. It was so strange you'll believe I imagined it."

"No, I can assure you I won't. You should know me well enough to know that, Stephen."

The owner of the second voice was clearly as intrigued as I. I recognised that voice now. He was a friend of mine, too — the local dentist, Tom Williams. He and his wife had recently been away for a holiday in South Africa. I'd thought they were due home later in the week but I must have been mistaken.

"Please, do tell me," Tom continued. "I promise I'll keep it under my hat."

"I'm not quite sure where to start. Let me see ..." Stephen sounded uneasy. "Do you recall my telling you that the deeds spoke of an old well in the garden?"

"Yes, I do. You thought it must be hidden under something ... a rockery, I think?"

"Yes. An odd place for such a large rockery, I always thought. Do you remember? That brick path led to it and then stopped short. There *was* a path around the rockery which led to the back gate, but it was of gravel, not brick."

"I remember," Tom assured him. "It looks quite different now, though."

"While you were away I thought I'd investigate. I got out my dowsing rods to dowse for the well and, sure enough, they indicated water beneath the rockery at a depth of some thirty feet ..." Stephen's voice trailed off.

"Go on," Tom prodded.

Stephen took a deep breath before he continued: "I waited till Mary was out for the day and then I dismantled the rockery. It took a brave man to do that without telling her, I can tell you! I took my courage in both hands, however, and removed the plants. To my surprise, I found that they were planted in amongst a load of bricks, as if a building had collapsed. I dowsed again and the rods still confirmed that there was water there so I laboured away, piling all the bricks up in one place, tiles in another and removing the rest of the rubbish and earth. I'd only just finished when Mary came home. She was livid! Wouldn't speak to me for hours because I'd demolished her precious rockery."

"That doesn't surprise me."

"No, I probably deserved it. But what I haven't told you is that when I'd moved everything away, I discovered that there was an iron coffin-like arrangement there, bolted down, rusted somewhat but impossible to budge. I didn't let Mary see that. I covered it over with dirt and waited ... and waited ... and waited until she was out for the day at her sister's ..." Stephen paused. "That was yesterday."

He stopped speaking. Tom (and I) waited. The silence grew unbearably until Tom asked: "So what happened?"

"I rushed down the garden as soon as she'd gone. It didn't take long to clear the earth away and then I had to wrestle with the coffin lid. Eventually, I managed to break the hinges and lever the top up. Sure enough, underneath there was a bricked shaft, covered by a round metal lid," he paused again and swallowed. "That was difficult to budge, too. In the end I got took hammer to it, tapped the lid loose. and levered it up. I was really sweating by this time, as you can imagine! So I went in for a glass of water and checked the time to see how long it would be before Mary came back. It was ten past three."

"What time does she normally get back?" Tom asked.

"About six."

"So you had plenty of time for exploration?"

"Yes, that's what I thought. I went straight outside and back to the well. It seemed to call me. The sun was blazing down and it seemed very cool and inviting. I noticed there was an iron ladder down the side of it, so I descended a couple of rungs. That was fine, they seemed strong, so I went further. I'd only been there a moment, I thought ..." Stephen's voice shook a little. "And then I heard Mary screeching my name."

"Screeching? That's a bit hard on her!"

"No. I *mean* screeching. So I came back up. My head was going round a bit but she was *distraught*. She'd been calling me for ages, she said."

"So she'd come home early and caught you at it?" I could hear the smile in Tom's voice.

"No. That's the strange part. It was half past six. I must have been down there *three hours*."

"Three *hours*? Surely not. You must have misread the time when you went indoors."

"I said you wouldn't believe me! But that's not all. I checked my watch. It had stopped at three fourteen. That would have been the time I went down the well." Stephen's voice was definitely shaking now.

"How peculiar!" commented Tom.

"Very. But that's not all, either." Stephen paused again but whether for dramatic effect or from emotion it was hard to tell. "Every clock in the house had also stopped. At exactly three fourteen."

Silence. Silence and a swiftly beating heart, followed by a swift kick in the diaphragm.

"That was strange, indeed."

I could imagine Tom clapping Stephen on the shoulder. I heard them move away. I'd been listening so intently that I jumped when I heard Mark's voice beside my ear.

"Ordering took ages," said he, reseating himself and picking up his tankard. "But the food shouldn't be long in coming."

"It's certainly cooler here in the shade," Mark went on, loosening his tie and opening the collar of his shirt. "You chose the right table."

"I have an uncanny knack of knowing these things," I told him. "Thank you for your reassurance today. I was a bit over-anxious."

"I'm lucky to have such a healthy patient. Talking of patients, I wouldn't normally discuss other patients with anyone outside the practice — but since you're a solicitor I'm sure you'll keep anything I tell you confidential?"

"Of course," I agreed absently, my mind still turning over the peculiar story I'd overheard. I watched the waitress bearing a tray towards us.

"A ploughman's and a chilli-con-carne," she announced. We accepted our respective meals and she swished away, her white apron accentuating the magnificence of her bottom.

I regarded my chilli-con-carne with not a little consternation. It was a very small portion and I was ravenous.

"Anything the matter?" asked Mark.

"Absolutely nothing," I mumbled, my mouth full.

"I don't know how you can eat a hot meal like that on a day like this," Mark commented, tucking into his ploughman's lunch.

His meal did look good: crusty white bread, a whole pot of butter, a huge slice of cheddar cheese, a small mountain of salad, homemade chutney and pickled onions. It also looked bigger than mine. In fact, a great deal bigger.

"As I was saying..." Mark swallowed a large mouthful of bread and cheese and took a swig of beer to help it down. "I would very much like you to meet a patient. Would you have a few minutes after lunch? She's the first of my afternoon calls."

I considered. I was longing for my afternoon rest and I knew that Mrs Pendant would soon be bringing me her deeds to check, but it was unlikely the visit would take long. Mark interrupted my cogitations:

"She's a lovely lady, you'll like her — and I think she'll like you. She's terminally ill, you see, and she was asking me if I could suggest a solicitor to make a Will for her."

"Oh dear," I said. "How sad. How long ...?"

"She has cancer," he said baldly. "Actually she's technically my partner's patient. Dr. Hadley finds it difficult to cope with the dying. Apparently she's had all the treatment the hospital can offer. She decided to come home to die because she didn't want to die in hospital. There's nothing more they — or we, come to that — can do for her. I try to visit each day to make sure she's as comfortable and pain-free as possible." Mark kept his eyes down and he applied himself with vigour to the plate in front of him.

"I see. Of course I'll come." What else could I say or do? "You say she wants to make a Will? I imagine she's on strong medication? If so, would you be able to certify that she is lucid and fully in possession of her senses?"

"Compos mentis you mean? Yes, I believe so. Would you need me to do that?"

"Shall we see whether she wants me to make a Will for her? I expect I'll get some idea of her mental state when I meet her. If she's obviously 'with it' I might ask you to be one of the witnesses. But I'm getting ahead of myself again. She hasn't even met me yet. She probably doesn't even know I exist."

"Oh yes, she knows all about you, of that I can assure you," he replied, looking mischievous. "It's the talk of the town that we have our own lady solicitor in Rype now. Elizabeth probably knows the colour of your hair and eyes, where you live and the date the baby's due."

I blushed. The heat suffused my face from neck to hairline. If he noticed, Mark gave no sign. He continued smoothly:

"Her name is Elizabeth Hudson. She used to sing professionally.

Opera, mostly. She's been ill a long time and unfortunately her family have fallen out with each other, and with her. She feels very much alone."

I'd finished my food but my stomach still felt as if my throat had been cut. The chile had been good but I was still hungry. I put down my knife and fork and placed a hand on the Bump, discerning my baby's heart beating under my hand. 'How lucky I am to be young and expecting to bring new life into the world' I thought, 'just as Elizabeth is preparing to go on a long solo journey.' A tear came unbidden to my eye.

"Elizabeth is not at all miserable. She's a formidable character. Just you wait and see. Now, that's more than enough of that, let's talk of things other than Wills and smuggling."

I was tempted to mention the conversation I'd overheard but it was not my story to share. I asked instead if he knew whether Tom and Joan had returned from their trip to South Africa and Mark replied that Bill, the Rype taxi man, had picked them up from Ashford station a couple of days previously. Ignoring the possibility of a discussion about apartheid, I turned the conversation to the beauty of the Cape, a place I had visited a few years previously.

Mark munched stolidly through his lunch while I chatted. Eventually, he wiped his mouth on a paper napkin and sighed.

"I'm pretty full now. How about you? Is there anything else you would like?"

I had been waiting for this moment. "Yes," I said. "*Another* chilli-con-carne!"

His eyebrows shot up. "You're joking, surely?"

I shook my head.

"Are you sure you can fit another one in?"

"Really. After all, I am eating for two," I said. Remembering my manners, I added: "Please."

As if I'd joke about something as important as food!

- 24 -

Of a Chase and a Fall

Annie is running, running ... running and laughing over her shoulder at Jack. Jack is hot in pursuit, gaining on her though she is as fleet-footed as the hares which race across the levels, barley coloured at harvest time, white as the snow itself in winter.

Annie's bare feet and legs are speckled with mud for it is raining and the paths are slippery. She ducks round the edge of the building closest to her and jumps the garden fence without faltering. Jack sprints past the house and on, on towards the church — but she knows that soon, too soon, he will realise he has lost her and will double back. She hears his racing footsteps falter, slow and cease entirely. He will be listening for a flurry of sound, for her feet flying over the cobbles upon the street, for her panting breath.

Annie backs — slowly, carefully, noiselessly — her skirts held high lest they impede her. She holds her breath and feels her heart trembling in her chest ...

And suddenly she is stumbling .... Her heel trips upon an object hard and solid and she is reeling backwards, falling head first through stale air. Tumbling, tumbling ... down and round, skirts veiling her head and bare legs flailing.

In the blink of an eye her destiny has altered. Her senses and her movements slow as though she is sinking slowly through water. All is dreamlike yet immutable. It takes an age for a split-second to pass and she is aware only of the closeness of a wall, nay, a shaft. She is falling, falling — but her motion is protracted, careful almost, small movements enlarged like a ship observed through a spy-glass. Now she is dropping through sea mist, damp and drear in its whiteness. Time is stilled.

She is aware of her destination, aware she is tumbling into the deepness of a well ... the water must be rising to meet her and yet still she is falling, falling, falling. Bricks are passing perforce though her vision, each distinct unto itself, so clear that her eyes gather tiny differences in shades of colour, conscious of the variation in each brick's size and shape, minuscule though it is. Her dropping is slow, slower, slower still ... and yet inevitable. She has no time to call out, no possibility of avoiding her fate. Only the slow falling.

Now the whiteness of the mist upon the water encircles her in its soft embrace. In a heartbeat her body will splash through the silver surface into the darkness of oblivion: she takes a breath, aware of her pulsing heart and knows regret as sadness wells in her — for the lips she has not tasted, the arms that have not held her close. She is already dead ... for there can be no escape for her. The prospect of life is hers no longer: never again will she breathe the living breeze of Summer, nor hear the waves upon the shore, no more will she feel the heat leap in her cheeks at the brush of Jack's hand, nor lie upon her stomach amongst the tides of waving meadow grass. Her wonder at the effervescence of the nightingale's golden song will cease to be ... and her love for Jack ....?

There comes a rushing in her ears ... a call so far, far away ... then Jack's voice suddenly loud in her ears, magnified by the walls around her.

"Annie! Annie! No!"

She reaches out towards the sound, and her body turns, slowly ... so slowly. Her hands touch something soft, her feet are caught in a heavy caul and she is smashing into oblivion.

She is drowning, drowning ... for she cannot get her breath and yet ... the water is not cold ... nor even wet. She fights to free her head of a dense substance that fills her mouth, her nose, her very ears. A substance that smells for all the world of something familiar — smells, so 'tis not odourless water in a well. Nay, nay ... and her heart leaps with sudden hope and instant laughter ... for the smell is of good Marsh sheep and the stuff is wool. Wool that is stashed high in bales, wool that is spread in fleeces one upon the other, wool that does not lie contained within the well-shaft but wool that stretches before her as far as her eye can see.

Darkness. Something blocks out the light ... no 'tis a personage. A man is descending towards her. Annie cries out as she shrinks back against the wall for he must be falling, falling as she has done and will surely crush her, push her deep into the smothering fleece and still her breath forever.

But the man is moving in a leisurely manner, his movements easy but deliberate. She catches her hand to her lips. Her eyes widen and she sees — dark with rust yet solid iron — a ladder built into the side of the well-shaft. The person is climbing down a ladder ... nay, is about to leap from it ....

And Jack takes her by the shoulders and shakes her hard.

"Annie. Annie."

His voice breaks and he crushes her to him. Feeling the blood suffuse her cheeks, she pushes him away. He checks himself and takes her small hand in his.

"All's well, Annie. Do not fret."

She hangs her head. "I am conscious thou hast saved me ...."

"Nay, Annie, 'twas our Owlers' wool did that!"

"So," quoth Jack, once he had checked that Annie was more shocked than hurt. "Thou hast discovered the secret hiding place of the Owlers' wool."

"I knew it was here," she responded stoutly. "Wast not my brother murdered when Pa took him an-owling?"

But she is looking around, eyes wide with amaze for she has never seen so much wool in one place nor smelled it either, for the close sweet-dirty odour is all around her and fleeces are stacked high about a cavern that opens off the well.

"Nay," said Jack, smiling now. "'Tis not so! For all Owlers are sworn to secrecy — especially from gabbling women."

Then the smile fades. Now what? Annie knows this hiding place and the entrance to it, a secret known only to sworn Owlers. Each Owler must swear upon the life of his family that he will keep silent upon all matters of these passages and rooms. A vow enforced with great brutality — for an unwise word or gesture might bring imprisonment or death to the Owlers, and ruin and famine to their loved ones.

"Gabbling ...?" Annie is incensed and lifts her fists to pummel him as of old.

He grips her wrists hard, she feels the indentation of his thumbs and knows she will bear bruises in the morn. Gasping in pain, she raises her eyes to his face. There she reads the grimness of mouth and eye, feels in her bones a Jack both cold and fierce. Afraid now, she falls silent and lowers her gaze.

"Come."

Jack releases Annie's left hand but keeps his grip upon her right wrist, pulling her past the fleeces to the wall of the cavern. His fingers find an indentation in the stone, comes the sound of an iron bolt sliding and a dark space yawns before them. Jack pushes Annie through the opening, his fingers fast about her wrist. She struggles a little but something in his eyes has warned her not to make a sound. He turns to close the door and they are in full darkness. Jack tugs her wrist and they begin to traverse this strange place. Whether it is well or passage, cavern or room, Annie knows not — knows not that it is a tunnel constructed wide enough to take a wool-laden cart. She feels her way along the wall, its dampness stealing into her fingertips.

A slight pressure in the air commands her to stop before Jack says the word. Once more he fiddles upon the wall and once more a door yawns open. They step into a chamber and Annie's fingertips tell her that it is bounded by dressed stone. The door creaks shut. Jack reaches into a crevice by the door and brings out candle and flint. Soon he has a flickering flame which he raises high. From shadows leaps a wide space bounded beneath and above by stone, its round arches echoing the time in which it was constructed, long before the church which rose above.

"Needs must I leave you here, Annie," Jack says, his voice rough — though why with anger or annoyance, Annie knows not.

"Nay," she pleads as her eyes fill with tears. Jack averts his own.

"Needs must I gather the Owlers here. Think on't — thou art a danger now."

"But I can fight! Sworn am I to avenge my brother ...."

But Jack is gone and Annie is left alone with the flickering candle to wait for ... she knows not what.

When the Owlers are convened some hours later, Jack speaks for Annie as does her Pa. On this one occasion, for lack of aught else to do with a fierce girl-woman who has fallen innocent into their secret place, 'tis agreed that Annie shall take the Owlers' oath on two conditions — that no allowance is made for her female sex and that she adopts a male disguise when she assists in running goods from cavern to beach and beach to cavern along the ancient routes, or rides with the waggons inland along the steep-cut Owlers' paths.

Thus Annie is become an Owler, thanks to Jack ... and her vow of vengeance still holds her heart in a grip of ice.

- 25 -

Of Entrainment and Singing

We left the pub by the front entrance into the High Street and made our way towards Elizabeth Hudson's flat. It was not far, only three houses further along from the Three Chimneys. We passed Stephen's house on the way and I couldn't resist looking through the windows. Mechanical clocks of all sorts crowded the front room. A swift glance took in three grandfather clocks and a wag-on-the-wall. A cuckoo clock marked two o'clock with cuckoos as breathless as if it had a heavy cold.

Mark grinned at my prying.

"It's all right, Hazel," he teased. "You can have a really good, long look. Stephen told me that all the clocks in his front room are for sale – in fact, he suggested that the grandfather clock there ..." He pointed to a beautiful mahogany-cased long clock with a polished brass face, "Would be a very appropriate addition to my surgery."

I stepped closer for a better view. "I agree with him. It would definitely give your room a certain gravitas."

The room was fascinating; it was literally filled with clocks of all sorts and sizes from mantel clocks of varying ostentation, to grandfathers, grandmothers, carriage clocks, cuckoo clocks, the wag-on-the-wall I had first noticed, and several others I could not categorise. My eyes fell on a simple Napoleon clock which I instantly coveted. Tom had told me that it was so named because its shape resembled that of Napoleon Bonaparte's headgear. I promptly put it on the list of things I wanted when I had my own practice.

I recalled Tom telling me that Stephen was an horologist, now retired. It was a subject which particularly interested Tom who himself enjoyed buying old clocks, usually in bits. He took pleasure in putting them back together and making them work again. Sometimes he had to make new parts or buy half another clock and cannibalise it. No wonder Stephen felt that he could unburden himself to Tom about his experience in the well, sharing, as they did, a passionate interest in clocks. Not only did Tom have an understanding dental-chair-side manner but he always had time to listen without judgement. A sympathetic ear, indeed.

An extraordinarily kind, self-effacing man in his middle thirties, Tom was tall, a little tubby, round-faced and brown-haired with huge, strong hands. I was always amazed that he could do such intricate work with them. He was the most gentle dental surgeon I had ever encountered. Tom had taken it upon himself to replace the teeth I'd lost in my teens so that I could smile again without self-consciousness. I was indebted to him for the help this gave me in overcoming my shyness. Even now, the thought of his kindness brought a lump to my throat.

Mark was saying something I didn't catch.

"Sorry, Mark. I was miles away."

"I thought so. I'm glad I didn't have to stand on my head to gain your attention! I was remarking that all the clocks are going and their pendulums are all in sync. Do you know why that is?"

"No," my smile deepened. "But I think *you* do — and I think you're going to tell me."

"I see you're getting to know me," he responded. "It's because, when pendulum clocks are close to one another, an interesting thing happens. All their pendulums ... er ... pendula? Never mind ... start to synchronise. Some chap called Christiaan Huygens noticed it in sixteen sixty something. They may not move in the same direction, but they will move at the same speed. If they start off differently, the slower one accelerates and the faster one slows down. It's called entrainment."

"That's *very* interesting. Would they all show the same time as well?"

"Of course not — unless they were set at the same time to begin with."

I took a last look round Stephen's room before we walked on.

"I suppose it's possible for all the clocks to stop at the same moment, too?"

Mark considered this.

"No, I think that's unlikely. They are all wound manually and would have a different cycle before needing to be wound again. But I have heard of clocks all stopping at the same time when there is a seismic event — or a cataclysmic one, like the eruption of Vesuvius that buried Pompeii and Herculaneum."

"Is this entrainment similar to the fact that when women live together they all tend to have their periods at the same time?" I asked.

"Yes, that's quite fascinating because it happens even if, say, one girl normally has a thirty-one day cycle and another's natural cycle is twenty-six days. After a couple of months their periods begin on the same day, sometimes even in the same hour."

We passed two more buildings before Mark stopped in front of a door, its grey-blue paint grubby and chipped. Taking a key from his pocket, he inserted it into the lock and laid a finger to his lips, whispering:

"Elizabeth may be asleep. If she is, I try not to disturb her. We can always come back another time."

We crept up steep stairs to another door, which Mark opened a crack.

"There you are, my darling man."

The voice was deep and vibrant — far from what I was expecting from someone so close to death. Mark opened the door and stepped into the room. I followed, leaving a space between us.

"And there you are, waiting for me, my dear Elizabeth."

Mark's voice was full of flirtatiousness. He crossed the floor to the bed, took the white hand from the counterpane and pressed it to his lips. He continued to hold it.

The atmosphere was oppressive. An occasional flutter of the long, white muslin drapes drawn across the windows revealed that one of the sashes was open but the air did not penetrate far into the room.

I scanned the huge room from the doorway. Dim but not dark, and dominated by a wide brass bedstead, the room was filled to overflowing with objects. A beautifully embroidered silk shawl hung on the wall above the bed-head and a collection of antique snuffboxes graced the mantlepiece. Beneath the mantle, a Victorian fireplace was tiled in turquoise. The ceiling was white, its frieze picked out in a pale shade of green. The high walls, which were of a paler shade of turquoise than the fire tiles, were hung everywhere with pictures behind which were lodged a profusion of photographs and theatre programmes.

"This is Hazel Dawkins," Mark introduced me. "She's the solicitor I mentioned. A little bird, by the name of Paul Stone, told me she's about to set up her plate here in Rype. Hazel, this is my friend, Elizabeth Hudson."

"How do you do?" I enquired formally, holding out my hand.

Surprisingly clear blue eyes inspected me — and then their corners wrinkled up in a fleeting smile that matched the one on her lips. Fine, very blonde hair fell in a fringe towards eyes set deeply into a sallow complexion. Her hand trembled as she lifted it from Mark's to touch mine briefly.

"Not very well, actually," she replied. "I'm better for seeing my dear Mark, though. And very glad he brought you with him. There's something I need you to do for me."

That smile again.

"I'll be glad to help if I can," I murmured.

"I need to make a fresh Will. My family have written me off as a nuisance. Only strangers come to care for me now. I seldom see my sister and never see my husband." There was a catch in her voice as it weakened and grew more husky. "He can't bear illness, you see. He pays for a nurse to come in and a cleaner once a week. But he ... he ... I never see him."

"I'm sorry ..." I faltered.

"It's all right, dear. Mark drops in most days and lifts my spirits with a song." I glanced at the doctor in surprise. He didn't notice because his back was turned as he pulled a chair closer to the bed, but Elizabeth did.

"I'll tell you about it all later, dear. There's only one person who deserves to have any of my money." Her eyes rested on Mark for a split second. "Will you come back soon so that I can get this all off my chest and die peacefully?" I seated myself beside her bed. She patted my hand.

"Of course," I agreed, feeling her hand's coldness. I covered it with mine and willed strength and vitality into her.

"Maybe tomorrow?" she suggested. "I'm at my best in the morning." The brightness in her voice seemed forced.

I opened my mental diary. "Yes, that will be fine. Shall we make it eleven thirty?"

"Thank you," she nodded in acceptance. "My nurse will have been by then. I should at least be presentable."

"I will need the names and addresses of two executors and the full names and addresses of your beneficiaries," I told her. "And — should your first choice of beneficiary die before you — do think about who else you would like to benefit from your Will instead."

"I understand," she said. "But that's most unlikely."

"I know, but the most important thing is that you do exactly as *you* want with your money. It's best to provide for every contingency."

"Good. That's settled then." Elizabeth looked relieved but there was the suspicion of a tear in the corner of her eye. She took her hand away from me and gave it instead to Mark. He smiled at her.

"Will you sing for me, now?" she whispered, looking up at him affectionately.

"Only if you will sing with me. A duet?" he suggested. "What about 'Somewhere'?"

And without waiting for her reply he launched into the song from West Side Story.

"There's a ..."

"... place for us," she joined him. Their voices rose and fell together in perfect synchrony and harmony; his, a mellow baritone, and hers, a deep, rich contralto at which her speaking voice had merely hinted. I sat there, spellbound by the beauty of it; the two voices interweaving with natural perfection in that darkened sickroom, transporting us all to another place 'somewhere'. When they finished she was breathless, but her eyes were sparkling and the smile on her lips was permanent.

"Bravo!" I cried clapping, regardless of the tears making tracks down my cheeks. "More!"

"That's enough for me," sighed Elizabeth. "Mark, sing 'Volare' for me?"

"Volare it is," he said, striking a pose at the foot of the bed.

His voice soared into the Italian song, reverberating in waves of captivating sound, raising the vibration in the room and enchanting both of his listeners.

"More!" I heard myself demand when the last note had died away and I was able to speak. Without further encouragement, he sang 'O Sole Mio'. We listened, enraptured.

As the last note faded, Mark looked at his watch and said:

"Elizabeth, I must fly! I'll pop in tomorrow afternoon to make sure Hazel hasn't tired you out." He kissed her hand at parting and with a brief "Goodbye till then," made for the stairs.

"Thank you for that wonderful treat," I said, trying to swallow my emotion. "I'll look forward to seeing you at half past eleven tomorrow."

I squeezed her hand in farewell and followed her doctor down the stairs.

"Sorry about that, Hazel. I find I have to go quickly or I'd never be allowed to stop singing."

"I gathered that! I have to go, too. I must put my feet up while I can. My doctor says so. But there's something I need to say. Do you have time?"

"Yes, of course," he answered. "I have to take the car for my next call. Let me give you a lift home and we can chat on the way."

Bruce would have known the make of Mark's car but I did not: suffice it to say it was a huge brute of a silver-grey sports car. He had left it with the hood down and the grey leather seats were very hot on my posterior. The dashboard was walnut veneered around an array of dials and switches. I was reminded of an exhilarating fairground ride as we accelerated up the High Street to Rose Cottage.

Mark drew the car into the kerb. Wonderfully enlivened, I said:

"Thank you for everything, Mark — the diagnosis, lunch, a client and most of all for the wonderful songs."

"I'm glad you feel better," he responded with a smile. "What did you want to say to me?"

"It seems pretty clear to me that Elizabeth wants to make you a beneficiary of her Will. That could be difficult for you if her family argued 'undue influence'. In other words, that you'd put pressure on her to change her Will in your favour."

"Yes, I know," he replied seriously. "I also know how shabbily she has been treated by her family — apart from one sister — since she's been terminally ill. She tells me her husband has practically deserted her now that she has very little money left. I only want her to die happy that she's arranged everything as she wants it."

"Very commendable," I applauded. "But there's another problem. If I ask you to witness the Will — which I will need to do to make it clear that she is of 'right mind', to use the legal jargon — any gift to you will be invalidated."

"Phew!" Mark let out a long breath. "That's actually a really good thing. Elizabeth will think she's done what she needs to do, I witness the Will, I can't take any benefit. And the result is...er...what is the result?"

"If she's made some alternative arrangements, the bequest to you would pass down to the next level of beneficiaries." I paused.

"And if not?" he prompted. "What then?"

"Then the Intestacy Rules would apply. The problem there is that they're complicated. Most of her investments and belongings would probably go to her husband, but not necessarily all of them."

"Well, that's good, too. You only have to make sure that she states alternative beneficiaries and then we're all happy."

"I'll do my best," I confirmed. "I'm really glad I hitched a ride but I mustn't keep you."

I began to struggle out of the low-slung sports car but Mark was there instantly, opening the car door for me, putting a hand under my elbow and heaving me out of the gleaming monster of a machine.

"Now — to bed," he ordered. I was glad there were no busybodies nearby.

- 26 -

Of Good Deeds and Bad

I waved goodbye to Mark. As I placed my key in the lock Poppadum barked her usual joyous welcome.

"I'm glad I've come at the right moment."

My hand jerked and I dropped the key. I spun round to find Mrs Pendant standing close behind me. She was carrying an enormous parcel.

"I'm so sorry I made you jump — it was quite unintentional," she apologised. "As you requested I've collected my deeds from the bank. There are far more than I thought. I expect you'll need quite some time to study them."

"Thank you," I said automatically. "I'll just ..."

I didn't finish the sentence because she shoved the parcel into my hands, bent down, picked up the key and handed it to me. I could hear Poppadum beating the door with her paws as if in time with her rhythmic barking.

"How kind of you," I said, flustered but accepting the key from her. "Um... I need to give you a receipt." Balancing the deed packet on the Bump, I flapped my key hand at the door just as Poppadum threw her entire body weight at it.

"No, no, that's quite all right, my dear," said Mrs Pendant benignly. "Take them back to the bank when you've finished with them. I think you have enough on your hands for now, so I'll bid you adieu."

She pirouetted on her left toe — easily for such a stout person — as if about to retrace her steps. Something made her pirouette back again. Poppadum was suddenly quiet.

"Beware!" Mrs Pendant warned. "I believe I've been followed."

Poppadum resumed her barking, the pitch higher and more penetrating, while I, confounded into silence, could only watch as my client whirled in the original direction and waltzed back whence she had come.

"Shhh," I hissed to Poppadum. Utterly no effect.

"*Be quiet!*" I roared.

The barking subsided and the thumping stopped. I managed to open the front door to a sheepish-looking dog, crouching humbly exactly where she was best placed to trip me.

"You're going to have to learn better manners," I informed her.

As if in agreement, she whined softly, licking my foot. I shut the front door and manoeuvred my way round her in an ungainly dance, gaining the sitting room with the package still intact, despite Poppadum's best efforts to demolish it.

"*Stop it!*" I yelled at her. "This is important. There are probably no copies of these deeds. These are the *only* ones. Do you hear me? Do you understand?"

She crouched down in utter abasement and rolled onto her back, legs in the air.

"Okay," I said, caressing the nearest foot. "I'm sorry for shouting at you." She righted herself and wagged her tail. "Out in the garden with you. You must be bursting."

I threw the deed packet onto the settee. Marching though to the kitchen, I opened the back door and let my neglected hound into the back garden. To my surprise, she'd barely set foot in the garden before she barked twice in a menacing manner and bounded back towards me.

At the same moment, I heard an odd scuffling sound from the sitting room and whirled round. Barking ferociously, Poppadum raced past me. I turned the corner into the room as a blue-jeaned leg disappeared through the front door. I glanced at the settee. No deeds. I couldn't believe it. My heart hammered somewhere near my throat and I felt nauseated all over again at the thought of losing them. The baby was going frantic too, and my breath came in staccato bursts. Putting a hand to my chest, I tried to run.

It all happened so fast it was something of a blur. The owner of the leg tried to shut the door. Poppadum threw her weight against it. The door sprang open again. I made it to the window in time to see the thief bang the gate and Poppadum leap over it, snarling and barking. She really did have magnificent teeth! Blue Jeans sped down the pavement but the weighty parcel slowed him. Poppadum was faster. She flew into his back, knocking him flat on the ground. She stood on him, panting noxious dog-breath in his sideways-turned face and growled through bared teeth. During this operation, which was worthy of a champion police dog, the deed packet flew up in the air and landed heavily on the grass verge.

My fleet four-footed friend had the situation well under control so I took my time in reaching them. Now that the shock of the intended theft had lessened, my panic subsided and anger flared:

"How *dare* you do that?" I screamed at him. "Break into my house and steal? How dare you?"

Poppadum, panting, grinned up at me, waiting for praise, but now she growled, low and threateningly.

"Good girl," I encouraged her.

"Call your dog off, Missus. He's hurting me," whined the would-be thief.

"Why should I?" I enquired, more cordially than the situation warranted.

I walked round him and picked up the deed packet.

"Pleeease! He's hurting me."

"Nonsense! You're just a wimp," I informed him. "And Poppadum's a girl!"

Hearing her name, Poppadum turned fast on his back and sank her beautiful white fangs into the thick material of his jeans in the region of his buttocks. She shook her head, snarling.

"Ow! Ow! Ow!" he yelled. I signalled her to let go. Obeying with reluctance, she sat down on him instead.

Behind me someone coughed. I swung round. A couple of middle-aged men were crossing the road towards us, their laughter barely contained. I swung back.

"Why *should* I call my dog off?" The whole scene was so ridiculous it was all I could do not to laugh out loud. I would have loved to have placed my foot on his back as in all the best hunting scenes, brandishing the deed packet on high in place of the usual rifle.

"I'm sorry, Missus," he snivelled. "I didn't mean no 'arm ..."

"Rubbish! You steal very valuable, unique, documents and you say you 'don't mean no 'arm'? Come off it!"

A snigger from behind, made me look over my shoulder: a few more people were ranged behind me.

Playing to my audience, I suggested: "You tell me why you stole these deeds." I raised them above my head like an exhibit in court. "And if I like the answer, I'll call her off. But it had better be good."

"'E told me to," whimpered Blue Jeans.

"Who?" I demanded.

"Can't tell you. 'E'd kill me." His voice quivered. He tried to push himself up. Poppadum snarled again, regarding his scruffy leather jacket as though she would like to kill it. Then it hit me. I'd seen that jacket only this morning in the doctors' surgery waiting room. I was instantly sure of it. I'd been so mesmerised by the jeans that I hadn't registered the upper part of his clothing.

"Very well," I said. "If you won't tell *me*, you can tell the police."

I'd seen Neil appear on his bike. He rested it against the wall of a nearby cottage and sauntered over.

"Hello Mrs Dawkins." He saluted me.

"What's going on here?" he enquired generally of the bemused onlookers. They had been eerily silent until that moment but now they all started telling him at once.

"The dog ..."

"... bit his backside..."

"... stole something..."

In the ensuing jabbering I quietly signalled to Poppadum who released the fellow but remained menacingly close to him. Blue Jeans felt the shift of weight and made a tentative move. Poppadum bared her teeth and snarled.

Neil moved quickly, grabbing the thief's jacket by the collar and hauling him to his feet.

"Adam Plackett!" he declared. "Why am I not surprised?"

Adam spat at him. Spittle missed Neil but struck Poppadum. Noting the light of battle shine again in her eye, I caught her collar by reflex action — only just in time to prevent her from launching herself on the thief. Unfortunately, the movement toppled me against Neil, who released his hold on Adam at the same moment I dropped the deed packet. Adam saw his opportunity, grabbed the parcel and took to his heels. I had enough sense to let go of Poppadum's collar and she flew after him. Quickly recovering my balance, I whistled her back but she took no notice.

We were back to square one. Everyone seemed rooted to the spot by the speed of Adam's escape. And the deeds were racing up the High Street again.

Adam made to push past an approaching soldier. The trooper's foot shot out, tripped him neatly and the unfortunate thief fell flat on his face again. With his left hand, the tall soldier caught the frantically barking Poppadum by the collar; with the right, he grabbed Adam by the arm as he tried to rise. He held them both easily, smiling jovially, until Neil had clipped some handcuffs on Adam and I had relieved him of my still-growling dog.

"Thank you so much," I grovelled. Now the emergency was over, shock was beginning to set in and I felt everything trembling, including my voice.

"My pleasure, ma'am." The soldier saluted me and I noticed that his uniform bore the insignia of the rank of Captain. He retrieved the deeds from where they had fallen on the pavement — by great mischance in dog excrement. He dangled the packet at arm's length by the red tape that secured it.

"Is this yours, by any chance?"

"Yes, thank you," I said making as if to take it but he held the packet away from me.

"It doesn't smell very nice," he remarked, and then grinned.

"Since our friend is within the strong arm of the law, I'll carry the parcel and escort you home. I must say, you have a fine protector in your dog." Poppadum wagged her tail.

He offered me his arm. My knees were weak and my tummy wobbling as the baby thumped me hard from inside so I accepted the courtesy with relief. Neil had the offender well trussed and was pushing him down the street towards the police station at the other end of town.

"The excitement's over," the policeman called back over his shoulder. "You can all go home." But the small crowd was already dispersing in a loud hum of comment.

"Would somebody wheel my bike back to the police station?" he shouted, plaintively.

No-one took any notice.

I bade my rescuer farewell at the gate and he handed me the noxious parcel by its red tape. I took it from him gingerly and headed straight for the dustbin in the back garden. The deed packet reeked appallingly and I couldn't wait to rid myself of it. But first I needed to fish out the deeds without getting my hands covered in excrement. Fortunately, they were bundled together with red tape and I managed to extract them without mishap. The packet was thrown into the bin and the lid replaced instantly.

I took the deeds indoors straightaway, through the back door. They accompanied me into the cloakroom where I washed my hands very thoroughly. Poppadum stayed in the garden while I made my ablutions, deciding to employ her excess energy in digging a hole under her favourite shrub. I gave dinner a fleeting thought but my bed was calling to me insistently. Now that the adrenalin had stopped pumping, all my tiredness went directly to my legs, turning them to jelly. The bundle of documents weighed heavily in my arms as I dragged myself upstairs. I was almost at the top when Poppadum's soft fur brushed my leg as she pushed past me into the bedroom. Despite my posturing over the boy I'd christened Adam Blue Jeans, the attempted theft of the deeds from under my nose had shocked me. My dog's protective presence was reassuring.

"He actually came *into* our home, didn't he, Pops? I don't feel very safe, do you?"

Poppadum regarded me with an inquisitive eye.

"That bed looks incredibly inviting," I remarked to her, lying down and allowing my weight to sink deep, my eyelids heavy as lead. Remembering that the back door was probably still open, I felt a moment's panic but no more: there was no way I could venture down those stairs again until I'd revived a little. I closed my eyes for an instant, winding my fingers in Poppadum's fur as she made herself comfortable on the mat beside the bed.

'I'll deal with it in a moment,' I thought, and fell instantly into a deep sleep.

I was woken by the sound of the telephone ringing. Sleepily I reached out a hand, pulled myself together and answered:

"Hello? Hazel Dawkins speaking." I heard a slight noise at the other end, nothing more. "Hello? I'm afraid I can't hear you." Still no answer. Annoyed now, I tried once again. "Hello? Hazel Dawkins here." Nothing. Not a peep.

I replaced the receiver and turned over. I fell back into sleep almost instantly. A sleep filled with fragments from the chase after Blue Jeans Adam. I could even hear Poppadum's furious barking. I drifted back to consciousness and realised that the barking was not in the dream.

Poppadum was beside herself, her barking becoming higher-pitched, interlaced with snarls. She had both front paws on the window sill and was looking out into the road. I crept up behind her and peeped.

Dressed like Adam, in jeans and T-shirts, two men stood on the opposite side of the road. I couldn't explain why, but somehow they exuded menace. I instantly bestowed them with the names Skinny and Heavy: Heavy was looking up at the bedroom window, his eyes seeming to note that it was only a few feet above ground level. I felt intimidated all right. And fully awake.

Poppadum still sounded ferocious: I needed calm in which to think, so I quietened her with a look. I risked a glance at the men.

They had turned away and were deep in conversation. As I watched, a white saloon car drew in to the kerb. The driver rolled down the window. There followed more conversation and much waving of hands before the occupant of the car got out, walked round to the boot and opened it. The other two followed him. All three were now obscured by the lid.

"You're imagining things," I told myself severely. "They were just standing there waiting for someone. Popsy's always barking at people from the window. Take your mind off it. Do something different."

I checked my watch. It was almost four o'clock. I'd been asleep for an hour. Bruce would be home at six o'clock and I would need half an hour to throw something together for dinner. I calculated that I had approximately an hour and a half in which to check Mrs Pendant's deeds, provided I started immediately. I took the bundle from under Bruce's pillow where I had hidden it, placed it on the table that served me as a desk and was about to untie the red tape when I heard Poppadum's warning growl.

She was crouching by the door, her nose almost under it. Instantly, I remembered that the back door was unlocked. My heart thumped; one break-in was quite enough for one day. I pushed the deeds back under Bruce's pillow again and peeped out of the window. Only one man stood there now. Skinny. Where was Heavy? My brain was working overtime. I imagined he must be round the back of the house. It was easy to open the gate and walk in — he would have no scruples about walking into another person's property. And he'd certainly be prepared for Poppadum for she'd made her presence well known; he'd guess — if he didn't already know — that I'd be a pushover in my current condition. My eyes fell on the telephone. I picked up the receiver: the line was dead.

Weighty footsteps thumped up the stairs. Simultaneously, Poppadum started barking furiously. I felt cold, cold, fear. Not panic, pure fear. At the same time, I had the expectant mother's urge to protect her unborn child, no matter what.

What could I do? My eyes fell on the yale lock on the bedroom door. We had left it there although we never used it. Fear gave me wings. I raced across the room and slipped the lock. The door handle twisted. It stopped moving. A hefty bang against the door as though someone had put his shoulder to it. More footsteps, lighter and faster this time. A yell. The sound of a fist connecting with flesh. Another punch. A heavier thump against the door. Cursing — and Neil's voice:

"Hazel. Are you all right? Hazel?"

I stepped back and sat down heavily on the bed, tears coming unbidden to my eyes.

"Y ... yes." A cross between a whisper and a croak. I cleared my throat and tried again. "I'm fine."

Pulling myself together in true British fashion, I crossed to the door, opening it to find one of the T-shirted men on the floor, his head bleeding a little and his hands cuffed behind his back. Neil stood behind him, panting.

"Thank you," I breathed. "How did you know? I couldn't phone out."

"I came back for my bike," Neil grinned. "I recognised a bloke standing outside — one we have been looking for. He took to his heels as soon as he saw me but I thought it suspicious that he was here so soon after ..." he broke off. "Anyway, I heard your dog barking and saw your garden gate was open so I thought I'd investigate."

Neil had used the next door neighbour's telephone to call for reinforcements and had also asked the telephone exchange to test my line. A kindly woman reported that the line was open but that they could not hear anyone speaking on it. The other end of the call was traced to a phone box around the corner from Rose Cottage.

"Usual way of operating," Neil had commented. "Ring the number of the house you want to burgle, wait till they answer and leave the receiver off the hook. The line is effectively put out of action."

"But our number is ex-directory. How could they have known what it is?" I knew the answer to my question as soon as I asked it. "I suppose someone must have given it to them, but who?"

"Ex-directory?" asked Neil. "Don't you use the number for work?"

"I'm not really working," I sighed. "I'm supposed to be taking a month off to prepare for the baby."

He and I had waited for the arrival of a squad car which had come the sixteen miles from Ashford. The intruder was bundled into the back, the police constables were told to look out for his partner and he was taken away for questioning at Ashford police station. Afterwards, I'd made us both a cup of strong, sweet tea which we had taken into the garden.

"Rype has never been so exciting!" Neil remarked, nursing his cup of tea in both hands and leaning his elbows on the garden table. "Tell me why anyone would want to steal those documents."

I'd been asking myself exactly that, all afternoon. What did the deeds contain that would make them worth stealing? They were only deeds, after all. Deeds were very useful for establishing matters of legal title to a property but otherwise had no value.

"I really don't know, Neil," I replied to his question. "But you can bet your bottom dollar that I'm going to find out – even if it kills me."

My remark was intended to be humorous, but the look Neil gave me was serious.

"Don't even joke about it," he warned. "Adam is just a petty criminal, and thick as two planks at that, but those others are real villains. They're well known to the police. We've been watching them for some time but haven't been able to find sufficient evidence to pin anything on them. Unfortunately, you said you left the back door open. Nothing was stolen or damaged and no-one was hurt. So, at best, we'll be able to charge them with attempted burglary and they may well be freed on bail."

This was not good news, I realised, but I was rather glad nothing had been stolen or damaged and I was certainly glad that neither Poppadum nor I had been hurt.

"Why have you been watching them?" I asked.

"We believe they're part of a very violent gang. That's all I can tell you," he said solemnly. "It appears that they want those deeds very badly. The sooner you rid yourself of them the better. In fact, why don't you phone Mr Stone and arrange to take them back to the bank now?"

This was exactly what I had been considering, but I'd seen a problem. Even if I arranged to take the deeds back immediately, the thieves didn't know that I'd been asleep and therefore hadn't had time to peruse them. They would assume that I had. They'd probably also assume that I now knew what it was that they wanted to remain concealed.

I explained my thinking to Neil. Much to his apparent dismay, he agreed with my deductions. We were still trying to come up with an alternative plan when Bruce came home. He sauntered into the garden from the house, looking hot and crumpled and not a little tired. He was pulling his tie loose as he came towards us.

"Hello, darl." Bruce spoke though a mouthful of curls as he kissed the top of my head. He held out his hand to Neil and grinned.

"I wondered whose bike it was in the front garden," he teased. "I didn't realise my wife was in the habit of entertaining policemen while I was at work! What's she done now?"

Neil shook Bruce's extended hand.

"Not quite what you think," he said, smiling. His face grew solemn. "Actually, she's had a very alarming afternoon and a lucky escape."

"Oh?" Bruce's eyebrows disappeared into the damp fringe decorating his forehead.

Poppadum rose from my side and butted Bruce with her head, asking for a pat. He complied absent-mindedly, his eyes asking a thousand questions of mine.

"Poppadum's the heroine of the hour," I said, stroking the part of her closest to me. "Sit down, darling, and we'll tell you all about it."

Between us Neil and I gave him a blow-by-blow account of the happenings of the afternoon. Bruce laughed when I told him of Poppadum's attack on the rear of Blue Jeans but sobered as soon as

Neil repeated the warning he had given me. My husband regarded me seriously, pulling at his lower lip, although his eyes still smiled.

"It's been so hot that I'm melting. And, come to think of it, I *do* think better in the bath," he informed Neil. "I'll go and do that now. Thank you for rescuing Hazel and for staying until I came home. I'm sure we'll think of a way out of this mess, but I'd be grateful if you'd keep us informed of what happens to your two prisoners."

"Of course," answered Neil, getting up to take his leave. "Take care of your wife, there aren't many as feisty as her."

"No, I know." Bruce winked at me. "It's taking me a long time to tie her to the kitchen sink."

I beamed at them. "Why, thank you, gentlemen both – I think."

Bruce and I escorted Neil to the gate. The policeman mounted his bike and pedalled home to his tea. We waved until he was out of sight.

My husband slapped my bottom playfully.

"Right," he said, "I'm off to the bath to mull this over, and, as you know, I don't mull well..."

"When you're hungry!" I finished for him. Laughing at our own joke we headed indoors – he to the bathroom and me to the kitchen. Poppadum looked at both of us, sighed resignedly, and then settled down facing the back door with her head on her paws. Her eyes followed my every move.

Bruce had his bath while I threw some spaghetti into a pan of boiling water and searched in the fridge and larder for something to go with it apart from the ubiquitous salad. I found an onion, one last clove of garlic, some streaky bacon, a tin of tomatoes and another of sweet corn. I fried the first three ingredients slowly together and, when they were done, added the tomatoes and sweet corn, a few herbs and some salt and pepper. In view of my disgraceful behaviour over the chilli-con-carne at lunchtime I had intended to forgo dinner but I found I was incredibly hungry. I blamed it on the adrenaline that had been pumping through my body. So much for the rest Mark had ordered.

My dear husband was not long in his bath and appeared as I

was tasting the pasta sauce. He tucked in the end of the towel like a sarong. Very sexy, I thought, admiring his powerful chest with its powdering of ginger hair.

"Hey Presto!" I said. "Dinner ready in fifteen minutes and quite palatable too."

He came closer:

"Take that smug expression off your face, woman." He took the spoon from me and turned off the gas. No doubt he had memories of our previous altercation in similar circumstances. "You have caused me untold disquiet and anxiety and yet you have the nerve to stand there smiling your come-on smile as if nothing had happened. Come here."

And with that, he gathered me tenderly into his embrace, rocking me gently and kissing my hair. The smug expression must have disappeared instantly for I found myself fighting huge sobs that began deep inside and threatened to overwhelm me with their power. I sniffed hard. And sniffed again, harder. But it was no good; sobs engulfed me. Bruce held me and rocked me and stroked my back and caressed my hair until the storm had subsided into sniffling wretchedness. My nose was running and my eyes swollen. I knew I looked a wreck; I certainly felt one. But the clean smell of Bruce's skin was comforting and I felt calmer. My heart throbbed with love for him. Even the incredible tenderness I was discovering for the new life within me paled into insignificance for a minute or so.

Then I felt a fluttering under my ribs and realised that my sobs must have been like a roller coaster ride for the Bump. I managed a watery smile and pulled away to blow my nose on the handkerchief Bruce offered me. My smile widened as I wondered just where he had found to secrete it on his person.

"That's better, Haze," Bruce said gently. "You needed that."

He took the hanky from me, wiped my eyes with a clean corner, found another dry part and held it to my nose.

"Blow!" he instructed. I blew.

"Thanks," I muttered into his chest hair. I was loath to draw away but I needed to breathe.

"Right," he said. "I have started mulling things over but ..."

"You don't mull well when you're hungry," I repeated obediently, happy now. "Dinner is ready – but I refuse to eat with an undressed man."

"Okay, watch this," he said archly, swinging his underpants (and his hips) suggestively before he put them on. I giggled, regarding the rest of his parody of a striptease artist in reverse until I could watch no more without stifling myself with laughter. I turned to the stove and dished up the meal. I thrust a plate at him.

"Take this, and hie thee thither instantly or I will be forced to frogmarch you to the table."

Unfortunately he complied. I would have liked to try the frogmarch.

Once we were seated opposite each other, with our toes touching on the deeds that I'd hidden under the table and a trencher of food in front of us, we ate in silence for a few minutes while Bruce continued to 'mull', occasionally grimacing at me foolishly.

"Behold! I have mulled," he finally declared.

"Tell me the result of your mulling, then."

- 27 -

Of Spies and Deception

"Okay, time to be serious. I'm not sure what's going on but, from what Neil says, you and the baby could be in serious danger. Actually, I think we must consider that you *are* in serious danger." Bruce's face showed his concern and his voice was grave.

I nodded. "Poppadum, too, I think."

The dog was under the table, still keeping me under close supervision. Her tail thumped as she heard her name.

"I've taken it that they won't try anything again this evening, now that I'm home and they've had a taste of Poppadum's medicine. However — and it's a big 'however' — I'm pretty sure they may try something else tomorrow. In fact, I'm concerned they might try something tonight."

"Yes, that thought had crossed my mind, too." I said, automatically putting my hand on the Bump, who was determined to have a share of the pasta, judging by the movement that was going on under my apron.

"I think you should go to your parents' tonight. Take the deeds and Poppadum with you. You can study the deeds there and see if you can find the reason for all this. I'll organise some tactics to keep them busy."

"What sort of tactics?" I asked.

"I don't know, I'll think of something. You just need to get going."

We had finished our meal. I rose to draw the curtains. Until that moment, I'd been careful not to look outside. I felt safe with Bruce but if I were going to drive to my parents' house alone, I wanted to check there was no-one spying on us. Poppadum shadowed me and jumped up, putting her paws on the window sill again.

I squinted up and down the road. Poppadum looked, too. Her tail gave a perfunctory wag. Then she pricked her ears and growled menacingly. Her hackles raised and her growls rumbled continually. I pulled the curtains closed. The street seemed to be clear, apart from the usual cars that belonged to our neighbours, but the hairs on the back of my neck were standing on end. I knew that something wasn't right.

"I can't see anything unusual from here," I told Bruce. "But Poppadum knows that *something's* wrong."

Hardly had I finished speaking than Poppadum started barking fiercely, her hackles up in a ruff round her neck. She ran backwards and forwards across the room, finally making a flying leap at the stairs and racing to the landing. I did my best to remain calm although even Bruce was looking alarmed at the dog's behaviour.

"I have a feeling I'm not seeing the whole picture. I'll go and check from the upstairs windows." I collected the plates together as I spoke.

"I'm coming with you."

He took the plates from me. I grabbed the deeds from under the table and took them with me as I mounted the stairs with a certain amount of caution. I wasn't entirely sure that I wanted to know what was happening outside. Poppadum had quietened although she was scratching at the bedroom door. I felt a little less apprehensive but the Bump was fluttering in a very agitated manner.

I heard Bruce dump the plates in the kitchen sink. There was a certain amount of banging of saucepans and a soft cursing and I thought he'd started the washing up. But moments later I heard his feet climbing the stairs. When he entered the bedroom, I had already drawn the curtains across all the windows. He found me peering through a very fine chink between the ones over the window that looked up the High Street towards the church.

"What is it?" asked Bruce, peering over my shoulder.

"See that white bonnet?" I enquired. "I think it's the same saloon car I saw earlier, when Heavy and Skinny were talking to the driver." Something else struck me. "Actually, I think I saw it before that when I was taking Mr and Mrs White's Wills to the bank yesterday."

"What white bonnet? I see no hats!" He was being facetious.

"Oh you!" I berated him. "I suppose you'd call it the hood, being Antipodean."

"Over there? Behind the black car? Is that ...? Yes, it is! You've got good eyes, Haze!"

I didn't care how good my eyes were. I shuddered. I was scared now. Bruce put his hand over mine.

"It's okay, darling. There are two of us, two of the finest brains in the country! We'll figure out a way past him."

I racked my brains for some way to distract our watchers so that we could slip past them. We needed a smokescreen. A smoke screen! That was it.

"I've got it!" I cried, turning so fast I nearly head-butted him in the stomach. "A smoke screen. We'll make a smoke screen!"

"What?"

I was excited now. "Leave this to me. I'm going to make so much smoke that you can report a fire. The fire station's just next door, after all." I was staggering towards the bedroom door as I spoke, Poppadum doing her best to knock me off balance, "We'll sneak out in the confusion. Now what will make the most smoke?"

I opened the door wide and stopped in complete confusion for I smelled ... smoke? I peered down the stairs and couldn't believe my eyes. A grey-white mist was rising towards me. I had no time to think what might be burning for the smoke was suddenly all around me. My eyes smarted; I started coughing.

Retreating into the bedroom I swiftly closed the door, stepping on Poppadum's tail in the process. She yelped and jumped back, hitting Bruce's shin as he rushed towards me.

"What is it?"

"It's full of smoke down there. Quick! Call the fire brigade."

"Already? That was quick work." He looked amused; Poppadum

raged at him, barking sharply in staccato fashion.

"No! Really! There's a fire down there." I managed to spit the words out between coughs. "Can't you smell it?" I had forgotten that his sense of smell was next to useless. "*Look!*" I yelled, backing away from the door and pointing to the curl of smoke making its way beneath it.

I grabbed the phone myself and dialled 999 feeling as though I were choking. The call was answered instantly. "Fire!" I sobbed down the phone, "Fire!"

Bruce grabbed a towel from the cupboard, made a sausage of it in a few deft twists and plugged the gap beneath the door. He opened all the windows, drawing back the curtains. Luckily it wasn't far to the ground — only about eight feet at the front of the house — but the casement was small and it would be difficult for me to scramble out through it. I saw him make a glancing assessment of me before he put a leg over the sill. Poppadum dashed after him in a crazed fashion, reminding him that I was still there in need of rescue.

All this must have happened in seconds but it seemed forever as I hung on the phone with one hand over my other ear to cut out Poppadum's noise.

Another voice, calmly asking me to take a deep breath and then give the address. I forgot the former and answered the latter:

"Rose Cottage, High Street, Rype," I coughed.

"Hello Hazel. Yes, I see smoke. We're on our way." It was David, the fireman.

The phone clicked down at his end of the line. I stood where I was, nursing the receiver, paralysed with indecision and a primordial fear. Bruce had all but disappeared. Only his fingers were visible on the sill as he kicked in the downstairs window. Glass splintered. Smoke billowed out into the street. I saw it curling past the window, thicker and yellower than before. A thunderous crash and Bruce's fingers vanished.

Fumes were seeping round the door frame; a stinking fog creeping towards me, thinning near the window where it was diluted by the air. Fortunately there was next to no wind. I gave myself a mental shake, slammed down the receiver and headed for the window. I had not quite reached it when it was filled by the black form of a man. I took a step back in trepidation before I recognised David's grin beneath the fireman's helmet. My knees shook but I managed to stay upright.

"We'll have you out of there in less than a minute," my rescuer promised cheerfully, wielding a screwdriver at the hinges of the casement.

He eased the casement from the window frame and passed it carefully down to someone. Shouts, joshing and laughter came from below — welcome and reassuring sounds — but I was finding it hard to breathe and was frantic for fresh air.

"Okay. It's all clear now, Hazel," David announced as he climbed in. "Let's get you out of here."

Suddenly I remembered the cause of all this. I grabbed the deeds.

"Is that important?" At my brusque nod, David took them from me and passed them into the waiting hands of his buddy below.

"Now you," he said and added jokingly, "I was thinking of a fireman's lift but I think that might have unfortunate results! Jim, down there, will guide your feet."

Poppadum watched as David helped me through the window.

"Good girl, Pops," I reassured her. "You'll be next. And if you're good you might get a fireman's lift." She wagged her tail uncertainly.

My exit was awkward but my feet had barely touched the ground before David landed beside me, Poppadum hanging limply over his shoulder. He set her down on her feet and she took up her place beside me. I took three gulping breaths and it was only when my breathing quietened that I noticed how many people were milling about.

Horace, from next door, was holding court by describing to a collection of neighbours how he had seen smoke pouring out of the kitchen window and had rushed to come to our aid, only to find Bruce hanging by his hands as he kicked in the downstairs window.

A familiar green builders' lorry was parked in haphazard fashion by the pavement and I saw Mark's distinctive vehicle parked more conventionally further along.

"Darling," Bruce pushed his way through the throng and grabbed my shoulders. "Are you all right?"

Flinging myself against his chest, I dissolved into racking sobs for the second time that night.

"I think that means 'yes'," he said ruefully to someone behind me. Then he bent his head and whispered in my ear.

"Now, Haze. It's all right. You left the spaghetti to burn on the stove, that's all. It's off now. Made a lot of black smoke, but there was no real damage. It brought out the neighbours and anyone else who happened to be passing, including Tom and our builder and not forgetting Mark — I'll get him to give you the once-over."

"Thank you," I sniffed, miserably. Then I registered what he had said and perked up. "No real damage? It's all right?"

"Keep your voice down," he hissed. "Yes, it's all fine. And your reaction was perfect. Do you think you can throw another wobbly?"

Perfect reaction? Another wobbly? I felt like hitting him. I was sure I hadn't left the gas on under what remained of the spaghetti. Surely he had turned it off himself, I thought, creasing my brow.

"We're lucky Mark was passing. I've spoken to him and told him about this afternoon. Tom too, he's *very* worried about you. They'll both help. Mark'll take you back to the surgery and then Tom will pick you up from there and run you to your mother's in his car. Big White Hood will be hoodwinked! I'll come over later when this is all secured."

He raised his lips from my ear and tucked me under his left wing, thrusting his right hand towards David and Jim who had already fixed the casement back in place and were about to clear the ladder and fire extinguishers away.

"Ta, Mates." Bruce lapsed into Australian. "That was real beaut! Good onya. Thanks a million. I owe you a grog or two."

They both shook hands with him and Jim bent to pick up the parcel I'd handed him. Bruce put his foot on it.

"No worries, Mate. Leave it there. I'll sort it later. Ta."

Jim looked surprised but shrugged and turned away as Bruce twirled me to face him again.

"Hurt your foot, did you, darl?" Bending down to rub my right ankle, he managed to pick up the deeds unseen and to bundle them inconspicuously under my smock. "Hold them close to you," he whispered.

Obediently, I put my hand on my belly, keeping the deeds in place and praying that babe would not kick too much. The Bump had been very quiet during the drama.

Bruce kissed me quickly, pointed me in the direction of Mark, who was standing talking to Horace and patted me towards him with that annoying habit of his — a playful slap on my bottom.

"There's Hazel!" exclaimed Mark. "Excuse me Horace. I must make sure my patient has come through this ordeal in one piece." He smiled at me and held out his hand.

An hour and a half later — it seemed much more — I was safely ensconced on the voluminous sofa in my parents' drawing room.

Mark had taken me swiftly to the surgery where he'd given me the suggested once-over, declared I was still alive and suggested that I gargle well with some disgusting red mixture unless I wanted my cough to induce labour within the next couple of hours. I obediently did as I was bid, the prospect of giving birth not overly appealing in view of the probable state of my home.

The red mixture not only looked foul, it tasted foul, but it did help the cough to subside. Satisfied that there was not much else he could do at that moment, Mark had given me the rest of the bottle of gargle, a bottle of Friar's Balsam which he had declared was still the best inhalant for respiratory problems, and a brief hug.

"Not very professional, I know," he'd said as he released me. "But you looked as though you needed it."

There came a soft double tap at the door.

"That's Tom's signal," Mark chuckled, opening the door to reveal Tom's solid shape outlined by the dim light of the hall.

"Your carriage awaits Ma'am!" Tom bowed, and offered me his

arm. I'm becoming accustomed to these old-fashioned manners, I thought, as I rested my hand on the proffered arm and resisted the desire to curtsey. Tom and Mark exchanged a speaking look. I registered that they were enjoying themselves; it was like a '*Boy's Own*' adventure.

"I've done my bit," Mark told Tom. "Now it's over to you. Take care of her. She's fine. I don't think you'll have to act as midwife tonight, but you might need to keep the windows open in the car. She still has the stink of fire about her!"

"Charming," I muttered under my breath.

"Sorry?" said Mark.

"Nothing at all," I said airily. "I'm sorry you've both been dragged into this but I do appreciate your help."

"Most dramatic thing that's happened to me since I was in the Army," observed Mark, shooing us out of the surgery. "Off you go!"

He picked up a bolster from his couch, locked the door to his surgery and all three of us walked along the corridor towards the car park at the back of the building. Mark had pulled his car in close to the door and Tom's was next to it. Both were in thick shadow. Mark turned off the internal light.

"Now for some sleight of hand," he whispered.

Whipping a piece of string from his pocket, he tied it round one end of the bolster.

"Does that look like a head?" he asked.

Not waiting for an answer, he arranged the pillow with the 'head' on his shoulder and his arm round its 'waist' as though he were supporting a person.

"This is supposed to be you," he explained, obviously enjoying the subterfuge. "I'm going to open the passenger door and put this on the seat. Funnily enough the interior bulb doesn't work. I'll keep talking to 'you' as if I'm going to take 'you' towards the hospital. Don't come out until you've had a chance to see whether anyone follows me. Okay?"

"Understood," Tom hissed. I nodded. Taking my hand from his arm, Tom held it tightly in his huge warm one. In the darkness, we made our way to the closest window and peered out, keeping well back so that we would not be observed should anyone be watching.

Mark opened the door and helped 'me' out.

"It's all right, we're nearly there now," I heard him saying encouragingly. "Hold on to me. That's my girl."

He opened the car door, managing to hide half of 'me' as he helped the bolster painstakingly into the seat.

"Deep breaths, now. We'll be at the hospital in a trice." The doctor banged the car door shut and dashed round to the other side. I smiled as I watched Mark's charade. Out of direct light, the bolster looked surprisingly convincing. Mark started the car and took off fast, heading out in the direction of Ashford and the hospital. I thought I heard another car's engine turn over.

Tom gave me the thumbs up sign and we waited, holding our respective breaths. I counted only four seconds before, sure enough, tail lights flashed past, the car heading in the same direction that Mark had taken.

"Now it's our turn," whispered Tom. "No!" I caught his arm. "Wait a moment."

From the tail of my eye I'd caught the red trail of a cigarette thrown down hurriedly. I drew Tom back further into the darkness. A figure detached itself from the shadow of the far wall of the car park, crept over to Tom's car and looked inside.

"I'm not having that!" Tom, incensed, strode towards the door. Before he reached it, we heard a couple joshing as they approached the car park. They seemed to be staggering along the road.

"It's no good! I have to pee." The woman's voice was high with laughter.

"Okay, go in there," chortled the man, guiding her towards us. "I'll keep watch."

On hearing them, the silhouette beside Tom's car had straightened.

"Ooh! There's someone there," the woman exclaimed.

Our shadowy friend made quickly for the exit. He passed close by them, walking fast. The man made a rude gesture and gazed drunkenly after him.

"Sodding pervert!"

The woman, obviously desperate, crouched by the wall. We heard the sound of gushing water as she relieved herself.

"Hurry up!" urged her escort impatiently. A moment later she swayed towards him and they were gone in gales of drunken laughter.

"Quick!" Tom drew me out of the door, locking it quickly behind us. He opened the rear door of his vehicle, a long station-wagon with room for dogs and children. "Lie on the back seat until we're out of Rype. Might be a bit uncomfortable but you won't be seen."

I was already halfway in by the time he had finished speaking, crawling along the seat in a manner that was anything but elegant. I curled up on my side.

"Ready?" Tom whispered. I gave the thumbs up sign. He closed the door quietly and whizzed round to the driver's side. We were away in no time.

He had been right. Lying on my side in a car careening through the side roads of Rype, was most uncomfortable. I felt sick and wanted to cough. I'd managed to refrain from doing either by the time he pulled over and stopped the car briefly in a quiet lane. He assisted me from the back to the front passenger seat which was much more comfortable.

Twenty minutes of rally driving later we were pulling into the drive of my parents' house. Thankful as I was for the help Tom had given me, I was even more grateful for the welcoming comfort of my mother's arms. Bruce had telephoned her so she was expecting me. She added her thanks to mine before we passed Tom over to my father who, clapping him on the back with a gruff acknowledgement of his help, led him off to the kitchen with the promise of home-made beer, to which they were both decidedly partial.

My mother led me to the bathroom where she helped me strip myself of my stinking clothes. I climbed into the bath she'd prepared for me. She sat on the bathroom stool while I, luxuriating in deep, hot, rosemary-scented water, regaled her with the events of the day.

"Bruce didn't tell me why you were coming so urgently," she said as my account drew to a close. "What an adventure! But you must be very careful. I'm going to ask Tom to move his car along the road."

She disappeared for a while and returned with some shampoo and the deeds.

"That's done. The car's down the track by the farm. We found these in the rear footwell. From what you say, they're the reason you're here. I thought I'd better bring them in case they went back with Tom."

"Phew," I gasped. "Thanks, Mum."

My mother smiled at my obvious relief. "Tom and Dad are having a chat in the kitchen at the moment but he'll be on his way soon. I've told him how grateful you are for his help but that you need to rest now, to recover from your ordeal. He understands and asked me to tell you that he was glad to help."

"How kind of him. You should have seen him and Mark, Mum! They were so excited to be doing something different from being Pillars of Society. They were like naughty little boys."

She laughed, the tomboy of her childhood surfacing for a moment.

"I bet it takes a while for his car to stop smelling of smoke. Talking of which, let me help you wash your hair."

Not many minutes later, I was ensconced with my feet up on the wide deep sofa in the drawing room, clean and sweet-smelling, swathed in an old soft dressing gown of my mother's.

Considering what had happened in the course of the day, I felt surprisingly fresh and awake.

- 28 -

Of Conveyances and Memoranda

From a swift perusal of the Schedule which listed all the deeds and documents in the legal title to Mrs Pendant's dwelling, it was clear that there was neither Land Certificate nor Charge Certificate. The title to the property had therefore never been registered at the Land Registry.

The Land Registration Act had been enacted in 1925 with the express purpose of giving state-guaranteed title to everyone who owned a registrable interest in land. Until then, the title had been transferred from one person to another by means of a deed called a 'Conveyance'. This is the reason that the process of buying and selling land, or of passing the legal title to it from one person to another, came to be called 'conveyancing'. Under ancient law, title to land had to be evidenced in writing. Generally a change in title occurred when land was bought and sold, but there could be other reasons. For instance, land might pass to a beneficiary under a Will, in which case the deed was called an Assent and had to be executed by the Executor of the Will of the deceased person.

Under the 1925 Act, state registration of title gradually became compulsory on the sale and purchase of land. However, there were so many titles to be registered in England and Wales that registration was brought in gradually, district by district. Kent had been one of the first of these areas of compulsory registration of title, registration in Rype's district having become compulsory in 1958 while down the road in rural Sussex it had only happened a year or two ago.

Thus registration was compulsory when any property in Rype was sold, but registration was not required where the title to the land had passed from one person to another in some other way. In such a case, when the title had never been registered, it was necessary to 'prove' the title by showing (through written documents, or deeds) the consecutive ownership of the land and the way it had passed from one person to another over the passage of time. Initially the ownership of the land had to be traceable from person to person through the deeds for at least thirty years, although latterly this period had been reduced to fifteen years.

I loved this part of the work of conveyancing. It often proved to be a combination of detective work and bringing the pieces of a jigsaw together. The old deeds, hand-written on vellum in ink, were beautiful but sometimes difficult to decipher. Land was often described as a 'piece or parcel' comprising a certain acreage or describing the boundaries by reference to the ownership of adjoining land. Where there *was* a plan, it was invariably hand-drawn and usually not to scale. Over time, the old estates were broken down into smaller pieces. In the nineteenth century, there had been a profusion of building developments. These often necessitated the provision of complicated arrangements and covenants with which both the purchaser and vendor, and their subsequent successors in title, had to comply.

Finding my way through all the verbiage and piecing together the title was an art form that I loved, so I was delighted that the title to Mrs Pendant's home had not been registered. I enjoyed the romance and mystery of the puzzle. Mother had supplied me with a clipboard, a large sheet of paper, pencils and assorted crayons, like a sick child kept in on a wet day and given the tools to draw a picture — which was exactly what I was about to do. As I read through the documents, juggling from one plan to another, I pieced together the legal history of the house and drew a map of connections.

It was not long before I discovered that Old Owlers had been in Mrs. Pendant's family for generations; in fact, my client owned part of one of the oldest houses in Rype. She had inherited it shortly after the War when it had passed to her under her uncle's Will. I was astonished to find that the Title started with an Act of Attainder in the sixteenth century, when the Freeholder, an Earl of ill repute, was found guilty of treason against the Crown and his lands were forfeited to the Crown by an Act of Parliament.

I recalled a dinner party where someone had asserted that the Crown meant the Queen. Having imbibed a glass or two too many, I'd pontificated — fortunately much to the amusement of our hosts and fellow guests — that 'the Crown (with a capital C) comprises the Monarch and the two Houses of Parliament: namely, the House of Lords and the House of Commons.'

Lands held by Peers of the Realm could only be forfeited by statute, and this was the reason the Act of Attainder was amongst the deeds. From an academic viewpoint I was aware of this, but I had never before come across a five-hundred-year-old, hand-written copy of such an Act.

I moved my fingers over the vellum which was stiff and yet fragile. Folded, the document was about the size of the Deed Packet which I had so recently disposed of in the dustbin at Rose Cottage. It was a little squarer than foolscap. My fingers traced the outline of three round objects. Gently, I eased open the Act's folds. I spread it out over the huge sideboard which was my mother's pride and joy, noticing that the black ink was faded where it had seen the light. Unfolded, the document was immense.

Inside, neat writing with extra tails and double S's looped across the whole surface making it much more challenging to read than the more usual round-hand or copperplate, which was easier to decipher. There were three metal tins attached to the bottom of the Deed. Flattish and round, each of them measured about three inches across the diameter and was over half an inch deep. I opened them one by one. They contained red-brown sealing wax into which the separate seals of the Houses of Parliament and the Monarch had been impressed. But there was a surprise in the last one that I opened — an old key. It fitted across the diameter of the tin with only a hair's width to spare. The sealing wax beneath it was scored and had crumbled a little. Odd. I replaced the key and put the lid back on the seal's metal container.

Reluctantly, I re-folded the ancient deed and put it to one side. The Act of Attainder might be interesting and the key intriguing, but neither were helpful in sorting out the present conundrum. Why had Blue Jeans Adam tried to steal the deeds? And where did White Bonnet fit into the picture?

"Now, come on, Hazel," I admonished myself. "Forget the old deeds. Start from the other end. The answer is likely to be in the Conveyance of part of the original house."

Resolutely ignoring my own advice, I picked up the Abstracts of Title. There were four of these amongst the deeds. The earlier three were handwritten but the most recent was typed. Resisting the temptation to go through the earlier ones, I opened the typed Abstract.

My mother came in bearing a cup of cocoa which she set down beside me.

"How are you getting on?" she asked. "Bruce just phoned to say he's on his way."

"I'm just wading through these deeds. They're fascinating, but I'm getting side-tracked."

My mother looked over my shoulder.

"What's that?" she queried. "It doesn't look like a proper deed to me."

"That's because it isn't a 'proper deed'," I answered. "It's called an Abstract of Title."

A perplexed frown wrinkled her forehead, so I launched into a detailed description of the conveyancing process.

"... And that is where the Abstract of Title comes in."

"Tell me again. I'm lost."

"Within a week after a sale is agreed, called 'exchange of contracts', the vendor's solicitor has to send to the purchaser's solicitor details of his client's title — deeds — to prove that his client owns that title and is able to convey the property to the purchaser."

Mother smiled and nodded at me to continue.

"The details of the deeds are written down in a summarised form which is called an Abstract of Title. You can see from this one here that it's basically just a list, in date order, of the deeds relating to the property. But it's more than just a list. It's a sort of legal shorthand setting out all the important parts of the various deeds and documents."

"What happens if there's something wrong with it?"

"Well ... the purchaser's solicitor goes through it with a fine tooth-comb. He has a week to ask questions called 'Requisitions on Title'. They're probably the most important part of the transaction because the vendor has to give satisfactory replies and if he can't the purchaser can withdraw from the transaction."

My mother nodded. "I see. And if everything's all right and it goes ahead there's something else to sign, isn't there?"

"Yes, nowadays the vendor signs a Transfer deed that is registered at the Land Registry after completion. Sometimes, if there are any special covenants or other provisions in the Transfer, it has to be signed by the purchaser, too. If the purchaser has a mortgage, he has to sign the mortgage deed as well."

"So if everything goes well ...?"

"The purchaser's solicitor hands over the money to the vendor's solicitor who gives him the Transfer and the other deeds in return. Once that is done, everyone moves out and in, and Bob's your uncle!"

"Thank you for explaining that, darling. Now you must drink up your cocoa. Bruce will be here any minute."

"Gosh!" I exclaimed. "I'd better get on and finish this."

"I'll leave you to it, then." She stroked my hair away from my brow and left the room.

I ploughed through all three Abstracts. Although the title was complicated, I managed to piece the patchwork of deeds together, comparing plans as the land boundaries shifted and changed over the centuries. The property had passed through various hands. Some of the lands it originally possessed were sold to a neighbouring farm. Others were re-acquired later. Adjoining parcels of land were purchased and added to the title. There were Indentures, Conveyances, Deeds of Mortgage, Deeds of Second Mortgage, Receipts, Releases, Official Copies of Probate, Assents,

Deeds of Rentcharge, a Deed of Arrangement, Assessments of Tithes, Leases, Counterpart Leases, Surrenders of Lease and assorted other documents.

'The only thing to do is to cut to the chase,' I thought. I picked up the latest Conveyance, dated 1923, which conveyed the whole house and garden, with the farmland it then possessed, to Arthur Chapman, Mrs Pendant's uncle. I turned it over. There was a memorandum on the other side setting out details of the Conveyance of part of the house and garden, but none of the fields, to a Mr Jeremiah Joshua Hadley in 1932. It was a very ordinary memorandum but I read it carefully. A plan was missing. Searching for it, I came across it in yet another document. Then I re-read the memorandum, referring to the plan, and then ... I read it again.

"Hooray!" I shouted. "I've found it!" I leapt up, heedlessly spilling deeds all over the floor.

The door opened. Poppadum flew in and jumped up at me. I managed to pat her and push her away at the same time.

"Down, down, you lovely, silly dog."

"Found what, Haze?" came a familiar, dark chocolate voice and, without further ado, I threw myself yet again into my husband's arms. But this time I wasn't weeping. I was laughing with triumph.

"Well, I must say," Bruce teased me. "It's good to see you're clean. But what have you done with this mop?"

My wayward hair had corkscrewed itself into ringlets round my head. Bruce straightened a strand which, gorgon-like, wound itself tightly round his finger. He used that curl to pull me even closer and kiss me. He tasted of mint toothpaste overlaid with beer. I realised that he'd had the opportunity to freshen up. His shirt was clean if not ironed; he still smelled slightly of burning.

"How ...?" I began, but he shut me up with another kiss.

"Come," he said, pulling me towards the door. "Your mother says that food is on the table. I know it's late to eat again but I must admit I'm hungry — and we can tell each other everything while we're tucking in."

"Me too," I owned. "But I must get these deeds into some

semblance of order first."

I was organising the deeds into date order as I spoke, bundling them together and tying them with the red tape.

"Did you find anything interesting?" Bruce was looking over my shoulder.

"Oh yes, indeed I did," I replied. "But, as you said, food ..."

"Tell me," he demanded.

I glanced at the old French clock that took pride of place on the mirrored sideboard. It was half past eleven.

"All in good time," I told him, skipping out of the door ahead of him, Poppadum at my heels.

"This is bonzer, Betty."

Bruce could never resist the alliteration of bonzer and Betty. Privately, when he and I were alone, he referred to her as 'Bonzer-Bet'.

The table was groaning with ham, hard boiled eggs, salad, bread, butter, jam, and an orange jelly and cream — what my family called high tea. Bruce and I sat in state. My father had toddled off to bed, muttering that he needed his beauty sleep and that he would see us in the morning. My mother set her chair opposite us, making small talk until we had eaten our fill, which didn't take long because Bruce ate fast and it only took a small ham sandwich to satisfy my midnight hunger pangs. When we'd finished, Mother leaned her elbow on the table and gave Bruce the Look.

"Now, Bruce," she said. "What happened after Hazel left with Mark?"

"Actually it was a bit of an anti-climax," he demurred as he sawed himself another slice of bead and smothered it with butter. "When I smashed the window, I got through it with barely a scratch." He turned his left palm up. It was crisscrossed with thin red lines that he rubbed ruefully.

"Oh dear!" Mother said, taking his hand in hers the better to inspect it.

"It's okay. It doesn't hurt," he said manfully, taking the hand back.

"Go on," I encouraged him.

"I ran in, grabbed the pan from the stove, chucked enough cold water in it to make the smoke even thicker and rushed round and round like a cut snake, waving the pan about all the while. Made me shed a tear or two but it had the desired effect."

"Was anything burned, damaged?" I asked.

"Nope, but I don't think you'll be using that pan again — and the whole place stinks to high heaven of burning pasta."

"Now that's something that puzzles me," I said, frowning. "I've been worrying over it. I'm certain you turned the gas off under the pasta pan. I suppose I must have made a mistake. But I can't think why I didn't notice when I went past the kitchen ..."

Bruce was grinning, really grinning, at me.

"You!" I declared. "It was you! You took the plates out. You put the gas on again." I reached across the table to pummel him. "You. It was you!"

"Ouch." He cowered, putting up his hands to defend himself. "I only did what you suggested later. You said you were going to make a big smoke as a diversion."

"Humph!" I snorted. "You might have told me!" I thumped him.

"Your reaction was perfect, darl." He was still grinning, despite the thumps. "I couldn't have expected more from a West End actress."

"I wasn't ... bloody ... acting! I was bloody scared."

"It made it all the more convincing. Well done, Haze."

"There must have been more than burning pasta to make all that smoke!"

"You can still use it ... I think."

"What?" I exclaimed. "What can I still use?"

"Your chopping board."

"Chopping board?"

"I spread a bit of butter on it."

"*What*?" I was aghast. Why had he done that?

"You said that before."

"Why *butter* it?" But I already had an inkling.

"Then I nudged it over the gas a bit."

"*Fat and wood? On the gas?*"

"It's a bit black on one side," he acknowledged. "The dishcloth's had it, though."

For a moment I was rendered speechless.

"But it made some great smoke, don't you think?"

"You didn't ...." I gasped. Bruce was nodding.

Poppadum had been quietly lying under the table but our raised voices must have disturbed her. She let out a series of short, sharp, high-pitched barks as if calling us to order.

"I *hate* you." I announced, getting up and walking round the table to press his head to my currently-ample bosom.

Poppadum looked from one to the other of us and back again with the air of a disapproving schoolmistress and retreated to her lair under the table. My mother's hand had flown to her mouth and I saw her shoulders shaking with smothered laughter but she pulled herself up straight and did her best to sound authoritative.

"I think you did very well, Bruce," she said, brown eyes still dancing and voice unsteady. "You provided a diversion — a *very convincing* diversion, it seems — and you're both safe here. It seems to me that this whole affair is bordering on farce. Tell me, Bruce, do you really believe that Hazel has been in danger since she was given those deeds?"

"Yes. Yes, I do," he answered, sobering. "In fact, I think the danger is considerable. Hazel's probably told you that the police think a drug gang is involved?"

"Where did you park your car?" Mother demanded.

"It's okay, Bon ... Betty," he stuttered. "I've parked it outside the pub. I went in, ordered a pint, went to the Gents and nipped out the back door."

"Did anyone see you?" she persisted.

"No." He was very serious now, voice low and eyes steady. "I took pains to make sure that I wasn't followed on the way here. I came through the lanes and I would have seen headlights behind me, I'm sure."

"Are you certain?" she pressed.

Bruce glanced at me but directed his words to my mother. "I am certain, Betty. Believe me, I was checking my mirror all the way here."

"Good," she sounded relieved. "Is anyone at Rose Cottage now?"

"I left Neil there," he said, directing the words to me. "Standing guard."

"Can this Neil be trusted?" asked my interrogator of a mother.

I laughed.

"Yes, of course," I said. "He's the local bobby. He'll get some reinforcements from Lightchapel if he needs them. And I've got the deeds here, anyway."

"Did you tell him you were coming here?" my mother pressed.

"I can't remember," Bruce said slowly. "He might have overheard me talking to Hazel but I'm pretty sure I didn't say exactly where she was going."

"Good," Mother said again, pressing her lips together as she thought. "Nonetheless, take the poker with you when you go to bed, just in case." Bruce and I exchanged a grin as she continued. "We'll leave Poppadum's bed in the dining room, as usual, but with the doors open. She seems to be a perfect burglar alarm and deterrent in one."

"Absolutely," I concurred. "I wish you could have seen her biting that chap's bottom."

Mother raised her eyebrows, amusement in her wide smile, "I wish I had, too." She stifled a sudden yawn. "Too much excitement makes me sleepy these days. Not at all how it used to be. I'll turn in now. You know where everything is. I'll see you in the morning."

She kissed me goodnight. Bruce leapt to his feet and took her into a bear hug.

"Thanks, Betty," he said. "You are true blue! And great in a crisis. Good night. Sleep well."

"I'll do my best," she smiled in response. "Good night, darlings." And with that she gave Poppadum a pat and left the room.

"Is the house *really* all right, darling?" I asked Bruce as soon as my mother had closed the door.

"Yes. Truly. There was no damage apart from the chopping board — which *might* have to be replaced — and a very disagreeable smell," he replied. "We might have to slap a coat of paint round the kitchen. On the other hand, it might just take a good clean. I opened all the windows and doors wide and let what breeze there was blow through."

"And you didn't hurt yourself?"

I'd only been half convinced by his showing of his hand. The window had splintered, of that I was sure.

"A few scratches when I pushed the window open. My shoes took the brunt of breaking the glass," he assured me. "My word, darling, there were a lot of people milling about — all concerned about you."

"Did you know them all?" I asked pointedly. But Bruce was still speaking.

"I'd barely got through the window and suddenly there were firemen everywhere. I pointed them up to the bedroom and told them you were still there. David was good. He and his buddy rushed out to get you immediately. Another fireman dashed into the kitchen after me. I only just made it to the stove ahead of him and pretended I was trying to put the fire out by running water into the pan. The poor fireman was quite shocked. I think he smelled the fat burning and thought I was pouring water onto it."

"So then you pretended you were looking for somewhere to put the saucepan down and ran round the house?"

"Something like that. Mark came barging in as I got to the front door. He was just going to bell-ringing practice at All Saints, apparently, saw the smoke and rushed in to help. Then Tom appeared. He said he was on his way home and couldn't believe his eyes." Bruce's eyes crinkled as he continued: "And I ended up with both of them — and the firemen — following me around and telling me what to do."

"And all the time I was so frightened." I was beginning to get angry.

"I really *am* sorry. I should have told you what I'd done. For a moment or two there I thought I'd done it only too well."

"Never mind," I said ungraciously. "Tell me the rest."

"Not much to tell, really. I rushed out of the back door, threw the pan down and looked up to see Horace. He started yacking, asking me where you were and what he could do. I got rid of him by asking him to go and tell anyone else that it was all under control — and then I quickly told Mark and Tom what was going on. They cooked up the rescue scheme between them."

"Funnily enough, I think they actually enjoyed it."

"Sure they did." He looked at me with grave eyes. "Anyway, I'd managed to take a good look round outside and noticed two men I didn't recognise. That was when I spoke to you and sent you off with Mark."

"Mark and Tom were wonderful!" I enthused.

"Tell me about it."

"Later. You haven't finished your story yet. Go on, continue."

"When Neil arrived — also concerned about you — I pointed the two shifty-looking blokes out to him and he nodded grimly. Said they were 'known to the police'."

"Did he know their names?" I queried.

"I didn't ask. I was too keen to make the place safe and get washed. Neil helped me knock a piece of plywood across the broken window. I made us both a cup of tea, had a shower, changed, and came here. The rest you know."

We had been clearing the table as we spoke. The dining room was back to normal and only the washing up remained. I peered under the table. Poppadum hadn't moved a whisker, but her eyes were following my every movement. She heaved a huge sigh and flopped over onto her side, eyes still fixed on me. I stroked her foot with my toe. I regarded the dirty dishes with a jaundiced eye. I was very tired but it didn't feel fair to leave the washing up to my parents in the morning.

"Your turn," said Bruce. "Tell me what happened to you."

I ran some water into the sink and threw Bruce a tea towel. We washed and dried our utensils while I regaled Bruce with my adventures.

He listened to me in silence, his expression growing more and more solemn as I described what had happened in the surgery car park. When I had finished my tale, which by chance coincided with the end of the washing up, he looped the tea towel round me and drew me to him, half playfully, but very earnestly nevertheless.

"This is not good, Haze. You must take care. Did you find anything in the deeds?"

I darted a kiss on his nose. "Yes, I did, but it's a bit complicated. I'll tell you in bed."

All at once I felt utterly exhausted.

"I *must* sit down," I said, as the room started to revolve.

Bruce grabbed my arm and plonked me into the nearest kitchen chair. I crossed my arms on the kitchen table and rested my head on them. I was not at all sure that I would ever be able to lift it up again. Even the Bump, who had been restive all evening, was quiet now.

"Poor old you," Bruce commiserated. "I'm sorry. You've had a very long and upsetting day. It's probably delayed shock. Here, lean against me."

He squatted down beside me; I did manage to move my head and rest it against his shoulder. Somehow, by some superhuman effort, he contrived to lift me from the chair and carry me to the bedroom. I had no idea how he managed to manoeuvre me through doors and into the bedroom. All I remembered was the comfort of the bed, my slight resistance to being undressed and the deliciousness of falling into a deep and dreamless sleep.

- 29 -

Of Love and Sisters

Jack. Oh! He is so handsome, he cuts such a fine figure. And he has come home at last, home to Romney Marsh and to me. Leastways, 'tis so I like to think, as I pinch my cheeks and bite my lips. Not that I have need of more colour in either — for I can feel the rush of blood to my face as I catch sight of him. I peep through the window and there he is — strolling down the High Street towards the cottage.

The window serves the room I share with my three sisters. And how they are teasing me and skipping round me and tying the strings of my best white pinafore! Now they push me from the room and retire in giggles to watch our meeting, squabbling forgotten quite. I imagine their tousled heads vying for space at the window. I smile even as I teeter at the head of the twisting stair. My heart pounds in my breast. I gasp for air. I cannot breathe. For a moment I fear I am laced too tight and I shall faint and fall. Then I hear a loud knock upon the door and my heart stops. But I breathe again.

Oh the agony! Oh the ecstasy! I set one foot upon the stair and the other follows. In the blink of an eye I am at the door, and opening it. He fills the doorway. The size of him! The man-smell of him. Blue, blue eyes, the careless grin, the sea-tanned skin. All are the same, yet not the same.

He senses my hesitation but will have none of it. He seizes me, huge hands meeting round my waist. I gasp — for he is lifting me high, high against his heart. I feel it beating strong and fast and mine matching it, beat for ecstatic beat. Together, the power shakes us. Then his lips are hard on mine, bruising them — till they open and his tongue invades me. He bends me backwards, forcing me to cling tight, tighter. Our bodies blend, mine fits his perfectly. I am one with his impatience, his longing: he hardens against me. Within me, a rush of warm, warm, molten love. But even as I am swept away in an anguish of wanting, he sets me back upon my feet, holds me at arms length.

We are both quivering, panting. We cannot speak, can only look deep, deep into the other's eyes. Then I cannot do even that. My eyes drop. I am ashamed. How could I behave like a common strumpet? Especially with this man whom I have loved since childhood. Shame pierces my breast with its keen sharp dart. And now my cheeks are flaming and my lips are throbbing with blood. I pull away and turn to run. But his hand darts out and catches my wrist in an iron grip.

"Nay, Annie. Do not run from me. I could not bear it."

He releases me and I rub my wrist, hold it with my other hand. Tears start from my eyes, I know not why. I cannot speak for there is a tumult of emotions in my chest — shame, frustration, anxiety, longing but most of all love.

"Nay, do not weep, Annie. I pray thee, do not weep."

And he is there before me, down on one knee, his face pressed into my apron which is creased beyond redemption by our passion. Still I cannot speak. Only my tears flow fast, unheeded. His words are muffled but I hear them.

"I beg pardon, Annie. I should not have acted so. Forgive me."

No words come. I can only shake my head from side to side.

He looks up at me, at my quivering lips, my trembling body and he is all contrition.

"Nay," he says again, his voice breaking. "Nay, I meant not to distress thee so. Forgive me. I have been gone so long. 'Tis but thought of thee has buoyed me up through all these months ...." And his dear eyes swim with tears.

My heart is aching but still I can force no words from my lips. I bend to take his dear head in my hands: kiss his wet eyelids tenderly and gently put my mouth to his. And now I can speak.

"Nay, nay. There is nothing to forgive. I am but ashamed that I should act so. 'Tis thou must forgive me."

Now he is swiftly on his feet again, clasping me to him. But gently this time. Then he holds me away from him, lowers his head until it is level with mine and looks deep into my swollen eyes. What I see there stops my tears and makes me smile with love. And he sees the reflection in mine eyes. Doubt falls from him and once again he sinks to kneel at my feet.

"Then — Annie, my Annie, if thou canst forgive such a great clod as I ... and perhaps understand how great is my need ... wilt thou be mine? Betrothed to me? My wife?"

Once again I am bereft of speech, so great is the exultation of joy within my tumultuous heart. But I can nod and smile and press his hands to my lips and raise my head and laugh out loud.

At the sound he leaps up once more and holds me high, high above him as if I weigh no more than a feather.

"Say Aye! I need to hear thee say it."

"Aye, I will! Now set me down."

He lowers me to my feet and kisses me tenderly on the lips.

"'Tis Beltane soon. Shall we be hand-clasped then?"

"Aye!"

And suddenly the world is a place of love and miracles and I am to be wife to this man I have loved forever and whom I feared never to see again.

Now there is a running of feet on the stairs and my sisters surround us in a dancing ring. Ma appears from the scullery, a cheesecloth dripping from her hand and her smile is as broad as the river Rother. Life is as sweet as the nightingale's song.

- 30 -

Of Theories and Explanations

The Bump kicked me awake in the morning. I lay for a moment, feeling drugged, as I surveyed the blue sky from an unfamiliarly familiar window.

My parents had kept my room as a spare bedroom for overnight visitors and for the odd occasions when Bruce and I stayed. I'd redecorated it when I came home for a few months after finishing university. All my parents had done to it since was to change my single bed for a double one, although this had necessitated some alteration to the placing of the furniture. So this morning, as I lay on my back feeling the busy movement of my baby within me, there was a moment of deja vu. But only a moment.

The door opened quietly and my mother appeared. Poppadum pushed her way through between her trousered legs and rushed to my side, shoving her cold wet nose into my offered palm.

"Ah, you're awake," Mother said, coming in. She bore a large mug of hot water with a slice of lemon in her hand. My favourite morning beverage. She put it on the bedside table.

"Yes, almost," I replied. "Thanks for the lemon water. I feel very spoiled."

I moved over a little and she sat down on the bed half-facing me. "Bruce has just left for work."

"Gosh!" I exclaimed. "What time is it?" The clock beside the bed read twenty-five to nine. I raised myself up on one elbow. My mother gently pushed me down again.

"Take your time, darling. Bruce crept out so as not to wake you and told me to leave you sleeping. He said he'd be back as soon as he could get away."

Fifteen minutes later, I made my way into the kitchen from

which wafted the delicious smells of coffee percolating and bacon frying. I was hungry. I decided it was something to do with being 'home' again. My mother always thought the answer to everything was easier to find on a full stomach and she was a very good cook.

I waltzed into the kitchen, closely followed by my dog who dashed over to her bowl and devoured the bacon rinds there.

"Hello, Old Girl," my father greeted me, not getting up from where he was installed behind the kitchen table with his newspaper. He pulled out the chair next to him with one hand. "Take a pew. How are you this morning?"

"Fine," I said, sure that he did not really want to know the ins and outs of my current state of health.

"Good," he grunted, pushing his glasses further up his nose and returning to his paper. A glass of water and a mug of milky coffee appeared miraculously in front of me.

"How hungry are you?" asked my maternal angel, going back to the stove.

"Not very," I responded, knowing that to admit to hunger in my mother's presence was to invite a meal of such gargantuan proportions that even I would have found insufficient room to accommodate it. "Although I must say that bacon smells wonderful."

"Just one egg, then."

She broke an egg into the pan, took a warmed plate from the oven, dished the bacon, added a fried tomato to the plate, lifted the cooked egg from the frying pan and passed the whole lot to me in the seamless pattern I knew of old.

I fell on the breakfast hungrily. Dad half-folded the paper and pushed it to one side.

"Now Old Girl," he said. "Your mother and I have been thinking ...." He glanced at my mother, who nodded in agreement. She sat down opposite us with her own mug of coffee nestled between her hands. "From what Bruce tells us, all this started when you took possession of those deeds. Is that right?"

"Yes, I'm sorry ..."

"There's nothing to be sorry about, sweetheart," he assured me, patting my hands. "The question is this: are you in danger? Apparently, your client hands you the deeds, you take them indoors and hey presto! A chap rushes in and tries to steal them. Is that correct?"

"Yes ..." I began.

"So the question we have to ask is: why?"

"Yes ..." I said again.

"And you thought it was something that was concealed in the wording of the deeds, I think?"

"Yes." This was getting monotonous. My mother took over.

"But what if it was something concealed *with* the deeds rather than *in* the deeds?" she asked.

"Er ..." I had not even considered that. I had been so focussed on finding the missing clue — one that I was sure was hidden somewhere in the wording of the documents — that I'd contemplated no other reason for the theft.

"Good point," I conceded, hitting my forehead with my hand in very dramatic fashion. "I didn't think to look in the deed packet. By the time it was retrieved from Blue Jeans Adam it was so covered in dog-pooh that I put it straight in the dustbin. I only just managed to get the deeds out unscathed."

My father took up the questioning again. "So you don't know if there was anything *else* in the deed packet?"

"No. Everything happened so fast."

"Did anyone see you put the deed packet in the dustbin?"

"I don't think so. But I was so keen to get rid of the sickening smell that I didn't notice."

I replayed the scene in my mind. The soldier had left me at the door. Adam and Neil had headed off in the direction of the police station and the rest of the crowd ... well, the last I remembered was that they were all going their separate ways as I was escorted home.

"But that doesn't explain ..." I began again, talking slowly enough for me to think faster than I spoke. "Maybe it's just a coincidence."

"What's a coincidence?" he queried.

"I found something interesting in the deeds – something that I thought explained why someone wanted to steal the deeds. But I see now it's unlikely to be the reason. What you suggest is far more probable."

"What did you find, then?" Mother was intrigued.

"A flying freehold, and an underground one," I said, offhand, as I marshalled my thinking apparatus. "But, *if* that was the reason for stealing the deeds, then presumably someone would have to know *what* the deeds contained – and that's not very likely."

"No?" Dad prompted.

"No," I said.

"Why do you say 'not likely'?"

"Because, now I come to think of it, someone would have to know what he was looking for – and the likelihood is that only an inquisitive solicitor, like me, would even think about it, anyway."

"It's a possibility, I suppose," said my father, thoughtfully. "But I think it was something *in* the deed packet. There's an easy way to find out, of course. Why don't you ring the policeman and get him to see if the deed packet is still in the dustbin and, if so, whether there's something hidden in it?"

Simple. Why hadn't I thought of that? No doubt I had been too busy following my own theories.

"I'll telephone Neil as soon as I've finished my breakfast," I agreed. My mother shook her head, and my father said:

"Might as well do it straight away, Old Girl. Get it over with."

Less than five minutes later I was sitting on the telephone seat in the hall having a conversation with Neil's wife.

"He's just left again, Hazel. He was up late, didn't come in till after midnight. He said he had to go and check on your house. You might just catch him there if you ring your own number."

"Thank you, Jane," I said. "Would you ask him to ring me as soon as he comes in – if I haven't managed to speak to him." She agreed and rang off. I looked helplessly at my parents who were both watching me from the kitchen doorway.

“Neil’s gone to Rose Cottage,” I informed them. “Apparently he was there till the wee hours and has just gone back to check everything’s still tickety-boo.”

I picked up the receiver again and dialled my own number. The phone rang and rang. I was just about to put the receiver back on the hook when someone answered.

“Hello,” came a man’s voice. The line crackled.

“Hello? It’s Hazel here. Is that you, Neil?”

There was a click and the line went dead. Perhaps I’d dialled the wrong number. This time I took pains to pull the dial all the way round with my finger as I dialled each digit of the number. It was answered on the third ring.

“Dawkins residence. Police Constable Havers, speaking.”

I sighed with relief.

“Hello Neil. It’s me, Hazel. I wonder if you can do something for me?”

“Hello Mrs Dawkins.” He sounded very formal. “Of course.”

The words tumbled from my lips. “I’ve just realised that there may have been something in the deed packet that Adam Blue Jeans wanted, not the deeds themselves.”

“Quite possibly, Mrs Dawkins. Have you found anything?” Still that formal voice.

“No, but the deed envelope was not very sanitary so I put it straight into the dustbin. I’d managed to extract the bundle of deeds first so I had no reason to look into the deed packet.” I had barely finished the sentence before he said:

“So you’d like me to check? I’ll do that straightaway.”

“Yes, please,” I said, but I had already heard a thud and I knew that he had put the receiver down on the table. Keeping my ear to the receiver and listening closely, I heard a quickly stifled oath, the sound of the back door opening and, possibly, a conversation.

Neil came back to the phone.

"Hello Mrs Dawkins?" Why was he being so formal this morning? I pondered this briefly and then I understood – he was not alone.

"Yes, I'm still here. Did you find it?"

"Yes, I did, Mrs Dawkins. Not a very pleasant object, I must say. Unfortunately it is completely empty."

"Oh!" I was very disappointed. I'd been certain he'd find a something intriguing inside. "Has anyone else been near the dustbin, do you know?"

"Not to my knowledge, ma'am," he replied, still distant.

"I should put it back then," I suggested.

"Well, actually, Mrs Dawkins, I suggest I take it with me. We may find some fingerprints on it."

"Very well," I agreed.

"Is there anything else, ma'am?"

"No ... I mean ... yes. Thank you for helping Bruce to make the house safe and for keeping an eye on it."

"I'm glad to have been of service."

"My husband will be driving me home as soon as he can leave work," I told my not-quite-so-friendly policeman. "Hopefully we'll be there in a couple of hours. There's no need for you to stay if you feel all's well."

"All's quiet at the moment, I'm pleased to say. I'll stay as long as I can."

"Thank you, again, Neil,"

"Goodbye."

My parents had been hanging on my every word.

"No joy, I take it?" My father enjoyed being pessimistic.

"No. The packet was there, but empty," I said. "Neil's taking it for fingerprinting."

"Are you sure?" My father's eyebrows leapt above the frames of his spectacles. "I thought the chap was apprehended in mid crime with numerous witnesses. I can't see why they'd need fingerprints to establish his guilt."

"Perhaps not," I dismissed his argument. "But they might find other fingerprints, I suppose."

Dad snorted.

"Yes, yours, your client's and everyone's at the bank to name but a few!" he exclaimed.

I changed the subject.

"Anyway, *anyone* could have seen me put the deed packet in the dustbin. They could have come back when the fuss had died down — or sent someone else. They wouldn't have had to go inside the house. No-one would know."

"So you think that we're right and there was something else in the deed packet?" Mother asked.

"Of course you're right," I acknowledged. "It's very obvious when you think about it."

"Good," she said, squeezing my arm. "Now let's have another cup of coffee and a natter until your husband returns and takes you away again."

Bruce appeared at half-past ten by which time I had telephoned both Mrs Pendant and Mr Stone.

I rang Mrs Pendant first. After the usual pleasantries, I thanked her for bringing me the deeds:

"I'm pleased to say that I've had the opportunity to go through them carefully and I think I've found something that will help with the problem of the roof. It's rather complicated so I'd prefer to discuss it with you privately. Could we meet tomorrow perhaps?" I asked. She agreed and we arranged a time.

"There's just one more thing, Mrs Pendant," I said, grasping the nettle. "I just wondered how long you had the deeds before you brought them along to me?"

"Not very long. I picked them up from Mr Stone yesterday morning and then brought them home to have a look at them myself," she replied. "They were very interesting, weren't they?"

"Very," I agreed drily.

"I deciphered part of one deed. A Conveyance, I believe. But my eyes aren't what they were and I decided it was best left to a lawyer. As I told you, I'm apprehensive of those youths who loiter opposite my house. I'm certain they spy on me. I thought it sensible to bring the deeds directly to you."

"Did anything else happen to you, or the deeds, before you gave them to me?" I questioned.

"Funny you should ask that," she said, sounding a touch disturbed. "One of those louts barged into me and I tripped. I'm sure he stuck his foot out deliberately. The deeds went flying. Luckily, I managed to regain my balance but there was definitely something peculiar about it."

"Why do you say that?"

"Well," she said, considering. "They usually think it's funny when they do something like that. Generally they'd snigger and joke amongst themselves but this time one of them grabbed my arm to steady me and another actually picked up the deeds and dusted them off under his sleeve before he gave them back to me. I was astonished. But ..."

I waited. She didn't continue so I asked:

"Did they follow you?"

"Yes, I was going to say that. But I'm not *entirely* certain. A couple of youths were definitely following me but I'm not sure they were the same ones. They all look the same to me in their jeans and tee-shirts."

"Was one of them wearing a leather jacket?" I queried.

"Yes, now you mention it, I remember thinking he must have been very hot, wearing all that in the sun. Why do you ask?"

I did not want to tell her about the foiled theft so I side-stepped her question:

"I'll tell you when we meet, Mrs Pendant. There's one more thing. I've finished with the deeds so may I return them direct to Mr Stone? I would be very unhappy if they were damaged while I had custody of them."

"Yes. That will be acceptable," she said formally.

"Thank you," I was about to end the call when she said suddenly:

"Mrs Dawkins?"

"Yes?"

"I wondered ... I mean, Petronilla wondered and I said I'd ask. Do you handle divorce?"

"Petronilla?" I asked, surprised. Then I remembered that livid bruise and the suspicion of a black eye.

"She banged on my door this morning in a terrible state of distress. She *must* have been to come to *me*. I calmed her and said I would ask you when we next met."

"No, I'm afraid I don't handle divorce but I could perhaps recommend ..." I said, thinking that now was not a good time to explain for the um-teenth time that I was giving up legal practice to have a baby.

"She only wants *you*, I believe. As a woman she thought you would understand."

"I'm sorry but I can't," I said firmly.

"Never mind. I'll inform her. Goodbye."

She hung up before I had time to respond in kind. I didn't bother to replace the receiver; I just pressed the bar and dialled the bank. Helen answered and put me through to Mr Stone. I told him I was anxious to return the deeds as soon as possible because I had no safety cabinet in which to store them.

"Bring them back anytime," he said expansively. I could almost see him waving his hands around. "Helen will give you a receipt."

Bruce's boss had been very understanding when he'd heard of the events of the previous evening, telling him to go home and look after his wife. My husband had left almost immediately and had no sooner set a foot in the door than my mother had pressed a bacon sandwich into his hand. He was still munching it as we bade a fond farewell to my parents, scooped Poppadum into the back of the old black Ford Anglia and headed home.

- 31 -

Of Rumours and a Plan

Many are the rumours that run across the levels like the bending of the marsh grass in the wind. And all of them pertain to the Eaglewood Gang. Rumours that they covet all the goods that other bands run through the moonless nights, that all contraband that passes through their territory is subject to their will, that they have taken full control of the swathe of country that lies between the southern shore and London, a stretch of land that runs from Devon to Kent.

Many are the stories that pass from lip to lip of dreadful acts of violence and of vengeance. Tales of punishment meted out to all who transgress the rules proclaimed by the Eaglewood Gang. Beatings, maimings and shootings are commonplace. All bow before their might. Yet they have one fatal flaw.

For now turn against them the Owlers of the Marsh and those other bands along the coast who smuggle commodities from France. The common enemy too, Revenue men, the Preventatives who seek to enforce the law against Fair Traders. Preventatives and Dragoons are keeping close watch upon the shore and upon the cliff where once the sea lapped ... ere the Marsh rose and banished it southwards to the Channel.

The reason for this turning is the latest whisper of deeds as black as boat-pitch, as dark and merciless as the devil's heart. Whispers that the Eaglewood Gang has taken prisoners and tied them upside down upon their mounts, stabbed the horses' rears with knives to set them galloping into the darkness, the screams and cries of the tortured gradually giving way to moans and then to silence — for they died hard, heads crushed by the hooves of their own horses.

All at the behest of one man, that associate of Satan, Big John

— he who killed Will the Saddler before he stole the Owlers' waggons and drove them through Rype for all townsmen to see and be rendered fearful.

Annie had been mounted there upon a horse, keeping to the shadows, instructed to watch, listen, learn and fade into the Marsh should danger threaten. She watched and listened well that night, and, ere she slipped away, she recognised her brother's murderer.

Annie tosses sleepless once again. Many a time she has risen before the dawn to run her fingers through her hair, twisting each lock in an orgy of thought and planning. Many is the scheme that she hatches, inspects and flings away. But tonight an idea becomes a plan; her mind turns it this way and that, inspects it from every angle and finds but one fault. Its weakness is that it depends upon Big John's two outstanding traits — his overpowering greed is as legendary as his sore distrust of all but his closest followers.

So Annie considers the scheme again from the beginning, adds a strand — and smiles. This time she knows she will have vengeance on Big John. And she will needs do no violence, for the Owlers will set a snare to rid them of the Eaglewood Gang for once and for all.

A whisper crosses the Marsh of a stratagem to draw the wool over the eyes of the Preventatives. There is muttering of a huge run of contraband, a simultaneous landing in two locations, two points on the bay's arc, two sites far apart on the Marsh coast. Rumours of the most lucrative goods run inland from the shore beneath the aegis of a single guide across the treacherous marshes; murmuring of a hiding place beneath the Ash Grove. Information that, meanwhile, a meaner cargo, landed at the Old Widow's Tap, well guarded and packed with ballast, will be carried through the secret cuts beside the wandering dykes.

A pretending turncoat, threatened by Big John, confirms the rumours. Later the man reports to Jack how the blacksmith relays the information to those vicious, avaricious few he trusts — then threatens dismemberment or death to the informer should any other learn the secret. Loitering near Big John, the 'turncoat' knows the man enticed by untold riches for the taking, hears him direct his many less-favoured men towards the Tap. The chosen few guffaw with laughter at the mis-direction.

Hearing this, Annie rejoices that her conviction is correct, that Big John himself will choose what he presumes the greater booty. Retribution is her sole intent; she alone to act the decoy, she alone to draw the black-hearted smith deep into the Marsh where his weight will drag him down to Satan, to the hell where he belongs; to lie beneath the timeless Marsh forever un-shriven, un-repented. A never-ending fit for this devil and for those who serve as henchmen to his murderous deeds. But Jack insists that he, and a trusted few — all of them keen of eye and acute of hearing — stand sentinels beneath the cliff, watching and listening for their antagonists' approach.

Concealed beside the ash trees' sacred circle, Annie waits and watches. Shadows shiver in anticipation; silver moonlight glistens on awakening leaves; silence weaves a spell of timelessness .... Then — a nightingale's sudden notes pierce the night. Scarce has the song echoed along the old shore cliff, than is discerned the tramp of hooves fast pounding from the north. First a hum, soon a murmur, then a rumble, thundering ever louder through the dark ... and Annie's fleet-footed gelding is racing along the causeway. A pause, a shout, a gesture and the Eaglewood Gang's leaders gallop after, horses' legs truncated by the rising mist.

Jack's heart throbs as he wishes her 'God Speed'. Resolutely he turns away, with his men rides swift as the sudden wind to Rype. Now they thrust attack against those who strive to take the lesser cargo.

Marshmen all are up in arms with spades and crooks and pitchforks, their aim revenge for Will the Saddler's death and more ... to strike so hard and fast that ne'er again will other smugglers venture on the Marsh. They know, too, that the Preventatives are hungry to supplement their meagre pay ... and there is a price upon the heads of the smuggling gang of Eaglewood.

- 32 -

Of Time and Tunnels

As we drove back to Rype, following the same route we had travelled with Joanna that Christmas Eve eighteen months previously, I reflected on the changing beauty and moods of the Marsh. Then we had been wrapped in a mild, pink mist, the sun a mere suggestion of brightness on the horizon; now the sun shone joyously from mid-heaven and green reeds decked every dyke, their verges high and white with the lace of cow parsley and the hawthorn hedgerows garlanded in white May blossom. Then, when the purr of the car's engine had been silenced, not a sound had disturbed the hush; now birdsong and the humming of insects' wings warred with the distant bleating of the sheep spread thickly across the lushness of the Marsh pasture. Then the air had been iced and scentless; now the breeze bore the sweet, lush fragrance of early summer flowers. Yet all these things were transient, changing through the seasons. The land beneath and the sky above were enduring, eternal; boundless as the timeless Marsh.

We wound down the windows, glorying in the day. Bruce stopped the car across the gateway to a field where we sometimes picnicked. Silently, we gazed across the flat expanse of green and white, watching the flight of a chatter of sparrows into the azure blue of the sky. Small, high pressure clouds, like tails of candy-floss, soared above us and the song of an unseen skylark floated down from high above.

The Marsh still kept us spellbound — its ever-changing sky-scape a welcome refuge of peace when pressure tended to overwhelm us; a cloud-scrying walk through its meadows never failing to restore equanimity.

Turning towards me, my husband took my hand in his.

"Only you could get into this sort of conundrum," he commented. "There's never a dull moment with you around."

"I'm glad about *that*, at least," I retorted. "I'd hate to be boring."

"Never boring, darl," he said. "You simply don't know how."

"I expect I could learn." I tried to look as though I were considering the possibility.

"Impossible!" Bruce dismissed the notion out of hand. "But I'm very worried about what's likely to happen next."

"Nothing, I should think," I told him. "I'm sure Dad's judgement is correct. You know what a good grasp of human nature he has. It's much more likely that something was hidden in the deed packet rather than in the deeds themselves. Someone must have checked the dustbin before we thought of the possibility. That's all."

"I don't want to leave you alone if there's any likelihood that they might come back."

"Huh! Fat chance of that," I scoffed. "They'll have skedaddled long ago. When they found whatever they'd hidden they'd *know* that I hadn't discovered it. Surely, there'd be no point in making bigger fools of themselves than they have already? It will all be fine."

I probably sounded more confident than I felt, for Bruce, after eyeing me for a long moment, sighed, re-started the car and muttered something under his breath that sounded like "I expect you're right."

I started singing to show him how relaxed I was and found, as always, that singing itself relaxed and uplifted me. Especially now, when the babe was kicking along in time with my ditty and Bruce was tapping the beat out on the steering wheel as he drove.

I was still singing when he drew up outside the bank, causing a few heads to turn my way in surprise as I hopped out of the car. I reached in for the deeds and then, on a whim, I fumbled with the red tape binding them together, eased out the Act of Attainder and opened the round seal tin which held that mysterious key. I handed the key to Bruce, who took it with a puzzled air. I hastily restored the deeds to order, my protruding middle forming a handy shelf for the purpose.

Less than five minutes later I was back in the car, minus the deeds but brandishing the receipt that I'd been given.

"I've never been so glad to relinquish documents!" I exulted.

"That calls for a celebratory pint," said Bruce, wheeling into the Three Chimneys' car park. He parked in his usual haphazard fashion and pulled on the hand brake. "Let's find your special table in the garden and I'll bring you some ginger beer."

"Oh!" I gasped, as a thought struck me. "What time is it?"

Bruce consulted his wrist watch.

"Just after eleven forty," he said. "Why?"

"I've got an appointment," I said breathlessly. "Thank God I remembered."

I was halfway out of the car before Bruce could respond.

"What?" he asked, baffled. "Where?"

"Not far," I said as I decanted the rest of myself. "This shouldn't take very long. Why don't you go and have a drink and I'll come back as soon as I can?"

"Okay, I'll be in the bar. As long as you're sure you'll be all right walking there?"

"Yes, I'll be fine. It's only a couple of houses up the High Street. I'll join you as soon as I can."

Poppadum tried to follow me but I told her to stay with her master. She grumbled as she reluctantly settled down again, turning her back on me to indicate her disapproval. Bruce blew me a kiss.

When I came to Elizabeth's door, it was ajar. I knocked but there was no answer. I waited for the length of a dozen heartbeats and knocked again. No response. I pushed the door open and called. Still no reply. I tried again.

"Hello? Elizabeth? It's Hazel. I'm sorry I'm a few minutes late." Still no response. I'd started up the stairs but now stopped to listen. I could hear nothing. Not a single sound.

'Strange,' I thought as I continued to mount the stairs slowly. 'Maybe she's in the bathroom.'

The thought was embarrassing. My heart was beating strangely, racing more than my slow ascent of the stairs warranted. That peculiarly uncomfortable feeling I had experienced on the night of the nightingale's song crept over me like a cold mist with a strong tinge of menace. Threat loomed in the lack of sound, as though all feeling, all light and noise had been extinguished. The baby was very quiet too. I reassured it with my hand. Movement was difficult, slow and deliberate, my feet feeling as if I were walking on the moon, without gravity.

It seemed ages before I reached the door to her room but it couldn't have been more than a few moments. The door was shut. I knocked tentatively and tried again:

"Hello? Elizabeth? It's Hazel."

Still no answer. Slowly turning the handle, I opened the door: for a moment the room remained empty but for the cold, noise-draining mist – then everything swam before my eyes, came back into focus and I saw her. Elizabeth was sitting up in bed in a colourfully embroidered silk bed-jacket. She turned her beautiful smile on me.

"Hello Hazel. How considerate of you to creep up the stairs. I didn't hear a sound."

"I did knock ..."

"Did you, dear? Are you sure? I fear I must be getting deaf. Never mind, you're here now. Come over here and sit on the bed." She patted it invitingly.

I went over to the bed, but pulled up a chair to seat myself.

"There's rather a lot of me at the moment," I explained ruefully. The Bump kicked me hard, seeming to take my comment personally, and I gasped a little. "I'm sorry I'm late."

"You're not late at all, Hazel."

Elizabeth reached over and took my hand.

"Just breathe deeply, my dear. Why, your hand is icy. You look very pale ... as if you'd seen a ghost."

I took a deep breath and smiled. The last of the mist evaporated.

"I'm fine, Elizabeth. Thank you for your concern. It was just ..."

I was not sure how to continue. Elizabeth's eyes looked shrewdly into mine.

"Ah, I see." It was a statement. "You were aware of the mist."

I looked at her in amazement.

"Yes," I said. "It made me apprehensive."

"I know, dear. I *know*."

"What is it?"

"It happens sometimes — usually on the full moon or thereabouts, I think. A cold mist envelopes everything and Time seems to stand still."

"Exactly," I said.

"That's because it does." Elizabeth's smile lit up her face.

"What do you mean?"

Elizabeth pointed to the clock at her bedside. It read a quarter past eleven. I gasped again. She pointed to the grandfather clock behind the door. "Look there, too." The grandfather's hands showed exactly the same time.

"It seems to happen when I have a very real wish," she said seriously. "I was worried that you'd arrive before I was ready. And you see — you are here in good time and I am ready."

I said, wonderingly. "But how?"

"A clairvoyant friend of mine believes there is a portal here in Rype. It's a place where the veil between the worlds is thin and different realities can bleed through. On occasion, Time stops here but moves on elsewhere."

"How does that happen?" I questioned. "Why today and not yesterday when I was here with Mark?"

"It has to be a very fervent wish. A wish strong enough to change Time itself," she said. "And yesterday, I didn't want to stop Time or change Time — I just wanted Mark to bring you to me."

I sought for the logical lawyer inside me who would dismiss such arrant stupidity. I failed. The feeling had been so strong, so all-encompassing. Nonetheless I made a great effort and managed to collect myself.

"Now that I'm here, what can I do for you?"

I fished in the bag my mother had insisted on lending me and found she'd had the foresight to put in a notepad and pencil. Not for the first time, I thanked God for my mother's thoughtfulness.

I took instructions for her Will and for a Power of Attorney, checking her family arrangements and giving her appropriate advice. By the time I'd made the most important points, and she had considered my advice and made the required decisions, she could hardly keep her eyes open.

"I must leave you to rest now. Mark warned me he would drop in this afternoon to make sure that I hadn't tired you too much. Let me make you comfortable."

"Thank you," she said when I had rearranged her pillows, removed her bed jacket and supplied a glass of water. "I *am* tired. I'll sleep now. Close the door downstairs, please."

She closed her eyes.

"Of course," I assured her. "I'll be in touch soon. I know you need these things as soon as possible. Sleep well."

She seemed to be asleep already. I straightened the bed cover and departed. Still spooked by the atmosphere that had surrounded me on my arrival, I descended the stairs fast and, in need of a potent jolt of normality, I made a beeline for the Three Chimneys, my husband and a glass of ginger beer.

I found him in the bar, as he had promised. He was leaning against it on one elbow, chuckling over a joke he was sharing with the barman. For a moment I went cold all over. A vague memory fleeted through my consciousness and I caught it as it was about to escape. Bruce's stance was exactly the same as Jack's had been in my dream of a couple of nights previously.

Poppadum, who had been lying at Bruce's feet, came instantly to me. I felt her cold nose in my hand, its familiarity bringing me sharply back to the present. Bruce turned and saw me, instinctively looking at his watch.

"That was quick," he approved. "It's not quite midday and I haven't even had time to finish my first pint."

The bar was dark and I needed the sunlight.

"I told you I wouldn't be long," I pointed out. "Let's go into the garden."

We were lucky; my favourite table in the garden was free. Bruce made sure I was seated as comfortably as my fecund state allowed before he went back to the bar to order my drink. Poppadum settled herself at my feet, her head on her paws. I bent over to pull her ears.

It was hard to believe that it was only the day before that I had been sitting in the very same place eating double chilli-con-carne and overhearing about peculiar goings on down a well. The thought reminded me that I had not mentioned the story to Bruce. Tempted to tell him about it, I remembered that it was not my story to tell — and I wasn't sure he'd believe it. I shivered. I hadn't completely believed it myself until I had that strange experience on the stairs to Elizabeth's flat.

Poppadum suddenly stood up, nose pointing at the pub door and I knew that, within ten seconds, Bruce would appear with his foaming tankard of Guinness in one hand and a glass of ginger beer in the other. I counted four seconds, the door opened and out walked Tom, carrying my ginger beer in his left hand and half a pint of bitter in his right.

"Ah! There you are," he declared as he caught sight of me.

He came across the lawn and set both drinks on the table.

"Met Bruce inside," he explained. "He said you were here, none the worse for the excitement of last night. I hope he's right?" He regarded me with his head perched on one side, like a bird.

"Yes," I said as brightly as I could manage, given that I had been looking forward to the illicit treat of having Bruce all to myself for lunch on a weekday. "Yes, I'm absolutely fine, thanks to you and our midnight ride to the other side of the Marsh."

"I hear the deeds are back in the bank and the whole of Rype's police force has been keeping guard at Rose Cottage?"

"Yes, that's right," I said. Good God, I thought, had Bruce been telling all and sundry at the bar about my adventures?

"It wasn't Bruce who told me that, if that's what you're

thinking." Tom must have read my thoughts. "Oh, no! You're the heroine of the hour. Everyone in Rype has heard of your exploits and the downing of Blue Jeans Adam."

I couldn't help chuckling but I had just taken a swig of my ginger beer and the result was a spluttering choke. Poppadum walked over to Tom and bashed him with her paw.

"Oh sorry, Poppadum," Tom chortled. "I know *you* were the real heroine."

He fondled her ears and then realised I was gasping for breath and thumped me on the back instead.

"Are you all right?" he asked, peering at me.

I managed an amalgamation of a cough, a smile and a nod. With the air of a gentleman politely ignoring an embarrassing incident, he continued:

"I passed your car as you went into the bank, and Neil is in the bar. He told me he'd spent most of the night at your place watching television while he 'guarded' it."

"I see." I'd recovered part of my voice, but couldn't ignore the amazing gymnastics which were going on beneath my smock. The Bump didn't like ginger beer too often, I gathered.

Poppadum dashed across the lawn to where Bruce suddenly erupted through the pub's rear door grasping two bags of salt and vinegar crisps in one hand, swigging from his usual pint glass of dark beer as he came towards us. He sat next to me, the chair so low that it was only with a struggle that he manoeuvoured his long legs under the table. Poppadum settled again at my feet.

"Neil sends you his best wishes, Hazel." This utterance crackled from behind a crisp packet that Bruce was tearing open with his teeth. "And asked me to tell you that all is well at home."

"That's good to know, considering that since this time yesterday it's been burgled, I've been attacked, we've had policemen swarming over it, firemen climbing into an upstairs window, another window's been smashed and boarded up and the whole place probably still stinks of burning pasta!"

Tom was looking at me as though I were a new specimen of

womanhood. Then he laughed.

"Well, I must say! I've never heard you with such an acerbic tone in your voice, Hazel. But you do have a way of making a point."

"Talking of points," said Bruce. "Neil asked if we had a cellar. What was the point of that? Does he think we're making illegal booze?"

"Probably just interested," said Tom. "This whole place is riddled with secret underground passages that lead from cellar to cellar. *Do* you have a cellar, by the way?"

"Nope," Bruce replied, offhandedly. "As I told Mr Plod himself, the floorboards are laid straight onto shingle. I do hope we have some foundations, though. I can't remember what the surveyor said about that."

"Do *you* have a cellar, then?" I asked Tom, intrigued.

"Oh yes," he said. "All the old houses have cellars. As I said, legend has it that they all used to be linked to the church crypt and used by the smugglers for distribution purposes. You know the old poem, I'm sure? How does it go now?"

"I'm sure I knew it once...." I was mentally pulling my hair out as I tried to remember Rudyard Kipling's poem. After a few moments I found I could still recite it word for word, and did so.

"Well remembered," commented my nearest and dearest. "But, if they used tunnels to move their stuff, the smugglers wouldn't have been riding anywhere would they? So horses' feet would not have been heard."

Tom grinned.

"Touché," I acknowledged. "But that doesn't explain..."

Bruce frowned at me warningly, intuiting rightly that I was about to recount our strange experience of a couple of nights previously.

"... How they got the contraband to the passages in the first place." I finished lamely.

"No problem there," Tom asserted. "It's said that the tunnel started at the shore — or not far from it."

"I can't see how there could be a tunnel all the way from the sea shore to Rype," Bruce said dismissively. "The beach is at least two miles away and it's nothing but shingle from there to here."

"Don't forget that the sea used to come much closer to Rype than it does now. There's been a lot of accretion to the sandstone ridge because of the littoral drift along the coast," Tom informed us.

"I'll take your word for that," Bruce conceded reluctantly. "But it's still shingle and there's no way you could excavate a tunnel under that. It would all fall in."

"I understand that the old tunnel ran from the low sandstone ridge at the western end of the bay, near where the Old Widow's Tap used to stand."

"The Old Widow's Tap?"

"It was a ramshackle tavern close to where the fishing boats beached. The fishermen would hasten there for a tot of spirits on their return to shore. Not that there are many fishing boats left nowadays. Rype used to have one of the largest beach-launched fishing fleets in the country," Tom mourned. "A great deal of the King's Navy was supplied by Rype-on-Sea in earlier centuries."

"How far was it to the sea in, say, the eighteenth century?" asked Bruce.

"I understand it was about a mile away. It's true that to reach Rype-in-the-Marsh from Rype-on-Sea they had to take a small craft along the King's ditch or cross the shingle on foot. But, of course in the old days everyone wore huge pattens on their feet, so they could cross it more quickly and with less effort," Tom answered.

I must have been looking puzzled because he smiled at me as he continued:

"Huge overshoes, rather like snowshoes. I've seen pictures of the women wearing them as they launched the lifeboat. Have I told you that it was the tradition round here that the lifeboat was always launched by the women? They didn't sail in it, of course — that was dangerous work for the men alone — but they always launched and recovered it."

"How interesting," I said.

"Yes, isn't it? It's quite unusual for women to be involved in that way."

We all looked up as a new voice called out to us:

"Ah, there you are Mr Dawkins ... Mrs Dawkins ... Hazel! I'm very glad I've found you." Mr Stone was waving in a friendly manner as he traversed the lawn towards us.

"Hello Tom," he continued. "How are you? It's been a long time since I've sat in your chair, I'm glad to say."

"Hello, Paul," Tom responded. "It's good to see you but you've reminded me that I'm going to have to make tracks back to the surgery. I have several teeth to extract this afternoon."

And with that, he stood up, quaffed the rest of his beer, wished us all a good afternoon and strolled away. Paul Stone sat down in Tom's place with a sigh of satisfaction.

"What a beautiful place this is," he commented. "How are *you*, Hazel? I was on my way to your house when I met Neil in the street — he told me you were here, by the way — and he tells me that all sorts of things have been happening in your neck of the woods, so to speak?"

"I'm fine, thank you," I replied.

"Yes, we've had an interesting time of it," Bruce said, determinedly off-hand. "But all's well now."

"Good, good. I'm glad about that." The bank manager took off his spectacles and polished them on a handkerchief which he pulled from his breast pocket with the flourish of a magician producing a rabbit out of a hat. "Hazel, I hesitate to ask, but could you see someone — a new client for you — this afternoon? I'm not sure there's anything you can do to help her but she really needs some legal advice." His candid blue eyes met mine and, for once, they were not twinkling. "The thing is ... she's '*in extremis*'. Really very worried indeed."

I looked from him to Bruce, who shrugged and said:

"If I know my wife, there's no way she can refuse an appeal like that. But, Hazel, please give us time enough to enjoy our lunch."

He'd hardly finished speaking before I'd answered Mr Stone's question in the affirmative and agreed to meet his client at one thirty – which gave us just under an hour to finish our meal.

"I really appreciate your kindness, Hazel," Paul Stone rose and, instead of shaking my outstretched hand, held it between both of his. "I'll put my office at your disposal since it's so much closer. Until I see you next, my dear ..." He was still holding my hand and now he pressed it to his lips briefly before he, too, departed.

On his way he passed the pretty waitress with the large posterior. She seemed to be heading in our direction.

"What are we having?" I asked Bruce who had apparently made a decision for me.

"You won't believe this," he said. "They actually had chilli-con-carne on the menu and I know how much you like it."

The waitress reached us and balanced the edge of her tray on the table.

"Two chilli-con-carnes!" she announced. I collapsed into giggles.

"You know," I said confidingly to Bruce when we finally found ourselves alone. "There's something fishy going on."

It was his turn to laugh.

"You can certainly say that! The understatement of the year, I declare."

"Maybe," I said, "But I mean that I'm sure there's *more* to this than meets the eye – it's a hornet's nest all right."

He laughed louder.

"Surely you can see that this is a *very* queer kettle of fish?" I demanded, surveying his amusement with annoyance.

Every time he tried to straighten his face it crinkled into chuckles again.

"It *is*!" I insisted. "It's a *complete* mares nest! *Why are you laughing at me*?"

"Well," he choked eventually. "I'm just amazed at the sheer *number* of clichés ..."

I hit him. Not hard, just enough to push him off his seat.

He looked up at me from the grass, a puzzled frown crossing his face before his grin returned and he launched himself on me, tickling me anywhere he could find bare flesh. Poppadum leapt up between us, growlingly telling us to behave. When we paid her no attention, she grabbed Bruce's trouser leg and pulled hard. The ripping sound as it tore brought us to our senses.

"Pax!" I cried, laughing breathlessly and holding up both my hands with the fingers crossed. "Pax!"

He and Poppadum eyed each other warily for a moment, she still with her teeth in his clothes. Eventually he disentangled himself and, having congratulated her on protecting her mistress, he held up his hands in surrender.

"Okay. I give in," he grinned. "Remind me never to take you two sheilas on together. Now, let me get this straight. You were saying something about a fishy kettle of fish — not surprising it's fishy if it's fish, I suppose? — more than meeting the eye of a mare's nest. Do I have that right?"

"Idiot!" I said, fondly. "You knew precisely what I meant."

"Of course I did," he acknowledged. His smile was gone. "I've been thinking about all this, too, but first tell me what you were going to say before the clichés be …."

"*Stop it!*" I yelled, laughter still threatening to break out. "Just be *quiet* and listen. It seems that Dad was right and that Adam Blue Jeans knocked the deed packet from Mrs Pendant's hands and hid something in it. He then followed her to my house. I expect he hoped to retrieve whatever it was quickly so that no-one would ever be the wiser. But he bargained without Poppadum."

"Neil comes along in the nick of time to arrest him," Bruce took up the thread. "And the deed packet is returned to you — covered in dog shit, it's true, so you put the packet in the dustbin, apparently unnoticed …."

"While Neil takes Adam Blue Jeans back to the Police Station under arrest …"

"And then someone else comes along and tries to steal it again

...” Bruce stopped and raised an eyebrow.

“... except that Neil comes back for his bike and stops them.”

“Or appears to.” Bruce’s face was grave.

“What do you mean? Appears to?”

“Doesn’t it seem to you that Neil is, very conveniently, always on hand?” Bruce looked me in the eye.

“It had crossed my mind,” I admitted. “He even stayed until you came home. I thought it was just to reassure me, but he was asking a lot of questions.”

“Those crooks must have been getting their information from somewhere,” Bruce declared. “And this all seems to revolve around Mrs Pendant, doesn’t it?”

“Yes,” I had to admit that my own thoughts had been following a similar pattern. “Of course, I took him there the day before, to investigate Mrs Pendant’s conviction that the house next door was being used for people-trafficking.”

We looked at each other in concern as we tried to puzzle out the problem.

“Did you ask her about the deeds when he was in earshot?” asked Bruce.

I tried to remember as I retraced the sequence of events.

“I think so, yes.”

“So he would have known she was likely to bring them to you if she had them there?”

“Yes, but they were in the bank,” I objected.

“Anyway, there was nothing in the loft to suggest people-trafficking, was there?”

“No,” I agreed. “But ...”

“But suppose it was ...”

“... Something else.” We finished together triumphantly.

“Okay, let’s go back a few steps,” Bruce suggested. “Try this for a possibility. Mrs Pendant is not completely dotty. Something is going on next door but she makes the mistake of thinking that Pakistanis are being smuggled into the country and that one of them has died there. Suppose, instead, that something is being grown there — cannabis perhaps — and supplied to local lads like Adam. Maybe there was a mistake, something was spilled, say, and went through Mrs Pendant's ceiling. You said there was a stain on her bedroom ceiling didn't you?"

"Yes," I agreed. "There was a strange musty smell in the loft. It was quite overpowering. I think that was what made me faint."

"Okay," Bruce went on. "Let's see... Perhaps the cannabis growers fear that Mrs Pendant suspects something so they follow her. She comes to see *you*. You act quickly and ask Neil to come and investigate. *If* he's a contact he would be able to tell them to clear everything away. You said he was there when you arrived, didn't you?"

"Yes, he was talking to the woman who lives there. She said her name was Petronilla De Cham."

"You decided to go there immediately after Mrs Pendant told you her story — which could have been difficult — but luckily they'd already cleared everything away. All Neil had to do was to go with you and make sure that you suspected nothing. He must have been horrified when you fainted. No wonder he carried you next door and away from the smell before you could suspect any funny business."

"But how does all this tie in with the deeds?" I asked.

"I'm not quite sure yet." Bruce pulled at his lip. "Tell me again what Mrs Pendant said on the phone this morning."

"She said she picked the deeds up from the bank yesterday and took them home."

"Suppose they were watching her, as she thought?"

"Very probably," I agreed. "Anyway, she said Adam bumped into her — deliberately, she was sure — and knocked the deeds from her hands. But, for once, he was not rude. He picked up the deeds and handed them back to her. She brought them directly to me and you know the rest."

"So he had the opportunity to put something in the deed packet, as your father thought?"

"Yes, and, as we've already said, I put the deed packet in the dustbin without looking inside," I reiterated.

"But you told Neil about that on the phone this morning."

"And he was still at Rose Cottage. Perhaps someone else was there too. He was very formal on the phone this morning. It seemed strange, but if there was someone there ... someone in the gang, maybe? ... that he was talking to? The man in the white car, perhaps?"

"You would have given them what they wanted."

"Oh dear," I said, deflated.

"Well, that's probably a good thing," Bruce said slowly. "If all the evidence is with Neil, *and* if he's part of it all, it means that they *know* you have no evidence and, as you said, they'll probably think it's safest to leave you alone. If they attack you it will draw unwelcome attention. If they leave you alone it will seem like some petty, drug-fuelled, attempted theft and will be quickly forgotten."

"This is all conjecture anyway," I reminded him. "How awful we'll feel if we've suspected Neil and he's nothing to do with it."

He sighed. "Well, whether he is or isn't doesn't really matter right now. The main thing is that it's unlikely you're in any danger for the time being. We'll keep an eye open though. They may watch you."

"Okay," I said, trying for a lighter tone. "I'll look out for a man in a white bonnet."

"Do that," Bruce urged. "And be wary of Neil, in a polite way. It's perfectly possible he's innocent. We could be barking up quite the wrong tree."

"Now who's into clichés?"

Poppadum raised her head. She looked resigned. It was Bruce who smiled. But he did not laugh.

- 33 -

Of Howls and Footsteps

Less than an hour later, I was installed behind Mr Stone's wide, wide, desk, enjoying the luxury of his huge leather executive chair. I had twirled round on it a couple of times. I'd been tempted to lean back and put my feet on his table but luckily dignity had prevailed and my feet were back on the floor when Helen showed in my new client. I rose to greet her.

"Good afternoon, I'm Hazel Dawkins. Do sit down. What can I do for you?"

"Mavis Blanchard," she introduced herself, icy fingertips glancing against mine as she bobbed down quickly.

I sat too. Thin, tall and red-haired, my latest client perched on the edge of her chair, clasping her handbag in both hands.

"I want an injunction!" she quavered. "I don't care what it costs — well, I do, actually — but I just can't take any more. They're driving me mad. Quite literally. Mad."

She had clearly screwed up all her courage to come. Her glittering eyes had been fixed on me; now they slid away.

"I'll need to take a few details before I can advise you," I said, wondering whether every client that Mr Stone sent me would be hanging onto their sanity by a thread.

"Of course," she whispered, her eyes cast down towards her handbag.

"However," I continued, smiling in an attempt to take the sting from what I had to say. "I should tell you that injunctions can be difficult to obtain. Although the Court will grant what's called an Interim Injunction immediately — provided we have sufficient evidence of harm or real fear — it may only last fourteen days. To make it permanent we will have to have very strong evidence."

"What details do you need?" she asked breathlessly.

"Your name, address and phone number to start with."

She supplied the information in a voice just an inch above a whisper.

"Thank you," I said when I'd finished scribbling down her particulars. "Let's start at the beginning. Who are 'they'?"

"I don't know exactly," she almost-whispered. "If I did, I'd have given them a piece of my mind before now. There are youngsters who plague me but I think this is something much more sinister."

"Okay," I suggested, considering the matter. "Let's put that to one side for a moment. What are the youngsters doing to distress you so much?"

"They keep me awake all hours. They bang on the window. And there are bloodcurdling screams and swearing. So much swearing."

"Do you know any of these youngsters?" I asked. "Could you give me their names and addresses?"

Miss Blanchard's long, thin nose twitched and she looked apprehensive.

"One or two I know. It's frightening when you're on your own."

"I know. I'm sorry to press you but can you give me their names?" If not, I thought wearily, this will go no-where.

Reluctantly. "I think they are Jimmy Gibbs and Matthew De Cham."

Interesting. That unusual name again.

"How old are they?" I asked.

"About twelve," she replied.

I laid my pencil down. "I'm afraid you can't take out an injunction against a minor."

She actually flinched.

"I suggest I have a word with our local policeman, Neil. He'll give them a warning and that should be the end of it," I said, thinking that calling on Neil to sort things out was becoming a habit.

She looked at me with horror.

"*No!* No. I've asked him already. Nothing helps. They think I'm mad." She leaned forward confidingly. "I hear things, too. It sounds as though things are moving under my cottage."

"What sort of sounds? Things?" I demanded.

"You'll think I'm mad, too."

"No," I reassured her. "I'm very serious. Something or someone has obviously frightened you very badly. I want to find out what it is. And then I want to see if there's anything I can do to help you."

"Do you?" she questioned, apparently amazed. "You believe me? And you want to help? Oh, thank you." And, to my horror, tears hopped down her veiny cheeks. She fished a handkerchief from her sleeve and blew her thin nose. I gave her a minute or two to compose herself and then I said, as gently as I could:

"That's right. But I can't help you unless you tell me everything."

Mavis took a deep breath, sniffed long and loudly, her thin nostrils pinching together, and words flooded out of her mouth.

"I live alone now. My mother died last year and I nursed her to the end. I am lonely and it's very quiet round by the churchyard. There's no traffic, you see. But recently..."

"How recently?" I interrupted.

She considered. "I suppose it started about three months ago. There was a lot of larking about in the churchyard by those boys — the ones I mentioned and their cronies. It had been so quiet until then."

"What did they do?"

"In the beginning they just rode around on their bikes, laughing and generally mucking about. It was a nuisance but boys will be boys... then one day I found them smoking. I said they were too young and that I would tell their parents if I saw them doing it again."

"And did you?"

"No, they seemed abashed. But the next day they were there again, smoking — and this time they had a bottle of beer. Actually it was probably more than a bottle. I was walking towards them, quite purposefully I expect, and the next thing I knew a beer bottle flew past my head — so close that I could feel it. Well!"

"Quite!" I said, with feeling. "What happened next?"

"That was the last straw! I marched up to them and said that I was going to report them to the police. That bottle could have killed me."

"Did you see who it was who actually threw the bottle?"

"No," she said slowly. "But I'm sure it was one of them."

"You're certain?" I pressed. "It was definitely either Jimmy Gibbs or Matthew De Cham?"

"N...no," she quavered. "I can't say it was *definitely* either of them. But I am sure the bottle was thrown from that direction by someone among their crowd."

"Thank you. And then?"

"After that it really started. That night they began banging on my window. I find dogs' excrement on my doorstep. They shout and yell and swear. They punctured the tyres on my bicycle. I haven't had a moment's rest. Even when they're not there I'm waiting for it to start again."

"Do they do it to anyone else?"

"No, that's the odd thing. They wait until I'm alone, when the neighbours are out or have their television on loudly — they're all deaf round me, anyway. I know one of my neighbours had a word with them and I expected them to start on her. But no, they're as sweet as pie to her."

"And you called Neil?" I queried.

"Indeed, I did!" she said indignantly. "He came round very quickly and spoke to them. I saw him. And I saw the rude gesture that Jimmy made in my direction, too, when Neil wasn't looking. In fact, I've called Neil several times but he tells me that he's never seen them do any of the things I've mentioned. And he says they deny it. But each time Neil comes everything gets worse afterwards. Oh dear." Miss Blanchard put her head in her hands and sobbed.

"What about the other sounds?" I asked when her shoulders stopped heaving.

She raised a tear-sodden face to me. I had seldom seen anyone look so overwrought.

"They're just terrible. Sometimes I think I'm going out of my mind. I thought it might be rats but if it is they must have hobnailed boots on." She attempted a watery smile. "There are definite steps going across the sitting room. Not one pair of feet. It sounds like a least ten pairs. All I want to do is to watch my television in peace. Is that so much to ask?"

She looked as though she were going to cry again so I asked quickly:

"Where were the footsteps? You say they go across your sitting room. Does it sound as if they are coming from upstairs, in the room above?"

"No. Funnily enough, the sound seems to come from underneath the house. Footsteps cross the sitting room and then lead to my stairs. But there's no-one there. Nothing to see. I wonder if the house is haunted?" Miss Blanchard stopped speaking, and her knuckles whitened as she gripped her handbag even more tightly. "No, of course it can't be. The Reverend assured me there was nothing untoward in the house. I ask you! No wonder they call me names."

"Correct me if I'm wrong, but it seems that you haven't actually seen anyone do any of these things? Even those you *think* Jimmy and Matthew are doing? Am I right?" I asked, softening my words by adding: "If I'm to help you, I need to know what hard evidence there is, you see."

Mavis considered for a moment and then said, with a firmness in her voice that had been absent before: "Yes, you are right. I haven't *seen* Jimmy or Matthew or anyone else do anything. But truly, Mrs Dawkins, it is very, *very* frightening. When it happens, I'm convinced I have intruders in the house. I ring Neil, as he told me to, but he always seems to be out when I call."

"Does this happen at any particular time?"

"No, but it's nearly always after dark. Sometimes it's three in the morning."

"Goodness me!" I exclaimed. "Are there any other sounds, apart from footsteps?"

She hesitated. "Yes. This sounds stupid, I know. I sometimes hear a scraping sound as if someone were dragging something heavy, or a rolling.... But you must think..."

"I think someone is trying to scare you very badly," I said firmly. "And the question is: *why?*"

Bruce was waiting for me in the car, his nose in a newspaper which he had folded into quartos and had propped on the steering wheel. Both the vehicle's doors were open.

"Stone the crows but it's bloody hot!" was his greeting. He folded the paper into a small parcel and stowed it under the dashboard before leaping out to hold the passenger door open for me. "Let's get you home."

I staggered wearily to the proffered door and collapsed onto the seat, exhaustion overtaking me. I was sure the baby was deep in sleep; I could feel an occasional stray arm or leg thumping against my ribs as he or she turned over. Poppadum rose from the rear seat to sniff the back of my neck in greeting. Bruce slammed his door shut and we were on our way.

Bruce had been right; apart from a faint smell of burning the house was none the worse for the smokescreen. The broken window-pane had been re-glazed and the afternoon sun was streaming into the sitting room. We wandered around opening all the doors and windows which our local bobby had conscientiously fastened before he left, and the house felt really pleased that we were home again. I was surprised to find it so clean and tidy — as though a good fairy had entered and waved a magic wand to clear all the smoke and anxiety away. I said as much to Bruce.

"That's because a good fairy *has* been and cleaned it for you," he said.

"Really?" I was amazed. "Who?"

"No idea, eh?" he teased.

"None." I wondered who would have been so very thoughtful.

"Marigold!"

"Marigold?" I asked automatically, slightly bemused. The only Marigold I knew was...

"Marigold Green, of course! How many Marigolds do you know?"

"Marigold?" I repeated, as if my gramophone needle had stuck on the name. "How did she know? How very kind of her." And to my dismay I burst into tears yet again.

"Come here, Haze," Bruce reached for me and pulled me against his chest, letting me weep. "You seem to have become quite famous here in Rype. I was almost swamped with offers of help to clear up. Marigold was the first and I thought you'd like her to be the one to do it. She certainly felt she'd like to help *you*."

"Really?" It was all I could manage, repetitive though my vocabulary had become.

"Yep. She said she'd heard from Phyllis White that you were a treasure. And she said that you shouldn't be doing that sort of cleaning work in your condition. I said I'd do it but she positively shooed me away to look after you."

"How sweet of her." I sniffed; my nose was running. I was tempted to wipe it on his shirt but he handed me a handkerchief before I could. I blew my nose and dabbed at my eyes, leaving daubs of brownish-black eyeliner and mascara all over it. At least I could wash this one, I thought. But I was annoyed and fed up with acting like a watering can as soon as something vaguely emotional touched me. I attempted a smile.

"Apparently Blue Jeans Adam is not very popular. Stories of your prowess in downing him have spread round the town like wildfire. When I was in the pub I was congratulated on having a wife with a great left hook! Though I was tempted to disabuse that particular chap of the notion, I thought better of it. I reckon anyone will think twice before taking you on now."

He kissed me, turned me round and pushed me in the direction of the kitchen. There was a note on the kitchen counter, kept in place by a vase of yellow tulips.

'*Dear Hazel,*' it read, '*I hope you will find everything back to normal. There's a cottage pie in the oven for your tea, and some broad beans in the fridge. Take care of yourself — good people are scarce. With best wishes, Marigold Green.*'

"No more tears, now," Bruce exclaimed, seeing the probability. "I prescribe a cool bath and then a rest. I'll fix dinner later, thanks to Marigold. Shoo!"

"Thank you, darling," I said appreciatively. "I'll phone Marigold afterwards to thank her."

The thought of a bath was wonderful; the reality was even better. I was lying there watching the Bump do its usual contortions when Bruce came in with a large glass of water.

"Just what I need," I exclaimed.

"I should know you by now," he grinned. He drew up the bathroom stool, dumped my clothes from it onto the floor and sat down. "Feeling better?" he enquired.

"Much," I responded feelingly.

"In that case, darl, we need to have a chat."

"I know," I said seriously. "It's my opinion that there's something more going on in Rype than we have discovered. Now all we have to do is to work out what it is."

"Yep. Easier said than done, though," Bruce commented. "But before we get our brains working on that ... what do you expect me to do with this?" He rummaged in his pocket and produced the key that I had handed to him on my way into the bank.

"Oh, that." I tried to sound off-hand. I had my own plan for trying to fit that key into a lock but it would have to be another time. My plan did not include Bruce.

"It belongs to Mrs Pendant," I went on. "I'll return it to her tomorrow. Just leave it on the oak chest with the others."

"Not good enough, Hazel!" His eyes were gleaming with amusement. "I know there's more to it than that. And you never did tell me what you'd found in the deeds."

I supposed I did owe him some explanation. Much as I hated to admit it, I didn't know the significance of the key nor quite what I'd intended to do with it. But I could tell him what I'd found in the deeds and it would be good if we could finally work out all that was going on. Bruce's reasoning skills would be very useful. I could see that my chance of a rest that afternoon was fast receding.

"Okay," I said. "Leave me for five minutes. Then I'll haul myself out of here and we'll see if we can unravel this mystery."

"Five minutes," he agreed, putting the stool back and picking up my clothes. "I'll put these in the washing basket and bring you some fresh ones."

I lay back in the bath.

"What do you think, Bump?" I asked. The reply came in the form of a kick behind my breastbone which took my breath away. "Quite right," I said. "I needed a kick. Saved me kicking myself. How could I have been so stupid as not to have seen it earlier? We must tell your Daddy."

Heaving myself out of the bath was tricky but I managed it without swamping the room with water. I swathed myself in a towel; Bruce had removed my worn clothes but he had not yet brought me the promised fresh ones. I would have to find my own. I opened the bathroom door and slipped. I felt myself falling, falling, falling ....

A peculiar feeling embraced me, a deep silence that was becoming slowly familiar. I blinked. I thought I had fallen but I was on my feet.

The room I had entered was the one in my dream. It was completely dark except for the glow of the fire. There was no sound apart from the creak of the rocking chair where a woman sat by the hearth, a baby in her arms. Her head was bent and I thought she was sleeping. The silence grew heavier, so heavy I felt I could hardly breathe. The pressure on my chest was almost unbearable and then, suddenly, pure and clear, a nightingale's song pierced the night and lifted the weight from my heart.

The woman's head came up and a joyful smile lit her features. She did not see me for she was looking past me to the back door, waiting. Simply waiting in anticipation. It opened, and there stood the tall figure of a man, silhouetted against the silvery light of a glorious full moon. He swept off a three-cornered hat to reveal dark curls. His teeth gleamed in a smile but it was the woman who broke the silence.

"Jack," she whispered, and I saw that she was trembling."'Tis, thee, Jack?"

He spoke not a word in answer, but strode across the bare boards and swept her, babe and all, into his arms. The baby was eerily quiet but the woman's sobs filled the room. I could feel the thump of their hearts.

"Hush!" the word was not spoken; rather, it reverberated through my head. She quietened and laid her cheek against his, her free hand coming up to press his head closer. He bent and picked her up; and, as he strode back to the door, I saw the love in their locked eyes and felt her tremulous, unbelieving joy.

"'Tis thee! 'Tis thee! I knew thou would'st return to us!"

He kicked the door closed behind them.

Silence descended again, oppressive and stifling. I waited for — what? I didn't know. My heart was beating hard, but through its pounding I heard the rhythmic thrum of hooves along a dirt track.

The thudding of my heart was echoed by a drumming in my head. I battled to open my eyes. As I did so, blinking and trying to focus, the night disappeared, the silence instantly dissipated and I found myself on the floor of the lobby outside the bathroom. Of Bruce there was no sign.

- 34 -

Of Confined Spaces

I was about to call him when I became aware of voices coming from the sitting room: Bruce's and a deep, resonant voice that I didn't instantly recognise.

'What now?' I thought, as the shout died on my lips. 'I'm lying on the floor, naked, not a clothe in sight, and Bruce has entirely forgotten me.'

Tears of self-pity rose in my eyes but I blinked them away. Tears were useless in my present circumstances. If I could just pull myself up into a standing position.... I took stock. The lobby was very small and I was very large. I must have passed out slowly for, instead of falling forwards or backwards, I appeared to have turned sufficiently to slide down against the wall flopping over on to my side. If I could reverse the process there was hope that I would be able to right myself. However, there were added problems: my head had wedged itself between the wall and the huge china vase we used as an umbrella stand, and one arm was trapped beneath me and thus virtually useless. With my free arm, I managed to move the vase sufficiently to enable me to raise my head a little, but there was no way I could push myself up sideways. There was only one thing for it. I pulled my knees up to my belly and, after a couple of false starts, I managed to roll over into something approximating the yogic 'pose of a child'.

My head was still trapped between the wall and the vase, my naked bottom was in the air and the Bump was squashed into my knees and complaining at the indignity by hitting out in all directions. I heard footsteps coming towards me. Our visitor probably needed the toilet that also opened off the lobby. The door opened outwards. Anyone opening it would discover me displayed like a biological specimen pinned to a board. Panic lent me strength. I finally managed to push myself back on to my heels and grab the hand towel that I had dropped. It covered most of the Bump but left my breasts bare. I did what any other woman would have done in the circumstances. I screwed my eyes shut.

I heard the door open. A soft fluttering. Then an incredulous silence. I opened my eyes a crack. Bruce was peering down at me anxiously.

"Darl! What are you doing down there?" I saw the emotions fleeting across his face: shock, concern, worry and ... laughter. How dare he?

"I fell, that's all." I said crossly. "You just try and get a great, lumbering body like mine up from this cramped, *minuscule* lobby. And that vase has to go!" I would have kicked it if I'd had a foot free.

Bruce bent to hide his grin and to pick up the pile of clothes he'd dropped.

"Here," he said, swathing me in a bath towel from the pile. "Don't get cold."

I glared at him. He grabbed me under the arms and tried to pull me up. The towel slipped. It was hopeless. There was simply no room to manoeuvre.

"Is everything all right?" the deep voice called from the sitting room.

"No, Doctor, I'm afraid not." Bruce answered before I could think of any way to stop him. "I need help, please."

I redoubled the ferociousness of my glare and hissed at him the worst insult I could find at the time.

"You ... you ... you ... bloody bastard!"

Dr. Hadley put his head round the door. He did not laugh. He did not even smile. I could have hugged him.

"Oh dear," he said as he managed to tread over me into the bathroom doorway. "I think this calls for a spot of nautical knowledge. I enjoy sailing, fortunately. Do you have another towel?"

Bruce nodded and went to find one. The doctor knelt in the

bathroom doorway and looked into my eyes as he took my pulse.

"You'll live," he pronounced. "Have you hurt yourself? Any pains in your back? A headache? Any sharp pains?"

"No, I'm fine," I told him, "At least, I will be when I can stand up."

Bruce reappeared and between them, he and the doctor threaded another towel under my buttocks. They both lifted me, a hand each on the towel and another under my arm ... pulled hard ... and I staggered to my feet. I could hardly stand, my legs ached abominably and my feet were full of pins and needles. Somehow they managed to manoeuvre me through the door and steer me to the settee. I settled myself there with relief; Bruce making sure I was well wrapped while the doctor politely averted his gaze.

"I'll make a cup of tea," said Bruce, disappearing into the kitchen

Dr. Hadley sat facing me, his face stern.

"Take care, Mrs Dawkins. A fall like that is not good for the baby."

"I know. I didn't fall on purpose. I must have slipped." I felt indignant.

"Nonetheless, take care," he said. "You seem to have been in the wars recently."

Something about the way he said it made me shiver inwardly.

"Yes, you could say that," I said, lightly. "Not intentionally, though."

"From what I hear, it appears you have become mixed up with the criminal element around here," he said, frowning. "I suggest you stop meddling and leave everything to the police."

"Well!" I was astounded by his rudeness.

He carried on talking over my exclamation.

"There's another matter. I understand from Mr Stone that you saw Mavis Blanchard this afternoon. That's the reason for my visit. I have come to warn you. Miss Blanchard has been a patient of mine for a long time and she simply cannot be trusted. Pay no attention to anything she tells you. She takes a great deal of medication to control her hallucinations, but they are getting worse."

"I see."

"Very silly woman at the best of times," he persisted. "Catherine Pendant is a similar case. Suffered a lot in the War. Still suffers from a persecution complex. Too much self-medication. Whisky usually. Ignore her."

"I see no reason ..." I began, but Dr. Hadley carried on peremptorily:

"You must tell me what that silly woman Mavis told you. I need to know, as her doctor."

"I'm afraid that is between me and my client, Doctor," I said as icily as I could, given the circumstances.

"Come, come, Mrs Dawkins, we are both professional people."

"Quite," I agreed. "As such, we are both bound to keep such matters confidential."

"Now, now, young woman, you know that does not apply between professionals. I insist. You must tell me."

I could feel my dander rising at this patronising speech. I took a deep breath to help keep my temper in check. I was even more annoyed that I was in the embarrassing situation of being undressed, which fact alone prevented me from rising in a huff.

Two could play at this game of hauteur, however.

"I fear it does apply to *me*," I informed him stonily. "I need express permission from my client before I can divulge anything that she has said to me in confidence. She has not given that permission and I do not intend to ask her for it."

The doctor stood up, drawing himself very straight. I drew myself up, too, ridiculous as I felt in my towel. I waited for his response with every sinew in my body tight and ready for action. Bruce chose that moment to reappear with the tea tray.

"How do you like your tea, Doctor?" he enquired.

"Tea? No, I don't think so," Dr. Hadley barked. "I'm leaving." Turning on his heel he said, curtly, over his shoulder, "You should shake some manners and sense into that ... that ... *young woman* you call your wife, Bruce. She has no idea how to behave."

Bruce's jaw dropped in astonishment. The front door slammed before he could shut his mouth. I held out my hand for a cup of tea feeling the smugness of the smile on my face.

I felt better after the tea. Better enough to get dressed in clean clothes and to laugh with Bruce about the doctor's patronising air.

"He's just an old fart," Bruce summed him up. "He thinks a lot of himself. And he's not alone in that. Everybody round here seems to fall down on their knees when he goes by. Even Blue Jeans Adam."

I raised an eyebrow in disbelief.

"Well, maybe not on their knees," he amended. "But they certainly do as he says. He must be most put out that a *young woman* is not prepared to give him the information he wants."

I was still nettled. "I know I'm in the right. How dare he ask me to betray a client's confidence? What's it to him anyway, I'd like to know?"

"I expect we'll find out in due course. Anyway, Haze, he's a respected figure round here so I humbly suggest you treat his information with respect and look at your clients in the light of it."

"All right, I will. But only for you." I agreed.

"Good. Now, what about this key?"

He produced it from his trouser pocket.

"Ah, yes ..." I murmured wondering what fabrication, or over-simplification, he would fall for. It was his turn to raise an eyebrow.

I decided to come clean.

"It's a key that I found in one of the seal tins attached to the Act of Attainder," I told him, noting that the eyebrow showed no sign of returning to its usual level.

"Oh, yes?" Bruce rejoined. "And what does that mean, precisely?"

"It's the Act that forms the root of Mrs Pendant's title to her house ..." I began, mildly enough, but he interrupted me, obviously convinced I was obfuscating:

"And you're telling me an *Act* had a *tin* attached to it? With a *key* in it?"

Annoyed now, I scrutinised him from under lowered brows; his colour was very high and his brows were drawn together in a frown. For a moment I struggled between reacting haughtily or humbly. I decided that a little humility would not go amiss.

"No, honestly," I said evenly. "I know it sounds ridiculous, but the Act of Attainder was sealed in the seventeenth century and the seals of the Houses of Parliament were literally impressed into soft sealing wax — so they had to be put into tins to keep the seals intact."

"You sure you're not kidding me?"

"Cross my heart."

"And there was a *key* in the tin?" Bruce was still incredulous.

"I know what you're thinking. I was *most* surprised to find it there."

"Okay, I'll take your word for it," Bruce conceded. "Why did you take it?"

"I don't know." I said hesitantly, forced to examine my motive. "It was on the spur of the moment. I suddenly thought that it might help us unravel a bit more of this mystery."

"What mystery? I thought we'd worked out a scenario." Still curt.

"True, we have, but I think there's more to this fishy business than meets the eye of the camel passing through the needle ..." I giggled.

Bruce refused the bait. He sighed.

"Behave, darling," he said wearily. "We have to work this out — and work it out *soon*. I can't have you fainting all over the place, let alone having arguments with all and sundry."

"All right. Let's see, we had agreed that ..." I counted the points off on my fingers. "One, there is something going on next door to Mrs Pendant. Two, this is probably something to do with drugs.

Three, something was put into the deed packet. And four, that something was probably collected — possibly by Neil who is always around at the appropriate time. Is that agreed, so far?"

"Yes, what else is there?"

"I'm thinking this may be tied in with something else. Do you remember that Tom was talking about all the secret tunnels round here?"

"Yes, of course. He said the tunnels ran from the shore!" He sounded disparaging.

"And Mrs Pendant was sure that there were people up in the loft?"

"Yes, but I thought we agreed they were probably cultivating cannabis." Bruce's brow furrowed in puzzlement. I rushed on:

"I know. But just suppose there's another racket going on. Mark was telling me that people trafficking is still rife and very lucrative. Suppose that the drugs — soft drugs after all — are eyewash. Suppose *someone* has found the old tunnels used by the smugglers and *is still using them*?"

"Good God!"

I laughed at the look of astonishment on his face.

"I know you think this is the product of an over-active imagination," I said. "But when I checked through Mrs P's deeds I found that, as she said, she'd inherited the house from her uncle, Arthur Chapman. When her uncle bought it in the nineteen twenties, Old Owlers was one dwelling but, probably because of the depression, it was divided into two residences in the nineteen thirties — one of which was sold." I paused.

"Okay, I'm following."

"Of course you are. But here it gets complicated. Shall we call Mrs P's half of the house 'A' and Petronilla's half 'B'?"

"Okay," he said, humouring me.

"Mrs Pendant's uncle kept A and sold B. With me so far?"

"Yes."

"Now, the interesting thing is that there's what's called 'a

Reservation' in the Conveyance — that's the Conveyance of B — reserving the right for the owners of A *to the cellar below and the roof space above B*," I informed him jubilantly.

"So?"

"So, Mrs P inherits her part of the house, Part A, after the war. She knows nothing about the cellar and you can only get to the roof space through Petronilla's half, Part B."

"And that means ..."

"It's obvious isn't it? The De Chams, or whoever owned B at the time, swopped one half of the property for the other. Mrs P is actually living in the half that was conveyed away. She's living in B — and Petronilla's living in A."

"But how come she doesn't know? Or does she?" Bruce was looking even more puzzled.

"She's probably never seen the deeds until now — and her uncle's solicitor was up in Leeds somewhere. He would have made sure her title to the property was correct and in order. That's all. The title *is* in order. He would have had no reason to think that the wrong half was empty. Mrs Pendant simply moved into the part that was vacant."

"How do *you* know, then?"

"There was a Memorandum of Conveyance endorsed on the back of the Conveyance to Mrs Pendant's uncle. It was in very small insignificant handwriting but, of course, I was looking for it — or, at least, for *something*. Originally there was a plan attached as well, but it had come away. I found it wedged inside the lease of A. That was the other part of the puzzle."

"A lease? I thought Mrs P owned it freehold."

"Yes, she does. Her uncle did, too, but he didn't live there. He leased his half — that's A — to a Mr Jeremiah Joshua Hadley in 1936."

Another unlikely possibility suggested itself to me.

"Oh!" I gasped

"What?"

I closed my mouth and smiled enigmatically — I hoped.

"Nothing."

"Hazel ... I know you. What aren't you telling me?"

"Something I haven't thought through yet. Something that has made me smell a rat — but it may be only a red herring!" I grinned.

"Hazel! I'll ... I'll ..."

"But," I went on quickly, before he decided to tickle me. "I think it's quite possible that the key I found in the seal tin is the key to the cellar. And, if it is, we could go down and see if we can find any evidence."

"Oh I see," he sniffed. "We wander into someone else's house, find a cellar door, open it, hunt around for evidence of illegal, and probably imaginary, people trafficking! All under the noses of some rather suspect people — and then what? If we find something we give it to *Neil*? Somebody we think is involved? You must be off your rocker."

"Nope." I said smugly. "I have a completely different plan. But right now, I have some Wills to draft for the Smiths and a Will and a Power of Attorney to draft for Elizabeth Hudson."

I got up, kissed his forehead and went to work in the bedroom.

- 35 -

Of Decoy and Chase

The silver light of a gibbous moon shimmers on the new green leaves of the ash tree. The horse stamps his foot and jerks his head, jangling his bridle. I sway with the movement, soothing him instinctively. The sweetish smell of horse is thick about me as I wait at the crossroads. Stiff as I am in every joint and sinew, my body screams for me to dismount and stretch my legs, but I cannot. Some intuition, some sense of impending doom, holds me motionless. I am aware it will not be long.

I flinch as the expectant hush is broken by the screech of an owl, eerie in the stillness that binds me to the saddle. The owl circles silently above me, seeking her tiny prey. I watch her until she slides away into the blackest of the shadows, where the sacred ash grove huddles beneath the escarpment.

My eyes seek the hallowed place where the Earth Mother is still honoured by man and maid on the sacred feast of Beltane, where they come in the dawning, clad in white and garlanded in green. May blossoms wreathe their brows as they stand side by side under a living canopy of ash boughs for their hand-clasping. A ceremony of rejoicing in union. A celebration of Life in dance and song. For this is the seven-treed sacred grove to which my beloved and I came not long ago; where we swore an oath to honour our love; and where, later, alone beneath the moon-silvered leaves, we became one in the flesh, too.

It grows cold now, and I shiver. I open my ears, listening, listening — a small sound trembles towards me; perhaps no more than a fluctuation in the air current. Then the liquid exquisiteness of the nightingale's song fills the air with its molten beauty. It is the signal. Jack's signal.

I fire my weapon into the sky and wheel my mount, pulling sharply on the reins. We race off into the night. Lying close to the horse's back, my head beside his ear, I ride hard. For a moment or two, as we gather speed, I choose those places where the low light gleams through the covering of cloud. I catch the sound of hooves in swift pursuit and know I have been seen. Now I guide my good companion into the gloom of the darkest shadows, allowing the horse to choose his footing on the causeway. He gallops smoothly on.

I risk a look behind. Shapes pursue us, legless in the mist rising from the Marsh, centaurs riding hard in a curved bow-shaped line. The triumph and excitement of the men who chase me is almost palpable. How long were they waiting close to the crossroads where I myself waited?

I let the gelding have his head. He knows these levels well. His hooves drum into the earth. I crouch low in the saddle, horse sweat hot-smelling in my nostrils. I cling to his mane. I risk another backward glance but I see nothing. I am sure we are gaining on our pursuers. But have they ridden yet into the trap? That part of the Marsh that is quicksand, that will swallow horse and rider whole?

The moon is hidden now, I have no bearings, all I hear is a thrumming, thrumming, thrumming. I know not whether it is my heart beating in my ears or the sound of pursuit. All I can do is ride....

- 36 -

Of Needles and Mysteries

The following morning I set off up the High Street once again, leaving my trusty Poppadum to guard the house from intruders.

The evening before, I'd been delighted to find that after my discussion with Bruce my brain was focussed and sharp. My creative juices had flowed so well and so fast that I'd completed the drafts of the Power of Attorney and Will much more quickly than I'd anticipated. I'd peeped into the sitting room to find Bruce mesmerised by the television so I decided to carry on and prepare the engrossments ready for signature. For once, the old typewriter had co-operated. Within a couple of hours the engrossments were ready for Elizabeth's signature. I'd also drafted the Wills for the Smiths.

Bruce had brought a cup of tea up to me and found me sewing Elizabeth's Will together with black tape with Poppadum curled up on the floor beside me.

"What *are* you doing?" he asked incredulously.

"I'm just sewing this Will together," I replied, unperturbed.

"*Sewing*?"

"As you see." I was enjoying teasing him.

"Why on earth ...?"

"I didn't have enough of that special Will paper. I've had to type it on separate sheets of foolscap engrossment paper — and that means it has to be sewn together."

"But I thought you said it all had to be on one sheet of paper."

"You're quite right. That's the best way for any document, especially for Wills. But if that's not possible, you can sew the document up like this." I waved the big-eyed needle, still attached to the narrow black tape. "The thing I *must* remember now is to make sure that the Testator — or rather, this time, the Testatrix — and the witnesses *all* sign their names on *each* page of the Will."

"I suppose you're going to tell me that's because you're not supposed to attach anything to a Will?" Bruce suggested.

"So you *were* listening. Now, do you know why I'm using *black* tape?"

"To sew it up?"

"Oh. You. Idiot." I chided fondly. "Yes, of *course*. But why aren't I using red tape?"

"Why do I have a feeling that you're going to tell me?"

"Probably because I am! It's a convention in the legal profession. Black for Wills; green for Agreements and other non-litigious documents; and red for Court documents and for binding up bundles of papers," I said, trying my best not to sound pompous.

"So that's where the saying 'too much red tape' comes from. I might have guessed lawyers were involved somewhere," Bruce teased.

I slipped the needle from the tape and tied the traditional double knot in the middle of the front sheet.

"There. Doesn't that look neat?" I asked, admiring my handiwork.

"Indeed it does," he agreed. "You had just the right amount of tape. Very clever."

"That's because I measured it," I said. "Two and a half times the length between the first and last holes."

"Holes?"

"Yes, I made them first, with the needle. Five holes about half an inch in from the edge. The first in the middle, the next two holes about an inch in from the top and bottom of the page, and the other two equally spaced between. Then it's just a case of ordinary back stitch, starting from the middle and ..."

"Very clev ..."

"I suppose it's more like a version of blanket stitch," I reflected, holding the document up the better to inspect the stitches that were oversewn along its length.

"Quite possibly, darl. Now, tell me – have you finished your endeavours for tonight?"

"Yes, it's definitely time for bed," I admitted, carefully stowing the Will and Power of Attorney away in a folder.

And so it was with some pride that I set off with my briefcase tucked under my arm into yet another warm and beautiful morning. The High Street was busy and it seemed that everyone I passed was as happy as I. Women smiled at me generously and men raised or touched their hats with a murmured 'Good Morning'.

Elizabeth's door was ajar again. On this particular lovely morning, however, there was no air of menace nor any strange atmosphere. I had a presentiment that Mark would be there, and, sure enough, I heard his voice upraised in song as I set foot on the stair. I paused long enough for him to finish his rendering of 'Dear Lord and Father of Mankind' before I entered.

This time he was seated on the bed, holding her hand; Elizabeth was lying back against the pillows, her face pale and her eyes closed. She was very still and for a moment I thought she had already passed away. Then her eyelids fluttered softly and her chest rose a fraction.

Mark looked at me and slowly shook his head, pressing a finger to his lips as he did so. Tears pricked my eyes and I began to retreat as silently as I could. Elizabeth must have heard me, for her head turned towards me, her eyes slowly opened and her hand moved convulsively on the sheet.

Blinking the tears away, I drew closer and stood on the other side of the bed from Mark. Elizabeth's lips twitched. She put her hand on her chest and slowed her breathing. With what seemed a stupendous effort she whispered:

"Have you brought it?"

I nodded, withdrawing the Will from my thin briefcase.

"I just need to read it through to you, Elizabeth, to make sure it's what you want. Is that all right?"

Her lips twitched into a half smile; she mouthed 'yes' though no sound came out. I sat on the bed and took her hand in mine.

"You don't have to speak. Squeeze my hand if there's anything you don't understand,"

The Will was short; it did not take long to read. I was very pleased that I had managed to take her rambling instructions and distil them into three pages of foolscap. Elizabeth appeared to be concentrating but the hand I held stayed still.

"Squeeze if everything is as you wanted your Will to be." I felt the soft pressure of her fingers. I looked at Mark, questioningly. I wanted to ensure that he had noticed. He nodded and reached into his medical bag.

"I have a pen here," he said, passing it to me. "Elizabeth, my dear, let me support you while I put this cushion in your back. There. Now you can sign more easily."

I checked the ink in the pen was blue, so that there would be no question that the document might be a photocopy, before I gave it to Elizabeth.

I held the Will firmly on top of my briefcase and offered it to her.

"I need one signature, here," I pointed. "However you normally sign a cheque."

She laboriously signed her name. Her signature was full of flourishes.

"Only two more, now. Here ... and here. Don't worry, I'll date it and Mark and I have most of the writing to do." I showed her where to sign at the top of each of the other pages of her Will. When she had finished I thanked her, quickly dated it and added my signature, name, address and occupation at the end of the Will. Then I added my signature below hers on its other two pages. I passed the document to Mark and he did the same before handing it back to me.

"There," I said, more briskly than I intended because I was keeping my tears at bay. "That's all done, now. You don't need to worry about it any more."

A beautiful smile lit up Elizabeth's face. Pulling Mark closer, she whispered something in his ear. His lips sketched a sad half smile as he raised his eyes towards the ceiling and his wonderfully rich tenor rang out in 'O Sole Mio'.

I watched as her smile broadened and then froze. A small choking noise came from her throat. Her eyes widened and grew still. Mark's voice broke. His eyelashes hid his eyes as he drew her fingers to his lips. Gently replacing her hand on the coverlet, he closed her eyes with his fingertips. He bent his head as if in prayer and I did the same. I was not sure what prayer to say but the words of the Lord's Prayer rose naturally to my lips.

We stood then and it was natural to move together. Mark put his arm round me in a one-armed hug.

It was only then that I remembered the power of attorney. No matter that she had not signed it, the document was quite redundant now.

Together, Mark and I descended the steps and there we parted, he to go back to the surgery and me to go on to visit Mavis.

Having carefully locked the door, Mark gave me a swift peck on the cheek before he dashed away. He would have to write out the death certificate but as the executor of her Will it was my task to make the funeral arrangements. The sudden transition from the stillness of death in Elizabeth's flat into the busy-ness of a sunny morning in Rype High Street was odd; it was as if I had walked into another existence.

I was considering this as I dropped into the bank and asked Helen to keep Elizabeth's Will in the bank's safe for the time being. I was not very happy about the safety of documents in my home.

I looked at my wristwatch. I had an appointment with Mavis Blanchard but not for another half an hour. I calculated that I had time for a swift visit to the undertaker whose shop was not far from the bank and on the way to Mavis' house. Pushing the door hard, I entered the low-beamed medieval building to the accompaniment of a clanging bell. Startled, I turned to find the melodious object hanging on a curved brass bracket on the back of the door and thus set ringing by my entrance. I was even more disconcerted by the apparition who unwound himself from a huge chair behind the small leather-topped table that acted as a desk.

When I'd entered the shop the Apparition had been hidden behind the newspaper he was reading. At my entrance, he folded the paper very slowly and unhurriedly uncoiled himself to his full height, stooping considerably to avoid hitting the ceiling. Dressed from head to toe in white, including the uppers of the huge platform shoes he wore, he regarded me through the small eyes my father would have called 'piss-holes in the snow'. A bulbous nose shone redly from a long face which was topped by a bald pate with shoulder-length lank brown hair hanging round the edges. I was speechless; he reminded me of a scarecrow and I wondered if he could speak. He soon put my mind to rest on that score:

"Good morning, madam," he welcomed me in a reedy voice. "My name is Ralph. Ralph Ralph to be precise. I'm minding the shop for Mr Clements who is otherwise engaged at present. How may I be of service?"

"Um," I said, dumbfounded by his name as much as by his appearance. "Um ... do you know when Mr Clements will be back?"

"Oh, he won't be long, madam," he assured me. The sound of a toilet flushing. I could feel myself blushing.

"I ... I'll wait then."

Ralph the Apparition offered me his chair. It was several sizes too large even for my increased girth and the arms were beginning to lose their filling, as though many an anxious person had clawed at them. Refusing with as much dignity as I could muster, I was pleased that Mr Clements took that moment to bundle himself into the room. He was short and round, his girth almost equal to his height, dressed in black and with an expression of unrelieved gloom on his face.

"Thank you, Ralph," he said, sonorously dismissing his assistant. The Apparition went out, setting the bell clanging again as he made his exit. Mr Clements reached up and stopped its sway with his hand.

"Ah, my dear," he said as he turned towards me. "How can I be of service?"

"Someone has just died ..." I began, the tears starting again. I sniffed hard.

"Oh my dear, you are so young. And with a baby on the way, too. My sincere condolences for your loss. May I ... uh ... ask ... who?"

"A client of mine," I said, briskly sniffing again, annoyed at the way his comments were peppered with 'dears'. "Elizabeth Hudson. I am her executrix, Hazel Dawkins."

I extended my hand. He shook it formally, retaining it as he said in his fruity voice:

"Ah, I have heard of you, my dear. Although I very much regret the circumstances, I'm glad to make your acquaintance."

He let go of my hand, rolled round to my side of the desk to set a chair for me and rolled back again.

"Please take a chair," he invited. He opened his notebook and took up a pen from the desk. I sat. It did not take me long to tell him what I knew and to invite him to telephone Mark for more information and to obtain access to Elizabeth's flat. I authorised him to collect the body and to lay it out. I also informed him that she had requested a simple cremation and that the funeral service would be held at the crematorium.

At this, he looked a little discomforted.

"Are you sure, m ... Mrs Dawkins? Do you not think it would be appropriate to have a service here in Rype? In my experience people do like the opportunity to say goodbye."

He had restrained himself from calling me 'my dear' and had consequently raised himself in my estimation. I paused.

"Thank you," I said at last. "I'll discuss the matter with Dr. Wilkinson."

"I believe Mrs Hudson used to attend the Friends' Chapel. Here is the Minister's name and telephone number. I imagine you would like to advise him of her death?"

"Thank you," I acknowledged again. "Is there anything else you need from me at present?"

"I imagine you would like a notice placed in the Kent Herald? It would be helpful if you would let me have the wording fairly soon. I will need the death certificate, too, in due course."

"Dr. Wilkinson said he will have it ready this afternoon," I said.

"Yes, that is the doctor's certificate. But you, as her Executor, will need to register the death at the Registry Office. The nearest one is in Folkestone. You will need to take Mrs Hudson's birth certificate and any marriage certificate with you, as well as the certificate Dr. Wilkinson will give you. It costs one pound fifty pence to register the death but I'm sure you know that. I imagine you will also need at least two copies of the certificate."

"Of course," I said, nodding, trying to appear as if I did this every day when it was must have been patently obvious to him that I did not. I had dealt with probate files often enough during my training as an articled clerk and subsequently, but I had never been an executor before.

"And then there is the question of the coffin, of course. Did Mrs Hudson give any specific instructions?" I shook my head. "I see she did not. There are a number of possibilities, but perhaps you would prefer to choose one at another time?"

"Yes, I do have something else I must attend to now," I said, standing up. "Thank you for your help, Mr Clements. I'll speak to the Minister and register the death as soon as I can." A thought struck me. "I wonder, do you, by any chance, have a pro forma for the newspaper notice that I could use, please?"

He smiled for the first time, passing me the paper that Ralph Ralph had been reading when I entered. "Not precisely, Mrs, Dawkins, but there are a number in here that you may care to peruse."

Trundling to the door, he opened it for me, stilling the bell with one hand, and bowed me out.

"Thank you for your instructions, Mrs Dawkins. I will collect

Mrs Hudson as you have requested. I will look forward to hearing from you further."

The old-fashioned words and his bow made me smile as I thanked him again and promised I would return soon. I put the newspaper in my briefcase.

Mavis' house was one of the terraced medieval cottages that ranged round two sides of the churchyard, which was roughly triangular in shape, the main road curving round the third side. I had left Mr Clements' establishment, walked up the path to the church and struck across the churchyard on the path that Mavis had mentioned. At the far end, a group of youngsters were hanging around, some on bicycles, others sitting on a low wall, smoking.

They moved to let me pass, their eyes cast earthwards, except for one who smirked at me, his eyes narrowing.

"Hello," I greeted him. "Can you direct me to number 3 Thatcher's Cottages, please?"

The youngster smirked a little more widely and I thought I detected a similarity to Petronilla De Cham. He was quite short and well-built, half sitting on a bicycle on which he was rocking to and fro in a manner that was somehow intimidating.

Off-handedly he jerked a thumb over his shoulder. "Third on the left," he said.

"Thank you."

As I set off, I heard a snort. I looked back and saw the little gang in a huddle around the boy. They were all facing me; there were some low-voiced comments I did not quite catch and a lot of sniggering. Just kids being objectionable kids, I thought, as I continued on my way, paying them no further attention.

"Hey! Mrs!"

The shout halted me in mid-step. I looked over my shoulder as the boy to whom I'd spoken drew his bicycle into the kerb beside me. I stepped back instinctively as he thrust his face close to mine and the stench of cheap tobacco hit my nostrils.

"If you're looking for Mavis," he said, with what I took for a sneer. "She's not there."

"How do you know?" I asked without thinking.

"I just know," he said sullenly. "We keep a look-out for her. She's a bit soft in the head. Doesn't know which way is up. Tells us off all the time — says we do things just to frighten her."

"Really?" I asked, my nose climbing a little too high for politeness. "And is she right, by any chance?"

"We can't help winding her up, but she's okay really, is Mavis."

I realised that what I had taken to be an unpleasant manner was, in fact, an adolescent combination of arrogance and diffidence.

"Why do you keep a look-out for her, then?" I asked as I walked on. He kept pace with me, scooting along on his bicycle.

"She's really scared by something. She thinks it's us, but it ain't."

"How do you know she's scared?"

"Policeman told us, asked us to look out for her."

"Oh, I see." Mavis had said Neil had spoken to the youngsters. "And you say she's not there now. Where is she, do you know?"

"Nope," he said. "Usually she would have been to the church by now. We ain't seen her at all."

"I take it you're Matthew De Cham?" I asked.

"Yes," he said, nodding.

We had reached Mavis' door. My escort turned the front wheel of his bike, about to turn back.

"Wait!" I demanded imperiously. "Shouldn't you be in school?"

"Nope, Mrs Dawkins," he shouted over his shoulder as he pedalled away fast. "It's half term."

"Of course," I shouted back, knowing I had been rather ungracious. "Thank you for your help."

'So Matthew knows who I am,' I thought. I was grateful for his information, such as it was, but I knew Mavis was expecting me and I didn't think she was the sort who would forget about our appointment. No doubt that was the reason she had not gone to the church.

Mavis' front door was of thick oak, banded with brass. Its brass ring handle also served as a knocker. Beside the door hung a doorbell, an old-fashioned affair with a pull handle. I pulled it hard. I could hear the bell jangling away but no-one came to the door. I tried again. Still no response.

Putting one foot across the bed of lavender that ran under the bow window of the front living room, I peered in. Heavy lace curtains crossed inside but there was a tiny gap through which I caught a glimpse of a tidy, rather shabby parlour. It was empty.

I grabbed the round brass knocker and struck it hard. To my surprise the door gave, swinging open to reveal a dark passage, the walls half-boarded and the floor covered in a rug that had seen better days.

"Hello!" I called. "Hello? Miss Blanchard? Mavis? It's Hazel Dawkins. Are you there?"

Still no answer. I hesitated on the threshold, unsure whether to go in or to leave. I was about to close the door, thinking that she must have forgotten our appointment. Perhaps she had made her way to the church by a route different from her usual one. Then I heard something. Not that I could make out what it was. I paused with one hand on the door and the other pressed to my belly to keep the baby quiet. The sound came again. An odd noise, like a cross between a thud and a moan.

"Hello?" I bellowed, listening hard.

The noise was repeated. It seemed to be coming from somewhere in the passage. It stopped. Silence. I ventured in, walking carefully along the rug. It was just as well I did, because I still managed to catch my toe in a wrinkle and had to steady myself, my hand making a hollow thump on the wall. The thump was answered with a long moan followed by a series of thuds.

"Hello? Mavis?"

I ran my hand along the wall. My fingers found a crack. Peering closely, I made out the edge of a door into what was probably an under-stair cupboard. But there was no handle. I walked further along the passage. The thumping resumed, faster, more urgent.

I opened the door at the far end of the corridor, my heart racing and my breath coming fast. A kitchen met my gaze, modern in the style of twenty years before, spick and span, and very empty. Turning to the left, I saw my instincts had been correct. A twisting staircase of bare boards led upwards but there was no way under it from this direction. I went back to the hall, patting along the stair wall. My heart was beating so hard that I could hear nothing else.

"I'm here," I called. "I'm trying to find a way ..."

My fingers met a chink in the wall. I pressed in, heard a slight click, and the door shifted inwards.

- 37 -

Of Darkness and Light

The door opened, as I'd surmised, into an under-stair cupboard, black as pitch inside but completely bare, as far as I could judge. I felt around for a light switch. There was none. All was silent now. I switched on the light in the passage. A single bulb swung from a socket above the stairs, the light it gave next to useless. I opened all the doors I could find. The parlour. The kitchen. The front door. Light flooded the passage but only lightened the gloom inside the cupboard a shade or two. Light enough, though, for me to see with panic-heightened eyesight, the edge of a trapdoor. Dropping to my knees, I knocked on it.

"Hello?" I called. There was a heartbeat of silence and then a slight thump and a mumble.

"Hold on," I shouted. "I'll get help."

A shadow fell across me and I nearly died of fright. The baby leapt within me. Doubled-up as I was, it almost winded me. Panic flooded through me as my brain worked overtime. I presumed someone had locked Mavis below, but suppose I had disturbed him. He might still be in the house.

"It's me, Mrs Dawkins," came Matthew's voice. "Did you say you needed help?"

Relief flooded over me, leaving me feeling as weak as a kitten. The babe's kicking became a fluttering.

"Yes," I managed breathlessly. "I think Mavis is trapped down here. Quick! Ride for the police!"

"Okay. Matt to the rescue!" he shouted, racing off. I could imagine him pedalling hard for Neil, beckoning all his companions to ride with him.

'Oh God!' I thought, 'We think Neil is involved in this.'

I dismissed the thought. From what Matthew had said, it seemed that Neil had asked them to look after Mavis, rather than to taunt her.

While these thoughts were racing through my head, I had the presence of mind to feel around the edges of the trapdoor with my fingers. Nothing, no catch or clip could I find. Of themselves my fingers widened the search. They found a brass ring, lying flat, let into the wood of the trapdoor. I scrabbled it into a raised position so that I could pull it. I heaved. The trapdoor did not move. I twisted the ring a little. It gave. I twisted it more and heard the click as the catch was freed, but the trapdoor remained obstinately shut. Anxious and apprehensive as I was, I had enough sense to pause and assess the situation.

There was not much room for me in the cupboard, which sloped sharply with the slope of the twisting stairs; I noted that the trapdoor was hinged so that it opened towards the back of the cupboard – but if I crawled into the deepest corner and heaved again I might just have sufficient strength and enough purchase on the brass ring to raise the panel from the floor. I had just completed my deliberations when the thumping suddenly recommenced, louder and more frantic than before.

Crawling into the corner I had identified, I set my back to the stairs, feeling the treads in hard ridges down my back, and tugged with all my might. For a long, long second nothing happened apart from a twinge in my shoulder – then the trapdoor leapt suddenly upwards and I toppled over, hitting my head hard on the stairs. Psychedelic lights flashed briefly deep within my head before blackness swallowed me whole.

A light shone in my eyes. It was painful; I turned my head and put up a hand to shield myself from its brightness. A gentle hand was stroking my hair and something damp was pressed against my forehead, so comforting that I felt I wanted nothing more than to allow the darkness to descend again. A flicker of thought dashed behind my closed eyelids and I forced them open, wondering where I was.

"Shhh ..." A kind feminine voice pervaded my semiconsciousness.

"Rest," she commanded. "'Twas a hard knock thou hast took to thine head. Rest now. I will watch."

My eyes closed of their own accord and I dozed, slipping back into unconsciousness where I dreamed of a voice calling me from a long distance away.

"Hazel ... Hazel ... where are you?" A familiar, much-loved voice. I wanted to respond; I opened my mouth but no sound came. The voice faded and another whispered:

"Rest now. Rest ... all will be well."

When next I opened my eyes, I found myself again in darkness apart from a flickering light. I watched the glow from beneath my lowered lids until it gradually materialised into a candle flame in a storm lantern. There was a movement close to me and a dark shape emerged from the shadows. It was a woman: a woman who reminded me strongly of someone — but, of whom, I could not recall. She smiled, a dimpling of the cheeks that lit up her face.

"Thou art awake at last," she said, and her voice was as warm and deep as her smile.

"What happened? Where ... where am I?"

"Do not fear. Thou hast but slipped through the veil. Thou art safe here."

"But where am I?" I gasped, disorientated, as my glance took in arched supports, brick walls, a low ceiling and the brown dress of my nurse. It was long — or would have been save that at present it was kirtled above her boot-shod feet — slightly threadbare, nipped in at the waist, high of neckline and long in the sleeve.

I felt the familiar movement from my baby and endeavoured to rise.

"Nay, do not move yet," she said, gently pressing me down as I tried to push myself up. "Think of thy babe ... for 'tis not yet time for her to be born. Breathe deeply, thus." She took a deep breath and exhaled slowly. I followed her example, feeling a tangible calm envelop me as my breath and pulse-rate steadied.

"Drink this."

She held my head as she pressed a cup to my lips. I was very thirsty. I drank. It tasted bitter.

"What?" I sighed but allowed myself to subside into sleep once more as her whispered words washed over me.

"'Tis nought but a sleeping draught."

When I next woke it was to utter darkness. My head ached badly but my senses were keen for I was conscious of the heart-beat of my child as we lay inert. The candle flame no longer burned, but I was aware that I was not alone, for I could hear others breathing close by. Someone snored and another was gasping as though in pain.

I stirred, and became aware that my head was pillowed in a lap. A face floated above me as the Lady-of-the-Lamp moved. She was sitting propped against the wall and I understood that my movement must have woken her.

"Hush," she said, holding a finger to her lips. "Others sleep nearby. Let us discover whether thou canst yet keep thy feet."

After supporting me as I raised myself into a sitting position, she disentangled herself and lit another candle. She encouraged me to stand, holding me steady against her; she smelled warm and musky with a hint of dampness.

"There is a bucket yonder." She pointed into the darkness. "Methinks thou must have need of it?"

I would have preferred to have kept my privacy but I was in no position to refuse her help. I needed that bucket very badly, and my limbs were strangely heavy and unresponsive. Between us we managed and afterwards I felt much better.

"Here, drink this," she said, offering me another cup, a golden one this time. I must have looked askance for she answered my unspoken question.

"Nay, 'tis not a draught, 'tis pure water from the well," she assured me, nodding towards a pail on a pulley over a dark round hole in the floor. The conversation I had overheard in the garden of The Three Chimneys flew into my mind and out again instantaneously. I thanked her and took the cup, spilling some of the water in my haste to slake my thirst.

"The Reverend lets us use such vessels for water only," the girl informed me. "We are beneath the church, in the crypt. The crypt beside the crypt. 'Tis here that we hide from our enemies in time of trouble."

"Enemies? Time of trouble?" I repeated, trying to make sense of what she said. I frowned in puzzlement. "You said I had slipped through the veil?"

"Indeed thou hast. Few are able to perceive the veil, fewer still trust their hearts and senses. But for those few who can see within, there is no such thing as Time. Thou hast fallen into the past. Sometimes we bleed through into the future. I have seen thee there, have I not?"

I contemplated her, slightly puzzled, for she did indeed seem familiar. It struck me suddenly, like an icicle down my spine. Jack's wife. She was Jack's wife, Annie, I was certain. I allowed the fact that I had managed to traverse Time to sink into my consciousness before I replied.

"And *I* have seen *you*, in my time. But what year is it now?"

"The Year of Our Lord seventeen hundred and forty seven," she replied. "'Tis a difficult year for us, the Owlers of Rype, for the Eaglewood Gang is wild and bloody in its intentions. They lust after our connections and have determined to wrest our goods and our lives from us."

The Eaglewood Gang. My heart beat hard in my throat, almost choking me, for I had heard of the Eaglewood Gang: they were the red-handed villains of every piece of smuggling history I had recently read. Indeed I had intuited that the strangeness I had become so aware of, the bending of Time, the presence of Jack and Annie, were all connected in some mysterious way with the Owlers who were famed across the Marsh for their daring and for their disregard of the Revenue Laws considered unfair and unjust by all and sundry. Even in the twentieth century there was felt to be something glamorous about the Marsh smugglers while the nefarious, black deeds of the Eaglewood Gang resonated with horror and disgust down through the centuries. They had been the bloodiest of the smuggling gangs that terrified and terrorised the whole of the south of England.

And those bloody, violent dreams that had tortured me of late .... I was sure there was some relationship between them and this barbarous smuggling gang. I recalled what I had read in the tourist literature. The Eaglewood Gang used to sit drinking at the Three Chimneys until they were so drunk that they could not stand. Until they reached that stage of drunkenness, they took delight in petrifying everyone in their vicinity. They meted out unspeakable punishments or even death to those who crossed them, the worst reserved for any whose smuggling routes they coveted or who might betray their whereabouts to the Revenue men.

So now, hearing their name spoken turned my knees to jelly. I felt compelled to find out more.

"Tell me, Annie — that is your name, isn't it?" I asked, somehow a little shy. Annie inclined her head in assent, as I continued:

"My name is Hazel."

"I know, for I have seen thee. From what year hast thou come?"

"Nineteen hundred and seventy six," I informed her, seeing her gasp and draw back. "Tell me, please — are the Eaglewood Gang close by now?"

"Indeed they are very near. We fear we have a traitor among us for they set upon us yesterday. I was set to draw them off into the sinking marsh and some followed me and died. I felt your presence then ..." she broke off questioningly.

"Yes, I remember. I dreamed. At least, I thought it was a dream?" I answered, haltingly.

"For thee, 'twas a dream. For me 'twas sore reality. The Eaglewood Gang killed two and wounded more. We have the wounded here."

She raised her arm and the light fell on the sleeping forms of many men, some with bloody bandages, others restless and wakeful.

"You must go to them," I urged her. "They need you. I am fine — well. You have taken such good care of me."

She smiled sadly, shaking her head. "I have done all I can do for them. Now they are in the hands of Christ and his Holy Father." She put her palms together, bowing her head and closing her eyes in swift prayer.

"But thee, Hazel ... " she continued. "Thou hast fallen through Time and for the moment it has ceased to run. See...." She indicated a huge clock on the wall. I could hear it ticking but the hands did not move. "The hands of the clock are stilled. When Time runs again it will be time for thee to return whence thou came. And for me, too, 'twill be time to return."

"So we are having this conversation in timelessness? How can that be?" It was a rhetorical question but she answered it with another.

"Know'st thou not that the veil between the worlds is rent, here in Rype?"

"I certainly know there is something strange going on. But what *is* this 'veil'?"

"I know not. I convey to thee that which Father Dann hast vouchsafed to me, no more. I know only that, on occasion, Time stoppeth here. I know, too, that I have glimpsed thee in another time ..."

I knew I had seen her in another time; and it was imperative for me to find out, while in this weird timelessness, whether time was running forwards or backwards. From the odd experiences of dream and vision it seemed that she had not yet reached that time when Jack had been killed so bloodily. Questions screamed soundlessly through my head.

If time were running forward for me from this space, was it running forwards too in the sense I had of her? Could I change things in my twentieth century present which would then change her future? Or was it all immutable? Had I pierced the veil at different scenes in a life already lived; a life in which she had suffered and lost and Jack had died young?

I had no way of knowing, let alone of understanding, but somewhere deep within me I was aware that I held her future in my hands — and also the future for all who lived in Rype in nineteen seventy-six.

Following on from this awareness, I realised that the glimpses I had had of Annie's life had not been consecutive. It seemed that I had been given brief vignettes of times of joy, apprehension, loss or pain. 'Strong emotion' was the key that Elizabeth had given me to the rift. Maybe, if I could find a way to change the events that I had witnessed which caused Annie so much pain, I could help her to live a life of happiness and contentment with Jack into old age. Yes! I felt a shiver raise the hairs on my arms and recognised it as a familiar feeling that I called 'the shiver of truth'. All my life I had felt it when I had found the intuitive answer to a vital question.

So — all that was required of me was to find and stop the Eaglewood Gang in their twentieth-century incarnation. That was all! Simple, really.

"Do you have a child?" I asked, urgently. It was imperative that I know for, in order to change the course of her future by my actions, it was crucial that I had lurched into her life before the scene in the Three Chimneys had happened.

"Nay," she said with her shy, gentle smile. "But I am hand-clasped ..."

"And his name is Jack." I finished for her.

"Indeed," she agreed, and then asked hungrily: "Hast thou seen our destiny?"

"I think I may have," I said, still pondering how much I should tell her, and whether that future was immutable.

"Tell me!" Annie's eyes shone as she clasped her hands to her bosom. "Are we happy? Do we have children?"

"Allow *me* to ask *you* something first," I beseeched. The girl looked disappointed but nodded in assent.

"You say you are 'Owlers'. What does that mean?"

"'Tis the name for those free-traders of the Marsh who trade at night, by the light of the moon. Or, to speak true, more often by the dark of it, so that we cannot be seen. Some say we are so-called because we use the hoot of the barn owl to signify our whereabouts to those who need to know."

"Thank you, Annie. Do you and Jack use the owl's cry to signal to each other?"

"Nay." The shy smile was back. "Jack does say 'tis too coarse a noise for the likes of me."

"So you use the nightingale's song?" I teased. "Even in the depths of winter?"

"Aye," she said, blanching, her hands trembling. "Pray, what hast thou seen?"

I couldn't bear to tell her the whole harsh truth, so I told her that part that I knew she wanted to hear.

"I have seen you and Jack deeply in love and married. I have seen you living at Nightingale Cottages. And I have seen you nursing a beautiful child who is healthy and the delight of you both," I obfuscated.

She clapped her hands in delight and her eyes shone even more brilliantly than previously, although I detected the sheen of tears.

Footsteps reverberated on stone stairs. A crack of light appeared in a corner of the room. A door groaned open and was quickly closed. A tall man, bearing a rush light, paused. Jack. Forsaking me, Annie flew across the room into his arms. He caught her close against his chest and kissed her hard.

"Annie, my love. Thou art safe, I thank God." Jack went down on his knees and pressed his face against her gown.

"And thou," she crooned. "Thou too art safe. I feared I saw thy horse lamed."

"Thou saw'st true, my love. But 'twas but a scratch for my Black Bess. We out-rode and outwitted them." He staggered to his feet, laughing and throwing his arms wide. "And behold! Unharmed also."

And, in that moment, the church clock began to strike. Time was moving again. I counted the strokes. One ... a pause as it reverberated down the centuries ... two ...

Soft mist began to twirl between me and them.

"Nay, I have not said ..." Annie turned toward me, distress in her face. “The Eaglewood Gang.”

Three ....

“I have seen them in thy time,” she cried. “They smuggle still ...”

Four ...

“But they smuggle persons, not goods.”

Five ... The mist was thickening. She was standing, it seemed, in smoke ...

“They have found our crypt beside the crypt.”

Six ... She was fading fast, her voice weakening.

“Like us, thou art in their hands.”

Seven ...

“But they ... and we ... are also in thine.” It was little more than a whisper.

Eight ....

She was almost hidden in the twirling, whirling, mists of Time.

“Thou hast the power to alter Fate ... ”

Nine ... No sound. Only the mist.

“The future rests in thine hands ...”

Ten ...

“Thou hast the key to the past... ”

Eleven ...

“... And to the present.” The gentle voice was no more.

Twelve.

- 38 -

Of Doorways and Buckets

I blinked. In an instant all had changed around me. Gone were Annie and Jack, the sleeping, moaning, wounded men, the clock and the well. I shut my eyes and took a deep breath.

When I opened them again, everything swam before my eyes before it steadied, coming sharply into focus. I was standing — one hand easing my back, the other calming my baby — close to the wall of a vaulted room. There were no windows, no furnishings, nothing but whitewashed walls with a painted frieze, the arched ceiling and a smell. A smell that reminded me of human excrement, mixed with damp. The floor was paved with stone that sweated. I was quite alone.

Then I realised the room was bathed in light and for a moment my heart lifted. 'There must be a window somewhere,' I thought. My hopes were dashed. The light came from emergency fluorescent bulbs that gave off a bluish tinge. Not daylight at all.

Panic rose in a wave from my belly; any moment the baby would feel it and try to kick its way out of its womb-prison. I breathed deeply, deliberately slowing my pulse rate; repeating "slow" as I inhaled and "calm" on the out breath as my yoga teacher had taught me, years before, when she showed me how to conquer my fear of examinations.

My knees gave weakly and I sank down onto a ledge that stretched along the wall. Although wide enough to support me it oozed damp. My eyes fell onto my thin briefcase which was lying on the floor and I almost cheered aloud. Seizing it up, I took out the newspaper Mr Clements had given me, and smoothed it beneath me. First hurdle cleared.

Next, I had to figure out where I was and how to get out. I was hungry, tired and battered. Escape was imperative, but how?

What had Annie said? We were in the crypt beside the crypt. So presumably, I was under the church. Interesting. Tom had said that there were secret tunnels running all over Rype-in-the-Marsh, their central focus the church. That being so, I reasoned, there should be more than one way out. From where I now sat I could see only stone walls, whitened with lime, and a frieze painted with a strange pattern of grapevines intermingled with cherubs and demons, but definitely stone. No doors. *No* doors at all.

'That's ridiculous,' I said to myself, crossly. 'If you got in here you must be able to get out.' A little sliver of panic chased the ice down my spine.

'Maybe it's a dream and you only think you're awake. After all, you've just been speaking to someone in 1747.' That was my fear talking. The pragmatic side took over. I pinched myself. It hurt.

'Of course, I'm not dreaming.' The annoyed Hazel was back. 'I've got a sore head with a lump on it. Someone must have hit me.' My fingers found the tender swelling on the back of my head and I kneaded it. That hurt, too. It also made me angry and my anger energised me.

'Right,' I said fiercely to the Bump. 'I don't intend to give birth to you down here. We must find a way out.'

The Bump kicked again, twice, in the same place. 'Okay,' I thought. 'We might as well start in that direction.'

I set off at an oblique angle, briefcase under my arm. Remembering that I had left the paper on the bench, I glanced back. And in that moment I saw it — a door, disguised by the frieze. It was right behind where I had been sitting.

'Of course!' I said to myself. 'You had to get in here somehow. A door was likely.'

My pleasure at finding a door halted abruptly as I remembered that I had been trying to let someone out when I must have toppled in — but then how had I come through a door? I searched the ceiling for a similar pattern. There was none. But, as my eye roved round the room, with that peculiar sight that is only available once activated, I saw many other doors. I counted a total of thirteen. Presumably each led to a different tunnel. Which one should I choose?

'Someone must have brought me,' I thought, wishing I could ask Annie which door to choose. I certainly had no wish to go back by the route I had come. I felt sure someone would have locked and weighted that trapdoor. I had to choose another door, preferably one that led into an intact tunnel, not one that had been blocked. It all came back to the same question; which door should I choose?

I retraced my steps and picked up the newspaper, folding it up small so that it would fit into my briefcase again. If I was going to get out it was important I left no clues for the smugglers to find — if there were smugglers and they were using this place. I caught myself up in the thought; my mind seemed to have jumped to that conclusion all by itself. My head was functioning well enough to know that.

Annie's voice sounded clearly in my head.

"Like us, thou art in their hands ... but they ... and we ... are also in thine."

I racked my brains. What else had she said? Something about altering Fate and having the key to the future? Her actual words escaped me — or did they? Words were slowly clarifying in my mind.

"Thou hast the key to the past and to ...."

Of course! I had the key from the Act of Attainder, *if* it were still in my briefcase. I hardly dared to believe it was there, but it literally fell into my hand as I scrabbled in the depths of the case. I made sure to replace the newspaper before I allowed myself to look closely at the key; I remembered that I had noticed some odd scratches only to dismiss them as unimportant. Now, as I peered closely, turning the key slowly this way and that, the answer shot into my mind.

VII. The Roman Numeral Seven. Did it have some significance here? I wondered, squinting at each of the doorways that now seemed so obvious to me — ah! The joy of knowing — it was clear that each bore a Roman numeral hidden amongst the painted vine leaves.

I approached the doorway marked VII in some trepidation. I

could see no keyhole. I passed my hands around the edge of the door, my fingers seeking one or some nook that might contain a catch, anything, to open it. I was spread-eagled against the door, feeling the upper edges, when I heard the footsteps. Not from a single pair of feet either. A number of people were approaching and they were coming closer very fast.

Panic was almost second nature now, but I positively refused to submit to it. Fear lent me clarity. The footsteps were coming from behind the door marked VI. I remembered that Jack's door had opened into the room. It was likely this one would, too. But which way? Did I go left or right? I chose my left, flattening myself as best I could against the wall, just as the leading footsteps came to a brief halt. The others, more uneven, continued.

People-trafficking. Annie had told me, but there was no time now for more than a brief acknowledgement of the fact. I heard a rasping sound close to my ear and a brick by my head moved outwards, nearly hitting me. The door was opening, inwards, and I was hidden behind it. I had made the right choice.

A burly male figure, clad in jeans and a T-shirt, his biceps muscling under the sleeves, burst through the door. I held my breath but he did not see me. He was shouting back through the door as he held it open. He had his back to me.

"Come along. Come *along*. Get a bloody move on. Quick! You bloody, coloured *bastards* — don't you speak English?"

A line of small short people, mostly youths, stumbled into the room. Grabbing each in turn, the man literally pulled them through the doorway. He pushed them roughly one-by-one into the centre of the room as he counted them:

"One. Two. Move, you bastard! Over there." He thrust the hapless youngster across the room. "Three, four, five, six ... you! Over *there,* I said!"

A rough shove sent the child — for he could have been no more than six — flying. As he regained his balance he saw me. His eyes widened and he fixed me with a stare. I put my finger to my lips. He made not a sound but his gaze did not waver. He stood still, slowly lowering the two green plastic buckets he was carrying to the ground. One was empty, the other half-full of water. I realised that the Pakistanis — for I realised now that Mrs Pendant had been right all along — were being marshalled into a rough circle.

"Seven, eight, nine ..." He paused in his counting to yell at those in the room. "Stop gawking, you fucking rats. Get your sodding pants down, and do what you're here for!"

They stood, uncertain. One squatted in the usual position adopted for waiting in the East. The trafficker stopped counting altogether. He strode over to the squatter, grabbed his arm and yanked it up behind his back, lifting him sufficiently to kick an empty pail under his rear. With his other arm,he tugged at the man's lower garments.

"Not *there*, you bastard! In the fucking *bucket*." He pushed the man's naked bottom onto the bucket. "And don't fucking spill any either. Dirty wog!"

He cuffed the man's head savagely. He scowled at the others, glowering at each in turn. They hastily did the same. I waited fearfully for his gaze to find me. The child was still staring at me but no-one paid any attention to him.

The trafficker's glare shone like a searchlight, turning inexorably towards me. I ducked as low as my belly would allow, hoping I was concealed behind the nearest immigrants yet fearing I was all too obvious. More and more people were crowding into the space, slowly blocking the doorway.

"*Move* will you? Don't bloody stop! Keep going!" A fresh voice was urging them on from behind. It reverberated down the passage.

My heart pounded so hard I thought it would be heard. I recognised that voice. Whatever happened, its owner must not find me.

What now? In a cold sweat, I found myself mumbling the Lord's Prayer under my breath. I squeezed my eyes shut and wished with all my might that I were back with Annie and Jack in 1747.

Whoosh! I felt faint and as if I were falling. A rushing sound filled my ears.

"Open your eyes, you silly galah!" The words, in Bruce's rousing voice, dropped into my head. Of course. Closing my eyes would not change anything. I would still be seen.

I opened my eyes. The room was misty, but the mist cleared quickly and I was back where I had been before. In the same room, just as it was. In 1747. Annie and Jack were in each other's arms, whispering sweet nothings. They must have felt my reappearance for they both started and whirled round towards me.

"What the devil?" Jack exclaimed.

"Quickly! We must go. The Eaglewood Gang are coming," I blurted. "I've just seen them!"

"What? Where? How?" Jack was dazed by my sudden materialisation.

"Now!" I answered. "Here, through that door – there." I indicated door VI.

It was Annie who leapt into action.

"Jack, guard that door! Lock it."

He flung himself across the floor, reaching up into the vault. There was a grinding noise.

"Done, my lovely!" he cried, but Annie was already waking the sleepers, helping them up. Intending to assist, I started forward but she forestalled me.

"No! They will be afeared of thee. They know thee not and thou wearest such strange garments. Jack, open the door for Hazel. She knows the way and hast the key."

"Which door?" Jack asked abruptly.

"The seventh," I replied.

Jack gripped my arm firmly, propelling me onward as he strode across the room. His hand went to the lever and another door gaped open. He thrust me through it.

"*Go*!" he commanded, his voice as deep and resonant as my own Bruce's. "I thank thee. But be gone."

He handed me a lantern and ushered me towards the dark opening. I threw one last look at Annie. She gave me a brief, sad smile as she worked to wake the last man. The others were rubbing eyes, snatching up weapons and forming a defensive ring.

"Follow me!" I yelled, hurtling down the passage, fumbling in my pocket for the key as I ran. I say ran, but the passage was not straight, it curved and curved again bending round and onto itself before changing direction completely and making a slow S-bend. I was completely disorientated as the light from the lantern flared against the walls, the shadows exaggerating the darkness ahead. I slowed. Footsteps trod hard in my wake.

I ran out of adrenalin. Suddenly. Lurching, tripping on an uneven part of the dirt floor, my shoulder smacked against the wall. The key fell from my grasp. Harsh breathing wheezed behind me as I sought for it beneath my feet. Candlelight glanced off metal. A thin hand darted in, picking up the key in one easy movement, and Annie was again beside me, supporting my exhausted, heavy body the few final steps towards the substantial, brass-banded door ahead of us. It was immovable.

"This lever!" Annie cried, seizing a long, iron handle in the wall beside the door.

Together, desperately, Annie and I tugged at it. A doubled, scraping, metallic sound. The door swung open and we were through into a wide space, where barrels lurked along one wall, half hidden from sight by straw and sacking. I threw a look around the cellar, for cellar it certainly was, and glimpsed steep steps leading up to yet another door, light filtering in around its edge. The key had indented my hand in red, I noticed, as I fumbled it into the lock. Annie's hand reached out and turned the key.

We tumbled out into the dark freshness of long grass. Above us hung a huge orange moon, lighting the way for the exhausted and wounded men who followed us into the open.

- 39 -

Of Women and Resourcefulness

The freshness of the grass is sweet beneath my face. I raise my head, dew cool upon my lips, cheeks and closed eyelids. For a moment I hang in timelessness, then open my eyes to the darkness of the night. A great orange moon hangs above but dark tumbling clouds are scurrying across the sky, the wind is freshening, turning to the West and soon, soon, the rain will be upon us.

How long have I lain in the grass? A moment? A minute? Too long. There is work still to be done.

Jack's long legs stride through the grass to me. He hauls me roughly to my feet and smooths my tumbled skirt. He holds me away from him, lowers his head, looks deeply into my eyes.

"Annie? Art safe? Uninjured?" he questions urgently, his voice uneven.

"Aye. And thee?" My voice matches his.

"I, also. Now ..."

"How many?" I beg.

"We are all free. We have five wounded, three sorely so, as thou know'st."

"And whole, how many?"

"Nay, here there is but thee and me. The others run the waggons inland."

The waggons! I had forgot that the waggons lay hid in the elm wood close by the Squire's manor. 'Tis no matter, I think, for he will have kept them safe enough. He has an interest in this cargo, in tea and brandy and good red wine.

A groan, deep and urgent from close beside me.

The injured man clasps his leg. Blood runs red through the ragged bandage I have fashioned and I know there is no time to rest. I take off my kerchief, fold it small and hard, press it to his wound.

"Let me."

Jack's strong hand takes the wad, pressing it harder to the wound than I can contrive. With his free hand he raises the man's leg to abate the bleeding, eases the man back into the grass. I am stripping the hem from my skirt, where it is yet frayed. Another bandage. I tie it hard around the man's thigh and Jack tightens it still more. The bleeding is ebbing. The man's teeth chatter. The smell of blood mixes with the cleanness of the air and now there is moisture falling from the sky in drizzling drops swiftly becoming thick and fast.

I must think. Think. Jack's voice regretting the lack of a waggon....

"Get them to the tavern," I command. "'Tis dry there and safer. And there is brandy for the pain. Stay there and guard them. I ride for succour."

Jack shoots a look at me but I am running as I speak, running hard into the wind to where my horse is tethered, concealed in the tavern's store, the tavern that is half hidden itself behind the dyke, beyond the bounds of Rype.

"Whither?" The words reach me through the wind, through the rain, above the pounding of my heart. But I perceive he knows whence I am headed for he can read my heart and mind as can no other.

I reach the hiding place. My trusty gelding eyes me wildly, his eyes rolling brown and white. I speak softly to him and he wickers. He and I have ridden hard already tonight but he knows I have need of him once more. His hoof rakes the floor in anticipation.

I shake myself free of my sodden skirt, casting the woman's garment to the floor, and stand revealed in the breeches that I wear beneath. A swift intake of breath and I fling myself upon a bale of straw, launch myself upon the strong, wide back and take his halter in my hand; no time for bridle nor for saddle. My knees sink into the gelding's chestnut flanks; he twists — and we are away, flying, flying across the Marsh along the road which lies low behind the dyke, beside the ditch. I allow my steadfast steed his head along the narrow, dangerous path and we ride hard, fast into the sudden summer storm, teeth bared. Before long, above the drumming of his hooves and the pounding of our hearts we hear the rolling rush of the breakers upon the shore. A light bobs in the darkness and we make towards the lantern swinging from the boat shed where the women are gathered, conversing together as they sew, waiting for their menfolk to return.

I leap to the ground. Wild and bedraggled I must appear, for the women, hardened as they are by labour at shore and home, the strong Marsh winds and the relentless sea, draw back from me. But soon they understand what is required and hasten in their pattens for the boat. Their skirts soon hitched up for the heavy work ahead, they take up the ropes and with a heave! and a ho! grandmothers and matrons alike draw the narrow shallow-drafted boat across the shingle to the dyke-ditch. Setting their brawny, hard-worked shoulders to its stern they chant and sigh as the boat begins to move. It slides with a splash into the water. Younger wives and children take up the tow ropes and they are away, heads down into the storm, singing through the blinding rain, the wind whipping skirts and shawls around their bony forms. Away into the blackness of the night, back whence I had ridden.

And now, once more, I bestride my faithful mount and ride, ride, ride into the night, though now the wind is at my back. I ride for the physician, who, blindfolded for the journey, will attend the wounded men if paid in gold. And gold we have a-plenty.

- 40 -

Of Past and Present

My back hurt. There was a kind of rhythm to the pain. Keeping my eyes sealed shut, I sought for it. A strong, sharp pain passed from left to right, taking my breath with it. I rode it, knowing it would ebb. As the pain receded, I opened my eyes. I blinked. And blinked again.

White light shone in my eyes. I was lying on my back on something solid.

"She's back with us," stated a familiar voice. I looked up to see Mark's concerned face peering down into mine.

"That's my gal." A large, warm hand squeezed mine and something moist dropped onto my cheek. Tears welled in my own eyes as I heard Bruce's voice. All at once, I felt safe.

"Where am I?" I asked.

I remembered asking the same question somewhere else. A long time ago, it seemed.

"You're in my surgery, Hazel, lying on my couch," Mark said. "You've had a pretty hard knock. How do you feel? Any dizziness? Nausea? Aches and pains?"

"No, just this ache in my back," I replied, although my head did not seem to be properly attached to my body. "Is it ... is it?"

"No, I don't think you've started labour yet," he replied, kindly and comforting. "But you *are* rather bruised. Do you remember how it happened?"

"Not a clue," I said, although some strange ideas were trickling into my mind. The pain was growing again. I held my breath to let it pass but with it came perspicuity, and I knew why I needed to keep my own counsel in Mark's presence. Mentally, I thanked the pain. It weakened and faded away.

"Stay still, Haze. You may be concussed," Bruce said gently, as I tried to move.

"I'm fine," I said, trying to sound fine. "I want to go home now."

It was imperative that I get away from Mark as soon as possible. I was sure he was implicated in all that I had experienced in the last — how long? It felt like weeks.

"If you're sure?" Bruce sounded doubtful; I was not certain whether he was speaking to me or to Mark.

"Quite sure," I said, firmly. The pain had not returned but the baby was giving me a good internal pounding. Thank God for that.

I moved like an old lady. I felt like an old lady. What was wrong with me? I laughed inwardly at my own thought. If I had really been through what I seemed to remember going through it was surprising I was here at all. And my back still ached. As we reached the car, I noticed that Poppadum was panting in the back.

"Bugger me, Hazel. What *will* you do next?" Bruce was all concern as he eased me and the Bump into the old Ford. "I take my eye off you for a moment and you're instantly in trouble."

Poppadum licked my ear.

"How come you're here?" I asked her.

She grinned her toothy grin and wagged her tail in response.

"No good you asking that pesky dog," said Bruce, as he started the car. "It's me you should ask."

"Sorry, darling. What happened? Shouldn't you be at work?"

"Would you believe it? I come home early to check you're okay and all you can say is that I should be at work. I'm incensed!"

I glanced at him. He didn't look incensed. He looked worried.

"Come on, darling, spill the beans."

"Okay, I'll do my best," Bruce promised, mock-frowning at me. "Here goes — but I warn you it's a long story. As I said, I decided to come home as soon as I could to make sure you were all right. It was lunchtime and I knew you only had to get that Will signed and see a client — Mavis, wasn't it? So you should have been at home. Poppadum was going mad indoors when I arrived, barking and whining and yelping and whining and barking and whining ...”

“I get the picture,” I said, “Go on.”

“I don’t mind telling you, I was bloody scared that something bad had happened to you. No sooner had I turned the key in the lock than Poppadum was out of the door, running up the High Street, still barking and whining. I called her. She came back *most* reluctantly. I grabbed her and pushed her back indoors, but she started barking again. I shut her in the dining room and went in search of you. You were *nowhere to be seen ...*”

“I know,” I said. “I wasn’t there.”

“Anyway,” he plodded on, ignoring me. “I opened the front door to look up the road and Poppadum burst out of the dining room and raced off before I could get a hand to her collar. She stopped, looked back at me and ran further. Then she repeated the whole performance. I guessed she wanted me to follow her.”

“Good guess.”

Bruce threw me a look of exasperation and continued:

“I raced back to the car, fired it up and followed her. She raced round to this place by the church. The front door was open and Pops tore in. I knocked and called but there was no response. Pops was scratching furiously by the wall in the corridor. In fact I think she made a hole in a scraggy rug. She yelped and snuffled and jumped and yelped some more — but it was only a wall.”

“Actually, there was something behind it,” I said.

“Of *course* there was something behind it! Who’s telling this bloody story?” he glowered. He didn’t usually swear. I had counted at least three swear words in his account. He must be very upset.

He pulled up sharply at the kerb outside Rose Cottage and came round to help me out of the car. As I unravelled myself I heard him take a quick intake of breath.

“Someone’s in the house,” he said. “I’m sure I closed the inner door. Wait here.”

“No way.” I exclaimed as I followed him, one hand on the Bump, the other on Poppadum’s collar.

* * *

Sitting on our sofa, speaking softly into a radio phone, was a tall man in the uniform of a captain of the military police. He stood up as we entered, stooping slightly to avoid hitting the beam.

"Roger and out." He switched off the radio and put it into his pocket. He held out his hand to me.

"How do you do, Mrs Dawkins? I'm pleased to be able introduce myself to you formally. I am Chief Superintendent Manning of the Metropolitan Police on secondment to the Military Police."

Mutely, I allowed him to shake my hand. Dark blue eyes held mine. His brown hair was greying at the temples and a tanned face set off the whiteness of his smile. He turned to Bruce, again offering his hand.

"How do you do, Mr Dawkins? I apologise for what must be my unexpected presence here, uninvited. I will explain."

Bruce ignored his hand.

"I hope you will," he said stiffly, clearly annoyed. "And quickly. My wife has had a very difficult and dangerous time today. She needs her rest."

I let go of Poppadum's collar. To my surprise, she didn't object to the policeman's presence. On the contrary, she walked over, sniffed his hand, gave a single wag of her tail and lay down on her bed, nose on paws, watching him. I sat down on the nearest chair. It would have been polite to offer tea but I had no energy left in me. Bruce seated himself in the other armchair and, after a moment's hesitation, the Superintendent — or as I thought of him, Captain Manning — lowered himself back onto the sofa. He leaned forward, his elbows on his knees, hands hanging loose.

"I apologise again for intruding in this manner."

"Apologise away — as much as you like," Bruce snorted. "How the bloody hell did you get in?"

The Captain passed him a metal object that resembled our front door key. It was our front door key — I recognised the red legal tape that marked it as our spare .

"As I said, I apologise. Constable Havers asked me to return your key," he said evenly.

"My bloody oath," Bruce muttered, anything but mollified. "Now what the fu ... dickens are you doing here?"

The Captain pressed his lips together and began again:

"Let me explain, as succinctly as I'm able. I have been working under cover for some time. A captain's uniform is very helpful because no one expects you to stay long — only as long as one's posting — and it gives one an entree into different social circles. Be that as it may," he paused. "I must ask for your assurance that what I have to say to you is in confidence?"

"Of course," I murmured, looking at Bruce who nodded curtly but said:

"I don't see why we should give you any bloody assurance! It'd be about as useful as an ashtray on a motorbike." He caught my eye. "Okay, okay, it's confidential. Get on with it, will you?"

Poppadum looked up sharply. She moved towards the door inquiringly. Then she settled down again, nose back on paws, ears forward and eyes brightly intelligent.

"Thank you. To continue: I am part of, a nationwide investigation into smuggling and people trafficking. This is not the cosy idea of smuggling that most people have. These crooks are extremely dangerous and very violent. They traffic in all sorts of commodities but mostly run drugs and alcohol, also dealing in diamonds and people. People trafficking is heinous. Many are kept as slaves, on little food and no pay, never having an opportunity to pay off the exorbitant sums they are charged for their passage. Girls, boys and women are kept in the sex trade. Some are as young as twelve, some even younger."

"Yes," I agreed. "I've been discussing this recently with my doctor."

He smiled grimly. "That would be Doctor Wilkinson, I presume?"

"Yes," I said again. "He was very hot under the collar about it."

"Really?" The tall man's smile widened. "He's certainly been collared now. We've just arrested him."

I was shocked into silence. Bruce was looking dumb-founded.

"I'll explain that later. Let me start at the beginning, when Mrs Dawkins here came into the picture." He turned towards me. "This is how I see it: you were consulted by a Mrs Pendant who finally found someone sympathetic enough to look into accusations that everyone else had dismissed as the ravings of a disturbed mind. You asked Constable Havers to take another look. Before going further, I should say that Constable Havers has been part of this investigation for a very long time."

Bruce and I looked at each other. Our surmise had been completely wrong then — but only if we believed what we were hearing. The tall man was still speaking:

"Your inspection of the roof space caused De Cham and his cronies to panic. Luckily for them, they'd recently cleared the roof space of any evidence because one of the workers had died up there."

I felt my eyebrows meet my hairline in surprise. Bruce gawped at him.

"Yes. Mrs Pendant was actually quite correct. Someone *had* died up there, of a heart attack. It wasn't a Pakistani, though. He was a local drug addict who worked there to feed his habit. You may have guessed by now? No? They were growing cannabis up there in very large amounts. You would not believe the amount of their electricity bills."

Bruce gave me a very pointed look which said: 'told you so'. I shrugged; I would have stuck my tongue out at him if we'd been alone. Captain Manning ignored us.

"Unfortunately, Mrs. Dawkins, you fainted. Constable Havers feared it was because of the overpowering effects of the drug in your ... uh ... *delicate* condition. He made sure you were out of the way before you recovered and put two and two together."

"I did not quite put that particular two and two together," I revealed wanly. "Although I did think he must have super human strength to carry *me* next door."

The captain smiled sardonically.

"We knew of the factory, of course, but we let it carry on because they were small fry. We hoped to catch much bigger fish. And now, thanks to you, we have."

"Oh?"

"Unknown to us, De Cham was dabbling in other things. Heroin to be precise. That brought him to the notice of a drug and people-trafficking cartel who think they own the right to smuggle hard drugs in this area. A very dangerous drug cartel. In fact, some people liken them to the notorious Eaglewood Gang of smugglers in the eighteenth century, guns and all."

"Oh Lord," I breathed. Bruce looked at me, perplexed.

"You've gone very pale, Mrs Dawkins. Are you all right?" The captain's piercing blue eyes fixed me to my seat.

"Er ... yes," I floundered. "I've heard of that gang, that's all. A very bloodthirsty lot, I understand."

"Precisely. When De Cham realised that he was being watched by a member of this cartel he panicked and asked one of the customers to hide the store of heroin somewhere he could recover it easily, on the basis that he took the risk and that the heroin was his when he regained it. They didn't know that *we* were watching the cartel watch *them*."

"Ah," I crowed knowingly. "Dad was right. Blue Jeans Adam hid *heroin* in the deed packet."

"Yes. And that's why I happened along at just the right time. It wasn't easy to extract it without your seeing and without stinking of dog excrement. I simply couldn't manage it. I didn't want to blow my cover so I asked Constable Havers to keep an eye on the house."

Out of the corner of my eye, I noticed Poppadum prick up her ears.

"We thought Neil was always about at exactly the right moment," put in Bruce. "We wondered whether he was involved."

"So it was you who was here when I telephoned," I exclaimed. Poppadum made a low grumbling noise, gathering her limbs together beneath her. I frowned at her.

"No," he sighed. "I'm afraid not. It was the man behind you. The one with the gun."

White Bonnet stepped out from the lobby. The revolver in his hand was pointed directly at the Bump.

- 41 -

Of Cops and Robbers

Bruce turned his head. His eyes narrowed as he saw the gun threatening me. He looked back at me, his face ashen. The mother in me grew fierce. How dare that blackguard threaten my child and the father of my child? How *dare* he?

Bruce must have sensed the rising of my fighting spirit for I saw him coiled to spring.

Poppadum, true to her sheepdog heritage, had slowly wriggled round the room, belly to the ground, hidden by the furniture. At my signal she leapt, snarling ferociously, at the hand holding the gun, knocking it upwards. In his surprise, the man pulled the trigger.

A shot rang out. The bullet hit the beam and ricocheted towards the couch, ripping into the fabric.

Poppadum sank her teeth into White Bonnet's arm. He screamed and dropped the gun.

Heavy rushed through the front door, waving another gun in my direction.

Neil erupted through the window, truncheon at the ready.

Bruce sprang at Heavy, dragging him to the floor in a rugby tackle.

The Captain strolled over, pulled out a handkerchief and casually, but carefully, picked up the guns that White Bonnet and Heavy had dropped.

A woman's voice rang out clearly. "Drop your weapon!"

I gulped involuntarily. I recognised that voice, although it was stronger and more vibrant than I had ever heard it before. How could that be? The last time I had seen its owner — just this morning — I'd been at her bedside as she breathed her last.

The room spun crazily around me. I closed my eyes.

For a moment nothing happened.

I opened one eye. Then the other.

Elizabeth was sauntering through the back door, pushing Skinny in front of her. She seemed to have something pressed into his back.

"Hello, Hazel," she said nonchalantly.

She was in full Customs and Revenue uniform embellished with gold braid.

"Call your dog off, Hazel," she went on. "We'll take over now."

The Captain jerked his head at Neil, who, blowing hard on his whistle, grabbed the blaspheming White Bonnet, clipping a handcuff to his free wrist.

Uniformed policemen surged into the room.

I called Poppadum, who let go reluctantly. She came back to me, growling warningly at the gunman.

Neil secured White Bonnet's other wrist and marched him from the room. Another police officer clipped handcuffs round Skinny's narrow wrists and led him away.

Bruce was sitting half on and half off Heavy, whose head was jammed into the headlock Bruce had perfected when he was a champion wrestler at university. At Elizabeth's direction, two police officers relieved him of his charge, cuffing the crook before they led him out of the back door.

"Great team work," approved Elizabeth, smiling grimly. "You can put the guns down now, Captain. They're no longer needed."

The tall man looked regretful as he laid the guns on the table.

"We'll check them for fingerprints," said Elizabeth. "Please leave them there, untouched, for forensics to collect."

Bruce stood, grinning like a Cheshire cat.

"Tea anyone?" he asked.

Elizabeth refused. Saying she had work to do, she left swiftly, promising that all would be expounded in the morning. The Captain accepted. Lounging back on the sofa after Bruce had vanished into the kitchen, he asked me:

"Are you sure you're all right, Mrs Dawkins?"

"I'm pretty good, considering."

The Captain smiled. "I'm glad to hear it. I'm sorry we were interrupted in so violent a fashion. I have a few questions to ask of you — if you're feeling up to it?"

"I'm fine," I reiterated.

"First, I need to put you in the picture about the *way* we were interrupted. I was expecting something similar because I'd been warned. But I'm afraid I couldn't tell you what might happen because it had to seem unexpected. The man with the gun has also been working under cover."

"Not White Bonnet, too?" I exclaimed, "There seem to be under-cover officers all over the place. You could almost say they're coming out of the woodwork."

"White Bonnet?" The Captain queried, looking flummoxed.

"In-joke between me and Bruce. It's to do with the car he drives."

The Captain's brow cleared. "I see. I think. Let's call him White Bonnet then, it's as good a pseudonym as any."

"Fine by me," I said.

Bruce appeared carrying two mugs of tea. He went back into the kitchen to bring me a glass of water, which I drained in one draught.

"The Captain tells me that White Bonnet is also under-cover," I told Bruce. "And he has still more to tell us, I think?" I addressed the last words to the man himself.

"Yes," the policeman said. "I've explained the situation regarding the drug cartel and the De Chams. Is that clear to you?"

Bruce and I exchanged a glance and then nodded in unison.

"As a result of this police operation — which has been mounted in conjunction with Customs and Excise — we discovered a link between the importing of drugs and people trafficking. As I've said, we know they're using a tunnel from the shore to bring the unfortunates inland, but we have reason to believe that there may be other entrances. Indeed, as you are probably aware, there are rumours that the whole of Rype is crisscrossed with tunnels and hiding places dating from the sixteenth century, or even before that."

He paused long enough for us to nod again, signifying that we were aware of the rumours, before he resumed.

"Once he had calmed Miss Blanchard, with the help of Doctor Hadley who gave her a sedative and left, Neil discovered the entrance to the tunnel that lies under her staircase. I presume that you also discovered it?"

"Yes, quite by chance. I was looking for Mavis," I explained. Bruce looked at me sceptically but said nothing.

"I'll take a proper statement later, please. What I'd like to know now is how you got out."

"It's a long story, Captain," I sighed. "I found another way out. I don't think the smugglers are aware of it."

"And it is ...? Where?"

A thought jumped into my mind with a heavy thud.

"Forgive me, Captain," I said, heart thumping. "But why should we believe anything you've said? You haven't shown any identification, however plausible you sound."

He grimaced.

"I do apologise, Mrs Dawkins. Of course, you are quite right." He reached into his jacket.

"Hold it right there!"

Bruce's voice rang out, a steely quality to it. The Captain's hand stilled inside his jacket. I turned. Bruce had a gun in his hand. His eyes were mere slits as he faced the other man.

"Take your hand out slowly ... *very* slowly," he commanded.

The Captain complied. The hand was not empty when it re-appeared. It contained his police identification. Both Bruce and I let out a long hissing breath of relief.

"My apologies," Bruce said, replacing the gun on the table beside the one recovered from Heavy.

"No. *I* apologise. I should have produced this sooner, as your wife was aware," the Captain owned.

Exhaustion threatened to overwhelm me. I wanted the man out of my house.

"I found another entrance, or rather, another exit, through the cellar under Old Owlers. In fact I have the key here," I told him, holding out the key that I had been unconsciously clutching; my hand still imprinted in red with its pattern.

"Thank you," he said, taking it gently.

"Oh!" I exclaimed as another recollection surfaced. "What time is it? I have an appointment with Mrs Pendant this afternoon."

Both men looked at me.

"*Honestly*," I added. Neither said anything for a moment then Bruce raised his shoulders in a shrug.

"Okay, I'll take you," he said. "But you have fifteen minutes tops. Then it's home and a rest for you."

We all departed together, leaving Poppadum in her role as guard dog.

Bruce ministered to me, understanding my utter exhaustion.

Although it had not taken me long to describe to Mrs Pendant what I had discovered in the deeds, she had been dumbfounded by the implications. I had explained that it would take a while to sort out the whole legal maze but that I believed she would be entitled to claim considerable compensation.

After the shock had waned a little, she had recollected that I was not feeling my best and she had insisted that Bruce take me home and feed me forthwith. Which he did.

He bathed my face and hands, undressed me and pulled a clean nightie over my head. Then he tucked me up in bed and went out to buy fish and chips.

I slipped easily into sleep, fish and chips quite forgotten. Later, I was aware of the baby's movements, a sort of dolphin-like motion within me — and of Bruce's long limbs surrounding mine. I clung to him. I grew hot and tossed the coverlet aside. I moved away from his warmth. Becoming cold and shivery, I wound the sheet about me. I lay on my back, my side, my stomach. Nowhere was the bed the right temperature; no position was comfortable.

Eventually, the call of Nature persuaded me to descend the stairs. I opened the back door, revelling in the sweet freshness of the dawn and the piping song of the blackbird. Peace comforted me, soothed and calmed the babe, and eased my wearied limbs. I climbed the stairs to my bed and slept again, the soft, tranquil sleep of the weary.

- 42 -

Of Squall and Shore

A flash of lightning woke me, bright in blackness. I waited for the clap of thunder, counting the miles. Ten seconds passed before the crash. Ten miles. Then the splash and patter of rain; quickly over. Lightning. A second crash. Five seconds. The storm was growing closer, fiercer. Rain fell from the sky in bucketfuls. I lay quietly, half-awake, allowing the storm's vitality to flow through me, feeling a vague sense of déjà vu, no more. The wind eased and the rhythm of the beating rain evened. I drifted into that strange state that is between sleep and waking dream.

Tall grasses sway and bend beside the way, their motion as easy and fluid as the men's movements are slow and halting. Jack is supporting two injured men. Limping along a path scarcely wide enough for one. Three others lead the way, stumbling in single file. One clasps his right upper arm with his left hand, blood running freely in channels through his fingers. Another holds his head in both hands, a bandage covering one eye, his ear a gory hole. The last staggers along with a hand to his thigh, a long bloody gash in his face. His shirt is ragged and stained with blood; his mouth is pursed in a soundless whistle.

The first of the rain has passed. Nonetheless, Jack's weather eye is upon the clouds and, sure enough, a summer squall is suddenly unleashed upon them; rain like rods beating down upon their heads. They are almost in reach of the squalid hedge-tavern. Jack shouts and, like crabs sidling along the shore, they make haste into the safety of the shelter.

Now Jack is there, encouraging, cursing, roughly tender as he assists them one-by-one into the comfort of the hay. He shouts for brandy. A small wizened creature of unknown gender appears at his summons, bearing a flask. But now Jack is out in the rain, staring through the curtain of water towards the shore, his whole being wrapped up in the thought of a girl, mounted on a huge chestnut gelding, pounding through the storm to the shore in search of help. He seeks with his thoughts and finds her, feels her intention and, knowing it, smiles.

The while he tends the wounded Owlers, adjusting bandages, giving them drink, applying what salve he can to pain, discomfort and wounded pride, he holds her in his heart and prays for her safety. Yet he has time, too, for thoughts of those who seek to rob them of their hard-fought gains.

When he hears the hauling song of the women fisher-folk rising from the greenness of the grassy bank, he springs to take the boat's bow rope, makes it fast to the hitching post. Women and children surround him in a rising wave, needing no summons to the aid of their menfolk. Rough but gentle hands convey them to the boat. But Jack has gone.

His black horse trots along the dyke path, slipping and sliding in the wet, gathering speed along the straight stretch towards the seashore. Now that the tide has ebbed, the rain has eased and the wind has dropped. Together, man and horse wing their way along the sand to the far side of the bay, slowing as they near the sandbars, which have fouled many a vessel in the past and will wreck many more in the future.

Jack marks three fishing smacks drawn up close by the ramshackle tavern known as Old Widow's Tap, boats which are unknown to him. Empty even of a sentry — a fact which speaks of arrogance — their presence is a sure indication of the Eaglewood Gang's intentions. At the sight, Jack's brow creases in thought. He knows his conscience will not allow him to hole the boats; they are but some poor man's means of livelihood. And yet he needs must find some way to delay the Eaglewood Gang for they have found this entrance to the shore tunnel, of that Jack is certain. The presence of the fishing smacks is evidence enough. And when he and the Owlers fled the crypt, Eaglewood men were fast approaching the door marked VI, the door from the shore tunnel. No doubt they will soon return bearing their booty. The shoreside mouth of the tunnel is well-disguised. Deep within the Old Widow's Tap, it lies concealed.

Jack's eyes fall upon a heap of fishing nets stowed in the prow of the nearest fishing smack, and his brow clears. He takes up the topmost three, sets his horse to drag them through the sand as he walks behind. Black Bess picks her way up the foreshore towards the shingle, treading delicately amongst the patches of pea beach. She halts without command at the familiar place. Jack stops too and stands motionless. Senses heightened and aware of danger, he listens. Only his eyes move as he searches the Tap's surroundings for any sign of life. It appears deserted.

Jack runs towards the tavern. Flattening himself along its side, he cautiously opens the door and peers within. The moon emerges from her veil of cloud and her beams penetrate the darkness of the entrance. Staring deep into its black heart, Jack lingers. He sees no movement, no flicker of candle nor storm lantern, hears no sound but the beating of the waves upon the shore. He smiles grim and resolute.

Hastening to his mount, he takes a rope from the saddlebag and pays it out along the shore. Next, he seizes the strongest, newest net and casts it over the roof. It catches on the pipe that acts as chimney. Cursing, he climbs gingerly upon the leaning shack and pulls it clear. The net cascades around the Tap. Another net follows the first.

"A catch, indeed," thinks Jack, stepping back to survey his handiwork. Alas, it will not hold determined men for long. But Jack is still toiling. He grabs the rope, passes it across the peeling timber door of the Tap and secures it to the winch of a rusting windlass. He sprints back towards the waiting horse, checks that the rope is fastened to the harness, then guides Black Bess twice more around the hut. He loosens the rope from her harness and knots its end to the winch. The Old Widow's Tap is wrapped as tightly as a child in swaddling bands.

Now he turns to the fishing smacks. Soon, they, too, are

swathed in nets. Although his hands are bleeding and his face and clothes bedaubed with sand, he is grimly jubilant. 'Tis done. The Eaglewood Gang's retreat is checked. But none too soon.

A musket shot cracks out, the report booming above the sound of the waves. Revenue men swarm along the beach on foot.

Oily Dick has done his work well; the susurration has travelled fast across the murmuring marshes, whispering to the Squire of the Eaglewood Gang's intentions and the placement of their boats upon the shore. Honour-bound as Magistrate, the Squire himself forthwith relays the rumour to the Prevention Officer ....

Leaning low in his saddle, Jack guides his mount skilfully behind the sandbar; slipping away like a wraith — but not before he has caught a glimpse of Eaglewood men caught in the trap, fighting like fish to escape the enveloping net that prevents their escape to the open sea. The Old Widow's Tap must be abandoned where it stands. But in a few weeks, or months, another Tap will arise further to the West, its back against the sandbar where the second entrance to the tunnel lies.

Once more upon the path — unseen, carefree and laughing now — he gives the horse her head and together they canter towards the copse called 'Songster Wood' where a certain maid waits astride a chestnut gelding.

It was full morning before the squall eased and the sun broke through, its brilliance throwing up rainbows through the raindrops on the window pane. Bruce thrust his long legs from the bed, stalked across the room and opened wide the window, his tousled red curls catching the sunlight, the fresh smell of after-storm whipping past him to fill my lungs. I felt refreshed and vibrant with life.

I laughed; and Bruce strode back to hug me to his bare chest, the hair tickling my cheek. Life felt good, very good. It was Sunday. Breakfast in bed day. Even better. Bruce brought toast and tea, butter and marmalade. We ate it together, sitting up in bed.

"Now, let me see," I said, licking the last of the butter from my fingers. "You had just followed Poppadum to a wall in Mavis' house."

"Is that whose it is? Yes, Poppadum made a great commotion there, barking and scrabbling. I grabbed her collar, but she wouldn't come quietly. She kept yelping and pulling and in the end I let her go. She had her nose close to that wall again in no time. Then there was a sudden crash like a door slamming but I couldn't see where. Poppadum backed away and the wall sort of opened. And out came this woman with wild eyes and hair screaming about all sorts of mad things — tunnels and smells and men with syringes."

"Men with syringes?" I queried, "Did she really say that?"

"Yes. At least, I think she *actually* said 'man with a syringe'. I was bemused because Poppadum had gone into the cupboard or coal hole or whatever it was, whining and pawing at something. I was about to go in when the woman — Mavis, was it? — flung her arms round me, pinioning my arms to my side. I tried to get free but she hung on for dear life, gabbling about how they'd come back for her but she'd pushed 'them' into the dark. It was crazy. Eventually she dissolved into sobs, slipping to the floor, hugging me round my knees. She kept begging me to save her. I really didn't know what to do. Especially when Poppadum started barking and whining, yet again, at something in the cupboard."

"Oh dear." I was hard pushed not to laugh at the picture of discomfiture that he had conjured up. "How did you get free?"

"I was saved by a boy on a bike, would you believe?"

"Quite probably," I said, "Go on."

"Well, this boy, who was about eleven or twelve I would think, came racing past on his bike, literally threw it to the ground outside and dashed in. 'Is she all right?' he asked. 'I've brought Neil, like she said.' And then he was shouldered aside by Neil who picked Mavis up from my feet and carried her into the sitting room."

"Well done, Matt!" I applauded. "What next?"

"Matt was it? Anyway, the boy kept asking 'Is she all right?' And I kept saying, 'She'll be fine' or something similar. Then he suddenly said, 'No. I don't mean Mavis, I mean *her*.' But right at that moment, Mavis started screaming again and Neil shouted at the boy to go and fetch a doctor. He looked at me oddly but dashed off on his bike. And that was the last I saw of him because Poppadum was off again."

"Off again?"

"She had been quiet for a moment. But suddenly she literally tore out of the house, barking. She didn't wait for me this time but I was after her at a run. No time for the car. I don't know how we got wherever it was. I could hardly keep up with her. My lungs were bursting as I came round a corner and there she was, and there *you* were. You were flat on the ground, out for the count, and she was licking your face."

He paused and I saw that his mouth was working and his eyes were wet.

"Oh Hazel," he whispered as he hid his face in my bosom. "You were so still, so pale ... I thought you were dead."

I held his dear head, and when he raised his face I kissed his wet eyes and his lips. My eyes were wet too.

It was in this state of mutual soddenness that we heard a loud knock on the front door. We both jumped. Swiftly wiping our respective eyes, I heaved myself up as Bruce went to answer it.

- 43 -

Of Truth and Deceit

I fixed my hair in the usual fashion when time was of the essence — by dragging my fingers through it. A quick slick of lipstick helped dispel the livid paleness of my face, which gave the lie to my earlier feeling of vitality. There was nothing I could do about the shadows under my eyes.

I could hear Bruce talking to someone who answered swiftly and easily. And then he must have brought her into the sitting room because Elizabeth's voice drifted up to me:

"I'm so sorry that I had to mislead your wife. Is she here?"

"Yes," said Bruce. "She'll be down in a minute. But I don't understand. What do you mean about misleading my wife?"

"She thought I was dying."

"Why?" Bruce sounded utterly confused. "You look perfectly well to me."

"Quite," Elizabeth's voice was clipped. "Indeed I am. But I should explain to Hazel personally, don't you think?"

I could delay my entrance no longer. I clicked the bedroom door shut and clumsily descended the stairs. Bruce came immediately to my side.

"There you are, darl. This officer would like to talk to you."

"Of course," I said, trying to second-guess what Elizabeth would tell me. "Good morning, Elizabeth. Would you like a cup of tea?"

She accepted and Bruce went off to the kitchen to make it while I invited her into the dining room. I thought an upright chair would be more comfortable as I ached all over after my escapades of the previous day. Elizabeth and I surveyed each other, neither really sure how or where to commence the conversation. The silence lengthened. Eventually neither of us could bear it any longer and both spoke at once

“I think I have ...”

“I’m sure you must be ...” she started.

“Sorry.”

“Sorry.”

We both stopped and waited. I waited a little longer than Elizabeth.

“You must be wondering exactly what has been going on,” she offered after a long pause.

“Yes, that’s very true. I must say I was *very* surprised when you walked in here yesterday. Luckily my baby seems to be sewn in. For a moment I thought I might give birth on the spot.” I had tried for lightness and she responded in the same vein:

“I’m relieved you didn’t. But there was no other way to come to your aid.”

“I’m glad you did, I can tell you. I was very nervous with that gun being waved around, especially since it was pointed at me.”

A sharp kick in the bread basket area reminded me that I should have used the plural. I ignored it. I would have to teach this baby manners but that would have to wait until after she was born. It was funny how I had accepted what Annie had told me; I really had no idea whether the baby was a boy or a girl.

“I will explain more, Hazel, but I wonder how much you know?”

“I don’t *actually* know anything,” I replied. “But there have been some clues. Some were things that did not quite add up. Others have just occurred to me.”

“Go ahead. Tell me. Let’s see if you’re right.” Elizabeth invited.

“First, I noticed how well you looked when I first came to see you with Mark,” I said, unable to resist the invitation.

Bruce brought in a tray of tea; I kept well away. My stomach was particularly sensitive today and I didn’t want to have to leave the room to be sick, especially as I was enjoying myself. I carried on:

“I’ve seen a lot of terminally ill people. It goes with the territory of making Wills. I know that their energy changes from day to day and, sometimes, even from hour to hour. But you were missing a certain pallor, a certain listlessness. It's hard to put a finger on it — which is why I didn't trust my instinct. But I had a sneaking suspicion that there wasn't much wrong with you, that for some reason you were putting on an act."

Bruce looked at me with an odd expression between amusement and respect.

"Well spotted. Did you have any idea what the reason might be?" Elizabeth asked.

"I thought at first that you just enjoyed having a handsome man singing to you. I thought that, if you'd been a professional opera singer, it would've been very hard not to have admiration and adoration — especially if you knew you were very ill."

"I see. Next?"

"Next, I realised that you didn't need a Will. At least not in the terms you instructed me to draw it. If Mark were the sole executor and beneficiary it was most unlikely that he'd actually be able to inherit all you appeared to own. He's in a difficult position as your doctor. There would have been a presumption of undue influence if the Will had been challenged, and it seemed likely that it would have been challenged if the situation between you and your sister was as you described. Remember that I asked you about that in great detail? I explained this to Mark and he pretended — at least I presume he pretended — that he just wanted you to die happy. Commendable. But, as I have said, you didn't appear to me to be as ill as he said you were."

"Good point, and ...?" Elizabeth was frowning.

"Thirdly, when I explained this to you, you made it quite clear that you wanted your Will to be drawn in precisely those terms. The only concession you made was to appoint me as the executor and you knew that I would be bound by the Solicitors' rules relating to client confidentiality. Apparently, not only did you have no real appreciation of the nuances of Mark's position, you wanted no-one else to have any idea as to how you were leaving your money. Now, while this does happen, it doesn't happen very often. In fact, once a testator realises that a beneficiary will be in such a difficult position, he usually takes my advice and makes other arrangements. But, of course, you didn't really have the sister or husband you described."

"Another good point," Elizabeth acknowledged. "Of course, we had to check your probity."

"I think you must have made up your mind about that already," I accused. "Or why would you have mentioned the rift? And why on earth would you have told me how to manipulate Time as you did?"

"T ... Time?" Bruce had just taken a gulp of his tea and this statement astonished him so much he choked. After I had finished smacking him on his back and he had recovered a little, I noticed that Elizabeth was watching me through slitted eyelids, a sardonic smile on her lips.

"Ah," she said. "Only certain people have the facility. Very few even notice when Time slips. Often they think they are daydreaming. But you *knew* immediately."

"Manipulate Time?" Bruce might have recovered his breath but he was still incredulous. "Is this something out of Doctor Who?"

"No," Elizabeth frowned at his flippancy. "This is deadly serious. Literally deadly."

"Would you care to explain to a mere mortal?" He was offended now.

"It's very easy, really," I attempted to explain. "Do you remember our experience by the churchyard at full moon? We thought we'd both seen a ghost? You remember I kept hearing things — the nightingales might have been real but they *felt* illusory — and feeling strange atmospheres? Well, the truth is that there's a rift here in Rype, a sort of tear in the web of Time. And, as Elizabeth told me, if you wish hard enough you can go through the web — and alter time."

Bruce mockingly shook his head.

"I'll accept we might have seen a ghost but I'm not buying the rest of it."

"Okay," I said, "I'll just say one thing more. Remember how

quickly I came back to find you at the Three Chimneys after I'd been to see Elizabeth? That was ..."

"Nah," he sneered. "Don't give me that. You were just quicker than you thought."

"Your wife is right, Mr Dawkins," Elizabeth stated. "Take it from me. But you do need to believe *and* you need to have some psychic power to be able to slip through the veil. Some people are born with the knowledge, some people work at it, occasionally a woman will develop that power in pregnancy, but everyone needs to *believe,* at least on some level, before it will occur. It's a facility that has been used in Rype throughout the centuries."

"I'll agree to differ," Bruce pronounced.

"Very well, Mr Dawkins. As you wish. That's up to you."

I said, "You might like to consider, darling, that someone who appears to be a very senior officer in Revenue and Customs, not only takes it seriously, but seriously enough to go into deep cover." I turned questioningly to Elizabeth. "At least, that's what I presume to be the case?"

"Quite correct, Hazel. In fact, although I am bound by the Official Secrets Acts in regard to detail, it's fairly common knowledge that during the War both sides resorted to the use of techniques that are often called supernatural. The two minutes' silence at eleven o'clock each day was one of them."

"I expect the same thing is happening now, in the Cold War, isn't it?" I asked.

"I cannot comment on that, at all," Elizabeth said shortly and I knew she was regretting the little she had said before.

"Well, I think it would be strange if the Russians *weren't* looking into it," I said.

We lived under the constant threat of nuclear war. The USSR was a very secretive regime, keeping its citizens firmly behind the Iron Curtain, as it was called. Every day, it seemed, we heard of someone being shot as they tried to cross the Berlin Wall into that part of Berlin held by the Allies. The Wall had been erected during one June night in 1961 by the East German Authorities. It was said that the President of the United States had only to press a red button in the Oval Office of the White House to start a nuclear attack on the USSR. The very idea made me feel sick and the squirm in my belly reminded me that I was still anxious about bringing a baby into this uncertain world.

"I think you're both talking absolute twaddle," Bruce exclaimed. "I don't believe a word of it. How can being at death's door be 'deep cover' anyway?"

Elizabeth and I exchanged a grimace. She inclined her head a little which I took as assent for me to explain.

"Suppose you hear that someone is terminally ill, on her own and deserted by her family? You wouldn't be at all surprised that she had visitors, including daily visits from her doctor, and, I would think, several from her priest or minister. Perfect cover for collecting information."

Bruce pulled his lip as he considered this. Elizabeth pressed her lips together. I continued:

"And, if she did go out, it would be most unlikely that she would be recognised for the simple reason that no-one would have expected to see her. All she would need is a wig and some glasses, and maybe a slight change of voice or accent, to become someone else entirely. Am I right?" I asked Elizabeth.

"Spot on," she agreed. "I'm Elizabeth Hudson when I'm dying and Janet Reed, her sister, when I'm not."

"Okay. I concede." Bruce raised his hands in mock surrender as he addressed Elizabeth. "So I suppose you recruited Mark to be your eyes and ears in places you don't go?"

"Precisely," Elizabeth confirmed.

"And I suppose you met him when he was called to the illegal immigrants who were found in some lorry or other?" I guessed.

"Right again,"said Elizabeth. "And you were right about the Rector, too. In fact it was he who first called us in. He was anxious about strange things his parishioners had glimpsed and peculiar noises that were heard. One of them, a Mavis Blanchard, was convinced she was possessed or that there was a ghost in her cottage. She even called him in to do an exorcism. But he could find no evidence of anything paranormal."

"Oh, poor Mavis!" I exclaimed feelingly.

"Then he found things misplaced in the church crypt," Elizabeth continued. "And wondered if Mavis was right after all. He decided to pray there in the crypt that night. He heard noises, similar to those Mavis had described, that called to mind the old smuggling tales, so he called us — and I drew the short straw."

"Ah. It's all beginning to fall into place now," declared Bruce, his brow clearing. "What I *don't* understand is how *you* got mixed up in this, Hazel?"

"I'm not quite sure either but I think it all started with Mrs Pendant, as the Captain said," I said slowly, the story unfolding in my mind mini-seconds before the words left my mouth. "All that he said was true. But we have to return to the drug cartel. They didn't know where the drugs had been stashed but they had Adam Blue Jeans in their sights and guessed that he might ... just might ... have hidden the heroin in the deed packet. When they saw him try to steal it they were convinced. But then, along came Poppadum, Neil, the Captain and you, Bruce, in that order. They must have thought that the drugs had been found. But they weren't sure of anything — so they kept watch on the house, as we know."

Bruce and Elizabeth both muttered in the affirmative.

"They didn't realise that I'd left the deed packet in the dustbin until Neil collected it after my phone call." I paused, wondering how much to say.

"Anyway, in the meantime, I'd been through the deeds and found that Mrs Pendant was, in fact, living in the wrong part of the house. The De Chams were living in the part that technically belonged to Mrs Pendant, and they thus had the use of the whole roof space *and of the cellar*!"

"Cellar?" Elizabeth looked at me sharply. "What cellar?"

"The one under Old Owlers, of course. I found that key in the seal tin attached to the Act of Attainder. It seemed to me that it had been hidden there. I have no idea who hid it. It could have been anyone. But I felt the *fact* that it had been hidden was very significant. I can only say that when I held the key in my hand, it felt important, as if it had been hidden for *a reason*."

"You certainly didn't tell me that," said Bruce. "There's no way ..."

I didn't let him finish.

"Of course I didn't tell you! You wouldn't have believed me."

"Of course I would."

"Well, you would have stopped me if you did," I retorted. "And I certainly didn't want that. Anyway, I thought the key had something to do with Mrs Pendant's property but what, I didn't know. I had a *feeling* that it was the key to the cellar and my intention was to find an excuse to get past Petronilla De Cham and try it ... gosh! Was it only yesterday?"

A wry smile from Bruce was my only answer. I swivelled towards Elizabeth.

"I set off to see you with your Will — over which I had laboured greatly, I may say — for signature, Elizabeth, and there you were, with Mark, engaging in an elaborate death scene. Why?"

"I knew it was the end of Elizabeth. We were planning a coup and I needed her dead. You were the right person to spread the word around Rype: a solicitor, someone with authority. In fact, I've already received condolences on her death."

"I see." It was my turn to smile wryly. "And I went straight round to the undertaker and spread the word exactly as you wanted."

"Yes, you played your part perfectly, even if it was unwittingly." Elizabeth applauded, clapping her hands slowly with a certain amount of irony.

"Glad to be of service," I discarded irony for sarcasm. "But I must inform you that I have a very large bill for you to pay. It took me most of the day and much of the evening to prepare your Will and Power of Attorney so quickly. So, for once, I feel I'm entitled to a proper fee." I was growing indignant, so I added hotly, "*Certainly* more than the usual five guineas."

"I quite agree, Hazel. Draw your bill up immediately!" Bruce broke in. "The person *I* feel really sorry for is the undertaker. Imagine the shock he must have had when he went to collect a body — and found it had walked!"

"*I* imagine your sister had to make a visit to Mr Clements to prevent him from collecting the body?" I asked Elizabeth coldly.

"I must admit," Elizabeth responded. "That I was not expecting you to act so promptly. I had only just become Janet again, when there was a knock on the door. I had to think fast."

"What *did* you say?" Bruce queried, fascinated.

"It was quite easy, really. I said that you had been mistaken, Hazel, and that Elizabeth had died in hospital. And then I got very angry, and very tearful, that you had interfered. I told him that it was *me...*" Elizabeth hit her chest. "Me, who was her sister *and* her Executor. And that I was instructing another firm of undertakers."

She caught my jaundiced eye and shrugged.

"I suppose I'll have to come clean with Mr Clements in due course," she admitted. I was slightly appeased but could not resist a sniff of disdain.

"Go on, Hazel. What happened next?" Bruce urged in what I knew was an attempt to distract me. I allowed myself to be diverted.

"As you well know, Bruce," I began rather sniffily. "I'd promised to go and inspect Mavis Blanchard's property but I was not sure which it was. Matthew De Cham showed me."

Elizabeth's eyebrows rose, but she did not say anything.

"Yes. He's a very nice lad, actually," I replied to her implied question. "Anyway, when I got there, I rang the bell and knocked but there was no reply. I was about to go away when I heard a noise — something that sounded like a cross between a thump and a moan. I tentatively pushed the front door and, *much* to my surprise, it opened. To cut a long story short, the noise seemed to be coming from the cupboard under the stairs, but I had a problem opening the cupboard door."

"So Poppadum was right. You *had* been there," Bruce interjected.

"Well, of course," I said, miffed. "That was where the noise was coming from. To continue: Matthew appeared and I sent him to get Neil. While he was gone I managed to open the door. There was a trapdoor inside the cupboard and I tried to open it. Then all I remember is blackness. For a while anyway."

"Why? What happened?" Bruce was all concern.

"I don't know. From what you've said, I think Mavis must have pushed the trapdoor back hard after I unlocked it. It probably knocked me out. I expect she thought I'd come to harm her or that she'd killed me. Either way, she must have been very scared and dumped me straight through it." I glanced at Elizabeth to see if she were following me.

"She was certainly distraught," Bruce agreed. "Then what?"

Luckily his interjection gave me a moment to think. A flicker of dismay crossed Elizabeth's face. Wondering how much I should divulge, I chose my next words with more care.

"I think I was knocked out for a while. When I came to, I had a lump on the back of my head. Here, feel it," I invited Bruce, who shook his head. "It's still tender. Anyway I was very dizzy and disorientated so I'm not very sure but somehow I found myself crawling along a passage into an old arched room. I tried to find a way out and had just found a door when I realised that people were coming. I was terrified. I thought they must be something to do with what had happened to me. I fled up another passage and came to a door. I managed to open it but I found myself in a wider, dark space. I crawled round it until I found an outer door. It was locked. I tried and tried to open it. Then I remembered the key in my pocket."

"Key? What key?" interjected Elizabeth sharply.

"The one in my pocket, of course," I said teasingly. "I told you I'd taken it." Elizabeth turned away, apparently unamused.

"Anyway, luckily the key worked," I went on, watching Elizabeth smother a yawn with her hand. "I staggered out into the open air and I must have fainted quite away ..." She was fiddling with her cuff now. "Because I woke up in Mark's surgery with my darling husband in attendance."

I smiled at Bruce. He took my hand and squeezed it hard.

"Oh Hazel. How could you frighten me like that? I shall never let you out of my sight again."

"Well you're going to have to," I retorted, as a griping pain ripped through me. "Because I need the loo. And I need it *now*!"

Elizabeth grabbed my wrist in a vicelike grip. There was nothing soft about her now, even those wonderful blue eyes were slitted, resembling hard blue pebbles.

"You're coming with me," she growled.

- 44 -

Of Birth and Death

The griping pain came again, and again. I gasped, doubling up.

"I have to *go, now!*"

With a quick jerk, I pulled my hand free, leaving Bruce to fill her in on the detail and to see her to the door. I headed fast for the toilet where I just managed to seat myself before my bowels literally emptied themselves, the hot griping pains taking my breath away. I wondered what I had eaten to bring on this diarrhoea and then I remembered that I had had practically nothing to eat the previous day and only toast this morning. The thought hit me suddenly. This was either a rehearsal for the birthing process or the real thing.

The thought had hardly reached my befuddled brain before the pain came again, really cramping this time, making me bite through my bottom lip. The salty metallic taste of blood in my mouth was quickly followed by another intense sensation of pure pain. This was no dress rehearsal, I gathered. This was the real thing. I called for Bruce. There was no reply. Pain. I called again. Nothing. Only the barking of a dog in the distance. Where was Poppadum? She had not left my side all morning; and as I had shut the toilet door, she had waited, very reluctantly, outside, slowly lowering herself to the floor in resignation.

This time the pain was so strong and cramping that it made me feel sick. I yelled. There was an answering congealed yelp from Poppadum as if she were being restrained by a tight collar, or as if someone had kicked her. Then silence.

"*Brrrruuuuuce!*" His name lengthened itself as a pain caught me in mid shout. This searing hot pain did not stop. It ripped up from stern to stem, completely immobilising me. Then nausea and sweating kicked in and I felt my waters break. I was doubled up on the seat, leaning forward as far as I could, praying that this would pass, praying that it was not my baby, not yet. Please, not yet. I wanted to be in hospital when the baby arrived; in hospital so that she could be born in the proper way with nurses and a loving husband in attendance, with gas and air, or whatever pain relief I needed ....

Waters gushed into the lavatory pan. I needed pain relief. I needed it now! The long spasm ended. Sweat dripped off my forehead, my nose. I licked my lips; they came away salty. I dared to breathe. Took a huge gulp. And regretted it instantly as toast came back up my throat. I retched over the tiny washbasin and was very grateful when nothing materialised. Spaaaaaasssssmmmm. Doubled up as I was, I felt the movement of something huge within me, tremendous pressure. The baby was coming! She was coming NOW.

Without thinking I eased myself off the toilet pan. My head found itself beside the pedestal and my knees folded up with my toes against the door. Pain. Pain. Gripping, griping pain. Pains were coming so fast I could only pant. It felt as though I was birthing a whale. How could something so big come out of me? I was not big enough. A huge, hot, pincer-like pain gripped both sides of my abdomen and I felt a shift, a loosening.

There was a sudden scratching at the door, a barking, yelping confusion of noise. I heard myself scream, a long, long, long primeval screech of protest, bordering on triumph, containing within it every emotion I had ever experienced — joy, fear, excitement, grief, delight, resentment, passion, guilt, bliss, anger, happiness, sadness, rapture, pride, elation — but most of all an overwhelming love. The love enveloped me as my body coiled itself for one last thrusting push — and the door was torn off its hinges, light flooded into the small place, as my husband's blanched, concerned face loomed above me.

The room darkened more as a black, furry shape launched itself over me, licking my face briefly with a foetid tongue before Bruce hauled Poppadum away. I saw his gaze fixed between my legs and allowed myself to come back into the world, away from the throbbing, aching, primordial hysteria into which I had slipped.

For the length of a heart beat I could feel the blood pooling there, between my legs; feel the softness of the slippery skin. I could smell the warm, brackish scent of my own flesh mixed with the metallic odour of blood; taste the saltiness of my blood and sweat. Then the hammering sound of my heartbeat drummed in my ears; my eyes were filled with shining, shimmering light in which fragments of stardust glimmered. I hung there for a moment — no more.

My body arched violently as it was racked with a huge volcanic eruption of pain and rapture; and a slithering, sliding, gurgling slipperiness broke free of my flesh — as my baby's head surged into the outside world. I gasped and felt the rest of its body twist; and twisting and twirling ... slip ... slip and slide into being. And I felt an orgasm of pure delight seize me as my strength returned suddenly. Adrenalin pounded through me and I sat up, careful to disentangle myself from the tiny body of my child.

Bruce was still peering at the baby which was eerily quiet. I thought babies cried as soon as they were born; the silence unnerved me.

"Quick, pick it up!" I commanded.

Bruce literally hopped from one foot to another.

"Er ... um."

"Quick! Quick, pick it up. It will be cold!" I repeated.

"My hands are dirty!"

Even in my heightened state I thought this very funny. "It's not exactly clean itself! Is it a boy or a girl?"

"I don't *know*."

"*What?!!!!*"

"I can't *tell!*"

I heard other footsteps and a warm, reassuring voice:

"My, haven't you done well, Hazel? And all by yourself." The midwife had arrived and swiftly took charge. "You have a beautiful baby girl. How clever of you to make it to the toilet."

And in no time at all the baby had been swaddled in a towel, Bruce had been despatched to make tea, the afterbirth was delivered and dealt with and I had been gently bathed and wrapped in the special nightgown I'd been saving for this moment. As my beautiful baby girl was placed into my arms, I sat enthroned on the sofa with my dog at my feet and my husband beside me. Basking in their adoration, I knew that this was the crowning moment of happiness in my entire life.

"Where were you?" I asked Bruce, sentiment making my throat rusty.

The mid-wife had finished her work, warned me that she would call in the morning to check that all was well and had left the three of us cuddled together in a morass of emotion. Poppadum had gone to her bed in disgust at the lack of interest in her.

"You may well ask," Bruce said, kissing my eyes. "I was having an adventure of my own before I was rudely interrupted by that perishing hound of yours."

"Adventure?" A huge lassitude was settling over me suddenly. It was all I could do to keep my eyes open.

"Are you awake? It was a very interesting adventure and I don't want you to go to sleep over the telling of it."

I threw off the net of tiredness and sat up straight with my baby girl in the crook of my arm. I knew she was the most beautiful, most adorable baby that had ever been born. Her little eyes were screwed up from the speed of her delivery but gleamed deep blue when she opened them; her skin was so soft; her limbs so plump and perfect; her fingers and toes so tiny and faultless; her little gasps of 'ah' so sweet; and her mass of fine, fine hair such an exact match of that peculiar shade of russet that was her father's. She was perfection.

"I know she's perfect," Bruce said, taking the words from my mind. "But you have to hear this."

"Of course," I said.

"I was just opening the door to show Elizabeth out when I felt something hard poked into my back.

'It's a gun.' Elizabeth said, 'I suggest you come quietly, so as not to disturb your wife.' Well — you can imagine my astonishment.

'I can't leave her.' I said.

'All right, I'll wait and bring her too. It's your choice,' she replied.

I thought of you, so nearly dead yesterday, and my heart was breaking.

'Where to?' I asked.

'Better you don't know,' she answered, prodding me hard with the gun towards a car that was parked right outside. 'Just get in.'

You won't believe this, Hazel, but I was sure it was the same car White Bonnet was driving that day we had the fire. And he was behind the steering wheel."

"White Bonnet?" I couldn't believe it. "But he was taken away in handcuffs yesterday."

"I know, I was very surprised when I registered that."

"What did you do?" I asked.

"I was most reluctant to get into the car but the feel of the gun in my back was very persuasive. I was about to comply when I thought I heard you call me. I turned my head quickly at the sound and saw Poppadum racing towards us. I heard you scream — it sent icicles through me — and I think Elizabeth heard you, too. Anyway, she turned, saw Pops and aimed a shot at her ..."

"At Poppadum? Is she hurt?" I panicked.

"No, no. Everything happened so quickly I'm not sure exactly what *did* happen but I think I shoved Elizabeth as she took aim. The shot went wide. Poppadum leapt at Elizabeth, I flung myself on the ground and Elizabeth fell flat on her back, her arm twisted behind her, the gun beneath her. I heard it discharge with a muffled thump and blood began to flow from under her skirt."

"Oh God! Is she dead?" More panic.

"To be honest, I don't know and I don't much care. Rather her than me or you," Bruce said grimly.

"What happened next?"

"There was a flurry of running feet, a car screeching to a stop, and the slamming of car doors. I looked up to see the Captain looking down at me. And then I heard you scream and Poppadum bark wildly. I rushed in to find Poppadum trying to get into the lavatory. You were wedged behind the bloody door so all I could do was wrench the bloody thing off its hinges ... and there you were, blood spilling everywhere." He paled at the memory.

"Not the best time to give birth, was it? But at least we'll never forget Jessica's entrance to the world, will we?"

"So that's her name, is it?" Bruce took the sleeping bundle from me and kissed the tiny forehead. "I thought you liked Amarella?"

"I know I did," I said, "But she's Jessica. She told me so herself. It means 'God is looking' and someone's certainly been looking after us! Jessica Jane, she told me. The words just popped into my head. The midwife agreed that the names suit her. Which reminds me, did *you* call her – the midwife?"

"I have not the faintest idea *how* the mid-wife got here," he sighed heartily, drawing me to him with his free arm. "But I'm damned glad she did."

We were just beginning to shake in the aftermath of all that had happened that day when there was another ring on the doorbell. Bruce went to answer it and ushered in Marigold Green bearing a tray from which the fragrant aroma of beef casserole escaped. I felt myself begin to salivate immediately.

"I'm not stopping," she said. "I know you will be tired and you must rest. But you need to eat and, from what I hear, you won't have had much time to cook today. Come on, Bruce, show me where to put this."

The tray was whisked into the kitchen. Marigold reappeared a minute later with another tray bearing my portion of the casserole and vegetables and a glass of Guinness.

"Very good for your milk," she smiled, indicating the glass. I thanked her profusely. "Now, introduce me to your first-born and I'll hold her while you eat."

"Jessica Jane meet Marigold; Marigold meet Jessica Jane."

I handed her over with more than a touch of reluctance.

Marigold rocked Jessica expertly, cooing at her while I tucked in avidly. I was absolutely famished. So was Bruce. He brought in his meal and shovelled it in as if he had never eaten before.

Marigold nodded at the rapidly disappearing food.

"That's not my only gift to you both," she said. "I bring news!"

"Oh?" I said, speaking with my mouth full — a habit I deplored.

"Yes! Rype has been alive with police all day, and customs officers too. I'm sure it hasn't seen the like since the bad old smuggling days."

This time I raised my eyebrows and kept munching.

"That's right," Marigold approved. "Keep eating and I'll keep talking. Things have been going on here right under our noses. Some drug barons discovered the old smugglers' passages and a big room beside the church crypt. They have been using them for years to bring in drugs. There's one passage that runs from the seashore to the church, apparently."

She was interrupted by a huge snort from Bruce who had such a huge mouthful he was unable to speak.

"Bruce thinks that's impossible because of the shingle," I explained.

"He obviously doesn't know that Rype has always been an island," she said, addressing me. "It used to be surrounded by the sea but it isn't composed of shingle. In any case, take it from me, there *is* a tunnel into the room beneath the church. Someone infiltrated into the cartel, I'm told, and someone else managed to locate another entrance — in fact, *two* entrances. Late last night the police caught the smugglers in a sort of pincer movement, coming down all three tunnels at once."

"Oh?" I mumbled, my mouth full.

"Oh yes! The smugglers were trafficking people, Pakistanis mostly, poor people who had paid a *fortune* to come to England. And do you know what else the smugglers did? They made those poor devils smuggle drugs, would you believe? Made them bring in heroin and cocaine so it wouldn't be found." Marigold was ostensibly disgusted but, nonetheless, was telling the tale with obvious relish. "Apparently, the authorities suspected this was all going on but had no proof. It was only by chance they found the entrance to the tunnels."

"Chance was it?" Bruce inquired, his eyes speaking to me over his plate.

"Someone – not a policeman or anything like that – worked it out, I'm told. I don't know who but rumour has it that it was a lady and had something to do with deeds." She looked enquiringly at me.

I had finished my main course and was about to start on the rhubarb crumble she had brought for dessert.

"Surely you don't think it was me?" I exclaimed. Marigold regarded me sideways but continued unabashed.

"Dreadful, dreadful business. Do you know, the police caught those poor Pakistani people *literally* with their pants down? The drugs were stashed in condoms which the poor things were made to swallow. Then they smuggled them into the country through the tunnels from the beach and made them shit (pardon the language) in a bucket so they could reclaim the lot. I hear they even put diamonds in the condoms sometimes."

"But what happens if the condoms split?" I asked aghast.

"I s'pose the person dies, don't you? No-one would know, would they?"

Horrified though I was by the thought of those young men being forced to carry drugs in such a manner, I was forced to agree that it was a very low-risk, high-gain operation.

"They're just mopping up the rest of the Gang, now," said Marigold. "I hope they get life sentences. They should be hung, really."

Inwardly, I agreed with her. Although I was generally against the death penalty and was glad that it had been abolished for murder in 1965, there were times I thought that the threat might still have acted as a deterrent.

"Who'd believe such happenings in Rype?" I asked. "And to think we chose to live here because it was such a friendly, sleepy little place."

"I know. But I've saved the best for last. Guess who the ringleader was?" Marigold was agog with the information.

"Funnily enough, I have an idea ..."

Marigold's jaw dropped. "Yes — but who?"

"It could be anyone." Bruce entered the conversation with a warning frown at me, "Who was it, Marigold?"

"I haven't the faintest idea," she said with a sly smile. "But I thought you might!"

"That was absolutely delicious food," I said. "We can't thank you enough."

"I'm glad you enjoyed it," Marigold dropped a kiss on Jessica Jane's forehead before handing her back to me. "I must be away to my own brood. I'll just take the dishes."

"No way!" Bruce butted in. "I'll wash them and bring them back to you tomorrow."

Scarcely was Marigold out of the door than the bell rang again. This time it was the Captain.

"I won't keep you. I know you've had a busy day." He glanced at the bundle that was Jessica and continued: "I'm here to thank you — and your dog — for the help you've given us in rounding up these villains. We had no idea there was another entrance to the tunnels, let alone two. We had reason to suspect that there was a tunnel from the beach but it took us a long time to find it, even with sniffer dogs. Perhaps we should have asked yours to help?" Poppadum raised her head and then sighed as she replaced it on her paws. "But what I'd really like to know is how you found the tunnel from the cellar at Old Owlers, Mrs Dawkins?"

"Now that really *is* a long story," I replied. "Would it suffice to say I discovered it from the deeds to the property? I'll be happy to tell you more soon, but not now." I clasped Jessica close and bent my head over her, only just managing to restrain myself from making goo-goo noises.

"Did you suspect that Elizabeth was involved?" Bruce asked bluntly.

"We knew, of course, that she was working under cover for

Customs and Excise. But we hadn't realised that she'd become so personally involved with the smuggling cartel. It seems that she'd become addicted to heroin as pain relief after a serious injury, so she was open to blackmail – and the cartel paid considerable financial inducements to turn a blind eye to their activities. Some people working for Customs and Revenue and also, I very much regret to say, several police officers, were on their pay list."

"So that was how White Bonnet came to be driving the get-away car," Bruce exclaimed.

"Yes and no. He'd been bailed by the police. But that would not normally have been the case after a firearm offence."

"How did he appear behind you so suddenly and silently?" I asked. It had been concerning me a little, recently.

"I have no idea, but I expect he slipped in the front door behind you."

"I'm sure that I would have seen him ..." I started, but the Captain was shaking his head in a dismissive but kindly manner. Maybe he was right: what other explanation could there be?

"Going back to Elizabeth's part in all this ..." the Captain resumed. "We knew, of course, that she liaised with Doctor Wilkinson about the drugs he found and the addicts for whom he provided methadone. We knew, too, that Doctor Wilkinson was also on call to the Customs Officers when they found any smuggled human cargo who needed medical attention. We believed that he 'protested too much' and that he was very much involved with the racket. In fact, he's completely innocent of that charge."

"Good." I said, relieved. "I couldn't believe that anyone so compassionate could be so vile. But even *I* wondered about him for a while."

"Yes, he is a good man. So is his partner, Dr. Hadley."

"Really?" I was astounded. "I had him marked as the villain of the piece."

It was the Captain's turn to look surprised. "Really?" he echoed. "He's been helping us with the victims. Why on earth would you think him a villain?"

"He warned me off his patients: something to which I took great exception! Especially as I was sure that both Miss Blanchard and Mrs Pendant were telling the truth – which, as it turns out, they were. And then I found out that he probably knew that Mrs Pendant was living in the wrong half of the property."

"What do you mean?" he queried, his eyes narrowing. He was no longer smiling and I could not put off further explaining in detail the result of my search into Mrs Pendant's title to her property. His eyes narrowed even more.

"And when I found Miss Blanchard in the cupboard she was raving about a man with a syringe," Bruce added.

"I suspect that Doctor Hadley, for all his charms, was over-medicating both women," I said. "So when Mavis consulted me and I started being nosy I reckon he decided it was time for her to disappear. I think he drugged her and pushed her through the trapdoor to be collected by the cartel and disposed of. After all, she was frightened enough to push me down there – so if you need another witness to the people trafficking, I saw it all: people and buckets, even children, before I managed to escape."

"How did you escape, Mrs Dawkins?"

"Actually, I only got out because I'd taken the key to what turned out to be the cellar below Old Owlers. I had a hunch it might be and I'd intended to check – I suspected Dr. Hadley knew something about that cellar. But, as it turned out, I was pushed into one of the old tunnels and only found the exit through the cellar by chance."

"There's not a lot of concrete evidence here, as far as Dr. Hadley is concerned," the Captain said regretfully. "Unless you saw him?"

I shook my head. "No, I didn't see him," I said, ruefully.

"Then we will have to see whether your surmise about Miss Blanchard is right and whether she would be prepared to give evidence."

"There's one answer to that," Bruce said. "Ask her."

"Actually, I *did* hear the doctor's voice when they were bringing in the Pakistanis," I revealed. "I'll be more than happy to give evidence against him."

Bruce was shaking his head at me, apparently wondering what other secrets I held, but he only said:

"In the meantime, Captain, I have two questions to ask *before you go*." The stress on the last words was clear. "First, why was White Bonnet waving a gun at us?"

"Another double bluff, I'm afraid. He's a policeman who has been working, under cover, for the cartel. He was sent by them to find out what you knew and, I'm afraid ..." he paused. "Whether it would be necessary to kill you to keep you quiet. He was playing a double or triple game. We're working on that now and we'll get the answer, have no fear."

"Oh!" Bruce and I exchanged horrified glances. He threw his arm round me and drew me close.

"And my second question. What would Elizabeth have done with me and Hazel?"

Once again the Captain paused. "I suspect that you, Mr Dawkins, would have gone with the cartel, probably dead, to feed the fishes on their next fishing trip for human cargo."

"Oh!" I said again. Nothing else came to mind.

"And Hazel?" Bruce pursued.

There was a longer pause as the policeman looked from one to the other of us.

"It's possible to make sure a woman dies in childbirth. And it was very convenient for them that you gave birth at such an opportune moment," he said, looking directly at me.

"And what would have happened to Jessica?" I whispered. I knew the answer before he replied.

"There is always a market for white babies."

I shivered and hugged Jessica tightly, almost smothering her. She struggled a little and I relaxed my grip. I found I was keen for the Captain to go and I was relieved when he made his exit immediately.

He turned on the doorstep, though, saying:

"But we did have you under surveillance, so you were reasonably safe. And I did send the midwife."

He saluted and left.

Poppadum took the opportunity to show her contempt for authority by yawning. Bruce and I laughed in relief. And, although it was still only seven in the evening, he and I went to bed to sleep, our little daughter safely in a moses basket by our side, guarded by the most intrepid dog in Rype.

As I slipped into sleep, I was aware of a gnarled old hand tucking me into my covers. Whisper soft, the hand stroked my hair and a tear fell from a sightless eye. Whether I dreamed it or not, I might never know: I imagined an arthritic finger gently chucking Jessica under the chin. And best of all, a blessing and the faint scent of lavender.

- 45 -

Of a Silver Coin

I heard it all happening in the room below as I lay in the centre of the huge double bed cuddling my sleeping baby. I knew that most new mothers were proud of their children but the pride I took in Jessica was indescribable. I believed that I'd achieved an amazing feat in giving birth — as if no woman had ever done it before!

I later realised that my euphoria was the aftermath of having experienced such an easy, quick, first labour. I learned subsequently that it had gone down in the annals of Rype as the fastest delivery in its known history. My level of adrenalin was no doubt exceedingly high. Although rather sore in the underparts, I felt absolutely marvellous and on top of the world.

I checked my appearance in the silver hand mirror my mother had given me as a memento of Jessica's birth. My features had already acquired the glow of motherhood, visible even through my carefully applied make-up, and my dark hair gleamed, well brushed and almost behaving itself. A half smile persisted round my lips no matter how hard I tried to look serious.

And I *was* trying to be earnest because, as I had remembered early that very morning, it had been arranged that Mr and Mrs Smith would call at half-past ten that morning to sign their Wills.

I had also recalled, much more importantly, that both Bruce and I had been so shell-shocked by the various events of the previous day that neither of us had thought to tell our respective parents of Jessica's sudden and dramatic birth. Knowing that my father habitually rose at six o'clock in the morning, I'd tiptoed downstairs: the kitchen clock showed that it was already a quarter past that hour. I remedied the omission immediately by dialling my parents' number. Much to my astonishment, my mother answered instantly. There was no preamble.

"Hazel's had the baby, hasn't she?" It was more statement than question.

"Yes, I have," I announced with jubilation. "And she's wonderful!"

"Hazel?" Mother sounded incredulous.

"Yes, it's me, Mum." Gleefully.

"Darling girl? Where are you? I knew something was happening! I haven't been able to sleep all night."

"I'm at home, and I'm fine," I assured her. "It all happened so quickly that I didn't even get *near* the hospital."

"Tell me *all!"* she commanded. My words leapt over themselves but it still took over half an hour to give her a full account. By the time our conversation ended, I was aware that both she and my father were fully awake, dressed and ready to drive down to inspect their grandchild.

I crept back upstairs and apprised a very sleepy husband of the likelihood that his house would be invaded by his parents-in-law within forty minutes — a fact which caused him to groan, possibly with relief but more probably with annoyance that his slumber had been so abruptly curtailed. He also decided to take himself off to work as soon as my parents arrived. He wanted to give his boss the news and arrange some time off.

"I want all the congratulations I deserve for fathering such a perfect child," he declared. "And I'm going to get them."

"What about me?" I demanded. "I had a bit to do with it you know."

He was about to reply when our mock-wrangling was interrupted by the eruption into the house of my parents. While Bruce introduced my father to the contents of our booze cupboard, my mother took charge of me and the baby so that, by the time Bruce had phoned his delighted parents in Australia and set off to work, he left us all in a state of elation.

Now I was sitting up in bed waiting impatiently for my clients to arrive — while downstairs happy chaos appeared to be reigning.

"Come in, come in ... do. The more the merrier!" I heard my father exclaim. I imagined him standing at the door, champagne glass in hand and spectacles slightly askew. "It's the best day of my life!"

"Come in? Are you sure? Is this the right house?" asked a wavering male voice.

"We have an appointment with Mrs Dawkins," I heard his wife explain.

"Yes, yes, I know," agreed grandfather Victor, no doubt standing back to give them room to enter the little porch to the cottage. "She's upstairs in bed."

I found myself smiling broadly as I imagined their mystified expressions.

"Is she all right?" Mrs Smith asked shakily.

"Fine. Absolutely fine. Do go up and see her. She's waiting for you," chuckled my father. He added, rather too gregariously: "And when you come down we'll do some serious drinking."

"Come along, dear."

Mrs Smith sounded nervous as she stepped into the porch, meekly followed by her husband. My father ushered them into the low-beamed sitting room and then my mother took over.

"My daughter is waiting for you," she said and again I could imagine her happy smile and the elegant wave of the hand holding a glass of champagne. "I hope you'll forgive her for not coming down. She had a baby girl only yesterday afternoon."

Suddenly all was clear. Their congratulations accepted and their protestations brushed aside, Mr and Mrs Smith were ushered into my sunny bedroom.

"Your clients are here, Hazel," my mother announced with the solemnity of a butler.

"I'm sorry I couldn't come downstairs to see you," I said, indicating Jessica who was sleeping peacefully. "As you can see, I'm marooned up here. But your Wills are ready for you to sign. Shall we go through them? And then, if you're happy with them, my parents can be the witnesses."

The Wills were approved, signed and witnessed in the nick of time for, as the Smiths turned to leave the room, we heard feet bounding up the stairs and a long-legged, uniformed man with short greying hair knocked hard but briefly before entering the room. Poppadum, who had already appointed herself my daughter's nurse and protector, rose from her place by Jessica's basket.

Instantly sizing up the situation, the Captain stood aside to allow Mr and Mrs Smith to slip from the room. They followed my parents down the narrow stairs but Grandfather Victor did not let them escape the celebrations.

"Have a drink! Got to wet the baby's head, haven't they, Betty?"

"It's our first grandchild, you see," Mother smoothed. "Do you have grandchildren? Do come and tell me about them."

Pulling my attention back from the happenings below, I smiled at the Captain only to find him studying me with an oddly soft expression.

"Congratulations!" he said, swiftly producing a magnificent bouquet of pink and white roses from behind his back. "These are for you, and I've left a very large bottle of champagne downstairs with your father."

"Th... thank you," I stammered in surprise.

"No! Thank *you*," he responded. "You were absolutely right with your assessment of that Pillar of the Establishment, Dr. Hadley. He was very hoity-toity when we took him in for questioning yesterday afternoon but after a night in the cells he was weeping unashamedly and begging for whisky, schnapps, gin, vodka, in fact *anything* alcoholic, when I visited him this morning. He's an alcoholic all right. Probably combines it with medicinal or other drugs."

"How sad," I whispered, tears welling, for I was so happy that morning that I wanted everyone's heart to be singing with joy like mine.

"Addiction like that is always sad," he agreed. "But don't waste your sympathy on him. One of the other members of that drug smuggling and people trafficking cartel has started singing ... I mean, turning Queen's evidence in the hope of a lesser prison sentence ... and will give evidence that the cellar beneath Old Owlers has been used for years by smugglers. And you can guess who the ringmaster has always been?"

"Dr. Hadley? Surely not?" I exclaimed. "I thought his involvement was recent?"

"Not at all," he countered. "It seems his family have been crooks and smugglers for years and years — in fact, probably for generations. Certainly we have evidence that he used that cellar, and the tunnels, for stockpiling and black market operations during the War. That is itself a reprehensible crime. And one which used to carry the death penalty."

"And all the time ..."

"Yes," he agreed again. "All the time he had the perfect cover as a very respectable and, I'm sure, respected doctor."

"Well," I said, briskly recovering myself, "I'm very glad I found those deeds and put two and two together. Who would have thought that rifling around in old documents could have unearthed a story like that?"

Again footsteps were heard on the stairs and Bruce burst into the room clutching a huge teddy-bear and a rectangular parcel wrapped in shiny red paper. The Captain excused himself.

As Bruce beamed at me and I beamed at him, we heard my father's inebriated jolliness:

"Have a drink, Captain! He's got to wet the baby's head, hasn't he, Betty?"

Bruce put the parcel in my hands, folding them over it.

"How are my lovely girls? I came home as soon as I could. Where's my daughter? Is she still as beautiful as my wife?"

Feeling ecstatically the worse for wear, I placed the little gurgling bundle in her father's arms, from where she stared at the teddy bear with a puzzled frown. She looked at her little right hand in a similar way and then waved it around in front of her face. The tiny thumb plopped into her tiny mouth and she sucked it, the picture of content.

I tore the paper from the parcel and my breath caught in my throat. There revealed, lay the most magnificent brass plate I had ever seen. It was about eighteen inches long and eight high, burnished to perfection and indented with black wax-filled letters, each over two inches high, the whole plate set on a polished oak board. The legend on it read:

H. DAWKINS LL.B.

SOLICITOR

I was speechless. Emotions warred within me. It was the most wonderful gift but ....

"It's all right, darling," my husband murmured in my ear. "You may never set it up, and that's fine. It's to show you how proud I am of you in your own right. And that I love you for *you* as well as for our little Jessica here."

"You silly, sentimental thing," I chided, tears of happiness clashing with my grin of delight as I threw my arms round him and our daughter.

A car door slammed nearby. A pause, a laugh, the sound of the vehicle turning and speeding away. A thump on the front door and Joanna's broad Australian vowels yelled:

"Bruce! Good on yer, Mate! Hazel, the original fairy godmother is here!"

The door was opened with alacrity.

"Come in, come in, my dear young lady! Wet the baby's head!" I heard my father enthuse and then there came a muffled oath and my father's bewildered voice.

"*Australian* champagne? Australian *champagne*? Since when did ...? What *will* they think of next?"

"I want to join the party!" I announced.

"But you *can't*," Bruce ruffled his hair distractedly. "You only gave birth to the child twelve hours ago."

"Just watch me," said I. "After all, it's Jessica's birthday party. I am definitely part of it and so are you."

I threw back the covers and swivelled my feet to the floor. As I drew on my frilly negligee I noticed something that glinted in a sunbeam, something small and round that I had found clutched in Jessica's tiny hand that morning. I picked up the old silver penny.

"Did you give Jessica this, too?" I asked Bruce, hoping I already knew the answer.

"What is it?" he said, taking it from me and looking at it with curiosity.

"A silver penny," I said. And smiled. Because I knew then it hadn't been a dream. "Actually, I think an old lady called Annie gave it to her. Crossed her palm with silver — and blessed her, too."

A faint wisp of lavender scent, quickly fading. My smile deepened and I said a silent prayer of thanks. Bruce juggled Jessica into the crook of one arm and took my hand.

"Okay, Hazel. Let's go."

- 46 -

Of Sisterhood

That night, as my sweet baby daughter murmured beside me, a golden light invaded my dreams.

Within the light Annie and Jack sat by the inglenook fireplace; Annie was nursing her baby and a boy of about two leaned against Jack's knee. It was a scene of perfect contentment and I made to steal away unseen, but, as they sensed my presence, both of them looked up and smiled at me. Jack gently dislodged the child onto the settle and drew out the rocking chair for me.

He returned to his family, holding them close, all of them watching as I settled myself and my baby into the chair. Jessica's little rosebud mouth clamped on my nipple as I offered it to her, the firelight glowing on my naked breast, as it gleamed on Annie's. Our babies' little hands kneaded softly. I felt the presence of Bruce behind my chair, his hand stroking my hair just as Jack's stroked Annie's.

In perfect harmony, our little families luxuriated in the peace of the firelight and then, without words, for none were needed, Annie smiled at me and I smiled at Annie and in that instant I knew that all would be well for both of us and our beloved men and children.

Together, Annie and I had bridged the years and with each other's help we had changed the course of history by trusting in the power of love and friendship to transcend Time. By joining hands we had defeated the malevolence that had threatened us and our dear ones. And we had brought life and peace to this small but special part of the world that was Rype.

The bond we had would not be broken. Though we might never again pass through the veil together, I knew that at times we would pass on the stair and I would feel the touch of her skirts, or we would sit before the fire and dream together, or meet in the space that was both my kitchen and Annie's porch, and in our different Time and differing realities we would feel that special love one bears a sibling and a benefactor.

The golden light faded and I heard again the soft little 'ah' sounds of my baby's sleep and my husband's gentle snoring. I slipped back into the unconsciousness of peaceful slumber.

Outside, the moon rose. A nightingale poured out its heart in song, singing of new life and ancient secrets.

Epilogue

Drug Cartel Infiltrated

In a daring raid carried out as a joint operation between the Metropolitan Police, the Kent County Police and H.M. Customs and Excise, a huge haul of drugs, valued at over a million pounds and reckoned to be the largest amount ever impounded in this country, was seized and the crooks arrested. It happened in the old smuggling town of Rype-in-the-Marsh on Sunday 20th June, in a dawn raid involving over fifty officers from the three services.

We are reliably informed that under-cover agents were used to infiltrate the drug cartel in an operation which had been planned over several months. The authorities believe the cartel to have been behind many other illegal activities which have blighted the lives of thousands of people in the local area.

In a surprise twist, a large number of illegal immigrants were also discovered. It appears, from first reports, that they have been used to smuggle in the drugs. Many of them were ill and starving and are now receiving medical treatment. A decision about whether they will be deported is to be made later.

Source: Romney Gazette dated 24th June 1976

Note:

The exploits of the ***Eaglewood Gang*** are based on the activities of the Hawkhurst Gang which caused mayhem on the south coast of England in the first half of the eighteenth century:

'The most notorious band of smugglers was the 'Hawkhurst Gang', which terrorised the country but were finally brought to justice.

In the Autumn of 1747 one of their cargoes of tea was seized and lodged in the Customs House at Poole. They attacked the building and took the tea away. As they rode away through Hampshire — for smuggling has no boundaries — crowds turned out to watch them and among them a shoemaker, Daniel Chater. A reward had been offered for information and Chater was overheard to say that he had recognised one of the smugglers. A Customs Officer, William Galley, was sent to question Chater and to take him before a Justice of the Peace. On the way they were captured by the smugglers and received such barbaric and inhuman treatment, before they were murdered, that the whole country rang with the news.

As a result, a huge reward of £500 was offered for information on the Hawkhurst Gang and seven of the ringleaders were brought to trial. All except one, who died in gaol, were hanged in 1749. Others were arrested and executed later.'

Source: Historic Hastings by J. Manwaring Baines FSA

Acknowledgements

In no particular order, the author gratefully thanks the following individuals for their comments, suggestions and encouragement which all helped to bring this novel to fruition:

Simon Maginn, Christine Warrington, Melvyn Montgomery, Vivien Ford, Anne Rix, Tricia Oakland, Wendy Booth, Christine Harmar-Brown, Patricia Marston, Roger Marston, Sophie O'Sullivan, Laura Barber, Judith Thwaites, Amanda Nicol, Sally McLaughlin, Mary Upton, Donald Eaton, Annie Goodsell, Stephanie Fox, Beverley Garner, Jason Worley, David Hobbs, Paul Pilon and my husband, Richard Eaton.

Cover illustration by Paul Pilon.
Cover design by Damonza: www.damonza.com

About The Author:

Retired from legal practice, Marion lives near the sea in the beautiful Sussex countryside with a long-suffering husband, a lazy Saluki and an urge to write into the small hours.

This is her first novel.

The second book in the Mysterious Marsh Series, *When the Tide Turned,* will be available in early 2014.

More information can be found at: www.marioneaton.com

Note from the Author:

Thanks for reading! My hope is that you have enjoyed reading this book. If so, here's what you can do next:

- sign up for an occasional newsletter on www.marioneaton.com
- leave a review on www.amazon.co.uk and www.lulu.com– a line or two is more than enough.
- and, of course, tell others about it.

  This will be of enormous help and will be hugely appreciated.

Thank you. Thank you. Thank you!